KISS OF THE PHARAOH

MARK D RICHARDSON

To Joe
Merry Christmas
and A happy New year

Mark D Richardson

BOOK TWO OF THE CASE FILES

KISS OF THE PHARAOH

by Mark D Richardson

ABOUT THE AUTHOR

Mark was born in Leicester in December 1961

Educated to A level standard and with a passion for writing, he designed school newsletters, produced many school plays; wrote articles in a teen magazine 'Look and Learn' and instead of the assigned English essay homework, created short stories on a regular basis.

After several writing courses and correspondence assignments, novel writing became a hobby. He started with a fantasy novel, followed by short story of a real life experience in the States, before constructing a rough draft of a thriller in the world of football.

But it was his passion for detective movies, spy thrillers, murder mysteries and whodunnits, that provided the material and inspiration for The Case Files.

Kiss of the Pharaoh is the second of many in the series. High energy, explosive thrillers set in a world of constant threat, a continual tale of good against evil.

ACKNOWLEDGEMENT

.

I would like to thank the people who have helped me to continue growing the Case Files universe.

To my wife Chris for her continual support and the labouring to ensure that the plot works and the characters remain grounded.

To Claire and Tony for their encouragement and constructive comments and to Mick for his enthusiasm and comparisons to authors I have no right to breathe the same air with.

And finally, to you dear reader for accepting my world of danger, espionage and mystery in a journey that I can assure you will continue to thrill and confound.

Enjoy the Journey

Mark D Richardson

FOREWARD

A NOTE FROM THE AUTHOR

Kiss of the Pharaoh was a difficult book to write when the whole world was gripped by a terrifying pandemic.

The truth is that the structure and format was penned in 2017 and writing began in May 2019, quite a while before any knowledge of such a virulent threat to mankind was realised.

Like everyone, it has been a struggle to remain focused when friends, family and associates along with people we never knew suffered immeasurably during these times.

Here in the UK, had it not been for the brave men and women of the NHS, who continue to show the dedication, determination and compassion to super human extremes, we would have lost many many more lives.

My heart goes out to those who have lost loved ones and to those who are still suffering today. It only makes you realise how precious life is and how easily it can be taken away, sometimes by elements that we are unable to control.

Mark D Richardson

1

Chewing gum, always chewing gum. Henry sat picking strings of gum from the sole of his boot after checking the shop and entering the fossil gallery. He had squelched only a few yards, but enough to mark the marble floors. It was a pain in the arse to clean at the best of times, but at night it was impossible to clear all the smudges. Daylight always highlighted them like a festering spot.

Every Bank Holiday the same. Kids, hundreds of them. Half of them don't even want to be here, but parents always think they will learn something. One thing was certain, if there was a degree in marble floor slalom, they would all pass.

As part of the security team it was important to protect the exhibits, this year in particular.

Manchester Museum was hosting a special Ancient Egyptian exhibition loaned from the British Museum. The sarcophagus of Sasobek, gold icons from the burial tombs and small trinkets discovered after many years of grave robbing.

The curators treated it like a royal visit, spending every day since its arrival emphasising the importance of the loan stock and its protection being paramount. The acclaim lauded on the security team to anyone who would listen was for the benefit of the insurance company alone, as it brought no bonuses, no perks, only more work.

Henry, along with Carl and Jock, made up the night shift. Tonight he was on fossils and the loan stock.

He sat close to the illuminated figure of Stan, an infusion of blues and pinks providing enough light for him to pick the glutinous goo from the grooves in his boot. Stan was the skeletal T Rex at the end of the fossil aisle, suspended in a running pose twelve feet in the air. An awesome spectacle when seen for the first time, but part of the furniture when seen every day. At night he was even involved in some of the conversations. Well, he was a good listener at least.

"Bloody kids, why can't they keep this shit in their gobs until they leave?" Stan stared down at him with sightless skeletal eyes as he shook the gum from his fingers into the bin.

"It's alright for you hanging around. I've got to clean this up." Stan didn't care.

"You know that's the first sign of madness, don't you?" Henry looked up to the balcony at the green face of Jock, illuminated by the emerald glow of the first floor.

"Come on mate, we're done. Time to get our money back. Need some help?"

Jock had completed inspection of the Living World and Carl was on his way down from Nature. It was close to break time, if he could halve Henry's shift they could get an extra twenty minutes.

"No, it's fine, Jock. I'll give the floor the once over and finish at the Exhibition. I'll be up in ten."

The cafe was on the fourth floor and the Exhibition was close to the elevator. With any luck they could squeeze out an extra fifteen minutes of poker, more than enough time to win another tenner. He was thirty quid up already and with two breaks left, the way Carl and Jock were playing he could see a fifty coming his way tonight.

He opened the cupboard and dragged out the floor buffer. A quick spin with this baby will have the floor shining in seconds. He whistled as he let the circular wheel buff away the blemishes. It was Friday tomorrow, his winnings will do nicely for a night out.

~

The Exhibition was impressive, the sarcophagus of Sasobek being the star attraction. It stood upright in the centre of the aisle on a stone plinth. In the gloom of the emergency lighting, the black silt-stone loomed over the exhibits like a giant shadow.

As he shone his torch across its surface, the true detail of this 600BC specimen came to life. The lid was finely detailed, carved with the features of Sasobeck wearing the wig of the Vizier, complete with beard and collar. The front of his intricately designed robe included the etchings of two hieroglyphic registers.

The rest of the exhibits, a collection of gold and clay artefacts, were held in blue-lit cabinets on either wall. An impressive selection found within the tomb at the time of the excavation.

Henry was pleased to see that the area was clear of any crap tonight. No discarded papers, crisp packets, empty coke cans left on the top of exhibition cases and best of all, no gum. Even the three mannequins depicting the servants of Sasobeck remained untouched on their podiums.

The other night one of the models had its tunic pulled up over its head, exposing the nappy like bandaging covering its genitals. Even worse, on the first night one of the bandages had been removed and stuck on its head like a turban, the tunic opened, its junk displayed to the world.

Reaching the elevator he paused before pushing the button to take him up. Something wasn't right, his inspection had been methodical, a task performed many times.

This time was different, only subtle but enough to make him

look again. He backed away, returning to the main hall to shine his torch over the exhibition. The beam illuminated something he hadn't noticed before. The mannequins; there were too many of them.

Two stood as before, in plain robes, holding a bowl to wash the body of their master during his journey to the afterlife. In the centre was the figure of a female. He wasn't an expert but if Henry had to guess, he would have said she was Cleopatra.

She wore a sheer dress covered in jewels. They sparkled as he moved towards her. Two coils of gold were shaped to resemble snakes cuffing her biceps. Across her chest a V-shaped necklace full of diamonds, pearls and multicoloured precious stones glimmered in the beam of his flashlight. When did they deliver this?

The reproduction was stunning. Her jet black hair had braids of coloured pearls hanging to her shoulders, the headband matching the jewels around her neck. But it was her face that drew him in; she was beautiful.

She was just as he would have pictured her. Clear complexion with black kohl liner outlining her dark eyes, and deep blue eyeshadow covering her upper lids. He could have been looking at a young Elizabeth Taylor from the movie; whoever modelled this was a craftsman, she looked so realistic.

Her head began to move, turning slowly until she faced him, her eyes locking onto his. She was smiling.

"What the hell?" He backed away as she began to walk towards him.

"Now Henry, that's not very nice. I can assure you I am not from hell." The woman had an accent, exotic but with an allure that reassured him.

"What… Who? Who are you? You can't be in here at this time of night." That's all he could think to say as she moved closer. Her walk was as exotic as her voice, all hip movement and nothing else, as she swayed towards him. Her head still, eyes focused on his, lips pursed, begging to be kissed.

He could only stare transfixed as she reached him, placing her arms around his neck and pulling his head towards her. The kiss was soft, sensual, full of passion. Her tongue pushed his lips apart, entwining with his own. He let it happen, what could he do? She was gorgeous, obviously knew him, from where he had no idea but he didn't care. One thing was for sure; this was better than poker!

He held her waist, feeling the softness of her skin as he pulled her close. Close enough for her to realise he was ready to take it further.

"Enough." The woman moved away; her breathing laboured, her voice soft.

"We can't here. Do you know anywhere we could get a little more comfortable? She stroked his neck, her touch gentle as fingers moved across his chest, past his stomach. She squeezed when she reached her intended target.

Henry swallowed back a gasp. This can't be happening! Instinctively he looked up, scanning the first floor balcony.

He expected to see Jock and Carl laughing down at him after pulling one of the many pranks they played on each other during the night shift. If this was one, then it was the best yet.

There was no sign of them which disappointed him a little, as if this wasn't a prank then the guys needed to see this.

"Who are you anyway?" He really didn't care who she was, he wasn't about to let this opportunity go, but he needed time to think. Where could he take her?

"It doesn't matter who I am, Henry. I have been observing you for weeks now. I wanted you from the first day I saw you, but I needed to find a way to be alone with you, in a position where you could not refuse me. I knew where you patrolled, your friend Jock told me; and here I am."

.   .   .

Her smile took away any doubts in his mind, its effect working wonders down below. He had to have her now, and he knew just the place

"Come with me."

He grabbed her hand, pulling her towards the lift. The elevator door opened immediately; it had been there for a while. Pressing B he pulled her towards him, the kissing firmer, more urgent as they descended to the basement level.

The staff room possessed a corner unit, brand new and comfortable. Jock and Carl were on the fourth floor, and the door had a lock. Perfect.

He tried to keep his pace even as they moved through the corridor. He felt like running but tried to play it cool, he didn't want to appear too keen. His heart was pounding, he was finding it difficult to walk and would explode if he didn't have her soon.

"Just give me a minute to freshen up, Henry" She removed his hand as they passed the toilets.

"I won't be a moment, get yourself ready for me. I have been waiting for this for so long." She licked her lips as she reversed into the ladies. He watched her until the door closed.

Sprinting to the staff room he set to work throwing everything off the sofa. He took the girly mags from the coffee table and thrust them into the desk drawers. Grabbing sandwich cartons, discarded paper cups and sweet wrappers, he pushed them into the over-flowing bin, shoving them down several times until the lid closed on its own.

The staff quarters had once been a storage room for unused or old display items before new health and safety directives were introduced.

Specifically, the museum was forced to provide an area for staff to take a break, a place of relaxation if required. Part of a new drive towards general wellbeing.

It coincided with the announcement that the museum was to be refurbished. There were high hopes of a modern state of the art rest area.

It didn't surprise them when it was unveiled as the old store room.

A carpet remnant left over from the refurbishment barely covering the centre of the room, an old desk with a defunct PC from one of the old research departments, a TV with a Freeview box and a kettle completed the makeover. At least they had a new sofa which was now free of any crap and dusted down to remove any crisp crumbs.

Thankfully the sofa came with a throw which will come in handy in the next few minutes.

She would be here any second and asked him to be ready. He was fine with that apart from the last item of clothing....should he leave his underwear on or not?

He chose not, settling himself on the sofa and covering his modesty with the throw. He tried several poses, trying to look alluring. He pulled the throw down to his waist showing his reasonably defined chest and his small crop of chest hair, but couldn't hold his stomach in enough to allow the sheet to stay flat. He tried laying on his side, leg up, resting his head on his hand, but with no arms on the sofa he couldn't support his head, his elbow kept sinking into the seat.

Henry decided, in the end, to lean back in the corner of the sofa, legs along the seat, facing the door.

The alarm sounded, wailing through the tannoy, shrill and urgent.

"SHIT!"

.   .   .

Henry leapt up, jumping over the back to retrieve his clothes, pulling on his boxers, stumbling forward as he snagged his other foot on the throw. Composing himself as best he could, he bounded to the door on one foot as his right boot struggled to stay on. His uniform thrown on haphazardly, his tie left behind.

The toilets were empty. He checked all four cubicles, each one devoid of an occupant. Ignoring the elevator he raced up the stairs and ran into the Fossil Hall to be met by Jock and Carl. Carl pushed buttons into the control panel, cutting the alarm.

"Where have you been, mate?" Jock noticed Henry's ramshackle uniform, in particular his open-necked shirt. The confusion on his face included a questioning look; he wasn't about to let this go without a full explanation.

"I got caught short." It was the best he could come up with as his head was all over the place. Where had the woman gone?

"Well, I think you might want to think of a better excuse than that." Carl was staring past the sarcophagus to the display area.

One of the doors to the ceramics was open.

2
___

It had been a long night. He managed to catch the bus just after the morning rush hour and huddled at the back of the upper deck, desperate for sleep.

The sun covered his face, making his eyes hurt. Even clenching them tightly failed to prevent the rays permeating through his eyelids like a red haze. His head was aching and he didn't have the energy to move away.

The police had questioned him as if he was an accomplice to the robbery.

A tiny sun disk amulet had been removed from the display cabinet. At only two centimetres high it had been easy to conceal. But several more valuable items were left behind which directed the questions toward the significance of the item. Why was it targeted? Who was the woman? Who did he work for?

Henry was too confused to provide sensible answers to any of the questions as he had no idea what was happening.

As far as he was concerned, he was a member of the security staff carrying out his duties when he was propositioned by a woman. He had enough about him to keep the real reason for taking her to the staff room to himself, preferring instead to explain that she wasn't dressed for the cool evening and he was going to find her a coat before showing her out.

This didn't go well with the investigating detective and he was taken back to the station and placed in a cell until they carried out further enquiries.

The cell had been cramped, furnished with one grey wool blanket that itched like crazy, a thin padded blue mat to lay on and a pillow that contained the feathers of a small chick.

After thirteen hours, a rubbery egg, a bit of stringy bacon, some dry toast washed down with a stewed cup of tea, he was allowed to leave.

CCTV placed throughout the museum captured everything. Thankfully there were no cameras in the staff room, but they showed the girl leaving the bathroom after he left her, and followed her back into the main hall where she opened the cabinet, removed the amulet, and disappeared into the night.

It was a relief to be cleared of any suspicion but the night in the cell had taken its toll. He had picked up a bug of some sort, probably from a real criminal detained there before him.

He felt awful. His head hurt, his chest hurt, he couldn't stop sneezing and he was sweating like a pig. It felt like the flu and it was getting worse, he was now beginning to shiver. The bus wasn't full and most of the passengers were in tee shirts and summer dresses, welcoming the sun as it blazed through the windows. It was going to be a glorious day.

He felt his chest tighten and managed to grab a tissue in time to smother his coughing fit, spasming as he tried to gather enough breath for the next bout. When it passed, he scrunched it up to return it to his pocket. His hand was covered in blood.

"Oh shit!"

3

One of the worst assignments for any agent is security detail, political conventions and open air rallies.

As he watched the audience take their seats for the President's speech in the open air rally outside the burnt out remains of the National Assembly building of Ouagadougou, Jack Case began to question, yet again, his motivation.

He was leader of the LARA wraith team, Land Air Reconnaissance Agency, a covert special forces team employed to aid world security forces against global threats. With no allegiances they were self sufficient and lethal.

The unit consisted of the elite from the armed forces and specialists in search and destroy missions, not babysitters for the International Monetary Fund to ensure the money was spent well.

Jack checked his watch, if anything was likely to happen it would be within the next thirty minutes.

As a francophone country, France had a vested interest in both security and the gold reserves. Burkina Faso, part of the Sahel region also involved NATO, and Ouagadougou being the capital of Burkina Faso and subject to many militant attacks, involved several joint security forces throughout the entire region. Who had employed LARA was known to only one man, Ed Ryker, head of the agency, after a tip off of a planned assassination of the President during his speech on public spending.

Intel suggested the attack could come from one of several factions, the Anusral Islam, the group for support of Islam and Muslims known as GSIM or Islamic State in the Greater Sahara known as ISGS, along with smaller militants building support against the Christian contingent of Burkina Faso.

"Jack, can you read?" Jack's earpiece crackled into life. It was Sara Moon, his eyes on the ground, in the air and through the airwaves.

Based at HQ in Central Operations she was his right hand, IT specialist, logistics expert and an experienced agent herself. She could track each operative and pinpoint targets, offering support when required. The PDA that all agents carried was their life support system, but it was Sara who kept them alive.

"Hi Sara, how's the weather?" He could sense her raising her eyes even from several thousand miles away. The operation was close to going down and Jack was as cool as ever.

"Same as always Jack, blue skies, sunshine and Central Operations more concerned about the mission than the continual perfect weather. Are you in position?"

From his post between the rubble of the former National Assembly building, destroyed during time of civil unrest, his vantage point covered the audience, the podium and the delegate's seating area.

"Yes Sara, I'm in position, hot, sweating, and picking up a little of the French dialect."

His understanding and willingness to learn a new language had never been a priority. It wasn't his problem, but he did admit that at times it could have helped, but his PDA bailed him out enough to continue his stance.

. . .

"Take that damned jacket off then, you are in Africa. Apart from warm downpours it's nearly always well over thirty degrees."

"You know that's not an option, Sara. What have you got for me?" He never left home without his leather, a jacket that he relied on either through superstition or as a talisman. It had saved him on many occasions, with its many cleverly tailored pockets whose contents could avoid detection even through the most vigorous of inspections. It was also damned comfortable.

"The gendarmerie have secured the borders at Mali and Niger as well as the main routes in and out of Ouagadougou. I have thirty in your vicinity, nothing else is showing up as yet. The President's cortege has just left the town hall, they'll be with you in ten minutes."

"OK, I'll check with Willy to see how he's getting on. How are we doing with the mines?"

The intel also reported a credible threat to all six goldmines which made Burkina Faso the fourth largest gold producer in Africa.

"Secured, and production has been halted for the next three hours. We've NATO forces on the ground, two of our men and gendarmerie in the surrounding areas."

"Great, I'd better get ready. Keep your eyes peeled Sara, out." Jack touched his ear cutting the call and looked around for the only gendarme who spoke passable English.

The area had been cleared of most of the rubble from the devastation in 2014 after the parliament building, along with many other political buildings were destroyed when the former President attempted to change the constitution. It took over four years to rebuild most of the buildings and along with it, the confidence of the people.

The National Assembly building however was kept as a burnt shell, a reminder to the people of Ouagadougou of the repercussions of civil unrest. It was also a statement from the government to demonstrate that governmental funds were being spent on the development of social services and not on their own resources.

It worked as far as bringing the community together was concerned, but over the past few years many more military forces had been drafted to fight against the growing terror attacks, and concerns were yet again surfacing that government coffers were being wasted on recruitment and training of a less than capable force to make any difference.

Terror attacks were still rife, unemployment was increasing and food stocks were at an all time low. This forced the IMF to intervene and a deal was struck to finance the economy, allowing the government to reduce the budget deficit to preserve the critical spending on social services and priority public investments.

The President and the Prime Minister were here to provide a united front, deliver the Social Services bill and confirm the economic growth report.

There must have been over a hundred already seated on the makeshift bleachers and more were pouring into the open square forecourt from all corners. They faced a stage bedecked in the colours of Burkina Faso, the red and green national flags waved gently in the breeze above, creating a rippling canopy roof.

Jack could see Willy over to the east, sporadically checking papers as spectators moved through the human cordons of the gendarmerie.

Wilbert Nwadike, twenty five, was one of the lucky ones offered a grant to study at the Dauphine University in Paris, culminating in a degree in Law. During this time he managed to pick up a rudimentary understanding of the English language and had been a great help to Jack so far.

"Hey Willy, just to let you know the cortege is on its way. Get the crowd seated as quickly as you can. We need to keep our eyes focused on the square."

"Yes, Mr Jack. Our work is moving through. Many will seat as we can." Jack got the gist, but he had to create a sense of urgency as he didn't want to be caught out.

"Right, close all other cordons, get your guys to point spectators to your position. Let's just leave one area to focus on. I'll take the podium and get one of your guys to take each corner facing the crowd."

Studying the crowd it was difficult to work out who were supporters of the regime, who were against or who were here for other reasons. The clothing, a mixture of loose fitting cotton shirts and pants, dresses and all in one tunics in a multitude of hues, just provided a blanket of colour.

Their faces gave nothing away as they were all stoic, expressionless, seemingly afraid to show their hand. No one spoke, staring straight ahead at the empty seating that awaited the government officials. Apart from the low hubbub of the crowd seeking entry, the silence from the audience was all the more disconcerting, as if everyone was waiting for something to happen.

"Jack, the cars are here." The crackle in his ear came from Sara. There was no need for the warning as the noise from the crowd outside had increased and the audience began to rise. There were chants of varying tones, some warbled calls, some screams, all building to a crescendo as some of the gendarmerie cordon parted to let the delegation through.

The President and Prime Minister, both sharply dressed in sober suits and tie, walked sombrely towards the podium, their faces expressionless as they focused on their destination.

Each was escorted by a soldier scrutinising the crowd, rifles held at their waists, fingers resting on the trigger.

The hubbub from the crowd began to subside as they gradually lowered onto their seats.

"Jack, do you read?" Sara came to life in his ear. Jack turned away from the crowd to hear more clearly.

"Hi Sara, what's up?" He could tell from her tone that she had come up with something.

"Not sure, Jack. Have you arranged a final sweep of your hotel?"

He looked past the crowd over to the only tall building within the vicinity of the square, his hotel. It had been emptied in the run up to the rally.

"No, Sara. It was done this morning and sealed off, guards to the front and rear."

"Well you have an intruder. There's someone on the rear stairwell. Take a look." He checked his PDA and could see the schematic of the surrounding area.

The square showed a blanket of green flashing dots representing the crowd and delegation within the confines of the barriers. Yellow dots highlighted the gendarmes positioned around the perimeter. Red dots indicated the crowd who were outside the square and as yet unchecked. One solitary dot flashed from the hotel, moving steadily to and fro as it ascended the stairs.

"I'm on my way, Sara. Keep me informed of the location." After hurriedly briefing Willie, Jack left him to take his position by the podium as he raced across the square, a gendarme stepping aside to let him exit as he headed for the hotel lobby.

He found the gendarme tasked with guarding the front entrance sprawled across the stairs, blood dribbled from the bullet hole in his head, dripping to join the red pool cascading onto the street.

Leaping clear of the corpse he pushed his way through the double doors and into the tiled reception area, scanning the room for the entrance to the stairwell. Two elevators positioned next to the seventies style oak reception desk were of no use as they had been deactivated that morning. He ran to the rear exit expecting to see another dead guard. There was nobody there.

"Jack, the intruder has stopped on the ninth floor in one of the rooms facing the rally."

"Yeah, and I've a feeling I know who it is." He spotted the door to the stairs.

"Sara, let me know if he moves, I'm on my way."

He pushed through the door and took the marble stairs two at a time. His footfalls echoed off the walls, there was no way the intruder could fail to hear him coming but there was no time to take evasive action. He had to get to the ninth floor.

By the time he reached the sixth floor he developed a steady rhythm, taking the stairs three at a time and gliding around the handrails to take the next flight.

It was his speed that saved his life as the bullet aimed at his head whistled behind him and crashed into the plastered wall, sprays of dust and chipping covered him as he leapt over the final four steps and rolled onto the eighth floor landing. Jack drew his Glock releasing a shot at the stairs above, the bullet sent a cloud of plaster into the air, missing his target.

He caught a glimpse of a military boot as it disappeared from view, the door to the ninth floor crashing against its frame as it was forced open.

Scrambling to his feet he gave chase. Reaching the door he eased it inwards a few inches with his foot, anticipating another attack, none came. Hearing the distinct click clack of a rifle being loaded a little way off along the corridor, he took a deep breath and launched himself through the door, rolling forward and in one continuous movement falling onto his stomach, his Glock extended ready to release a bullet.

The corridor was lit with a faint green hue from the emergency lighting, the wall lamps having been disabled, it made detection near impossible. His eyes didn't take long to adjust and confirm that he was alone. Eight doors down, a thin shaft of light shone onto the hall carpet, this could either be a trap or the room he needed. He had no time to make a decision either way but favoured his odds. If the assailant was concentrating on him then the target was safe for now, if it was the correct room he would be on him in seconds.

The carpet smothered his footfalls as he approached the open door. Flattening against the frame he risked a glance through the opening.

He could make out a tripod and the butt of a sniper rifle, just as he'd feared. But there was no one behind it, which meant he was either waiting for him to enter or it was a trap. In his current position he could see the length of the corridor on both sides; empty.

The door opposite was shut which would only compromise the gunman, as Jack would have him as soon as the door moved inwards. He had to be inside.

A stand off was an option, wait out the rally. He had sight on the gun and could react as soon as the gunman took hold of the rifle, but he was sure that if he was an Islamic insurgent, he would not wait around for long. Besides that, Jack was not one to wait around either and he hated surprises. There was only one thing to do.

Staying with his back against the wall, he used his heel to push the door inward. Light from the room spread into the hall illuminating the orange, black and gold angular designs of the carpet.

A bullet burst through the door at head height, shattering the door frame inches from his ear, exactly as he expected and needed; the location and position.

Jack squatted and launched at the door, rolling into the room with his Glock at the ready. He fired a volley into the far corner behind the now open door, hoping that he had his calculations right. He had...

The gendarme fell to his knees, blood spluttering from his mouth as his shattered lung expelled more than just oxygen. As he collapsed forward, with his dying breath he shot one last bullet, shattering the window sending shards of glass onto the street below.

Jack moved to the window and looked down at the crowd, most were standing and staring towards the hotel. In times of crisis there were two types of reaction, freeze or flight. The crowd were of the former, nobody moved. Scanning the podium Jack searched for Willy and found him close to the delegation in the same stance as the others, staring straight at him.

He was a hundred yards away at least but he was hoping that his cut throat action, waving his hand under his chin from side to side, would bring Willy into action. They needed to get the officials away from the site as it had been compromised and it may not be the only threat. Willy gave him the thumbs up, moving towards the President to escort them away.

The rifle was an American M40A5 sniper rifle with suppressor and day scope, accurate at a thousand metres. It was unusual to be American, but as some were taken from fatally wounded US servicemen during the Middle East conflicts, it was impossible to tell how the insurgents had obtained it.

He peered through the scope and wasn't surprised to see the face of the President within the viewfinder. At this short distance he could see the sweat begin to materialise across his balding scalp.

Willy whispered into the dignitary's ear and began to escort him away. The escort by the President's shoulder pushed Willy away making it clear that it was his job to guide him to safety.

As Willy staggered backward, the escort placed his hand on the President's forehead, yanked the head back exposing the dignitary's throat and grabbing a knife from his belt, lifted it towards the exposed flesh. With no time to think Jack pulled the trigger, the shot at such a short distance blew a quarter of the man's head away, the knife falling from his grasp as he fell back into a row of seating, sending chairs across the podium.

The crowd erupted in hysteria, trying to climb over each other to escape. Women screamed, men yelled and guttural chants filled the air.

'Shit!' This was all he needed. Jack bolted out of the room and leaped the stairs.

"Sara!" He shouted as he reached the third floor. "Get some support to the square, we have several situations and I'm not sure how many more we'll have."

He was the only LARA agent in the area with a team of poorly trained soldiers as back up. If there were more threats he couldn't rely on Willy and his even less capable comrades.

"Done, Jack. Mike and Rory are on their way from the mines, they'll be with you in fifteen minutes."

That was Sara all over, she could second guess agents before she was needed. The mines were at least twenty minutes away, so she read the situation and acted as soon as he entered the room in the hotel.

"Great, keep your eyes peeled, I've a feeling this isn't the end."

He left the hotel, leaping clear of the corpse sprawled across the front steps and headed towards the square.

Something was wrong. He hadn't noticed it as he descended the stairs while communicating with Sara, but now it was evident. The crowd had quietened.

~

Entering the square he was surprised to see it as full as before, although this time they all stood in silence.

At the podium the President, the Prime Minister, what was left of their guard detail and Willy stood stationary, their eyes trained on the crowd. It struck Jack that everyone in the square was facing centre.

He eased his way through the throng until he was in front of a solitary figure, the crowd spread around him at a respectable distance.

He was sweating profusely, his ebony skin glistening in the sunlight. Wearing a traditional embroidered tunic of deep blue with a leather waistcoat hanging open from his shoulders, Jack could see the wires and blocks of C4 very clearly. In his right hand he gripped a metal tube, wires leading back to the vest, his thumb pressed firmly on a button at the top of the tube…A dead man's switch.

"Allahu Akbar, Allahu Akbar…"

repeating the phrase over and over again without taking his eyes off of the President, as if in a trance. He took no notice of Jack as he approached his right shoulder, which wasn't good. He had to draw his attention for fear of surprising him, causing his thumb to slip off the trigger.

" Come on fella…" Jack moved slowly into the man's view. The eyes snapped to his as he moved past his peripheral vision. Jack stopped, holding out his hands to show that he came in peace. The chanting stopped.

" Come on fella…" He began again. " Is this really worth it?" He couldn't think of anything worthwhile. He knew that this terrorist was intent on blowing himself and everyone around him to pieces. It was the will of Allah, a promise of vestal virgins and a wealth beyond imagining. He needed to distract the insurgent somehow, to give him time to think.

He took a slow step towards him, more of a shuffle in an attempt to glide, while keeping his eyes locked on the bomber's determined stare.

"How old are you?" Again not the best thing, but he needed to get within arms length. He looked no more than early twenties, if that. The beard often makes the face look older than it is, and this guy was a young man. Yet another, brainwashed or influenced by an indoctrination of lies and fantasy.

"Come on son, how old are you… twenty one, twenty two?" He could see the young man's eyes relax from their intense stare as he watched him, his arms extended, offering a form of mediation, a calming voice, waiting for an answer, a simple answer.

The young man noticeably calmed, although he began to shake. Jack moved another shuffle step forward, he was now two arm lengths away.

" Nineteen." His voice was soft, nervous, lacking any conviction. His face changed from fierce determination to one of fear, his eyes began to flit from Jack to the crowd around him, occasionally flicking left and right, checking for any movement. It was not a good sign.

He eased another few inches towards the bomber while thinking of another question to bring him back to neutral again.

"No!..."

A shout from the podium caused everyone on the square to turn to the front. Willy was wrestling with another of the Presidential escorts, the loud crack made everyone dip their heads instinctively.

Jack dived at the man, catching him by the hand as he fell backwards, making sure that his own hand gripped around the dead man's switch over the bomber's. His face was covered in blood as the ruined carotid artery from the young man's open neck wound pumped life away from him and into the agent's face.

The crowd broke apart and ran for their lives, shouts and screams filled the air as they fought to leave from all directions. Jack smothered the body of the dying bomber along with their entwined fists with his own, ensuring that however hard he was kicked, jostled, fallen on, the switch would remain down.

As the noise subsided to a distant furore, he began to hear the sickening gurgle from the wounded man's mouth as he tried to swallow, but without a larynx and destroyed oesophagus, it just sent more blood into the air. Another sound reached his ears that caused Jack to move closer to the bomber's vest. It was a beep, quite faint, but definitely a rhythmic beep, a rhythmic beep that matched perfectly the spurts of blood squirting from the ruined neck.

"Sara..." He was panicking now as he feared the worst.

"Jack, thank God. How are things?"

"No time for pleasantries Sara, I'm lying on a suicide bomber with a dead man's switch that is killing my hand. I hear a beep... should I be concerned? I've a feeling I'm in trouble."

His earwig fell silent as Sara investigated. The beep was constant but the rhythm wavered, sometimes speeding up, slowing slightly, skipping a beat and catching up with itself.

.   .   .

"Jack, it's fine as long as it keeps beeping. I assume he is alive?"
He feared that would be the answer.

"He's going Sara, half his neck has been blown away. He's got minutes at best."

"Then get out of there, Jack. Leave now…"

She knew what she'd said as soon as it left her mouth, but it was Jack and she cared for him. More than she should and more than she would like. They agreed to not let it get in the way of missions and nine times out of ten it was never an issue, but occasionally that one percent reared its head, normally when Jack was in trouble. He was now in desperate trouble.

"It's linked to the heartbeat, Jack… a fail safe to ensure that it explodes whether by the bomber's own hand or should he be taken out."

"And in particular to avoid a situation like this. Great. Give me a minute to think, I'll get back to you."

"No Jack, I'm here to support. I'll stay right here." She was not going to leave him, not at this time.

"Sara, I need time to think and I don't have a lot of that. I'll get back to you. Out."

"Jack. No!…" Jack used his free hand to rip the earwig from his ear and shove it into his jacket. He needed the short time he had to work a plan.

Over at the podium he could see Willy escorting the shackled guard out of the square. He was obviously an insurgent and had shot the bomber to ensure the mission would not fail. So far it had, but not for much longer.

His eyes moved to the blackened beams from the destroyed National Assembly building poking up behind the makeshift podium. He really hoped that the devastation had been total, he had an idea.

"Willy!" He shouted across the square.

" Over here, I need you, quick!"

He waited for the gendarme to hand the insurgent to a colleague, before sprinting to his side.

. . .

"Give me a hand, Willy. Help me up and lift this man onto my shoulders. Take his legs."

They hoisted the dying man onto Jack's shoulders, allowing him to hold the dead man's switch in his right hand and the legs with his left. Blood was still oozing from the bomber's neck but it had slowed and the beeps now close to his right ear became more erratic, stopping on occasion which made Jack instinctively close his eyes to wait for the end. They needed to move fast.

"Guide me through to the Assembly Room Willy, then leave as quickly as you can." Jack took the lead.

"No Mr Jack, I will be your escort. It is my duty." Willy took over the lead and led them around the podium and into the skeletal ruin of the burnt out building.

The acrid smell still hung in the air, emanating from the now char-coaled beams that once held walls and a roof. The area was covered in debris and waste dumped over the years by locals, adding an additional aroma that was sticking to the back of Jack's throat. He tried to keep inhaling to a minimum for fear of gagging and drop-ping his passenger.

"Take me to the centre of the main building, Willy. Then get out of here."

Willy looked at Jack and was about to argue when he saw the urgency in the Englishman's face. He needed to move fast.

Lifting debris from their path, the gendarme cleared a swift route through the rubble, throwing brick on top of brick, sending corrugated sheets and timber flying left and right and kicking general rubbish out of their way. Suddenly he stopped and raised his hand.

"We cannot go further, Mr Jack. The floor is no longer a floor." Willy turned, looking for an alternate route.

"No, this is fine Willy. It was what I was hoping. Now move to the edge of the building and get ready to run."

The gendarme looked at him quizzically, he wasn't about to leave their visitor and protector on his own.

"Willy, go! I'll be right behind you."

The beep slowed…almost inaudible. It was now or never.

"GO!" He barked the order so loud he was sure Willy jumped a few inches from the ground as he began to back away. He then returned to the task at hand, hoping this would work. To be honest with himself, he had no choice.

In front of him was a gaping hole where the roof had collapsed through the floor during the fire, exposing the basement. He had guessed right.

He bent his knees until he was on haunches and let the legs of the bomber slide down his back and onto the floor. A gurgle came to his ear and with it globules of blood…small globules, remnants of what blood was left in the young man's body as he twisted away keeping hold of the switch, until the bomber's body was lying face down in front of him.

Placing his free hand on the dying man's head he pushed forward, sliding the body towards the hole. Once the legs were over the edge, the rest of the body started to follow suit, slipping slowly into the basement. Taking his hand away and grabbing the dead man's switch with both hands he let the weight carry it over. Jack went back onto his haunches as he took the weight until only the bomber's hand, along with both of his were visible. Suddenly the beep stopped, replaced with a continuous high pitched whine. The heart had stopped. It was now or never.

As soon as Jack let go the explosion knocked him backward, along with concrete, beams and rubble. He scrambled to his feet as he felt the floor move and started to run, a beam from the roof joist crashed behind him in the exact spot he had first got to his feet, he felt a jolt as the floor dropped an inch, it was about to fall in on itself.

He could see Willy at the edge of the building some fifty feet away, he was holding his hands out as a mother would to entice her child to run into her arms. A hole appeared in front of him as floorboards gave way and dropped into the void, this was going to be close.

. . .

Leaping over the expanded hole, his landing caused the remaining floor to steadily fall around him. He could see Willy still, but he appeared to be taller, Jack was slowly descending past ground level. With ten feet to safety he leapt forward, flailing arms and legs like a long jumper to add extra momentum.

He crashed into Willy's midriff and grabbing hold for dear life, the two men rolled out of the Assembly room and crashed into the rear of the podium.

~

Jack lay on his back and took in deep breaths, staring at the blue sky, beautiful blue sky and fresh air, sweet clean fresh air. Nothing mattered for a moment or two as he felt his heart reduce from the pounding in his chest to a steady thump that he could still hear in his ears.

Willy lay alongside, mumbling something incoherent, but he could guess it was a prayer, thanking his God for getting out alive.

"Well, that was close." Jack finally broke the silence as he began to feel human again.

Where the Assembly building skeleton had once stood, he could see only trees, bushes and shrubs. The whole shell had fallen in on itself.

" I think our government will be very pleased." Willy was following his gaze to the hole full of rubble in front of them.

"They have been trying to arrange funds to pay for the full demolition of the building. You have done it for us, Mr Jack."

Jack gave a wry smile as he thought of everything they had been through in the last hour. Willy still had a pragmatic view of the result of all the devastation, turning it into a positive. One thing was sure, with Willy at the helm of the Burkina Faso gendarmerie, they will be alright.

. . .

Taking the earwig from his jacket he placed it in his ear and getting to his feet, left Willy to look over their demolition project. He activated the speaker.

"Sara, all done."

Jack was reporting in as if he'd just finished decorating a house or taken out the rubbish. All done, that was it. Sara, relief flooding over her, collected herself for fear of tears, clearing her throat several times to avoid it breaking when she replied.

"Good to hear." She tried desperately to keep her composure.

" The dignitaries are back to their offices and safe, Mike and Rory have captured three more insurgents in the melee as the crowd dispersed. They will be continuing the investigation in the city. The ISGS has claimed responsibility, but we can't be sure if they know they have failed. NATO are sending over troops to clean up in the next 48 hours. They'll be increasing security for a while."

That was music to Jack's ears, he was going home. Back to Marizian and his small but adequate safe house overlooking Mount's Bay and the beautiful Cornish coastline. A place where he was known as Matt Collins, IT consultant for a global network group. He was rarely there these days, but the villagers knew enough about him to keep his cover intact.

It would be great to be back, take time out to relax as a normal human being. Run along the sandy beaches, a pie and a pint at the Jackdaw, playing pool with the locals.

He could almost smell the clean air, the stale beer and the fresh fish caught only that morning and displayed by the harbour to be the main course for that evening.

" Ed wants you back here, Jack." Sara burst his idyllic bubble with those six words.

" Hang on, Sara. I should be on R&R. Can't someone else take it, whatever it is?" He wasn't about to volunteer for more missions just yet.

There were times that he wished he could stop taking any missions at all. He was tired, stressed and at times, had enough.

But it didn't last, he knew that. He had been military most of his life and he knew nothing else.

"We are all on it, Jack. This is global and a biggie. All leave has been cancelled and all field agents are active. You need to get back here, Ed will explain everything. "

"Wow, that sounds serious." His interest had been piqued.

"What can you tell me, Sara? Can you get me intel to digest on the trip back? Ed will expect us to be in the know."

"Not this time, Jack. It's need to know and I can't fill you in until you get here. But you have a special assignment, that's all I can tell you. A plane is waiting for you at the airport, get there as soon as you can."

"Oh come on Sara, how long have we known each other? This is a secure channel, surely you can give me the SP. What is it all about? Give me something." Jack found it strange that Sara wouldn't let him in on what was going on. She was normally on his side.

"All I can say Jack, is the world is dying, we are dying, and if we can't come up with a solution soon, it could lead to the end of the human race."

4

Rachel pushed the control for the doors to slide clear, allowing Gerard to enter the chamber. As the door closed behind him he disappeared for a few seconds in a fog of cleansing aids before a tone registered at the desk. She opened the main doors to allow access.

"Is he there?" Gerard entered reception and headed to the executive suites.

"Yes, he is, and he is not in the best of moods." Her board lit as a call came into her headset.

"Good Morning, BioTane, how can I direct your call?" She waved Gerard through as she pushed the buttons to connect the conversation.

Not in the best of moods, when was he in a good mood? Gerard was on treatment duty, never the most pleasant of tasks, but essential to remain employed.

Hopefully, this one will last a little longer. Last time was only a week, before that they managed to stabilise it for nearly three. They were playing a cat-and-mouse game and for now, the mouse was winning.

Holding his breath, he pushed open the door initialled CEO and entered the room.

Dr Gordon Nightly sat by the window on the Eames lounger, his feet resting on its ottoman. He was covered in a throw up to his neck and from the sound of his laboured breaths he was going downhill again. He moved his gaze from the view outside to the movement at the door.

"Is it improved?" His voice hoarse from his last racking coughing fit.

Gerard moved to the side table and removed the steel bowl full of bloodied tissues.

"There are improvements, we have managed to stop the reproduction before the gene pool restructured. But it is starting to become unstable to the extent that it is beginning to swap genetic signatures. We may not have many more opportunities."

Nightly rolled his sleeve above his elbow and offered his arm to his aide.

"And what of the immunes?" He watched as the needle entered his vein through the bruised pin cushioned skin of the crook.

"Nothing yet. We thought we were close but we lost two of our more hopeful subjects."

Gerard finished the treatment, placing the syringe back into the medivac. The recovery would be rapid and he wanted to be clear before his patient became well again. It was a race against time with everything else he had to do.

"Send Stacy to me in forty-five minutes. Now go." Nightly pulled back his sleeve and returned to the view of the gardens.

Gerard left the table, silently making his way to the altar by the hearth. Kneeling on one knee he bowed his head…

"Oh Ra

You God of Life, you Lord of Love, All men live when you shine.

You are the crowned King of the Gods.

The Goddess Aset embraces you,

and enfolds you in all seasons.

Those who follow you sing to you with joy,

and they bow down their foreheads to the earth In gratitude for your radiant blessings."

He stared at the disc on top of the falcon headed statue of Ra - Horakhty, deity of the sun, and rising backed away until he reached the centre of the room. He could hear the throw being moved aside, a sign that he should be leaving.

"I will arrange your meeting with Stacy." He said without looking back.

Once the door was shut behind him he closed his eyes for a few seconds, relieved that his shift was over. With any luck they would either have the cure or Nightly would be dead before he needed to do this again.

Nightly finished wedging the knot of his tie in between the stiff collar to establish perfect symmetry. Checking that his receding crown was suitably hidden he ran his fingers through the front of his hair, ensuring that his black locks were slightly lifted at the front to give the impression of a full head of hair.

Through the reflection of the mirror he stared with longing at the model of the obelisk, in particular at the pyramid shaped Benben Stone.

"I must taste the fruits of the tree of life. Soon it will be mine."

. . .

He turned just as the sun appeared overhead. It was close to midday and the rays began to enter the room through the pentagonal pyramid styled skylight. As the seconds moved towards noon, each of the five sides created their own shaft of light, crawling across the floor until they reached their destination, a golden disc positioned at five quadrants of the room.

As the clock chimed the first peal of twelve, the discs diverted the light into a criss cross of beams each ending at an ornament. The first shone on the pyramid atop the obelisk, the second on the statue of Bennu the phoenix, the third shone on the golden cat Mau and the fourth on the sun disc above the head of the Ra - Horakhty. As the four radiated the sun's rays, the fifth hit the mirror causing it to move aside to reveal a small tree bearing fruits of a pear, designed to grow in the shape of a tear, their golden skin glowing in the light like jewels.

Picking a fruit from one of the branches Nightly took a bite, closing his eyes as the bitter sour flavour filled his mouth.

"Oh RA God of Life, you Lord of Love, All men live when you shine."

He spoke with the conviction that flowed through his heart, filled his senses and reaffirmed the pledge that, as the descendant of Amenhotep IV he would fulfil his destiny, eat from the true tree of life, and live a life eternal.

5

Stacy Mickelson loved San Francisco, the culture, the way of life and most of all the weather. After leaving MIT she wasn't sure where in Biochemistry she would realise her potential, until she was approached by BioTane four years ago. It was an offer she could not refuse.

She had been monitored carefully by the Gordon Nightly foundation, a fund that ensured he obtained first dibs on the Alumni and she possessed everything they needed. Now she was here, now she knew what she was tasked to do, she realised why she had been chosen.

Being from the Bronx was good grounding. Having a criminal record from theft to murder was not a prerequisite, but it helped profile her. That was 10 years ago, enough time to turn her life around, and with an intelligence bordering on genius she was perfectly malleable for the BioTane project.

To the world BioTane was a pharmaceutical giant, leading the way in wellbeing, pioneers in stem cell research and leaders in the development of cures for the blight of mankind. They were one or two stages away from a cure for most cancers, no more than three years away from the reversal of dementia and ready to deliver to the world a remedy to eradicate rheumatoid arthritis.

. . .

Internally, BioTane was the front for a quest for immortality, headed by a man who by rights should be over 3000 years old. Gordon Nightly was born into a wealthy family of oil barons, part Texan and part Middle Eastern through ancestry. The Nightly family can be traced back to Africa as most can, linked as far back as 1345BC where the line completes with Amenhotep IV. Either through a freak of nature or a genetic breakdown, Gordon Nightly has the genome similar if not identical to an Ancient Egyptian.

During his growing years Nightly became fascinated with his ancestors, in particular the earliest, even practising the worship of the sun to the horror of his orthodox family. As he reached his teens, his health began to deteriorate. He suffered from anaemia, constant iron deficiency and eye infections. These were seen as illnesses of the modern age that could happen to anyone, it was just that Nightly had drawn the short straw and suffered from several conditions where most people would only have one or two.

Then there was the hospitalisation. Two occasions in particular that gave cause for concern. He was rushed into hospital at the age of 14, complaining of severe pain in his eyes, and swelling that caused one eye to close. After an emergency operation they managed to save his sight and in time he made a full recovery. Tests however had shown traces of galena, cerrusite, laurionite and phosgene, four chemicals high in lead.

The school he attended was quizzed about the chemicals used in science classes and discounted as none of the elements were present.

Nightly was asked to recall if he may have been in contact with any other chemicals. Had something been thrown into his face or had he ever painted his eyes? All were strenuously denied.

The last question was asked specifically because of his interest in ancient Egypt, as all four chemicals were used as make up by the Pharaohs, as eyeliner and eyeshadow. Having exhausted all avenues it was a throw away line from the surgeon, quickly discounted by all as more of a quip than a diagnosis.

It was the second admission to A&E that caused most consternation to both medical staff and his parents. At 17 he had become listless, drained to the extent that he found even walking exhausting. There was also the acute stomach pains and no appetite which became so debilitating that his screams of agony had him admitted directly into emergency surgery.

The operation uncovered two Schistosoma worms in his intestines and stomach with several eggs flowing in his bloodstream. Again he made a full recovery after removal and a blood transfusion, but as Nightly had never travelled to Africa, the Middle East or Surinam, it was near impossible that he could have been anywhere to be infected and there was no doubt that he only bathed, drank or swam in clean clear water. This time there was no quip, but Nightly knew that it was systemic in ancient Egypt.

By thirty five and with a doctorate in biochemistry, Nightly inherited half a billion dollars and the oil business after his parents were killed in a car crash off the coast of Mexico. His devastation caused him to turn his back on oil, selling the business for less than half its worth to start BioTane. He had two motives, the first to create a powerhouse; the second to employ the best biochemists, researchers and developers in the world with the specific goal of self discovery and once confirmed, his ultimate goal.

He set out a series of tests, programs and procedures to build a genome map of himself, he had too many questions, too many insights and too many thoughts to imagine that he was like any other human being. But he needed the expertise to confirm it, and within ten years he obtained the answer.

Through extensive tests, research, and numerous comparisons, he was found to have mutations in 95% of his mRNA which caused the amino acids to produce proteins identical to those of the DNA of tests made on bone and tissue fragments from 3000 to 4000 years ago; the DNA of a Pharaoh.

It pleased him, gave him comfort and reaffirmed what he always knew. His faith, his goals and his destiny were preordained. He surrounded himself with a trusted core to help with his creation and a team of explorers to find the final piece of the puzzle; the key to eternal life.

Stacy was a major part of his inner temple or the 24 as he liked to call them, one of the biochemists tasked to create the pestilence that he needed to become the saviour of mankind. A pestilence that would be so devastating, so cruel, that he would not only be seen as the saviour, but as a true god. A descendant of a true servant of the Sun disc, with the power of RA- Horakhty himself.

She wanted to believe in her boss as she was the one who discovered his mutated genome and it was irrefutable that he had the DNA of an ancient race. But she was also a realist and she understood that a chemical reaction can sometimes be more hit and miss and in this scenario, a miss could wipe out the human race.

His plan was simple but flawed. Create a world pandemic, provide the cure, elevate BioTane into the world leader, destroy the competition and then provide Utopia; the chance to live forever.

It could be seen by some to be megalomania, but those in the know were more than aware that it was the natural thinking and desires of a Pharaoh, a world leader, a man who wanted to show the way. The rewards were incredible, one of her main reasons for seeing this through. She was four months away from her thirtieth and she was already a millionaire.

But if she wanted it to last, in fact if they all wanted it to last, they had to find the cure faster than they initially thought, and again it was down to Nightly.

He developed a strain of pneumonic plague modified to be resistant to all current drugs…it was a risk as the Y.pestis was unstable at the best of times, creating its own way of subverting the human immune system. Currently there are five different drugs administered to counteract the disease, only one of which will work in any given prognosis. By Nightly altering the pathogen-associated molecular patterns he had effectively given the PAMPs a brain, it could now mutate as and when it was threatened, making it impossible to treat.

She thought back to when the inner temple were summoned to a general meeting six days ago.

"Here we go, and about bloody time." Mitch Dawson looked at the others around the table; the scientist, the three chemists, the three immunes, his fellow commander Mel, and their Scorpion team.

Every one of his men looked uncomfortable in their suits, but it was a Nightly thing, he expected every one of the 24 to be executives and fatigues weren't suited to the mahogany boardroom.

"This is what we've been waiting for boys and girls and trust me, it'll be worth it." Half was for effect, the other was that Mitch got to know Nightly more than most.

As a mercenary, a gun for hire, he was ready for anything as long as the price was right. Two million dollars bought him for life.

Nightly just wanted a crew to search the globe for an artefact, an ancient scroll of immense power apparently, some sort of roadmap to a weird field of reeds. He wasn't concerned what it was, he just needed to find it. The problem was, nobody knew where it was, where to start, or even if it had been discovered yet; they just knew that it existed.

They'd scoured most of the globe starting with the obvious, Egypt, and found nothing. They learned from sources that it was buried in a Sun temple with one of the lesser kings, as legend has it. But as only two of the fifteen or so that were purportedly built had so far been discovered, it could still be out there somewhere in the sand. But it paid the bills and he was more than happy to continue to cash the cheques.

They only had to resort to fire power on two occasions so far. Once in Columbia where a collector of ancient treasures assumed they were after his drug trade, and again in the north of Moscow where this time, a collector, also an active member of the Bratva, thought they were Soviet police. That one ended with a few less members of the Russian mafia by the time they had finished.

Nightly entered the room, a smile crossing his face as he saw all 23 present. Good, what he was about to tell them would affect them all

"Good morning everyone, another fine day forecast for Frisco and an even brighter day for BioTane."

His smile broadened as he looked at the faces in front of him, each one in turn, savouring his inner temple; the 24 who would change the world. He was about to press the start button and he was finding it hard to control his excitement. He wanted to tell them now, get it out in the open, but first he had one thing to do.

He opened the aluminium attache case and turned it around so that the contents were there for everyone to see. Inside were twenty vac tubes, each containing a red translucent liquid.

He slid the case towards Dawson.

"Take one, Mitch, and pass it on. Lincoln, Aya and Lacy you don't get one."

He watched as each took a syringe, looking from the liquid to Nightly, questioning the intent.

"OK, now don't worry, this is perfectly safe. I want you all to administer a shot and I'll explain everything. "

He waited as the room went silent.

Mitch was the first to comply, a hiss from the vac as he injected was followed by fifteen more as the rest of the Scorpion team followed suit. Next came the scientist, Saul Milliner, leaving the biochemists still staring at the vial.

.   .   .

Of all of the 24, the biochemists were always going to be the ones to take their time as they tried to break down the chemicals they were about to push into their bloodstreams. Without the means to analyse, read the report, double check their findings and retest just to be doubly sure, they were faced with the biggest quandary.

Gerard Payne was the first to administer, part through curiosity, but mainly because of the money. He was more of a mercenary than some of the Scorpions around the table when it came to the mulla. Drew Templar was the next. The quietest of the group, he did his job, kept his nose clean and hated making decisions, so he would always go with the majority.

"What's in it?"

Stacy wasn't about to stick anything in her without knowing the facts and the boyish enthusiasm of her boss worried her.

Nightly gave her what he hoped was a more than winning smile. He thought there would have been more dissenters than just Stacy, but he definitely knew she would be one of them, hence the reason for hiring her. He needed his biochemists to question everything and not be afraid to start again. To rethink, rework and strive for perfection, but time was running out. August was the deadline and everything was in place; or it would be once he set the wheels in motion.

"Stacy, I'm glad you asked, that is what I pay you for. But I also pay you for your loyalty and trust."

His expression changed. The smile disappeared, replaced by a glare that most around the room had seen many times. A glare that made it very clear that there was only one way to be part of the 24; total compliance.

"All I will say, for the moment, is that it is for your protection. Now hurry along so we can get started. I will give you until I return to my seat. More than enough time."

He took two items from the case, slowly walked around the table and placed one in front of Lacy and the second with Lincoln. Returning to his seat, he stopped for a few seconds behind Stacy for effect. He smiled as he heard the hiss of the final vac tube expel its contents.

" Good, now let's begin."

Nightly livened the video wall behind him. An image from an elcc-tron micrograph filled the screen, a mass of blobs and swirls, linking and rolling over each other.

"This, ladies and gentleman, is the Yersinia pestis bacteria. As we know, the Pneumonic plague. We have been working tirelessly to develop the pathogen to ensure there is no known cure and thanks to all your efforts we have achieved our goal. I'd like to congratulate each and every one of you for your dedication and hard work so far."

He allowed his smile to drop once again, this time to be replaced by a look of resignation.

"But, we have run out of time to develop our cure. August will be here before we know it and we have much to do in the coming weeks. So I have come up with an incentive, an incentive that will ensure we all benefit from untold riches for the rest of our lives, fame normally reserved for pop idols and movie stars, as the saviours of all mankind. This, ladies and gentlemen, is the ultimate goal, the reason BioTane was formed. To make the world a better place, to eradicate all illness and to make the earth healthy forever."

They were waiting for the catch, there was always a catch with Nightly, but he liked to stretch it out. He changed the screen to an image of a parchment, an ancient scroll, full of hieroglyphics, blurred to avoid translation. The figure underneath stated; winning bid $12 million.

"And this is what we have been waiting for."

The image was from the dark web, the scroll had been found

and was available to the highest bidder. The figure changed to $15 million.

" I have information that says it is somewhere in Cairo. Mitch and Mel, get your crew down there straight after this meeting. The rest of you, Aya I need you in Egypt, Lacy you are to head to the Americas and Lincoln, I need you in Asia. Stacy, Drew and Gerard; I need you to save my life."

The room sat in stunned silence as everyone focused on the man in front of the screen. Nightly, a satisfied grin on his face, took his seat at the head of the table.

"I have injected myself with the bacterium, and have full blown Pneumonic plague."

He held his hand in the air to stop the buzz of questions as they flew from all directions.

"Wait everyone, all will become clear with a little more patience." He loved to build the tension and he could feel it filling the room.

The biochemists sat open mouthed, the immunes understandably were surprised but had no fear of being in the same room with him, which is more than can be said for the Scorpion team. Some stood up from their seats, moving to the back of the room. Those that didn't started shouting expletives, some of which he had never heard before.

"Alright people, calm down. The vaccine you injected yourself with is a refined strain of Y.Pestis F1+V antigen created by myself. It will prevent you from contracting the disease carried in the atmosphere, and none of you are my type, so a kiss is out of the question. But I thought we should up the stakes a little as we are running out of time. Stacy, Gerard and Drew, get to work on a vaccine to prevent me from dying. Remember, unless you find a cure, all of your funds, any future funds and your careers will cease…"

Again silence, he was enjoying this.

"...But, that's not going to happen as I have every faith in my team, which is just as well as I have one other thing."

He pointed to the thin tubes that he had passed to the two immunes.

"Leave them sealed for now. You both have a lip balm that contains a high strain of the pathogen, I need you to use it during your trips; get close to people, drink in every bar, be promiscuous, over friendly. I need you to spread the disease while we work on the cure... Oh, and Aya, good work in Manchester, the balm has proved its worth. Right, I think that is all for now. Any questions?"

"That's it for now. Any questions? Yes I have a question...Have you gone fucking mad?"

Mitch could not believe what he was hearing, He knew Nightly was strange, different, but this was the edge of madness.

"You are ready to start the spread of a plague around the world; you have given yourself a death sentence and we have no way of stopping it. What happens if you can't find a cure? What happens if you die? Where does it leave us, the people we infect, the world we live in?" He wasn't one to panic normally, but he was now shitting himself.

He was a soldier not a chemist, he had no way of altering the path and he had a team, who by the looks of them, were ready to down tools and run for their lives.

" Ok, I'll answer that very simply." Nightly was on a roll, he felt empowered, confident. This was exactly what this needed.

"If I die, the world dies with me. But that is not going to happen. I have every faith in my team, and I will head the research. Between the four of us and the rest of the lab technicians we will not fail. I just need my Scorpions and immunes to do their part. So enough chat, let's get to work."

.   .   .

Nightly closed the attache case and calmly left the room leaving the twenty three staring at the closed door trying to digest what they heard.

~

Stacy could hear Nightly finish his prayer to RA and upon entering the room he was just settling himself behind his desk.

"Ah, hello my dear, come in and take a seat." He gestured for her to sit in the leather chair at his desk.

"So, are we confident this one will work?" He felt strong again, healthy, the wheeze from his chest cleared and he could breathe deeply from the air conditioned atmosphere without coughing.

"I can't be sure, sir. The pathogen mutates faster then we can catch it. The PAMPs are setting a defence at everything we throw at it. With the last vaccine we managed to trap everything before the mutation started, but there are too many strands to be sure we caught them all."

She was more hopeful this time than she was with the past two attempts, but they were running out of options.

"Well we know we can stave it off once it starts, so at least we can keep me ticking over. Once we get the scroll, along with the antidote, we can begin our work."

"That's true sir, but I can't be sure that the vaccine will work and we won't have time to produce enough to cover the casualties that are being infected by the immunes. We are losing our test subjects daily, two more died this morning."

There were volunteers drafted in through adverts to test a new drug for the cure of the influenza virus, with the incentive of a big pay cheque. Most of the subjects were students who were more than happy to be part of the test to help pay their college fees.

They were told that they would experience cold like symptoms which was perfectly normal, and all seemed to be fine at the beginning.

. . .

Nightly had also initiated a research program of his own that uncovered a number of asymptomatic subjects around the world, immunes he liked to call them and discovered three in particular, Aya, Lacy and Lincoln who showed signs of a ruthless single mindedness that made them easy to enroll as interns at BioTane once the $500,000 was deposited into their accounts.

Although resistant at first to the idea of being carriers to spread the disease, a further cash injection, and an assurance that it was for the good of mankind seemed to do the trick.

The less fortunate volunteers however weren't so lucky; they lost five so far and the intake had dropped dramatically.

"Well I wouldn't concern yourself too much for the time being, my dear. I have no intention of releasing a vaccine that might work. We need the cure."

"But people may die before we can conclusively prove the vaccine works." She didn't want to hear the answer, but she knew it was inevitable.

She had become a biochemist with the sole intention of saving lives. But the money and kudos of her role at BioTane had a part to play in her lack of reaction to the answer she was about to hear.

"Sometimes in our quest to cure the world, to create a healthier lifestyle, to live longer lives, there are casualties along the way. We'll just call it collateral damage for now. But how much collateral damage is in your hands, my dear. I suggest we get back to the lab."

6

Jack tried to relax as the 767 levelled at thirty four thousand feet, but as ever his mind was preoccupied with what was coming next. He flicked through the movies, found nothing he fancied, tried a few podcasts but kept drifting and missed several portions of the conversation. By the time he concentrated again he was completely lost.

Special assignment? What had Ed got for him this time? His last assignment was meant to be an escape from the front line, a way of recharging his batteries. A murder in a quaint English village, a favour for one of Ed's cronies. It was sold as an easy case based in the heart of the British countryside. It turned out to be a chase across the northern hemisphere to stop a megalomaniac from trying to blow up the world.

LARA were assigned missions that were either diplomatically erroneous or covertly funded by those who had no choice. All assignments were cleared by Ed Ryker, former wraith, now head of Land Air Reconnaissance Agency, and a man not to be messed with. An American with the diplomatic charm of the English and the ruthlessness of a Russian Oligarch. He was quite a mixture and most of the time it was a challenge to recognise which head he had on from one day to the next.

. . .

He commanded a global force of wraiths, all ex special forces from every government agency, with skills that covered all eventualities. Jack reluctantly became Ed's right hand man due to his success rate, his own ruthlessness in completing missions whatever it took, and as he found out from a few in the force, he began to mirror Ed in his younger days. The last part galled him, as some within the ranks, the likes of Riggs for instance, had great pleasure in announcing that dad was on the comms for him.

On the flip side however, it did have its benefits as he was able to run missions his way, and that was important, he had always been responsible for his own actions and would never change.

It was impossible to second guess the assignment and with Sara tight lipped, he knew it was something that he wouldn't like. He could imagine Ed perfecting his best diplomatic stance on arrival, he did the same with the village thing and look at how that turned out.

Ordering a coffee and a chicken sandwich from the trolley, he read through the inflight magazine and wondered if anyone had ever bought the model of the aircraft they were flying in. It helped to take his mind off things, feeling himself drifting as tiredness began to spread through his body. Pulling the eye mask from the seat pocket, he reclined, letting the darkness and the hum of the engine lull him to sleep.

F ifteen million dollars, that's probably twelve million pounds in todays currency. Not a bad day's work. At least it will cover the Inca trip, three icons and four clients vying for ownership.

Tia Stirling sipped some of the Sakara gold and looked across the Nile, savouring the low alcohol lager as it helped relax her after the twenty day expedition. She wasn't going to risk anything stronger, as much as she wanted to, as she needed her wits about her when she dispatched the scroll. She wasn't expecting trouble but it was a first if there wasn't any. If it was a bounty that no-one tried to steal from her, beat her to the prize or put her through hell trying to protect it, it wasn't a bounty worth hunting.

Since the find eight days ago she had been pursued from the burial site, shot at several times and had it not been for Karim's expert driving through the northern streets of Cairo, the taxi would have been rammed off the road twice. She was safe on the moored Le Pacha 1901. The giant floating palace on the banks of Zamalek housed nine restaurants, a casino and several bars, all heaving with tourists. Her pursuers also knew that she wouldn't have the scroll with her so they were just warnings, letting her know that they were there. She carried her revolver and Kabar just in case, but for now she was going to use the time to relax.

Johnny's bar was the closest to the Le Pacha entrance, ideal for slipping in and more convenient to slip out. She sat on one of the high stools at the main bar in front of the wall of spirits of every brand, brightly backlit in golden yellow fluorescence. The mirrored backsplash of the serving counter was ideally positioned to see anyone entering.

For the first half an hour she had no problem in identifying new drinkers as her striking looks were a magnet for any male wishing to try their luck. She had changed from her preferred khaki shorts and loose top to a figure hugging navy jumpsuit and bolero jacket, an accessory needed to cover her holster. Her dark hair, loosely plaited, fell down to her belt line. Swept back from her face it exposed her clear tanned complexion, emerald green almond eyes and full lips. She required little make up to enhance her natural beauty. It did however hide the razor sharp tongue that quickly dispelled any impression that she was available. Before long she was given the space she needed with seats clear on either side.

Her mobile vibrated, it was the buyer.

"Hello... Yes I have it. It will be with you the day after tomorrow as agreed." She moved her phone from her ear and switched to her account screen, using her thumb recognition to log in. She smiled as she saw the $5 million finders fee sitting there.

"Yes, it's there, nice doing business with you."

Beckoning the barman she ordered a bottle of Krug Grande Cuvee 166. Time to celebrate, champagne now her preferred refreshment.

Tia turned her back on the family business ten years ago as salvage just wasn't cutting it any more. Her father was happy trawling the seas for sunken treasure, pirate ships, war galleons and merchant vessels from yesteryear, but her fascination for the history of the trove was more alluring than the cash it brought in.

Dad was great, he put her in touch with one of his buyers who had a requirement for an Inca idol reportedly hidden in a jungle close to Machu Picchu, Peru. With a small expedition she studied the area, researched the idol, worked several maps and charts of the surrounding terrain and eventually, through knowledge, determination, and a large stroke of luck, she managed to find it. The idol was discovered in a hidden burial chamber within one of the network of caves leading from Cusco all the way to Machu Picchu. The exhilaration of the find, the knowledge she unearthed created such an overwhelming sense of satisfaction that the money she received, although considerable, became secondary.

It was now a passion that gained her a reputation amongst the well heeled as the one to go to for the valuable and the hidden. This latest job was commissioned by a billionaire Sheikh, born in Eritrea from Bedouin ancestry. A scroll of immense importance apparently. It was full of Hieroglyphics which she was sure, if she had long enough, she could have made a good attempt to translate, but with fifteen million pounds resting on its recovery and delivery, a clear photograph of it will do for some free time research.

She commissioned two locals to assist in the recovery. Malik and Ishmael had been recommended through connections she had built within the Bedouin community, no group better to understand the lay of the land, even better at misdirection until the time or money suited them. They told stories, offered guidance and assisted in many fools errands with no promise of an outcome, stretching it for as long as the ruse lasted or until the fee ran dry.

Tia had been warned many times that they were untrustworthy, too dangerous to even consider a commission. But for her it was a challenge, a way of proving herself in her chosen career and more importantly, gain the trust of the people she needed to fulfil her assignments.

. . .

Two hundred and fifty thousand dollars as a deposit helped for starters and after travelling twenty kilometres west of the necropolis of Saqqara they were attacked by three bandits. One was dispatched with a bullet through the head, a knife across the throat finished the second and the last had his neck snapped by her own hands. This helped to convince her two guides that she was serious and it would be unwise to double-cross her.

They led her to an area they insisted hid one of the undiscovered solar temples of Sahure, which although seemingly genuine, she did expect more of a challenge to reach her goal. After one not so elaborate trap and a couple of dead ends and double backs, she came across an ornate box within the walls of a simple sandstone chamber, nowhere near any temple or shrine. If she didn't know better she might have thought that this may have been a plant and the bedouins were in possession of the scroll all along. But it was well worth the additional two hundred and fifty thousand dollar finders fee.

It was only after she left in Karim's cab, evading several tails, that she suspected that they were trying to get the scroll back. She had a feeling this wasn't the last she had seen of them.

"Now that is a sad sight. A beautiful girl sitting alone with a two hundred dollar bottle of champagne and no one to share it with."

She turned to look into the face of a handsome man, oozing with a charisma that suited him.

She guessed military, both by his mannerisms and his tan chinos, khaki shirt and C crown fedora tilted forward just above his eyes. Instinctively she placed a hand on her lap, just inches from her knife.

"Now now, Miss Stirling, there is no need to slit my throat. I have a proposition for you."

His smile showed a confidence that she could tell came from back up. Looking in the mirror she spotted them immediately, three in total, all in black tee shirts and chinos. Again their demeanour screamed military.

"Go on." She remained calm, keeping her hand in her lap, poised and alert.

"My employer is in need of an item you took possession of this week and is willing to pay you double the current offer."

He called the barman over and ordered a bourbon as he let his words sink in.

Tia tried to hide her disappointment, she was sure she had covered her tracks to ensure she remained under the radar. But it is necessary to use a system that is assumed to be trustworthy, only to realise everything has its price.

"I guess Malik's price was accepted. How much? A quarter mill, half?" She knew instantly the bedouins had sold her out.

She was still learning her trade, but she made a mental note for next time.

" I assure you that it was money well spent. You have to understand Miss Stirling, that what you have in your possession is the key to saving mankind. It will allow the world to thrive, save millions of lives and create a future that we can only dream of."

"Well it's a pity I don't have it any more, Mr…?" She thought she may as well know the name of the man she was about to dispatch.

" Mitch…Mitch Dawson." He extended his hand in greeting. This was too easy.

Tia, accepting his handshake and matching him grip for grip, swivelled, pulling his arm over her shoulder sending him flying over her head onto the bar. The momentum carried him over the edge. The three black tee shirts made a beeline for her, but she was too quick. She jumped onto the bar, ran along towards the entrance and leapt through, narrowly avoiding a young couple who were entering arm in arm. She stooped to pick up his hat and handed it to him, mouthing an apology before disappearing into the night.

"Shit!"

Mitch eased himself up and flapped his fedora against his leg to straighten the crumpled top, pushing it back onto his head to avoid the bump that was beginning to form on his crown.

"You ok, boss?" Bamford offered his hand from the other side of the counter.

"Yeah, I'm good. We need to get after her, we have to get that scroll before it leaves Cairo."

He ignored the proffered hand and straddled the bar, clearing it easily. He had to give her credit, she had a good knowledge of martial arts, that was one hell of a throw.

They didn't have a lot on her as she had only just started to make waves, but her father, Josh, had a fearsome reputation in salvage, fighting his way through powerful corporations, mob bosses and pirates to get to the top of his game. So far, the Stirling girl had uncovered some important artifacts and she was collecting commissions over and above the established hunters, which in itself brought its own dangers. It was definitely a case of like father like daughter.

His mobile rang as they left the boat and entered Sharia Saray Al-Gezira street. Mitch weaved through evening diners as they searched for a place to eat.

"We've lost her, boss. She headed towards Zamalek and disappeared in the crowd. Wes has gone over the 26th July bridge into town and I'm in Zamalek. She's gone, boss."

He wasn't surprised. With a fifteen million dollar pay cheque she had more than enough incentive to disappear.

"Get Wes to go to the hotel, she'll need to return at some stage."

He cut the call and headed towards the bridge. It was going to be a long night.

Sensible shoes, one thing she always promised herself whenever out of her work outfit, and tonight was the first time to test the theory. The Prada espadrilles performed well as she managed to nimbly weave through the crowds and onto the Sharia Saray Al-Gezira without incident. She had no idea who was after her or why the scroll was creating so much interest; all she knew was that she needed it gone.

They would expect her to go back to her hotel and by now she guessed they knew that it was the Grand Hyatt, meaning she would need to go over the 26th July bridge to get to it. As she crossed the intricately designed marble forecourt of the Cairo Marriot, she knew what needed to be done. Ignoring the stone lions guarding the entrance she passed through the golden archway, pushing open the double doors to the first telephone of the row of six lining the walls next to reception.

The call was answered after three rings.

"The Grand Hyatt Hotel, good evening, Fadi speaking. How can I help you?"

It was going her way, Fadi was working reception tonight.

"Hi Fadi, it's Tia."

"Miss Stirling, are you lost?"

The concierge took his job seriously, having visions of one day running his own hotel. He knew every guest by name, knew their likes and dislikes. He organised the newspapers and trips tailored to the clients requirements, which made him almost instantly the guy to go to.

"Fadi, can you do me a favour? The package I asked you to post tomorrow, I need it doing now, this minute. Can you do that for me?"

If they can get the courier to the dispatch office in the next hour she could get it out of the country before morning.

"Of course, Miss Stirling. I'll arrange for a courier as soon as we finish the call. Is there any other business you would like me to attend to?"

She knew the code.

"No, thank you Fadi. Ten thousand Egyptian will be added to your account first thing in the morning."

Five hundred pounds was well worth it to ensure the safe delivery of the scroll.

"It's always a pleasure, Miss Stirling. You know where I am if you need me for anything at all."

Tia was satisfied. She could relax now as there was no one better in Cairo to get the job done than Fadi. His recommendation came from several quarters, all in a related industry; either relics, salvage, bounty or treasure. Fadi was the man and as long as he was looked after, he would look after you.

Now it was time to look after herself. There was no way that she could return to her hotel until she was sure that the scroll had gone, which gave her four hours to kill.

Walking along the impressive highly polished marble hall of the Marriott, she took in the splendour of the Egyptian mosaic trimmed brown and gold walls, interspersed with evergreen plants in beige ornate pots, gold framed paintings and porcelain statuettes of maidens in various poses. She followed the signs until she came to an intersection, heading for the lavish drapery surrounding the golden doors of the Omar Khayyam Casino.

The room was a buzz of excitement. Punters filled the air with a low hum of enthusiasm as the roulette wheels ticked and rattled, fruit machines whistled and beeped as they rolled their reels to a fortune and croupiers called out the results from the craps tables. The decor was a mix of beige and brown with large chandeliers dotted across the ceiling sending a warm golden light over the throng. The floor to ceiling windows were draped Arabian style in gold silk, styled as an entrance to a bedouin tent. The whole decor created a soothing ambience that suited her right now. She settled at the long bar, ordering a strawberry daiquiri while she checked the menu for a light snack. She decided on the Hawawshi, fancying the chilli minced beef to compliment her chilled drink.

The nearest roulette table had a space near the bar, becoming an ideal distraction while she waited for her food. She liked the odd flutter and she could afford a wager or two. Changing 2000 Egyptian she played red and watched as the wheel stopped on red 32, decent start… now her number 18 red, the ball bounced across 7 moved around the wheel as it slowed…it bounced several more times and settled into 22 black, one number away…

"Oh, bad luck…one away." A voice consoled her from over her shoulder.

"Well you know what they say, the house always wins." She smiled as she turned to the bar and came face to face with the man from Johnny's bar…Mitch something.

"Hang on Miss, I'm just here to talk." He held his hands up in surrender as he prepared for an attack.

Again she made a mental note to be more efficient at covering her tracks, as the speed he got here he may as well have been following her from a foot away.

She barged past him, forcing him a pace backwards; his hands still raised.

"I have nothing to say. As I told you, I don't have it and I have no interest in anything you have to say."

Her Hawashi was waiting for her as she reached her seat, she pushed it aside and look a long draw of her daiquiri, her appetite waning.

Mitch moved alongside her, just far enough away to be at arms length. He gestured the barman for a bourbon, hoping this time that he had a chance to drink it.

"Miss Stirling, I represent BioTane Pharmaceuticals and we are currently trying to prevent a world pandemic of biblical proportions. The scroll that you have in your possession could very well be the key to saving the world. It is imperative that we get hold of it." He left the part out about the fact that it was BioTane who started the pandemic.

He wasn't paid to complicate matters.

Tia looked at the military man in front of her, rugged, stocky and obviously confident. Her throw must have caught him completely off guard as she could tell that if she tried it again he was ready for her. She felt no fear, the job took care of that, but she was wary as she had made too many mistakes lately and one more could be fatal with the way things were going at the moment.

" So, a pandemic of biblical proportions; interesting hook line. But I'm not the type of fish that is willing to take the bait. As I said already, the new owner has it now. I was commissioned to retrieve and dispatch, exactly what I have done. I've been paid and I'm going home in the morning."

Mitch took his phone from his pocket and handed it to her. It was open on the World News page. The first headline she saw was:

'PLAGUED: World Health Authority in turmoil.' Today the World Health Authority released an update on the sudden outbreak in

cases of the pneumonic plague reaching developed countries for the first time since the 1300s. The last reported epidemic was in Madagascar in 2013 where 89 people were infected, with 39 deaths.

So far, in the UK, there are 230 cases reported, 300 in France, 270 in Spain and over 1000 in the USA. There is continual news of other countries reporting cases every day throughout Europe, Asia and the Americas. All medical attempts to treat the illness have so far failed, although scientists are sure that they will shortly have it under control. Only one death has been reported so far, Mr Henry Billingham from Salford, Manchester, England, who succumbed to the disease yesterday. Reports as yet to be confirmed indicate that he may have become infected during a robbery at the Manchester Museum just over two weeks ago. As of yet there has been no confirmation of this from the National Crime Agency in England, although it has been confirmed that the Greater Manchester Police headquarters has been quarantined after a high level of staff have become infected. They are all currently being treated at Manchester Royal Infirmary. More information will follow.

Tia flicked through the various news sites throughout the world and they all carried the same headline. Being stuck in the desert for several weeks had left her devoid of news, but this was incredible. She handed the mobile back to Mitch and took another draw of daiquiri, she needed something stronger.

" How can this happen? Where has it come from..." She didn't really know what to say, but he certainly had her interest.

"That isn't important now, Miss Stirling. It's the scroll; we need it and we need your help."

She prided herself on her confidentiality, and in her job it was vital to keep her clients protected for many reasons. But this was unbelievable, if this scroll is that important then she should help. Her conscience was stabbing at her from all directions. What should she do? She didn't trust this man but the evidence was overwhelming, she had to think. She signalled to the barman for a JD and coke, tall glass, lots of ice.

" Look Tia, do you mind if I call you Tia?"

She nodded, they knew enough about her already.

"Look Tia, we are willing to pay you double your fee for your co-operation to get the scroll back for us and for this." He slid a small zipped pouch across the bar to her.

She unzipped the wallet and opened it. It contained a small vial and a syringe.

"What's this?" She kept her eyes on the contents.

"Insurance." Mitch explained

"It will help hold off the infection. It's no guarantee, but so far it's proven effective. It's yours if you help us."

The words registered in her head, although not as Mitch intended.

"You'll give it to me if I help you? What about the people infected, the ones dying?And is this a bribe? Are you telling me that I can be protected only if I help you? Who the fuck do you people think you are!"

Some of the players turned from their games as she remonstrated with the man at the bar.

" No, calm yourself Tia, that wasn't what I meant. It's yours, take it, but it's pointless to give to those already infected, it would do no good. This is similar to the flu jab, it will help but won't guarantee protection, but ineffective if you already have the flu. I'm sorry for sounding callous, it wasn't intended. We just need your help."

Her JD and coke arrived which she quickly gulped down to calm herself, letting the caramel with the sour mash aftertaste warm her throat. There was only one thing for it.

. . .

"Tell me what's on the scroll and I'll consider helping you." She watched as his face noticeably brightened.

"I can't tell you exactly what is on it, no one can yet. But it contains the location of an ancient temple that holds the answers to mankind's existence, including the eradication of this disease. But we only have until August, in fact, just over a month from now." He watched as her mouth tightened, her eyes fixed on his.

Emerald green gems of beauty, her full sensual lips had a symmetry of perfection. Her shimmering black hair, tied back in the longest plaited pony tail he had ever seen, emphasised the contours of her face, the high cheek bones angled down to a near elfin chin, a small dimple in the centre. He could feel his heart speed up as she kept her eyes on his. He took a sip of his bourbon, letting the burn break her spell.

"This is more than I can take in for now and I am not going to retrieve the scroll for you..." She held her hand up to prevent his objections.

"...But I will give you the details of my client and you can negotiate with him yourself. I am sure that if you tell him what you have just told me, he will help. I know him, he is a kind man, a family man, but be under no illusions Mitch, he is not one to mess with. If anything he could provide you with a copy I'm sure, at a price."

She wasn't about to tell him that she had her own copy. Her excitement was hard to keep at bay, but she could see her next quest before her eyes.

"A copy will not be good enough, the scroll has to be at the location. Don't ask me why, I can't answer that. All I know is that it has to be the original parchment."

Tia opened her purse, tearing a sheet from her tiny notebook. She wrote across it before handing it to him.

. . .

" Abu is a reasonable man. I'm sure, if the price is right, you can negotiate."

Sheikh Abdurrahman Rashad Bin Al Sharraff was a billionaire, the Middle East's foremost negotiator for all things from oil to cotton. A shrewd businessman with a taste for anything expensive. £15 million to him was nothing, but she wasn't about to lose it.

There can't be any harm in a simple phone call from BioTane with a financial incentive to help save mankind. Abu loved attention and knowing him as she did, he'd make sure that his name was at the forefront of whatever the discovery was.

"Here's the details, just his name and a phone number. Keep my name out of it, whatever happens I cannot be involved. Say you mugged the courier, sweet talked the dispatch office, anything, I don't care. But this hasn't come from me."

Mitch finished his bourbon, pushing the note into his breast pocket before smiling and extending his hand.

" Thank you for your help, Miss Stirling. I hope we are able to meet again under different circumstances."

She looked at his hand and decided against shaking it. She half expected him to return the favour from earlier. Instead she just smiled.

"Take care, Mitch. I hope you succeed in your quest, and thank you." She held up the medipac as they nodded to each other before he moved away and left the casino.

After he disappeared from view she moved to the end of the bar to the telephone and dialled.

"Fadi, Tia again... great, thank you for doing that. The client will be pleased to receive it a day early. Anyway, can you get me on the first flight to London, just charge it to my account...No, I'm going straight to the airport. Can you store my belongings and book me a three week stay starting next weekend?...No, that's fine...fifteen thousand Egyptian for your trouble, Fadi. See you next week."

She needed to get home to her office, she had some deciphering to do...but first things first. Get to the airport and buy a charger, without her mobile she felt naked.

8

After twenty hours in the air Buchanan needed a drink, a good old American coffee. The Arabic ahwa was like treacle, it blew your head off, and the Neskafe alternative was a cheap instant rip off. He decided there was nothing better than returning to his own country, appreciating the familiar food and drink that he had consumed all his life. It really was the taste of home.

He watched the girl pour a black American from the pot sitting on the heater, breathing in the perfectly filtered blend as she placed it in front of him. Grabbing a bagel for good measure he sat at one of the tables in the concourse.

San Francisco International was a busy airport and this afternoon was no exception. Business travellers, tourists and commuters going about their business in a typical manic state, either running to the terminal, rushing to the exits or bustling around the stores getting last minute items before their flights. For those with time to spare, or like him, just taking a break, the concourse seating areas were a great place to people watch. It also gave him a moment to decide if the mission had been a success. They hadn't retrieved the scroll, according to Mitch the girl had already dispatched it to the new owner. Whether that would satisfy Nightly was anyone's guess.

. . .

The boss was becoming more erratic as it neared August, to do with some special ritual or something. Whatever it was, it was way over his head, but it was making him weird. The guy had purposely infected himself with the plague, how fucked up was that? When he signed up for the Scorpion team it was drummed into him that they were tasked with the protection of BioTane. They were also assigned to travel the world to obtain specific minerals, herbs or plant cultures from some of the most remote areas, fraught with danger from the terrain as well as its inhabitants.

Borneo had been a challenge, they lost two men to an indigenous tribe of some god forsaken mountainous forest, all for the sake of a plant, a rare orchid. Two good men killed by a poisonous dart that took days to work, the screams until they eventually succumbed was the stuff of nightmares. Some nights he could still hear them when his mind flashed back to past events just before sleep took him. Nightly insisted on bringing them back to BioTane so that he could study the poison and the effect it had on the internal organs. 'For the sake of science' was his favourite phrase; heard many times before and after each assignment.

Had it not been for Mitch, who he served under in Afghanistan, he would have walked away, but he was back with his old team. The money was good and he owed his former commander his life. He had no allegiance to Nightly, the guy was a freak, but he rarely had to deal with him directly. He doubted if the scientist even knew his name.

" Is this seat taken?"

He looked into the eyes of a stunner. Mid thirties if he was to guess, blonde with a slight reddish highlight which worked with her tanned skin. Her summer outfit of tight tee shirt and figure hugging shorts outlined her full figure, which made it all the more difficult to remain focused on her face.

"Yes, sure." He gestured for her to sit.

He took the tray from her, allowing her to hang her bag on the back of the chair before placing it in front of her as she sat facing him.

"Thanks, where are you headed?" She poured her soda into the glass, taking a sip while maintaining eye contact. Her smile was infectious.

" Oh, no…I've just arrived. I'm just taking a break before I head off home…You?"

"Oh, I'm going nowhere and you won't be either unless you tell me what I need to know."

Her smile continued to shine, but he wasn't sure if he had heard her correctly.

"I'm sorry, what did you just say?"

She continued to smile at him.

"I have a .22 automatic pointed at your groin Mr Buchanan, take a look. Be careful though, any false moves and it will go off. Go on, take a look."

He looked around at the counter. The service girl caught his eye and smiled back at him as she dried a cup and placed it amongst the others. Across the concourse he saw an airport cop directing an old lady towards the correct terminal. He was too engrossed to notice anything unusual. Like a guy sitting at a table facing a beautiful girl who was smiling at him, even though panic was written all over his face.

He risked a look under the table, straight into the barrel of a silencer fixed to a Ruger SR22. He sat bolt upright staring at the girl in disbelief.

" Wh…What do you want?"

He held onto the edge, pushing himself further back into his chair. His mind was racing, what should he do? If he stood she may miss, but the Ruger, even if she nicked his leg, would cause catastrophic damage. If he pushed the table into her, the gun would go off as the Ruger had a feather trigger.

"Where is the scroll?"

She kept her voice calm, a matter of fact question while keeping her smile intact. Anyone looking over would see two friends enjoying each others company over a coffee.

"We don't have it." What did she know of the scroll? Who is she?

"Pity. Who has it, Mr Buchanan?"

Her smile faded to a tight mouthed grin, her eyes showing her disappointment.

"I don't know. Some girl…Tia Stirling had it up for auction, she sent it to the winning bidder…I really don't know who it is, I swear."

He was telling the truth, he could see that she knew that too. He needed to keep her talking while he thought of a way to get out of this.

"What is the scroll to you?"

It was a start.

"The same as it is to you. We are after the same thing Mr Buchanan, to save mankind."

He wasn't expecting that. He was sure this was a robbery, he assumed they wanted the scroll for financial reasons. Maybe to resell it to a higher bidder, or as in the Stirling girl's case, to retrieve it for a collector.

"Who is your employer?"

He needed to report this back, this was huge.

"My employer is of no concern of yours, Mr Buchanan. Just tell me, who has the scroll?"

Her face had changed to one of determination, she was tired of his answering a question with a question. It was delay tactics, something she used herself, but she didn't have the time to go around in circles.

"Who has the scroll? This is your last chance, please don't waste it."

He had no intention of wasting time, although he began to relax a little. He couldn't be sure but it seemed that they shared a common goal, perhaps there was a way they could work together. It was worth a try.

"Look, let's calm this down, shall we? The Stirling girl gave the information to Mitch Dawson, my direct boss. Let me get hold of him, I'm sure I can arrange a meeting. He's gone home for the day, but will be back on Thursday. I can arrange a meet for then?"

That should work. Mitch needed to know that there was another organisation out there searching for the scroll and at the same time he can get this woman to move her gun away from his crotch. He was relieved to see the smile return, it looked like it had worked.

"Thank you Mr Buchanan, that has helped immensely. I can see now that you were telling the truth, you really don't know who has the scroll."

There was a soft click and a bump, a little like the popping of a cork. At the same time Buchanan heard a crack of splintering wood˙ from the back of his seat. Looking down he saw the blood flow from his stomach onto the floor, he watched as the red pool began to spread between his feet, although he couldn't feel his feet, he couldn't feel his legs either.

He looked across at the woman, there was just an empty chair. A few yards away he could see the distinctive red highlighted hair swaying away from him before it disappeared in the crowd of people walking towards him. He should get up and warn the others. As he grasped the table to lift himself free his shattered spine broke in two, his body toppled sideways followed unnaturally by his pelvis, that in turn dragged his useless legs with it. Buchanan was dead before his broken body hit the floor.

Gabrielle placed the mobile phone to her ear waiting for the call to connect. She was far enough away to ensure the screams of panic wouldn't interrupt her conversation. Looking at the board, it indicated that her flight to Boston was boarding.

"Hello…"

The authoritative voice had been expecting the call and was ready for the good news.

"I don't know the location, but I know who does. It's Mitch Dawson. He wasn't on the flight, so I can only assume he has travelled home. I'm on my way back and will see you in the office in nine hours when I'll brief you on the rest."

"…I assume there are no loose ends?"

It was a pointless question.

"Caelan, it's me you are talking to. I'll send my team to LA, get to Mitch before he gets back to San Fransisco. He'll be alone but I'll need my best men. Mitch won't be a pushover. See you later."

She cut the call as she rounded the corner to her gate. Buchanan was easy, Mitch was another matter altogether, highly trained, brutal, and intelligent.

He wouldn't go down without a fight, but she wasn't right for the job. Someone else could have the satisfaction of killing him, she was still revelling in the satisfaction of their divorce.

9

G ordon Nightly hated waiting, he was impatient at the best of
times and one of his pet hates was 'hold' music. He had so
far listened through a Beatles track, some god awful girl band and
now some rapper wanting to rape his girlfriend at gunpoint. Who
was this man? Finally the music stopped.

"Sorry for the delay, Sheikh Rashad Bin Al Sharraf is ready to
speak to you now."

Ready to speak to me now? Fucking cheek!

"Mr Nightly, it is a pleasure to speak with you. Your reputation
precedes you." Abu had obviously done his homework.

"The pleasure is all mine, Sheikh Rashad."

He wasn't about to address him fully, he had no need to impress
and as the Sheikh couldn't even address him as doctor, there was a
mutual distrust.

"What can I do for you, Mr Nightly?"

He could read the man just through his tone and his pleasantries,
he wasn't here to waste time. Abu liked that in a man, straight to the
point and blunt with it. But there was an undertone that made him
wary.

"I would like the scroll, Sheikh Rashad, and I am prepared for
you to name your price."

That really was straight to the point. He had come into possession of the artefact only two days ago. Miss Stirling had failed him with her promises of anonymity, he would need a word with her father.

"I'm afraid that the item is not for sale, Mr Nightly. It belongs in my family, an item of significant importance both in terms of the heritage and the secrets that it holds, written long long ago by my ancestors."

Abu gave enough to see if he could bring Nightly's real intentions to light.

"A secret? That is intriguing. My interest is purely as a collector. I too have roots to a bygone age and I am always on the lookout for interesting artefacts, particularly new finds."

What did the Sheikh know?

It was an unexpected turn of events. He had a dossier on the Sheikh from birth, but apart from his birthplace of Eritrea, his main focus had been on his business dealings, his family, his weaknesses. The latter proving to be the most difficult as Sheikh Rashad was a shrewd operator with a reputation as a manipulative negotiator who kept any frailties well hidden.

He hoped money was the key as, like all the super rich, everything has a price.

"Eternal life, Mr Nightly. As a scientist with a reputation for eradicating disease, it must be very alluring. The problem is that it belongs to me and if it is true, I will be the one to make the discovery. It also makes sense that should there be such a discovery, the value would be immeasurable. I have my doubts that my forefathers, simple tomb builders, would have made such a discovery and there is certainly a doubt as to whether the ancient script can be translated, being that it would have been written in the twenty fifth century BC, many years before the language became formalised. But I will have fun trying."

The Sheikh made his position very clear.

"I can certainly see that it brings a challenge …"

Nightly had one more proposition, this had to work.

"…But what if I were to mention that should I take possession of the scroll, I could guarantee the eradication of every known disease, condition and malformation for the whole of the human race. I could also stop the pandemic we are currently facing around the world, as well as curing those already afflicted."

He was reputed to be a family man, this has got to sway him.

There was silence from the other end of the line. The Sheikh was obviously mulling it over, probably calculating a price in his head, a price to test his resolve. He was ready for him, money was no object, he had to have the scroll. He heard a rustle in the earpiece and an intake of breath, he was about to get the figure.

" I tell you what, Mr Nightly. When we have made the discovery I will give you first refusal on the understanding that it is manufactured, acknowledged, marketed and distributed under my family name. I retain all rights, and we will agree a percentage as profit to BioTane over and above the initial fee agreed for purchase. If it does exist, and if you claim it will do what you say it can do, we will make more money than either of us, even in our privileged position, could ever dream of."

"NO…"

This wasn't supposed to happen. He needed the scroll for the last phase of his plans and he was running out of time. August was approaching fast, any delays and too many would die, he wouldn't be the saviour of mankind. This could not happen, he won't let it happen.

"Sheikh Rashad, let me stress…."

He was cut short.

"Enough, Mr Nightly, I have made my offer. I need to begin the translation and the longer we continue this fruitless conversation the longer it will take to get you your solution. I will be in contact if we find anything, we can then begin our negotiations. We will be in touch."

He held onto the receiver for several seconds after the call ended, staring at the figure of RA, focusing on the sun disc on his head.

Replacing the handset he pulled the sun disc amulet from his drawer, running his fingers over the minute blue glazed disc, feeling the cool surface radiate a tiny surge through his hand. Sitting it on the desk, he stared at the minuscule artefact Aya had retrieved from the museum, in particular, the tiny hole bored into its top. He longed to know its secret, he had to know it. For that reason, his alternative strategy will come into play.

The Sheikh had been given the chance to be part of the journey and offered a substantial sum for the privilege. He will now pay in another way.

He picked up the handset and dialled.

"Lacy, hello my dear. Well done for your work so far, we have encouraging reports that the hospitals are becoming overwhelmed. I now need you to focus on one man for us. You need to fly to Massachusetts, you are going back to school."

Before entering the office, Gabrielle Millson grabbed a coffee and relaxed under one of the corporate red umbrellas of the open air North Plaza, sheltering from the scorching midday sun. The trip to Boston had been uneventful, allowing her to strategise her meeting with Caelan before he started firing questions and theories at her. Kendall Square was beginning to fill as the offices spilled out for lunch. In a few minutes the plaza would be full of scientists, secretaries, analysts and chemists, all theorising, speculating and bitching about their current programs.

BioScience was as boring as it sounded and she wasn't one to involve herself in anything to do with the industry, apart from the money that could be made.

Aruman Technologies were making a mint, but Caelen wanted more. Especially after things exploded a week ago when news came in that BioTane were close to a cure for the current spate of pneumonic plague sweeping the globe. A plague that showed every sign of being engineered, something to do with anomalies in its make up. Caelen was sure that it was Nightly. He had no proof, but he was a rival both in the sciences and some sort of ancestral conflict that she neither understood or really cared about.

It was some secret society mumbo jumbo from thousands of years ago, originating from Egyptian times. But to the two scientists it was a way of life, a religion, something that brought a war of attrition they had been waging for years. Whether it was the latest discovery or a revolutionary drug, their battle for supremacy within the biosciences was as fierce as any in the corporate world. The Microsoft and Apple rivalry of the chemical world.

Discovery of the scroll however certainly raised the stakes. It was a monumental find and Caelen was determined to have it under any circumstances. It was a find that will change the world apparently, something that had to be achieved by Aruman Technologies, in particular by Caelen Khan.

She had done her job identifying Mitch as the one with the information on the buyer, a complication she could have done without. She knew that they would run into each other sooner or later and it wouldn't be pleasant. But even though she would shed no tears to hear of his death, she didn't want to be the one responsible.

Two tours of duty and a three year marriage had ruined them both. Afghanistan had been the hell hole where they first connected. They were part of the International Security Assistance Force operation in Marjah, a section of the Helmand Province that still held a number of Taliban insurgents. The expectations were that they would receive no resistance once the size of the American force was realised. How wrong could they be.

After four years of negotiating past human shields of mainly children, indiscriminate suicide bombers and the loss of countless comrades and even closer friends, they made the stupid mistake of marrying during their rehabilitation back into civilian life.

One PTSD sufferer in a relationship is bad enough, but a husband and wife combo was a disaster waiting to happen. The disaster came with the death of her mother. Despite the fact that Mitch was the one with his hands on her mother's throat, the one who slit it with the kitchen knife, the one who claimed she was an insurgent sent to seek revenge for the Marjah victory; he was exonerated. Gabrielle's PTSD had now transferred from Afghanistan to small town Micanopy, her Florida hometown, her mother's home. A house she inherited and never visited. Oh yes, not be a single tear would be shed when Mitch was pronounced dead, not one.

10

Mitch Dawson loved the neighbourhood, one of the quieter areas of Berkeley, close enough to cross the bridge to Frisco but far enough to leave BioTane behind. The leafy suburb of California style bungalows allowed the sun to bathe the streets from sunrise. He needed a few days every now and again to recharge his batteries, forget about the job and do nothing in particular.

After returning from Egypt the night before he had risen early, taking to the porch with a pot of coffee, three newspapers and this months Sports Illustrated. The sun was already warm but comfortable and the avenue soon began to populate with dog walkers, joggers and commuters. It took him twice as long to read through all the good mornings, the how've you beens and the nice to see you agains, but he enjoyed it as he felt part of the community for a short while, a place he belonged with people who knew him just as Mitch, the guy from the bungalow who worked away a lot.

At lunchtime he entered town heading for Fourth Street, stopping at Peets Coffee for a recharge of caffeine and a ham and swiss toastie.

The traffic was light and the shoppers thin on the ground which helped to calm him before the meeting he had decided to attend while in town. A few diners relaxed with their feet on the provided footstools, basking in the sun as it burned over the patio. Their heads back facing skywards, occasionally taking a break to sip their iced teas and coffees.

He envied their carefree lives, a life of the mundane, a structured existence where work was Monday to Friday, weekends reserved for family and friends, holidays preplanned. It was a life he would not have considered as a younger man as he belonged to the Marines and it suited him. He saw the world, made lifelong friends and had no time to think for himself. It also exposed him to horrors no man should ever be forced to experience, loss of friends in ways no amount of grieving or time can erase. The agonised screams and helplessness that conflict provides in spades.

It damaged him irreparably and had it not been for Nightly's pills he'd either be dead by now or incarcerated, either in the joint or in a mental institute. Nightly developed a formula to control and maintain the neurotransmitters serotonin and norepinephrine levels of the brain to a normal level, a PTSD Eradicator, PTSDE he called it. So far it had worked, he had not had an attack for over two years, not since the incident with Barbara.

During the trial Nightly used his influence with the Courts to be summoned as the expert witness. He provided the jury with such overwhelming evidence as to the effects and repercussions of PTSD, even going to the extreme of including a layman's explanation of the mechanics of the brain. By the end of the trial the jury understood more about the destructive nature of a fucked up neurotransmitter than they did about the man who had caused the death of the woman.

The terms of his exoneration included a twelve month internment at the BioTane medical facility to continue treatment as a lab rat in an attempt to find a cure. The PTSDE was almost there, twelve more months of his brain pattern data along with the other five trialists and production would begin.

He was still a killer, but his brain could now associate with those that he was paid to kill, leaving the demons to run around somebody else's head.

Mitch made his way from Fourth Street to Eighth, and entering the Community Centre he found them in the main hall. His footsteps echoed around the room as he crossed the highly polished floor towards the therapy group who all sat together in silence. Three from his unit, Budge, Foreman and Duke along with four others, two of whom he had seen before. The eighth man seated within the circle rose to greet him.

"Sergeant Dawson, good to see you again."

The man extended his hand as he moved towards him. Receiving it warmly, Mitch smiled.

"Hello Major, been a while."

They walked back amongst the group and sat on the two vacant chairs facing the others.

"Right guys, shall we start? Who wants to tell their story first?" The Major looked at them each in turn, waiting for the first to speak.

Mitch didn't need this anymore, he was one of the lucky ones. The others had no access to the PDSTE. They would eventually, but for now they had to make do with the therapy and drugs currently available to them. He'd be here as often as he could, for his unit, for his colleagues and more importantly, his own sanity.

It was good to catch up with the guys and encouraging to see that they all seemed to be improving, apart from Duke. He still had a few issues; looking around at times with a jolt as they were having a beer at The Albatross, only to look back, relieved that nobody was there.

He knew that feeling, convinced that you were being tracked, somebody was creeping up on you or was in hiding nearby ready to jump on you when you least expected it. It could hit at any time. Someone offers you a knife to carve a turkey at Thanksgiving, all you see is an insurgent rushing you with their machete, ready to plunge it into your body.

It was still warm in the early evening, perfect for the two mile stroll back home. It gave him time to clear his head from the alcohol, the therapy session and the reunion that reminded him of darker times. He needed to get refocussed as Nightly was on a roll and it would only escalate once he got hold of the scroll.

His phone vibrated in his pocket, he'd forgotten to take it off silent.

"Dawson." He answered the call from Nightly.

"Mitch, where are you at this moment?" He could hear the tension in the boss's tone.

" A mile from home. I'll be back in fifteen, is anything wrong?" He knew there was.

"Buchanan is dead."

Straight to the point as usual, as subtle as a brick.

Mitch stopped in his tracks. Not Buchanan, his right hand man? He'd been with him from the start of the Scorpion team, had helped put the team together. He classed him as one of his few true friends. They had the same sense of duty to the job, the same sense of humour and an uncanny knack of second guessing each other. Their relationship helped him through the darker times.

"What happened?"

. . .

He was hoping it was an accident although he'd heard of no planes going down. Car accident on the way back from the airport perhaps?

"Shot and killed at Frisco International. It was a hit."

"A hit? For what? We weren't on any assignments, just the scroll retrieval and we got what we needed...or the best we could get to allow us to find the scroll. Who did this?"

His cell was silent for a moment as Nightly considered how to answer without causing his best man a meltdown.

"The only information we have is that he was seen at a table with a woman, quite striking, a blonde with distinctive red highlights, tall, slim and sporty looking. She left just before Buchanan collapsed..."

Nightly waited a moment for the information to sink in before he continued.

"...A silenced .22, through and through, cut his spine in half... and Mitch...she blew his balls off."

Mitch closed his eyes as he let the information sink in. Gabrielle was back in service and she was out to hurt him.

"I need you back here, Mitch. Civvy street has just become a danger to you and the scroll will be mine in a few days. I need my best man to lead the way."

Nightly wasn't wrong. If she was now active he should start looking over his shoulder. She knew how to push his buttons, knew him better than anyone and could use that knowledge to bring him down. One of the ways was to choose targets close to him.

"I'll grab a bag and be with you in a couple of hours." He had already packed for a long stay away, but he needed time to collect his thoughts and the bourbon on his mantle would help to stabilise him before he set off.

" No, Mitch, I need you here now. Make it an hour...I have plenty of bourbon here. One hour."

The line went dead.

11

C aelan Khan paced the boardroom waiting for his head of security to show her face. Where was she?

The scroll will be in Nightly's hands soon and he wanted Gabrielle to step up to the plate. He couldn't have Aruman Technologies implicated in any of this as he was close to a breakthrough, one that would need both medical council and military support which required high level clearance.

Using nano technology and cell regeneration it could soon be possible to treat and cure cancers, mental defects and his piéce de résistance, repair wounds, even bullet removal with instant cell regeneration in the field. It would put Aruman Technologies at the forefront of the bioscience world and make Caelan Khan a pioneer. It would have been the pinnacle of his career had it not been for the news of the scroll. He had been late with his bid, but knew who he was up against. The Atenist, Nightly.

Being of Nubian blood, a descendant of King Piye and of the cult of Amun, the Atens were an enemy of beliefs...worshippers of the sun disc and believers of their own self importance, separate to the rest, as was demonstrated when the Pharaoh Amenhotep IV created a new capital, changed his name to Akhenaton - the servant of Aten, banning all other religions and destroying all other idols other than that of the Sun god. Gordon Nightly was without a doubt a worthy descendant of the self important.

But it was the scroll, the key to eternal life that provided a common goal. They both had to own it, find its secret, it was their right, their destiny.

BioTane had stolen a march on Aruman when they announced the cure all. A bold attempt to eradicate the world's ills. In tests it had proven successful and the published papers seemed to stack up.

At the same time however, came the outbreak of the plague. A particularly robust virulent form of pneumonic plague, immune to any traditional treatment due to its genetic morphing. It was too coincidental to announce one minute that there could be a cure for all diseases and days later have a world pandemic that will need such a cure. The medical council had reached out to all pharmaceutical institutes in the US to assist and they were all working feverishly to try to determine the best way to combat the disease. It came as no surprise when BioTane announced that they were close to a solution. Nightly was playing with the world's health and if he wasn't prevented from recovering the scroll, he would hold the world to ransom. A typical Aten trait.

He stared out of the window at the buildings in the Kendall Square district of Boston, a biochemical hub sharing space with a growing clutch of tech start ups. It was an impressive complex employing 50,000 technologists, close to MIT, which helped capture early drafts of the brightest students, and having the largest skyscraper, an ideal base to grow the Aruman empire. With his current breakthrough he could grow tenfold, with the secret of the scroll he could own Kendall Square.

He turned at the dull ping that came from the back of the office. The benefit of making all of the internal walls glass, he could see

Gabrielle leave the elevator and make her way across the floor towards him.

She was a danger to his business but right now a necessity. She had approached him eighteen months ago as a security consultant, demonstrating her abilities by showing his vulnerabilities both inside his office and out. She had intel of plans of potential espionage, threats to the business as well as to his own life along with other members of his staff. She was convincing enough for him to take a chance on her for one month to prove herself.

Within twenty days she uncovered two biochemists leaking information to competitors, three technicians who were redirecting copy emails and a security guard who kept a log of Caelan's whereabouts, a security guard with a link to the Boston mob.

He had no hesitation in offering her an open ended contract as his Head of Security. Within six months she had recruited her own personal army, all off the books and all mercenaries. This had proven to be a shrewd move as once he became aware of the disappearance of all of the conspirators against him, he felt it best to remain oblivious.

There was one exception however, one task that they had in common for totally different reasons; Caelan for the sake of his company and his ancestors, for Gabrielle it was personal.

They were hell bent on the destruction of BioTane.

12

Mitch pulled his gun as he approached the bungalow. Dusk smothered the street in a misty red haze as night began to fall. Porch lights illuminated every house as they prepared to hold the darkness at bay. Except for one.

As the sensors were hard wired to the secondary grid they would light even during a power cut.

The bulb may have failed, but he wasn't taking any chances after the news he'd just had from Nightly.

Ignoring the porch he made his way down the side of the house and silently unlatched the gate, stooping below the window and positioning himself to the side of the back door.

He strained to hear through the distant chirrup of the crickets, leaning forward until his ear was in touching distance of the frosted glass. A dog barked from one of the gardens behind causing him to start, he followed with a cuss before stopping suddenly as he heard another sound from inside the bungalow. A sound he had heard many times before, sending a chill through his spine.

"Stay hidden, he will be here in moments."

The language was Pashto, a language he lived with for many years when serving in Afghanistan, a dialect of the Taliban.

He moved back and rested against the wall, closing his eyes

tightly to push the memories away. This wasn't happening. His defences were down, Gabrielle had spooked him and he was having flashbacks.

He could feel his heart banging in his chest, pulsing in his ears. His breathing began to accelerate until he could feel himself panting. He was on the verge of an attack, if he wasn't already in the midst of one.

He could recall the look of horror on Gabrielle's face as she stared at the crumpled form of her mother, covered in blood, her throat oozing as the jugular pumped the life from her. He recalled dropping the knife as the turban disappeared, the loose peraahan tunbaan cloth shirt and pants changed into the summer flowers of a light cotton dress and the rough beard and tanned skin transformed into the pale terror filled face of Barbara, his mother in law.

"Check the back. He is a skilled warrior, he may already be with us." The voice was clear, unmistakeable, definitely Pashto.

Mitch could only stare as he saw the handle turn and the door swing open to reveal a hand and the sleeve of a loosely fitted cloth robe. He watched as the barrel of an M16 poked through the gap followed by a head masked in a scarf tucked into his turban, leaving only the eyes exposed. As their eyes locked Mitch pushed the door closed, a sickening crunch came from the head as it smashed against the frame, the M16 dropped free.

Grabbing it he faced the barrel away from himself and shot three blasts into the turban sending it flying across the kitchen, still gripping a portion of head and brain.

A flash from the hallway caused him to dive behind the serving island, sliding to a stop as the kitchen was peppered with gunfire.

"You son of a dog."

The voice came from the hallway as another round was sent into the kitchen. Crockery, pine and glass filled the room, shattering all around him as he huddled behind the island.

With his back against the oak surface Mitch tried to decide

which side to send return fire. To the right faced directly down the hall, to the left would provide an angle which may hide the gunman. But he would be favouring his right hand, easier to release a volley at speed.

He looked at the debris on the floor in front of him as he mulled over his decision and his eyes fixed on a sizeable shard of glass that had imploded during the last attack. The reflection of a boot, closely followed by another, made his decision for him.

He swung to the right, out into the open, and sent two bursts of rapid fire into the advancing body of the intruder. The gunman toppled forward, his tunic covered in an ever-growing dark stain.

Mitch stared at the body for several minutes looking for movement. Seeing nothing he stepped over it, collecting the fallen M16 and moving into the hallway, checking each room until he reached his office. He tried the light but as expected they had cut the power, which had saved his life. They hadn't been able to extinguish the porch light so had disabled it at source. It proved one thing, they weren't locals.

His bag was in full view and taking a few spare clips from the cabinet and the last cash from his safe he headed back to the hallway. He needed to move fast as the police would be here at any minute. The gun battle will have woken the whole neighbourhood and he didn't fancy being around when they arrived.

He looked up, watching as the lampshade swayed on its cable. It was followed by a creak as one of the rafters bore weight.

Pointing the M16 at the ceiling he pressed the trigger.

"Son of a bitch!"

The curse was definitely American. He pressed the trigger again sending neat holes through the plaster.

"Ok...Ok wait, stop please. I'm coming down."

"Send your weapon down first motherfucker, then haul your arse down here." He kept the rifle aimed at the attic cover as it slid backwards, followed by the steps as they unwound and slammed into the ground.

The M16 was lowered on its shoulder strap and clattered to the floor. Slowly, using one leg as the other ruined limb hung uselessly in the air, the man made his way down the ladder, stopping at each rung as the pain racked through him. He wore the same outfit as the others, although his turban had unravelled and was falling down his back. As he reached half way, Mitch grabbed the cotton trousers and yanked him off the ladder. He waited for the screams and moans to subside before he started the questions.

"Who sent you?"

Mitch moved the barrel of the M16 towards the stricken man's face. He tried to back away but his wrist was broken, he collapsed in pain as he put his weight on it. The barrel was pressed into his cheek.

"I'm waiting…"

" We were after the scroll, you were our target to get the whereabouts."

The distant sound of sirens began to reach their ears. The Police will be here in a few minutes, he had to work fast.

"And I guess when you had the information you had the order to take me out?" He pressed the barrel forward, pinning the mans head to the floor.

"Yes, yes we were. I'm sorry, we had our orders. Just get it over with." The insurgent gritted his teeth, closing his eyes tightly as he waited for the explosion.

Sirens were getting ever nearer. Mitch needed to move, but not before he had the answer to his first question.

"Who sent you?" He watched the gunman's eyes pop open and deliberate on his odds.

He was likely to be killed by this man so why not tell him, he would be dead anyway if he was taken into custody. His body relaxed as he resigned himself to his fate.

"Gabrielle Millson."

He pulled the gun away and held it down by his side. He expected it, but it still came as a shock. She had even set them up to imitate the Taliban, an attempt to cause him mental as well as physical harm.

He needed to act quickly as the sirens were nearly on top of him. Any moment now he would hear the screech of squad cars halting in front of the porch.

Rifling through his bag he grabbed a zip tie and wrenching the injured man forward, ignoring his protests and squeal of pain as the tie cut into his broken wrist, Mitch propped him against the wall. Running into his office he rifled through the top drawer, the drawer he used most, and found what he was looking for.

Returning to his captive he grabbed hold of his blonde hair, pushing back his head until he could see his face in the fading light. Biting off the lid with his teeth he took the indelible marker and scrawled on the gunman's forehead.

Stepping back to admire his work he smiled before giving the man a friendly pat on the cheek.

"Good Luck."

Mitch grabbed his bag and ran to the back of the house. The screech of tyres came as he hurdled the fence at the rear of the garden.

No one noticed him cross two more lawns, reappearing three streets away to make his way to the bridge.

13

"Shit!"

Gabrielle poured a coffee and sat at her desk staring at the print of Salvador Dali's The Persistence of Memory. The melting clocks in a disjointed landscape, a subject apt for the situation she found herself in, a depiction of mortality melting away, the swarming ants demonstrating the decay as time moves on. It was a smack in the face, letting her know that the hunt for eternal life had eluded her and every minute, every hour, every day the scroll is out of their reach, the older they become. It was her favourite painting, but in the current situation it was mocking her.

She was waiting for Caelen to demand her presence, which was unlikely to be pleasant. She had no excuses. She had gone with Ardman, Coates and Roach, all capable, all able to speak Pashto and good soldiers. But this was Mitch, and he had proven to have lost none of his battle hardness. Her phone buzzed at her desk; here it comes.

"Hello." She didn't need to wait for long.

"I think we need to get together." The phone went silent, Caelen had no more to say.

The elevator seemed to travel faster than usual. When she was in need of speed it took an eternity, now she needed it to take its time she was on the top floor before she knew it.

Caelan was sitting in the boardroom at the head of the table. It was one of his black days, his black polo neck matching his Armani suit, contrasted only by the gold of his Rolex.

He was leaning back in his chair with his elbows resting on the arms, his two forefingers protruded from his linked fingers pointing into his chin, in deep contemplation. His Mediterranean colouring appeared darker in the warm lights of the ceiling. The long streak of silver, the only blemish in his shoulder length black hair, seemed to sparkle like a bolt of electricity. His pronounced nose flattened as he moved his head toward the female as she entered the room.

"Sit down, Gabrielle." He pointed to the chair at the other end of the twenty-two seater table, positioning her eight metres away from him, a ploy to demonstrate his dominance.

"You have failed me." He spoke softly but with purpose.

It couldn't have been more menacing had he shouted at the top of his voice directly into her ear.

"I know that, I've lost three good men. But I have another way."

She wasn't going to take this lying down and she certainly wasn't going to be treated like a silly little girl. Caelen had other ideas.

"You will do only this."

He rose from his seat and opening the door to his drinks cabinet he withdrew a package. Walking to her end of the table he tipped the bag, letting the contents spill onto the glass surface in front of her. She looked at the air tickets, one way to Cairo International, the flight time was midnight tonight.

The passport was for a Lynn Sayer, same age, same place of birth, but the photograph was missing. She saw why from the last item, Natural Auburn hair dye. She looked questionably up at her CEO.

"I have two options. I can either turn you in and claim that you were planning to sabotage my company, or I can utilise you for the task ahead. As I know that you still have your uses and we are too close to change the whole of my security detail I have decided that you can make amends. I also have a feeling that this failure will only add to your determination to complete the job."

Gabrielle narrowed her eyes as she listened to him.

"Surely I am still of use to you here? I have an idea to guarantee the capture of the scroll." She hadn't, but she would come up with something to avoid being packed off out of the way. Caelan raised his hand to stop her.

"No, we have to get you out of the country. You will be travelling as Lynn Sayer to Egypt where you will await my instructions as to the next part of your mission. Once there you will be Gabrielle. It will only be for a week or two until we find the location we seek. You will then be tasked to take the scroll and follow its instructions once it is in our possession."

Gabrielle was intrigued, but still unsure why she should lay low until then. She was an asset to him. It was one screw up and he was right, she would be more determined to succeed the next time.

"I don't see why I can't remain to fulfil my obligation. I will not fail this time. Come on Caelan, give me one more chance to nail Mitch; I can get the scroll, I know it."

Caelen looked down at her with no emotion. His brown eyes bore into hers as if trying to see inside her head. He leant forward until he was inches away from her. Again his voice was quiet, but menacing.

"You will do as you are told. I expect you to be on the flight this evening and await further instructions from me. I am sure that you could have continued your mission had we lost all of your men. It would've been simple as the attack could not have been connected to Aruman. But Coates survived, he is currently in custody in downtown Berkeley. That is why you have to leave tonight."

She wasn't slow, but she couldn't see his point. Coates would not divulge any information, his military training and his loyalty to her ensured that. This didn't make sense.

Caelan, seeing her confusion, gave her the final piece of the puzzle which convinced her that she definitely needed to leave that night.

"When Coates was arrested his face had been marked with a pen. An indelible ink marker across his forehead. Your ex husband had written 'Property of Gabrielle Millson'.

14

Somewhere in the northern hemisphere in a valley overlooking a lake, Jack watched a heron dive into the water as he walked across the glass corridor, a tubular link between the various departments of LARA Headquarters.

He paused for a second and waited, taking in the spectacular panoramic view of the snow capped mountains surrounding the complex, marvelling at the green splendour of the rolling hills, settling back to the clear azure lake matching the sky above. The heron appeared one hundred feet or more from his initial dive as it remained submerged until finding its prey. He watched as it flew majestically into the air with lunch in its bill, flapping body, fins and tail, with no hope of escape.

As he entered the elevator for the next floor he tried to remember the last time he had been here, which was difficult as the years seemed to meld into one.

It was maybe two, three years. If it could be avoided he tried to find a way. It was another pet hate, officialdom, offices, protocol, leading to either a dressing down or a security update, new tech, new procedures and countless new rules, hours of listening to waffle.

'Just let me know what it does, why it does it and how to switch it on.' His standard stock response to new technology. He didn't care what it was made of, how long it had been in development or which spotty oik had come up with this latest marvel, he just needed to know if it did the job.

Another reason for avoiding the place began to flutter in his stomach, he could feel it moving up, settling around his chest, flicking at his heart, letting it beat just that little bit faster. He found himself moving his hand over his shaved head making sure that it was smooth, checking the stubble around his strong jawline for any gaps. He looked at his reflection in the highly polished steel doors, hoping that the redness had disappeared from the whites surrounding his ice blue eyes. There was nothing he could do about the crows feet, slightly furrowed brow and the scars, but he convinced himself that it gave him character.

He berated himself for being like this. It was years ago, a lot of time had passed and many discussions since convinced them that it should stay in the past.

But it wasn't easy for either of them. In another life they were a perfect fit, it was meant to be. Their destiny. LARA put paid to it all. It nearly cost them their lives, could have destroyed the company and cause repercussions around the world had they not succeeded in their mission by the skin of their teeth.

That was the one and only time he had felt fear and not only for himself. The decision was very clear, he was always at risk and he knew the score, but he would not be responsible for risking another life through an emotional attachment, an attachment that could bring mistakes, misjudgements and ultimately, death.

. . .

As the elevator slowed to a stop and the doors slid open, she was standing at the entrance. Her sultry hazel eyes looked into his, sharp, clear and focused, but with an inner warmth.

"Hi Sara." He entered the floor and kissed her on the cheek, keeping it brief, ensuring that her alluring aroma didn't draw him in.

"Hi Jack, welcome home."

She let go of his waist as quickly as he moved his lips away, it was awkward for both of them.

"He's in his office, waiting for you. This is yours." She handed him a manilla folder which he opened for a quick glance.

It was one sheet of paper with the image of hieroglyphics on a parchment.

"And this is?"

He watched her push her blonde hair aside allowing it to settle down her back. He was glad she had let it grow. As a former agent she kept it just short of shoulder length, but now as head of strategic she could be herself again, feminine, voluptuous and alluring.

"I've got no idea Jack, but it's the topic of your meeting. They will explain when you're in there."

"They? So we have a guest?" He was now intrigued.

"Sort of, why don't we get a move on and you'll see for yourself."

She walked ahead of him towards the executive suites, leaving him enough distance to appreciate her form as she swayed across the floor, the emerald green dress flowing gracefully as her long legs strode on. He smiled as he followed her, pleased that he had made the trip.

15

Gordon Nightly had been expecting the call sooner or later but now it was here he couldn't contain his excitement.

Rachel informed him that Sheikh Abdurrahman Rashad Bin Al Sharraf was on the line and returning the courtesy, he decided to let him wait.

Pouring himself a generous measure of Louis XIII cognac from the decanter, sniffing the floral, leather, fruity notes, he took his seat behind the desk. He took a sip of the smooth liquor and toasted the telephone, in particular the line that was flashing to indicate that his search was over; the scroll was his.

"Sheikh Rashad, what a pleasant surprise. I must apologise for the delay, but as you know, our research is critical in the current climate." He relished a little payback; now for the home run.

"You have translated the scroll already? You have an impressive team."

Here it comes… He couldn't resist a wry smile as he waited for the real reason the Sheikh had called.

" Mr Nightly, thank you for taking my call. I am in urgent need of your services."

'I bet you are' he thought, trying to wipe the smile from his face, and failing miserably.

"Of course, Sheikh Rashad. After all, we have a common interest. What can I do for you?"

The line went quiet for a while as the Sheikh chose his words carefully.

" It is my son, Mr Nightly. He has the plague."

The final word was all but spat through the receiver as Sheikh Rashad came to terms with the fact that even billionaires can be subject to the scourge of disease.

"Oh dear, that is awful news. How did he get exposed? Has he been anywhere that could have put him in contact with carriers?" He tried to remain sympathetic, but inside he was doing cartwheels.

"Sami has been at MIT for the whole semester. The University sent him home yesterday and by the time he landed in Dubai his condition had worsened. My medical staff are at a loss. Mr Nightly, I fear losing him. I need you to find the cure."

Touchdown!!

" I understand…" *'more than you know.'*

"… And we are close to a cure, but this is an unusual strain of pneumonic plague. Every time we think we are close, the molecular structure changes, fighting any remedy. I am sure we will get there, but it is taking longer than we hoped."

'Not long now.' Nightly took another sip and waited.

"Time is not on our side, Mr Nightly. I need you to save my son. If I need to send him to you it will be done. If you need to be here I will make all the arrangements. If you need any materials, resources, money to accelerate your research, it is yours. Just tell me what you need Mr Nightly and it is yours. Just tell me what you need to save my son."

He should reward Lacy, her short trip to MIT had proven successful. She was a pretty girl and confident. It was odds on that a billionaire's son would be the centre of attention for most of the females at any university. A new arrival with the looks and physique to attract most men was certain to grab his attention. Whether he chose to or not, Lacy had succeeded in her mission. It only needed a kiss. It was not his concern if it took more, he had achieved his goal.

Nightly let the silence stretch, giving the impression he was deep in thought. He took a sip of the heady cognac, enjoying the warmth as it slipped down his throat.

" The scroll, Sheikh Rashad. I need the scroll. Without it the world is in peril. We may find a cure tomorrow, or it may take weeks, months or heaven forbid, years. Millions will die before this time and that could include your son. We have developed a decelerator, not a cure, but at the moment tests have shown that it slows the illness and in some cases stabilises the patient, keeping them alive until a cure can be found. The scroll contains the antidote, as well as the secret to prolong life. It can eradicate the illness and many more like it. It can cure the world."

There was an audible sigh through the receiver as the Sheikh prepared to speak.

"I will arrange a copy to be sent to you via email straight after this call. If you can arrange for the decelerators to be prepared immediately, I will send somebody within the hour to collect them. I pray that it will bring the result you require."

"It won't. I have to have the original."

Nightly expected the initial offer.

"That, Mr Nightly, is out of the question. We spoke of this only days ago. It is to remain in my family."

"Then your son will likely die, Sheikh Rashad. The contents within the parchment are key to the discovery. It has to be with me when the location becomes clear. Without the original, the sequence will fail." He took a gamble, just to test the resolve.

"Keep your son cool, administer the antibiotics regularly and pray that he survives in time for us to administer the cure. I will be in contact once we are successful. Good afternoon, Sheikh Rashad."

He kept the receiver to his ear and waited.

"WAIT!..."

It didn't take long for the Sheikh to answer, part in fear and part anger.

"…You can have the scroll, I will lend it to you until the search is over. But I will produce the translation, which will be shared with you once I have it. I will also provide an escort. I need to guarantee the return of the scroll and its continual protection up until that time."

The Sheikh added conditions which Nightly expected and perhaps additional protection enroute could be of assistance, bearing in mind there were others after the secret.

He didn't believe that Gabrielle Millson was working alone and the search could be long and arduous. It would be better for others to have his back rather than looking over his shoulder himself. He decided that the compromise was worthwhile after all, once he performed the ritual the scroll would be destroyed anyway.

"You have two weeks to translate the scroll as August is fast approaching. We will then have a fortnight to reach our destination. I will have the decelerators available for collection within the hour. I will provide five weeks supply, enough to stabilise your son until our return. But be assured Sheikh Rashad, delay and not only will your son die, you will also kill millions worldwide. You see, the decelerator holds the illness, but once it is stopped the disease will multiply tenfold, the patient will die in hours."

"Is that a threat, Mr Nightly? It appears that you have the contingency pre planned. Is there something you are not telling me?"

Sheikh Rashad dealt with many of the world's biggest scoundrels, some of them world leaders and he could always see through them, play them to his own benefit. But Nightly had a hold on him, his son, and he felt exposed. He had to even the odds.

"I am in no position to threaten you, Sheikh Rashad. My only interest is in the survival of mankind, which now includes your son. All I will say is make haste as time is a wasting. I await your call once the translation is complete and I can take possession of the scroll."

. . .

Nightly cut the call and sat back, finishing his cognac, gasping in satisfaction as the last large swallow settled inside.

Pressing the extension for reception, he waited two rings before it was answered.

"Rachel, get hold of the 24 and advise them that I expect them in the meeting room tomorrow afternoon at 4PM. Pull everyone away from their tasks. No excuses, no exceptions. I assume we have the replacement for Buchanan?"

"Yes, Mr Nightly. Marcus Laine is being brought in by Mitch. I will make the arrangements for 4PM tomorrow."Nightly cut the call and poured another drink.

This one was to toast himself.

∼

Sheikh Abdurrahman Rashid Bin Al Sharaf stood outside the clear polythene of the isolation unit erected in the master bedroom. Sami was laying on his back, his head sunk deeply into his pillow, his eyes wide open staring at the ceiling. A doctor in full bio suit was waving a light over each pupil looking for a reaction, there was none. A second doctor was looking over the many machines monitoring vital signs, he was writing furiously on his clipboard.

Without warning Sami shot up from his pillow, coughing uncontrollably. The doctor rushed to grab a cloth to cover the young mans mouth but was too late to prevent the Sheikh from seeing the blood splatter across the sheets. A tear fell from his eye as he watched his son struggle to breathe, wanting to rip the plastic restraining wall away and comfort him.

He watched helplessly as Sami was restrained as he continued to cough, rocking to and fro as the convulsions took hold. The Sheikh continued his vigil until his son calmed and with the help of the injected sedative, sank into the pillow, his eyes slowly closing until he was still.

. . .

Walking into the hall he took a deep breath. His son will live, he would make sure that he does. He knew his billions were useless at this moment in time, he had to place his trust in a man he'd never met. One with a brilliant medical mind, but a disturbing belief in the hieroglyphics of an ancient scroll. He had no choice, but he needed assurance. He would ensure that his best interests were being served. He didn't give a damn about the millions dying around the world, his only concern was the health of his son.

He knew what he needed to do, knew the only way to gain the assurance. The only option he had.

"Jakub!" He shouted along the hall, waiting as his bodyguard left the study and walked towards him.

A mountain of a man whose soft features belied his muscular physique. His shaved head and perfectly shaped goatee shrouded soft coffee coloured skin, small rounded nose and large piercing blue eyes emanated kindness, a total contrast to the brutality he demonstrated in his role as protector.

He bowed slightly as he reached his employer.

"What can I do for you, Abu?"

Only close friends, trusted partners, his four wives and his personal bodyguard were allowed to address him in this way.

" I need you to make a call Jakub, and I need you to stress the urgency. A matter of life and death. Explain the situation with Sami, express the need for immediate assistance at any cost and tell them that they will be assigned to assist a killer in saving the world."

Jakub widened his eyes with interest but decided against asking any more, he would find out sooner or later. He turned to head back to the study.

"Oh and Jakob…" The bodyguard turned to face Abu.

"Insist that we are assigned their best man… Insist that they assign Jack Case."

16

"Jack!"

Lindsay looked up from pinking one of her Chinese evergreens and ran into his arms.

She wrapped her arms around his neck, shears still in her hand and stared at Sara, a wry smile on her face. She knew the feelings they had for each other and took advantage of the situation.

She could be such a bitch. This all started after Sara was appointed head of strategic, a role that took her into higher management, far more important than Ed Ryker's PA in Lindsay's mind. She was full of her own self importance and to have to serve this girl teas and coffees at the high level meetings that she was excluded from really riled her.

Sara couldn't help smiling back, her head slightly tilted to show her derision. Lindsay had been Ed's PA forever and during that time she transformed her mahogany and beige office into an evergreen tropical garden. Every available space contained a plant, from bonsai to the two thuja conifers nearly reaching five feet that sat either side of her desk. She had to admit that it did liven the place up and the aroma, sweet and aromatic, reminded her of the scent of an English garden in the summer.

·   ·   ·

"Put him down, Lindsay. I need him in here." Ed's distinctive voice boomed through the comms, the all seeing eye was waiting.

Lindsay pulled away from Jack and brushing down her skirt turned back to her pinking, but not before Sara caught a glimpse of the redness beginning to creep along her face, caught like a naughty school girl. Her smile was genuine this time.

"Well, I'll leave you two boys to it. Be nice."Sara entered the elevator and offered a cursory wave as the doors closed.

She hoped he would stop by before he left, even if it was just to say goodbye.

She managed to catch the nod of acknowledgment from Jack before the lift took her back down to Strategic.

~

Ed Ryker stood looking through his main window, a floor to ceiling, wall to wall sheet of impenetrable glass. He was standing, hands behind his back, taking in the panoramic mountain view.

It was the stance he took when expecting visitors, his way of showing that he was alert, focused, even though he appeared to be concentrating elsewhere. Whether it was OCD or a subconscious form of power play, it was a ritual that he felt compelled to perform.

As the door opened he caught the reflection of a big man enter his office. Even in silhouette he was instantly recognisable.

"Take a seat, Jack." He stayed a moment, eyes remaining on the mountain range until he heard the soft whoosh of leather as his guest settled in his chair.

He turned to face him and smiled.

"Hello Jack. Good job in Faso. How are you feeling" He sat in the other visitor chair, preferring to be on the same side of the desk.

"I'm fine, Ed. Got some rest on the plane and now I'm intrigued…" He held the manilla folder in the air to indicate he had seen the contents.

"…I guess it has something to do with Egypt?"

Not difficult to ascertain as the sheet was full of hieroglyphics, but with LARA it was never straightforward

" All will become clear when our guest arrives...Drink?"

Ed moved across to the bar and poured himself a bourbon, looking to Jack as he gestured with the other empty glass.

"Just water, Ed. That'll be fine." He wanted to keep a clear head for what he was about to learn.

He watched his boss pour the drink and flick a switch on the console beside him. The enormous window began to mist over, as if condensation had suddenly appeared inside the pane.

As Ed moved back to take his seat, Jack looked him over. He was late fifties, tall and thick set, his muscles still well honed, he guessed from the gym below.

His waistline gave the only sign of age, beginning to extend to match his well built chest. He had a full head of hair, which still retained its brown colour without a hint of grey. It was slightly darker than the tan. He definitely looked after himself.

By the time Ed took his seat and handed him his drink the misting at the window had transformed the glass into a wall of brilliant white. It flickered at its centre as a black cube appeared, spreading out until it dominated the window. The cube came to life and showed the video link to someone Jack instantly recognised.

A handsome man looked back at them. Clear olive skin enhanced by a neatly trimmed beard shaped around his chin, finishing at a point just below the centre of his mouth. His immaculate black hair swept back leaving his mesmerising amber eyes to eclipse his roman nose and dominate the screen.

"Hello Abu." Jack couldn't help but show surprise, as it was definitely unexpected.

" Hello Jack. It is good to see you again, my friend. If only it was under different circumstances, I am in desperate need of your help."

What has she done now? His first meeting with the Sheikh had been in Venezuela, after he rescued his daughter Zabrina from kidnappers. A rescue that was made far more difficult by the headstrong shaykhah and her belligerence throughout most of their escape. He wasn't surprised that she had got herself into another situation.

" Zabrina? Is she OK?"

"Zabrina is fine Jack, she has grown into a lovely young woman, something that I can put down in no small part to you. No, it is my son Sami. He is dying."

A second cube widened out of the white wall, expanding until at its optimum, the screen came to life with a graphical map of the world. A high percentage of red covered most of the image. Sara's voice added commentary.

"Jack, the red marks the contamination areas and as you can see, it currently covers seventy percent of the map. It's increasing at a steady rate of one percent a week."He had been away for less than a month, this was news to him.

He wasn't one to keep abreast of world news and even on the flight to HQ, he avoided catching up.

"Contamination? What are we talking, Sara?"

"Pneumonic plague, a strain of which has the CDC and health authorities worldwide unable to contain or cure. There are reports of mounting deaths daily."

Jack stared at the screen, his eyes focused on Britain and in particular the south of England, his home. It was relatively clear to the west, although London and the east seemed to be mainly red and creeping into Sussex, it wouldn't be long.

"Isn't pneumonic plague cured with antibiotics?"

"Normally it is. Historically an outbreak such as this hasn't been seen since the thirteen hundreds, known as the Black Death. The biggest outbreak since then has been eighty nine known cases of infection with nineteen deaths in Madagascar in two thousand thirteen. But this strain is fighting any antibiotic and according to the World Medical Council, any other treatment. It seems that the molecular structure of the pathogen is changing its structure within the gene pool, randomising its genetic make up."

"And my son has been infected, Jack. Which is why I am asking you to help my family once again."

None of this made any sense. Where had the disease come from? The big one seven hundred years ago was caused by rats, and in African nations it can be carried by flies and mosquitos, but it escalated due to poor hygiene and most of the world had improved a hundred fold in cleanliness.

It was also something way out of LARA's remit. What use could they be?

" You know that we will always do what we can Abu, but what can LARA do to assist your son? This is surely a major medical emergency?"

" I need you to assist my son's killer in a search for a cure."

Both Ed and Jack stared at each other, the head of LARA shrugging his shoulders. This was news to him too.

"Hang on, Abu. Are you saying that you know who is responsible for all this?" Jack sat forward staring into the Sheik's eyes.

He was a shrewd operator, he had to be as the Middle East's foremost negotiator, a man with both guile and common sense. He would not have made a statement like that unless he was sure.

Jack became interested.

" Dr Gordon Nightly, CEO and Founder of BioTane Pharmaceuticals…"

Sara started the story, the map disappearing to be replaced by the image of the sharp features of a smiling Gordon Nightly. A press photograph, pristine in expensive suit, immaculate coiffured hair and a winning smile. His eyes however showed no emotion, seemingly staring straight through the camera, the two green orbs just a decoration with no interest in the world around them.

"… also, and this will take a little explaining, he is of the high order of Aten and direct descendant of Amenhotep IV, Pharaoh of Egypt in 1353BC."

Jack and Ryker studied the screen displaying the strange sculpture of what appeared to be a pharaoh.

The sculptor had exaggerated the features, giving it an elongated and narrowing of the neck and head, sloping of the forehead and nose, a prominent chin, large ears and lips, spindle-like arms and calves, and large thighs, stomach and hips. It was as if someone had created a caricature rather than a flattering depiction of the subject.

"This is Amenhotep IV…" Abu continued the commentary.

" …Probably the most influential of all of the early rulers of Egypt. His primary wife was Nefertiti and his son, Tutankhamen. But more importantly he was the first to practise monotheism, the belief in just one god. He declared that the god Aten, represented by the sun, as the only true god. He changed his name to Akhenaten, to pay homage to his chosen deity and destroyed all statues, tombs and idols of all other gods. This created a radical change throughout the whole of the Egyptian culture at the time…"

Jack was thankful for the history lesson, but there were more important current issues that needed answers.

"What does all this have to do with this Nightly character?"

The Sheik stared from the screen, his mesmerising eyes narrowing as he portrayed a flicker of annoyance at being interrupted. Jack settled back into his chair to listen to the remainder of the story. Best he let Abu finish.

" After the death of Akhenaten, his son Tutankhamun reinstated the many deities worshipped by the Egyptian people and the Atens were driven into the shadows but thrived as a secret society which has stood the test of time. Similar to other societies that have survived throughout the centuries, such as the Freemasons for instance. This is where Nightly comes in, Jack..." Abu paused for a moment, either waiting for another interruption or more likely making a point that he did not want further interruptions.

"...Throughout the centuries man has been searching for the secret to eternal life. The Egyptians were one of the pioneers and passages from the Book of the Dead tell of the journey to the afterlife, a journey that is reliant on the completion of many tasks until the final task decides the destiny of the traveller; either to die a second time or enter the gates to the afterlife.

Many believed that the afterlife was in fact a continuance of life and as the years developed and redefined the journey, many believed that it was the secret to eternal life.

Nightly was born of Egyptian lineage, and with a rare genetic condition. He has the genes of an ancient Egyptian, an anomaly recognised in less than a hundred subjects throughout history. This is the driving factor, he feels the secret is his right."

"Jack, I can tell you have questions and can see by the way you fidget that you wish me to get to the point. So I will finish with the following; Nightly is after the secret to eternal life, he requires the location hidden in an ancient language written on a scroll by my ancestors from Eritrea, hieroglyphics like no other, written specifically as a gift for their own people."

"I have the scroll and Nightly has been searching for it in his quest to uncover its secret. Upon learning of its existence he created a plague from ancient times, using it to infect every nation across the world and then notifying the World Medical Council that he was developing a cure. It was his way of taking control, forcing the medical world to rely on BioTane. His last obstacle was me, I was not prepared to trade the scroll under any circumstances, having been hidden from my family for so many years. This led Nightly to infect my son, a heinous act to use Sami's life as a bargaining tool to take the scroll for himself. We now have no choice, until he finds the location he intends to hold the world to ransom."

The silence was almost tangible as it hovered over the room. Sheikh Abdurrahman Rashad Bin Al Sharraff stared at the two LARA agents as they sat impassively in their seats, mulling over what they had just heard.

For a race steeped in religious belief, a history moulded by many scholars, with teachings of many different worlds, different lands and tremendous rewards, Abu was sure that the scroll would indeed show the way. Western culture would have a different view, he was sure. But he hoped that he could rely on LARA, for the sake of Sami, for his own faith and for the future of mankind.

"Wow! That was not what I was expecting..." Jack said to no-one in particular.

"... So let me get this straight. You are saying that this mad scientist Nightly has spread the pneumonic plague around the world so that he can use a scroll to find an elixir or whatever it is, so that he can save the world from a disease he started? That does not make any sense. "

Ed Ryker said nothing, but a slight nod to Jack in agreement told Abu that he still had work to do.

" Oh, Gordon Nightly is far from a mad scientist, he is nothing short of genius, but along with his intelligence comes a drive to be the best, number one in his field and the riches that come with it.

But he wants total control, the go to guy for all medicines worldwide. He currently has the World Medical Council sanctioning his hastily developed drug program that stems the effects of the plague, stabilising the patient until they can develop a cure."

" So a quasi good guy? A knight in rusty armour." Ed chipped in, purely to confirm that he was beginning to get it.

" In a sense Mr Ryker, you are correct. It is a form of Munchausens by proxy. Once he knew that the scroll existed he produced a genetically modified form of pneumonic plague, resistant to all known drugs, a plague that morphs, ensuring a cure can never be found. As a way of providing him an insurance policy against anyone else using the scroll, he has given himself the disease, guaranteeing that should he die, the secret dies with him and…he will ensure that mankind will follow."

Jack went to the drinks cabinet and poured two bourbons. Handing one to Ed he took a sip of his own and moved around the desk to lean against it and look up at the five foot face of Abu.

" What's the plan, Abu? I'm not sure how LARA can help. This guy seems off the scale and who's to say he will find what he is looking for? You know treasure maps, ancient scripts and legend rarely uncover what they are supposed to."

Abu was prepared for this. There was a solid plan, a dangerous one and one that will test LARA to its limit. But if anyone could achieve it, Jack Case could.

"I am employing LARA as part of the search party to find Aaru, the Field of Reeds, the destination of the source of eternal life. The scroll describes the location, for which I have several learned scholars trying to decipher as a matter of urgency. We have uncovered the first few lines and I am confident that we will have the rest shortly.

You will also be tasked to protect Nightly at all costs and ensure that he reaches the destination. Should he die…all is lost."

Jack was beginning to see a clearer picture. It was a LARA mission alright, something the organisation was formed for. With a pandemic hitting the headlines, the world health authorities stretched to the limit and governments struggling to avoid worldwide panic, this was a mission under the radar.

"OK Abu, I get it. Under the radar, get this Nightly character, find what he's looking for, then bang him up while he works on fixing his mess. As long as we maintain the story that BioTane are working on the cure, commissioned by the Medical Council, we can avoid any have a go heroes from trying to get at him."

Sounded pretty straightforward, apart from the fantasy at the end of the rainbow. The problem will come if nothing is found... Jack caught sight of Abu shaking his head... There was something else.

"Sorry Jack, I'm afraid we have a complication. Caelen Khan; CEO of Aruman Technologies.

Khan is after the scroll and will stop at nothing to get it. Aruman are direct competitors of BioTane, worth billions and just as determined to dominate the pharmaceutical world. He is also of the Cult of Amun, followers of the king of the gods Amun Ra.

He has forces on the move trying to locate the scroll, knows Nightly has knowledge of its whereabouts and has already taken drastic efforts to recover it. He had one of Nightly's security staff killed and made an attempt to eradicate his head of Security. He is a dangerous adversary, Jack."

Finishing his bourbon and placing the glass on the desk, Jack walked back to Ed and took his seat. He could see from his impassive look that Ryker was mulling over what he had heard. Planning the strategy in his mind, assigning the team, checking every eventuality and the contingencies required should there be deviations.

His expression changed as he came across an issue, something in his mind that was bugging him. Narrowing his eyes he looked at the screen and addressed the Sheikh.

"Sheikh Rashad, you seem to be very well acquainted with the current situation. In fact some of your intel leads me to believe that you know much more than you should. Is there something you are not telling us?"

The smile radiating from the screen was not of a man being caught out, more an affirmation that his decision to employ LARA had been the right one.

. . .

"Mr Ryker, I can see that you are a man who likes detail. I too have a policy to never embark on any task, business venture or strategy, without knowing everything I can before making any decision to proceed. You are right, I do have more information than I should. In my line of business, shrewd investments are the cornerstone of growth. Invest wisely and you reap great reward, Investing blindly impairs the vision until darkness decides your fate."

"I was advised to invest in BioTane two years ago when they began testing the cure-all drug. It would revolutionise the medical world and the rewards potentially astronomical, but before a decision could be made I needed inside information.

Nightly has a trusted team around him, known as his inner temple, the Twenty Four."

"This group are the eyes and ears of Nightly, seven in his security team representing the seven scorpions who guarded the goddess Isis. Fourteen scientists, immunes and support staff, representing the body of Osiris, torn into fourteen pieces by the god of Chaos, Set. Then the last three, the high order, Apophis the deity of Chaos, Sobek the deity of pharaonic power, fertility and military prowess and Anubis, god of embalming and guardian of the gates."

"One of the the twenty four has recently come under my employ, enabling me to gather the information I have imparted here today. It is also the reason I know that he gave my son the plague, a reason that once a cure is found and the world is safe, Nightly will be punished for his attack on my family."

The venom in his last sentence was clear. Abu wasn't about to allow Nightly to get away with the attack on his son.

"Well it looks like we have some work to do, Sheikh Rashad. We will come back to you in a day or two with our strategy and we'll be ready to get the job done." Ed needed time to think through the mission, it was less seek and destroy, more support and protect, but from the sound of it, no less dangerous.

Abu had other ideas.

"You have one day, Mr Ryker. Aaru needs to be found and the tasks completed by August fifth, nineteen days from now. Failure to achieve this will mean that all of our efforts are in vain. My son will die and once he has drawn his final breath, mankind will follow."

17

A s he studied the faces around the table, Gordon Nightly couldn't help but feel immense pride in his creations.

The room was full of the best the world could get. The best physicists, the best chemists, the best scientists and the most loyal of subjects to ensure that the destiny of the world was in his hands.

He had spent his life searching for the key to his existence, his destiny, his true vocation. It was here, the time when Aten would shine his light for all eternity.

"The time has come, ladies and gentlemen. Ra - Horakhty is ready to bless us with his presence; we have been given the key to unlock the door to his Kingdom and fill the world with his exultant light."

The twenty three sat expectant, waiting for the news, their instructions, the next stage in the operation. Except perhaps Marcus Laine, Buchanan's replacement who looked confused as he attempted to feign interest. No matter, he was the muscle, Mitch will get him up to speed soon enough.

. . .

"The scroll is ours. We can now begin our quest. Mitch, your team will meet with representatives of Sheikh Rashad in Cairo. The Sheikh has allowed the use of the scroll under escort, I trust we will ensure that the journey to Aaru is without incident."

Mitch gave a slight nod as Nightly looked over to him. He wasn't over enthusiastic about escort duties, but if they can find the location quickly he could leave them to look after themselves. The important thing was to find this cure or whatever it was to put a stop to this insanity. Nightly was dying and he was determined to take everyone with him. Mitch also had the added complication of his ex wife on the loose, making the mission hazardous. His team would have their work cut out.

"Good, good…Now Stacey, I believe you have some news?"

Stacey opened her file and stood to address the room.

" We believe we have identified the rogue gene within the pathogenic structure and are working to slow down its reconstructive morphing to enable us to disable the change. So far we have three patients who are showing signs of slight improvement during our tests, but it is only temporary as we cannot completely stop the gene from transforming at the moment."

Mitch wasn't totally up on his chemistry, but understood that they were close to a fix.

"So, how long are we talking, Stace? Before you have a cure."

Stace! who the fuck did this Neanderthal think he was? Only one person had ever called her Stace; an ex boyfriend. His bruised bollocks were a testament to her anger at the abuse of her birth name in such a crass way.

She decided to ignore the prick, directing her answer instead to Nightly.

"We are several days, if not weeks away before we can be confident we can stabilise the morphing and another month or two before we can work through the strands to create a vaccine. I am confident we should have a batch ready in three months."

"Well that's us knackered. In three months time there'll be no-one left!"

Had these lab rats listened to what was going on in the outside world? Three months and there will be no need for a serum. There wouldn't be anybody left to give it to.

"Your understanding of basic chromatin dynamics seems to have eluded you, Mr Dawson. The latent and lytic stages of a pathogen are complex, believe me when I say three months to identify and neutralise the abnormality is a near miracle."

Saul Milliner, senior scientist in both age and stature, preferred to keep quiet at meetings. He found that too many questions led to false promises and traps. When there are millions of lives at stake there was no time to second guess.

He preferred to provide guarantees and solid facts to back up their findings, which was more of a challenge than anything he had faced before with Nightly at the helm.

But he couldn't sit there and take the criticism from the uneducated in front of him, particularly as his team had already performed several miracles over the past few months, including a treatment that slowed the effects of the disease dramatically. Without it, half the world's population would have perished already.

Mitch stared at the older scientist, refusing to look away as the chemist held his gaze, unblinking below thick grey eyebrows.

"Sorry Doc, but I'm not concerned about how it's fixed, or made or transandigitalised…I just know that we don't have three weeks, let alone three months."

"… And we will have to wait no longer." Nightly had to interject as time was wasting and a battle of brain against brawn would lead nowhere.

. . .

"We are confident that we can contain the slowing of the effects for the foreseeable future, certainly until we find Aaru. We shall continue to produce a vaccine after this time, purely to increase the BioTane market share and establish our place in history as the company that saved the world."

He could feel the tension in the room as some struggled to accept the reality of what lay ahead. He wasn't expecting a round of applause, but he was somewhat disappointed that the enthusiasm he had hoped for wasn't there.

"Ok... we still have a long journey ahead and our time is short. You all have your tasks and I know that your dedication and loyalty is without question. May the light of Aten surround you for all eternity."

The group left the table in silence, each deep in their own thoughts, choosing not to interact until they were safely amongst their peers.

"Mitch, stay behind will you. We have some things to discuss."

As his head of Security took his seat alongside him, Nightly's feeling of excitement, the bursts of exhilaration that made his heart flutter, the anticipation of what was to come started to wane. The task he was about to assign Mitch will test his right hand man to his limit. But for the sake of all he had worked for and to ensure the rise of Ra-Horakhty, he had no other choice.

"How are you, Mitch?" He genuinely wanted to know, but a level of empathy was required as he carefully manoeuvred the conversation to its conclusion.

"I'm fine, sir. It's my ex wife that's causing the problem. As always her timing is impeccable, but I won't let it affect the mission. I'll put a stop to it"

"Mitch, how long have we known each other? It's Gordon, please, no need for formalities. You are not to blame for Gabrielle, there is a far greater threat to our cause, one who has influenced your ex wife to serve a disbeliever, a Nubian who favours the cult of Amun, Caelen Khan."

Mitch narrowed his eyes at the mention of the Boston billionaire.

Aruman Technologies, the reason he was appointed in the first place, a competitor ruthless in his push to make his company the world leader in pharmaceutical distribution. So ruthless in fact that Mitch uncovered two saboteurs in the research lab, a mole in administration and before he was able to take over the whole of the security detail, a guard who had records of Nightly's every move. Industrial espionage wasn't new to him and he wasn't naive enough to believe that Nightly hadn't been doing the same thing.

What was new was the ancient link, the Egyptian connection. This changed everything, it also explained the appearance of Gabrielle. Industrial espionage had now become a war.

"Why wasn't I made aware of this connection? Gabrielle is an assassin, and a good one. What the hell were you thinking?" It came out louder than expected but he hated being in the dark, particularly in his role as Nightly's supposed protector.

" It wasn't necessary to let you know. You needed no distractions"

Nightly's matter of fact response made the hairs on the back of his neck bristle, Mitch's anger trigger, he was ready to explode. He closed his eyes as he clenched his hands together under the table, holding on tightly to ensure that neither became a fist.

"And you felt it best to keep silent until after one of my best men is killed! Jesus, Gordon, what the hell!" Mitch left his seat, knocking the chair to the floor as he strode to the far end of the room, the thirty foot table between him and the man he wanted to kill right now.

Placing both hands flat on its surface he shook his head slowly, another mechanism to calm himself. As he felt his composure return, he raised his eyes to look at his employer.

. . .

"I had the right to know."

Nightly remained composed, his eyes fixed on the military man. He took a deep breath before speaking, he couldn't afford to lose him.

"Mitch, you are right. I would have let you know sooner had I known the extent of Khan's determination to beat us to Aaru. But I was as surprised as you when Gabrielle appeared in San Francisco. He has shown his hand, we need to be extra vigilant once you begin your journey."

"Well for a start we need to up our security here, I will leave four of my men behind."

"That won't be necessary, Mitch. Khan will not threaten BioTane with a public show of aggression anymore than I would Aruman. For our empire to succeed we need to keep our conflict out of the news... This is personal."

Mitch, his anger receding, moved around the table, picked up the fallen chair and sat back down.

"So, what next?" It was the reason Nightly kept him behind, may as well get on with it.

"You and your team are in danger as soon as you leave the building as are all my staff. We will use the accommodation block until you report that you have found Aaru. Once I receive the information I will meet you at the start of the voyage to eternal life, we will journey together to our destiny and the reawakening of mankind"

As a gun for hire, in the guise of a security specialist, Mitch made a point of never building a relationship with his clients, always complying with their instructions and successfully completing assignments, no questions asked. But Nightly was different.

Although he was without doubt an intelligent man, the madness in his eyes, his mannerisms, his very psyche as he discussed his Egyptian heritage intrigued him, even scared him a little. As his obsession for the scroll and the search for this Aaru began to really take hold, he was drawn even closer to the man, needing to learn more about him and his motivation.

He admired the man's commitment, his work ethic, the way he treated the people around him. But most of all he found that his passion for his life's work, the quest to cure the world of every known disease by putting the world in danger as well as himself, was so fucked up that he was fascinated to learn what else was in store.

"You will meet the Sheikh's representative, an archeologist by the name of Faversham, in Cairo. Details of the rendezvous will be waiting for you at the airport once you land. You will take Aya along with your team as she has not yet completed her work."

"Woah! Hang on, we are going to have our work cut out keeping the Sheikh's man safe, adding one more will just add a further complication."

Nightly's smile, sardonic, patronising, made Mitch's hairs prickle on the back of his neck.

"Aya is more capable than half your team, Mitch. She can take care of herself. You can also forget about the protection of the Sheikh's representative, they have their own contingency. His Highness has hired a security agency made up of ex military, an elite group called LARA. Their leading man, a guy called Jack Case, will ensure that the scroll is delivered to Aaru and then returned to the Sheikh.

You are there to protect our interests until the time comes when I call upon you to perform a task that is vital to the success of our quest. Once we enter Aaru, I need you to ensure that the scroll remains in our possession. I need you to dispose of Jack Case."

18

"Cambridge! When did this happen?"

"Your friend Abu, Jack. He has a problem with the scroll's translation." Sara handed Jack the file.

Her smile, a telltale sign that he wasn't going to like it.

"You have to be kidding me. Is that a real name?"

He looked at the image of a man perhaps late thirties, early forties, full head of blonde hair with a stylised fringe more suited to a member of a boy band than an English professor. The staged shot, head turned and slightly tilted forward, brown eyes staring directly at the camera. A typical model pose that made him look like a film star.

He stared at the name for several seconds but couldn't see how it matched the man in the photograph, Professor Ignatious Faversham.

"Abu's team have only managed to translate the first few lines of instruction from the hieroglyphics and have no confidence in completing the task before it's too late. Professor Faversham is an Egyptologist at the University of Cambridge, an expert on Eritrean history and through his studies of The Rosetta Stone, claims that there are more languages hidden within the Egyptian and Greek scripts which will help in this translation. Oh, and he's a bit of an adventurer, rock climber, deep sea diver, sky diver and arrested several times for BASE jumping from prominent buildings in his youth. I think you'll like him." Sara couldn't disguise the snigger in her voice as she finished her sentence, Jack will hate this.

"Don't tell me. He's coming with us? "

"Yep, he has to. For a start he can translate on the go and get this, if the Field of Reeds actually exists, there are some tricky obstacles to navigate before you get there and according to the Sheikh, the professor would provide the best chance of succeeding."

Jack slumped in his chair, resigned to yet another babysitting assignment. This was the part of the job he found the most difficult. It was another dangerous assignment with several elements in play. The psycho pharmacist in search of some ancient hocus pocus that can cure all, a competitor who will stop at nothing to get the scroll and beat him to it, and a bacteria in the air with no cure. Now, just to make things interesting, a roadmap with directions that no one understands apart from a daredevil English professor, who will need to be protected at all costs until he uncovers the secret to The Field of Reeds.

"So, Cambridge it is then."

Jack collected his PDA, checked his passport one last time before tucking it into his jacket and turned to Sara.

"Good to see you, Sara. Keep us safe." He pulled her into his arms and kissed her cheek, the hug remaining until the warmth of their bodies began to rise, pulling away just as the memory of a previous encounter threatened to envelop them.

Sara watched Jack as he walked away from her to meet the car taking him to the airport. His six foot frame disappeared from view without a backward glance, she half expected it but it didn't stop the skip in her heart, the tiny flutter of disappointment.

" Take care, Jack."

19

'The World Health Organisation has today confirmed that the Y.Pestis pathogen has escalated the number of cases of Pneumonic Plague to global pandemic levels and has officially declared the pathogen a global health emergency.

Around the world, medical services are at breaking point. Many hospitals are overflowing with confirmed cases of the plague with more being reported every day. Several countries have closed their borders in an attempt to contain the spread of the disease, which has culminated in areas of quarantine growing in some cases to include whole states. In the US, Virginia has been designated as a quarantine state with schools, Universities, sports arenas and industrial parks being converted into makeshift hospitals to cope with the influx of infected. Other countries have followed suit with Australia, China, Germany, Sweden, South Africa and Argentina all designating whole regions as expanding quarantine zones.

One company however is close to creating a vaccine to combat the disease. San Fransisco based BioTane are currently producing a serum that has noticeably slowed the virulence of the pathogen. CEO Dr. Gordon Nightly has declared that a cure is less than a month away, leaving the world holding its breath awaiting the news that could very well save the lives of millions of people.

In other news...'

. . .

Gabrielle Millson switched off the TV.

Nightly was surging ahead and Caelen was becoming more agitated. Her trip to Egypt as Lynn Sayers had been uneventful but no sooner had she landed and cleared Customs she received the news that Khan was sending a squad to ensure that the scroll was in their possession sooner rather than later.

It was a bad move, they needed to wait for the location to be uncovered before they took over the operation. There were too many unknowns between now and then. They had no idea if the scroll had been translated fully, if the location had been mapped out and more importantly, who they were up against.

She had received intel that the scroll was under the protection of an agency task force led by a guy called Jack Case, a military man with a list of accomplishments on his CV. There was a small contingent which included Mitch, tasked with finding the location of a place called Aaru, some link to a Field of Reeds or something.

She needed to know where their rendezvous point was, to make ground before Khan's team got here. She had to get her boss back onside and quickly.

A cough confirmed that she hadn't killed him…yet.

She faced him and concentrated on his good eye, the one that was still open slightly, despite the surrounding weals.

"There you are! I was beginning to think you had left this party early." Taking a bottle of water from the mini bar she unscrewed the top and knelt in front of him.

Lifting his chin to make it easier to swallow she trickled the cool liquid into his mouth and waited for the coughing to stop before she began to question him again.

" Come on Neill, you know full well that Mitch wouldn't just dump you here without instructions. Where is the rendezvous?"

He stared at the woman but he really wasn't here. It was like looking through a window, observing her from afar. He couldn't move his hands as they were bound behind the chair he was perched on, he could feel the soft velour of the seat pad on his buttocks, he was naked. It was impossible to cross his legs to try to cover his modesty, he couldn't move, his ankles were strapped to the chair legs.

He remembered the meal, a lovely Hamam Mahshi washed down with a glorious white. Pigeon wasn't an everyday choice of meat in New Jersey, but when in Rome. The way it was marinated and slow roasted was more succulent than any chicken he had ever tried, which was a lot, and with far more flavour.

He was enjoying it so much that he hadn't even noticed the woman as she sat at his table. They locked eyes as he sipped the Sauvignon. She was mid to late thirties, blonde with a slight reddish highlight which worked well with her tanned skin. Her brown eyes swallowed him whole, perfect clear whites and a hint of mischievousness that alleviated the surprise of her presence.

She had just arrived on vacation and was looking for some fun. Now, Adam Neill was never one to look a gift horse in the mouth and after a couple of bottles and a few shots later they were back in his room. That was where it became hazy. He could remember her undressing him, the kisses, undressing her. The next thing he remembered was the pain of the marble statuette taken from the bedside table as it crashed into his face, the bitch screaming questions at him until he passed out.

"Who are you?" He was still wasted.

He felt no pain, a surreal out of body experience, but had enough about him to remember not knowing her name.

"My name is not important, your destination is. Where are you meeting your colleagues? What are your instructions?"

" There are none, apart from checking in to our hotel. We are to wait for a call, that is it." His mouth dried up again, he needed more water. Coughing, he was hoping she would oblige… She didn't.

Walking behind him she loosened the cord that had been tied just below his ribs, securing him the chair's back. She tightened it with such force that the air in his lungs burst from his mouth.

Returning to face him the woman asked the question again. This time with a slow deliberation that made it all the more menacing.

"Where is the rendezvous?"

" Listen you fucking crazy bitch! I told you, we are waiting for a call. How many more fucking times...Jesus!"

Neill screamed through gritted teeth as he found it difficult to breathe and talk at the same time.

With a strength that surprised him, the woman grabbed the back of the chair and dragged him across the floor, coming to rest in front of the full length mirror fixed to the door.

He stared at his naked frame, shocked at the sight of his ruined face. His left eye was barely open, but it was in far better shape than his right, blackened, bloodied and swollen to the size of a golf ball. His nose was broken, misshapen with congealed blood from his nostrils surrounding his mouth. He stared at the woman standing behind him, the softness in her face replaced by a malevolence that took away any of the beauty he had seen in the restaurant.

She moved away from him, collecting her coat and handbag from the bed before returning and facing him once again.

"Well Neill, it appears that our short liaison has ended. I must say that it wasn't pleasant, but a girl has gotta do what a girl's gotta do."

She scratched his stomach, quite hard. There was no pain, but he could feel that she had put all her effort into it. It wasn't until he looked down and saw the knife appear from the long red line that had been drawn across his waist that he realised the scratch hadn't come from her nails.

As the woman left the room shutting the door behind her, he was left staring at himself, studying the line that began to open at his stomach.

He looked on mesmerised as a thick pink worm began to appear from the opening, slowly at first and as the worm came free, it cascaded from his stomach, swirling neatly between his feet. It kept coming, bringing with it more blood than he had ever seen. His ears were filled with splutters and squelches as his insides began to congregate at his feet. He tried to keep his eyes open as the macabre scene unfolded before him, but his one good eye began to feel heavy and he found it difficult to support his head.

As he began to drift, he felt pain. For the first time he realised this was going to hurt.

As Gabrielle pushed the button for reception and watched the highly polished brass doors of the elevator close, she couldn't help but feel frustrated. She hoped to have gathered the information she needed first time and she was sure that Mitch's crew would have an itinerary. She now realised she needed to find another way.

Neill obviously had no knowledge of the rendezvous as she was sure that he would have broken before she had to conclude their meeting. It spoilt what she hoped would have been a productive evening.

Neill's fate was already sealed, but it didn't satisfy her as much as it should. The salvia she had put in his drink will wear off soon and he will suffer excruciating pain for a few hours more before death takes him. She could imagine the screams emanating from the room, the sight greeting the hotel staff as they investigated the noise, the horror that would haunt the finder for many months. But failing to gather what she needed took the edge off a little.

Leaving the elevator and heading past the busy reception desk she noticed the signs to the bar.

It cheered her up a little, she could do with a drink.

20

A fter walking through departures at Heathrow, Jack was struck by the sense of foreboding that greeted him as he headed for the Underground.

For an airport that handled over one thousand aircraft a day, servicing half a million passengers, it was more like a ghost town. Apart from the half full plane load of passengers from his flight striding through the concourse heading for the exits, there were less than fifty others milling around the huge expanse of Terminal Three. A lot wore wafer thin blue face masks, keeping a distance between themselves and other shoppers. Even couples walked apart from each other as they moved around the concession stands.

He had observed on the news that a lot of flights had been grounded and most of the major cities in the UK had begun to introduce a lockdown. Businesses were allowing staff to work from home, schools were closed and the advice from the Government was to avoid crowds wherever possible. It was a similar story throughout the world, with many hospitals fit to burst and the death rate increasing on a daily basis. There was no doubt that the plague had developed quickly, but it hit Jack harder as he saw the impact it had on his own country.

The digital signage, normally a hive of activity as it flicked from departures to arrivals, gate to gate and flight to flight, now stood still with only arrivals highlighted on half of the screens. Jack had been on one of the last flights allowed onto the runway before the airport closed for incoming aircraft. There was no doubt this Nightly character had a lot to answer for and once this was over he would make sure of it.

The tube ride to Kings Cross was long and again unnatural. There couldn't have been more than a dozen passengers for the entire journey with hardly any more joining en route. He felt as if he was on a quarantined vehicle as he stood out as only one of three passengers with their faces uncovered. It crossed his mind to look for a mask seller before he continued on his journey, but as he was assured it was close contact and not an airborne risk, he settled for keeping well away from any other passenger.

The link from the Underground to the train to Cambridge was a long tiled tunnel, intersections leading through to alternate exits, linking travellers to different routes through London. Along the centre ran a tubular steel rail designed to keep the crowds flowing in one direction east or west, normally a hive of activity as commuters rushed from terminal to terminal. Today it was empty. The only sound coming from his footfalls echoing off the porcelain.

The announcement over the tannoys that the Government had advised against any unnecessary travel seemed to have had an effect. It appeared that the city was heading for a lockdown. Pubs were closing, restaurants, theatres and clubs closed. Leisure centres, gyms and swimming pools shut to encourage social distancing and now stores were taking it upon themselves to cease trading until the threat was eliminated. There really was no reason to leave the house other than to replenish food stocks, but with the amount of panic buying reported throughout the country, for many it was a wasted journey.

A man appeared twenty yards ahead, staggering along the corridor using the wall for support. He looked the worse for wear and by the looks of his bedraggled state, one of London's homeless. He was dragging a tattered haversack behind him, his blue bedroll neatly rolled across the top. His head, covered by a ripped beanie, was lowered which pushed his unkempt beard forward. As he trudged along Jack couldn't make out a face, but from his gait he didn't seem to be a young man.

He began to cough, a slight wheeze as he tried to suppress it in the silence of the tunnel, but he was struggling and soon began to hack, bending forward as his lungs expelled the mucus that forced its way through his tubes. An eruption of thick, nearly black blood splattered on the floor in front of him.

Jack stopped five yards from the old man as he continued to vomit blood, gasping in air between spasms. Straightening to take in more air, he spotted the younger man in front of him. Wiping the blood from his mouth with his sleeve he moved away from the wall and dropping his bag, staggered forward, arms outstretched towards the man who was staring at him quizzically.

"He..he..he..lp…help me…"

He struggled to get the words out as his lungs no longer functioned. He tried to suck in much needed air, but nothing came…he felt himself topple forward… then everything went dark.

Jack watched as the man died in front of him, stepping back as the impact of the headlong fall sent a spray of blood towards him as the dead man's face smashed into the tiled floor.

He found himself transfixed, unable to move as he let the last few seconds register in his brain. The full extent of the horror that this scientist had inflicted on the world was right there in front of him.

How long the old man had lived on the streets, had survived the cold wet nights and the relentless fog of London's traffic, the odd doorway here, a park bench there, building up a strength, an immunity that allowed him to weather the hardship of his failed life, only to be struck down from being exposed to some manufactured bug. It angered Jack to the core.

His job was to protect the son of a bitch, escort the madman until he found his treasure, with the outside chance that they will find a cure. A cure that was too late for many, like the old man in front of him. LARA were assigned to assist a serial killer, a premeditated murderer, a psycho.

Having been through the horrors of war, the futility of innocent victims dragged into the crossfire, his role as LARA's head of the wraith team was supposed to be to protect the lives of the innocent, to act swiftly and eradicate the threat under the radar. This situation was not what he signed up for.

There were times when he felt that enough was enough, his time had come to pack it in. To get away from it all, let the worries of the world pass him by and for some other schmuck to clear up the mess. But he knew it could never happen. He had sold his soul to the cause. Just as he was ready to end it, something stopped him, his sense of purpose, his duty to protect the innocent. Like the old man sprawled in front of him, an innocent man caught up in another man's fight.

As he rounded the end of the tunnel he took the stairs to the main terminal and headed for his train, stopping briefly to inform a station attendant of the man in the tunnel, a man that he wanted handled with dignity, to be covered until the authorities could collect the body.

A man who gave him the purpose he needed to get this job done, to find a cure for the other innocents of the world and to bring to justice the person responsible.

He would not rest until Gordon Nightly was made to pay.

~

Walking along Hills Road towards the University buildings, Jack was not altogether surprised at the sparse pedestrian presence or the lack of cars on the road, but similar to the rest of his journey across the country it nevertheless exuded foreboding. Fear had gripped the nation and many had taken notice of the Government warnings to stay indoors to prevent further spread of the disease.

. . .

He passed an old lady reading the notice pinned to the closed doors of the Catholic Church of Our Lady and The English Martyrs, a stunning Gothic revival construction with a spire that could be seen for several miles. It made notice of the closure of the church for the foreseeable future and instructions on how to attend mass and enlightenment online.

She turned to face him, instinctively stepping back to keep her distance. She wore a light blue face mask under her hat, her wide glasses covering the rest of her face.

"What is this world coming to, huh? You can't even get to God without switching on a bloody computer!" She waited until he was well away from her before she scuttled away muttering to herself.

These were unprecedented times, when a whole country was in virtual lockdown, the way of life had changed within weeks.

Cambridge, a thriving university city with a tradition spanning centuries, a city of great learning, where students traveled from all over the world to study in its prestigious halls, was practically devoid of any learners. One or two cycled past him, their mouths covered, heads down, earphones filling their ears with a playlist that helped push away the horrors of the radio, television and tabloid news, as more deaths were reported daily.

By the time he reached Downing Street and entered through the archway into the gardens of the Museum of Archeology, he was beginning to think he had made a wasted journey. It was deserted.

He was in a courtyard surrounded by an architectural mish-mash of buildings, from Elizabethan through Georgian to Victorian along with several additions from the modern era. Palladian windows of the Renaissance period, large arched central windows with two smaller rectangular side sections filled the east wing, square Edwardian sash windows dominated the west and a variety of post Victorian to modern double glazed filled the north.

A manicured lawn surrounded by a low perfectly squared hedgerow dominated the centre of the yard. The four large benches positioned along its edge faced a solitary oak tree that towered above the rooftops, probably the oldest original piece of the entire area.

But it was to the south that completely threw the already quirky architecture into chaos. The McDonald Institute of Architectural Research was an octagonal building built in the nineties, modern brick and beige fascias housing black framed fully glazed windows. It sat on its own, separated from the rest of the architecture, either as a testament to the changing face of the generations or as an embarrassment for breaking with tradition and conformity. Jack felt it fell into both camps.

As he pushed through the glazed double doors he came face to face with a young woman, who he assumed was a student. The purple hair, saggy oversized mustard coloured jumper acting as a dress, the black tights and military black boots didn't make him immediately jump to conclusions. For all he knew she could have been a lecturer with the amount of files she clutched to her chest, she may be on a marking assignment.

He stopped to keep the door open for her. Careful to position himself behind the glass as she passed. She nodded in appreciation as she exited.

" Excuse me, miss. Is this where I will find Professor Faversham?"

The girl looked back and smiled at him, a lovely wide grin of immaculate veneers.

"Iggy? Sure, he's in there." She nodded in the direction of a door to the right of the central stairway.

Iggy? Well that answered one question. He wasn't as pretentious as his name suggested. But then, only time will tell.

Entering the classroom Jack was surprised to see that the decor was far from what he anticipated at one of the foremost seats of learning. He hadn't expected antique desks and well worn high back wooden chairs, but the formica tables and plastic chairs of varying colours seemed so far out of place that the only thing missing was the counter to order his burger and fries.

The traditional blackboard had been replaced by a state of the art electronic white board, it was illuminated with the dissection of an Egyptian pyramid, scribbles from an array of different coloured marker pens highlighted the various chambers.

Pictures, photographs and etchings from tombs, archeological digs and historical finds were pasted around the rest of the walls, no uniformity, no particular order, as if just thrown up wherever there was a convenient space.

A crash, a shattering of broken glass and a curse came from an open door in the corner of the room.

"Oh, bugger!"

Cups, pictures, books and several boxes fell into the room followed by the body of a man clutching some clothing and the rung of a still connected step ladder. Dust, sheets of paper and several ornaments flew around the body as it crashed to the floor.

"Bloody hell!" The man exclaimed in clear concise English.

Jack went over to assist and stooping over the man, extended his hand.

"Professor Faversham, I presume?"

Staring up at the man standing over him, Ignatious Faversham was struck by the steel blue eyes that seared into him. His shaven head and fine stubble along with the misshapen nose added to the menace. This man wasn't to be messed with, but he wasn't in the best position to defend himself. He had no weapon, his gun was in the vault, his knife in his back pack and besides that, he had a step ladder firmly pinned to his body by the box of manuals that had fallen out with him. To add insult to injury, a floating sheet of A5 swept gently over his face, tucking neatly under his deep fringe as it swooped in to land.

He blew hard to move it away, but the thick blonde strands held it firmly in place. He tried again…harder this time, but to no avail, the paper hovered above his mouth, a rasping sound filled the room as it fluttered furiously, refusing to budge.

Moving the paper from the prostrate man's face, Jack threw it aside and pulled the ladder off of him.

"Hello professor, Jack Case, LARA."
    The relief in the professor's face was evident as the agent helped him, the weighty box of books and ladder swept easily aside, crashing to the floor behind him as he struggled to his feet.
    " Oh my…yes of course…Commander Case…Mr Case… Commander…yes…yes …of course…yes…hello."

Faversham grabbed Jack's hand with both of his and shook furiously, partly through relief, partly through embarrassment and definitely through excitement. He was about to go on another adventure.
    "Just Jack, professor, that's fine." He prised his hand away and took a step back, fearing he was about to be hugged.
    "Yes, of course Command…er…Jack. Welcome to Cambridge. Yes, very good." He looked at his hands, tutting as he looked back to the LARA agent.
    "Oh…Hang on…Yes…of course…sorry..here, have some of this." From his pocket Faversham pulled out a bottle of bacterial hand wash and squirted some into his hand before squeezing some of the contents into Jack's.
    "Sorry, keep forgetting…can't be too careful these days."

This man is an idiot Jack thought as he watched the guy bumble around, picking up papers, throwing them back down, picking up a leather jacket, rifling through several boxes before taking out what he was looking for and dusting it off on his leg before placing it on his head. He stood before him, his blonde hair swept back and partly concealed by the fedora, slightly battered, but dust free.

. . .

"So…I gather we are off on an adventure?"

The boyish charm and glint of enthusiasm in his eyes forced Jack to smile.

"Yes, it appears so. I understand from the Sheikh that you are making headway on the translation?"

"Oh, the scroll! Yes, indeed. Here we are." Professor Faversham moved to the desk in front of the whiteboard and punched into his laptop.

The screensaver dissolved away and the image of the pyramid was replaced by the scroll. The hieroglyphics clearly visible on the sharp LED screen.

He watched as the first three lines faded away and English script replaced symbols.

'To the West of the Nile Delta. Where the palms hold the moon. At the top of the…'

"That's where we are so far. But given a week or so, I should have the rest."

"Well professor, that's pushing it…I don't think we have that long."

"Ah, yes you are right. The 19th month of Thuthi…I have that part here…" Moving the mouse across the screen he highlighted another section of the scroll where the word Thuthi came into view along with the figure 19.

"By my reckoning, this relates to the 19th day of Thuthi…a season of the 360 days of the Egyptian calendar. It is the day of the festival of the goddess Nut and Ra… In our own Gregorian calendar, August 6th. Eleven days from now."

"Then we should get a move on. How long will it take you to pack, professor?"

He looked over at Jack and smiled.

Closing his laptop, he wrapped the cables together and walked over to the store cupboard. Climbing over the fallen ladder and manoeuvring past the scattering of boxes, he disappeared.

After a little more rustling, a metallic clank and a few more clatters, Professor Faversham emerged wearing a backpack over a tired leather jacket, wheeling a holdall behind him. He walked past Jack and opened the door to the corridor. Taking off his fedora he offered it through the doorway and looked back at the agent.

"Shall we?" He waited for Jack to leave the room before locking the door behind him.

"One thing Mr Ca...Jack. Call me Iggy, I find professor can be rather tiresome when we are out in the field."

21

M ido Ganin looked up at the fan swirling from the ceiling above his head. The windows were open, his office door was wedged open and yet he was still sweating like a pig. All the swirling was just pushing warm air from one corner of the room to another and then back again.

The air conditioning had failed over a week ago, but due to the Egyptian government imposing a social distancing order, their maintenance crew were refusing to enter the General Intelligence Directorate building unless it was devoid of Secret Service personnel, which was impossible.

He took a draw from his cigarette and tasting the salty sweat soaked filter, stubbed it into the overfilled ashtray sending used dog ends onto his desk. He picked a loose strand of tobacco from his mouth and spat the remainder onto the floor.

The stench of stale body odour and spiced food from discarded lunches filled the air, not as bad as before as he was getting used to it, but once he left the office it made Cairo smell of pure clean air.

This global pandemic had begun to affect the whole of Egypt. Deaths were increasing every day even though they were being offered some wonder drug to prevent them. Crime had grown as the need for food and supplies brought panic throughout the community, seeing people robbed at knifepoint for their shopping.

The GID were tasked with protecting the border lockdowns, monitoring the airports and more importantly the ports as pirates used the Suez to distribute contraband as quickly as they could. Gun battles began to litter the shorelines as desperate traders both legal and illegal tried to deliver ashore before the port closures.

They were stretched and it was only going to get worse. As the phone broke the silence he popped a cigarette into his mouth, lighting it before lifting the receiver.

"Ganin." His abrupt manner normally returned a garbled retort as the caller struggled to compose themselves.

But he was greeted with silence, a silence that once broken by an American accent made him exhale a cloud of smoke and stub out his newly lit cigarette.

" So Mido, you have news?"

This was more than abrupt, it was menacing...the tentacles of Caelen Khan stretched across the globe and he knew that the answers were already with him. It was a test to ensure that he was keeping up.

"Yes Caelen, the Cambridge professor will be arriving at Cairo International at three this afternoon. He will be with the LARA agent Jack Case. My men are in place, awaiting their arrival." As he waited for a response he flicked open the pack and placed a cigarette in his mouth...Lighting it he took a longer draw than before, holding his breath, slowly exhaling through his nose.

"And Dawson...?" Mido sat upright and stubbing out his cigarette scattered stinking dog ends across his paperwork.

Mitch Dawson was of interest, being the head of Gordon Nightly's security force and leading an expedition through Egypt for some item that was important to both Aruman and BioTane.

. . .

"No sign of him yet Caelen, but we have all routes into Cairo monitored. We will find him and deal with him."

"Well I suggest you get out from behind your desk, Mido, and
join your team. I'm not paying you to push a pen. Dawson needs to
be stopped."

Mido took another cigarette from his pack and once lit he took a
lengthy draw, welcoming the harsh burn within his lungs. This time
he kept it alight, he needed to calm himself.

"I'm behind my desk, Caelen, to sort out a fucking mess of your
doing! Your psycho bitch has been here less than a day and already
she has gutted a member of Dawson's team in one of our finest
hotels. I have the authorities on my back looking for answers, even
the Prime Minister is wanting a report. This is not what we agreed."
The silence allowed him two further draws, each as deep as the first.

The room began to mist over as the thick smoke swirled around,
propelled by the useless fan above his head that only served to keep
the smoke away from the ceiling.

"Yes, I admit that I have an issue there, but she has a job to do and I
am confident that she will succeed in her task. The added complication of a score she has to settle has somewhat increased her enthusiasm. Get Dawson and I can assure you that my agent will play nice
from then on."

Mido ignored the sardonic tone, his arse was on the line on this
and he needed to nip it in the bud. Dawson was the key to getting
the authorities off his back and once they moved out of Cairo the
military could have the headache. He just needed to secure his turf.

"Leave it with me. I'll let you know when we have him in custody.
In the meantime, keep the bitch on a short leash for a day or two.
When he enters Cairo we will have him and he is all yours." He
didn't wait for an answer, slamming the receiver down and pulling
it back up to his ear as he dialled.

.   .   .

" Omar, get yourself back here. I have a job for you."

Replacing the receiver, Mido pulled another cigarette from its packet. This job will be the death of him.

22

After a five hour flight Jack knew more about Ancient Egypt than he had ever known and to be honest ever wanted to know, but once the professor started he didn't stop. From the history of the scroll, its Eritrean roots mixed with the scripts of the Pharaohs, the story of Amenhotep IV, the Aten influenced faith of Gordon Nightly and the conflicting faith of Amun Ra, favoured by Caelen Khan. The only belief that linked the two factions was the search for eternal life, something that Faversham finally explained as the aircraft began its descent into Cairo International Airport.

"… The scroll is supposed to hold a route map to the entrance to the Duat, the Egyptian Netherworld or the realm of the dead. It is a journey through twelve gates of hell, twelve chambers guarded by gods and monsters, a test of resolve with a reward of the weighing of the heart before entrance to Aaru and the afterlife."

Jack looked over at the professor whose eyes remained on the pad as he scribbled furiously, taking short breaks to re-read the scroll stuck to the seat back of the first class passenger in front.

"…And you believe all this, do you?"

Peeling the wire framed glasses from his face, pinching the top of his nose to relieve the tension beginning to tug at his eyes, he stared at the agent with a touch of distain. This was his territory after all.

"I am an archeologist, Jack. I have seen many things throughout my travels that should not exist.

The Baghdad battery for instance, a ceramic pot made by the Parthians in 250BC who by inserting two different kinds of metal into a vinegar solution produced enough current to electroplate gold or the Antikythera Mechanism discovered on an Ancient Greek ship in the Aegean Sea, a shoebox sized cabinet consisting of thirty gears that when operated by a handcrank could calculate dates, astronomical phenomenon and chart the position of the sun, moon and planets, as well as noting when eclipses will take place. It should never have existed because it was used over fifteen hundred years before it was even proven that the Earth revolved around the sun.

So, when the question of do I believe in the afterlife, the netherworld and monsters and gods, my answer will always be, I don't know. Because until it is proven either way, man will continue to strive for answers."

Jack could see that as a plausible answer. He felt the same when it came to religion. He could not believe that the world was controlled by one man, and there was plenty of proof that the earth was created by the Big Bang, a scientific phenomenon, the splitting of atoms, biological morphing and regeneration.

He was unwilling to admit that it was not plausible, but without the proof he preferred the logic of science and as religious factions evolve and develop year on year, there were far too many 'one true gods' to choose from, to even start guessing who spoke the truth.

"Throughout all of the many studies of Ancient Egypt, the scroll of Aaru has always been one of the myths that crosses my desk from time to time, and mostly either fakes or scrolls of interest, but not startling, like the passing of a new law, or the announcement of a new Pharaoh. But this one, this one is different. The parchment is authenticated as being from the period. The weird cipher, a mixture of Eritrean and Egyptian script, the placement and the wording all new to us…"

Ignatious Faversham pulled the wire frame around his ears and set the lenses with his fingers to make sure the glasses were comfortable before flicking through his notebook, stopping at the page he needed.

' To the west of the Nile Delta, where the palms hold the moon.
    At the top of the noon sun, on the 19th day of Thuthi.
    After the night of the full moon, when the blind shall see…'

"That is as far as I can go for now as the script has changed. I have a feeling that there is a key to the final passage, a cipher that is not clear. It's as if the writer has created a code within the script, as if there is something else needed to finish the final passage. But we have enough to start our trek across the desert, dear boy."

The young professor's boyish smile lit up his entire face. Jack could see the excitement in his eyes, heard the catch in his voice as he spoke of the trek across the desert. He watched as the professor packed everything into his leather filo, slowly and cautiously rolling the parchment within its cellophane sleeve, being careful not to crease it. He was watching a man full of enthusiasm and dedication to the task at hand, meticulous in his preparation and focused on his goal.

Jack had to admit that Faversham had grown on him and along with it, his enthusiasm. It really did feel like they were going on an adventure. But he also knew that they had a world in crisis, and if this did prove to be nothing but a myth, then many of the Earth's inhabitants were doomed.

. . .

As the announcement came of their final descent, the two men sat in silence, each concentrating on their role in the expedition. Both determined to succeed and find the key to the survival of the human race.

23

C utting the call he knew that he had made the right decision. It was the only way he could live with himself after all of this was done with. He closed his eyes for a moment as he brought everything into perspective.

One of the benefits of booking VIP is that when you arrive early, a long wait for your target becomes a pleasurable experience.

Mitch Dawson had spent many occasions cooped up in a rental car through the night, or staring through binoculars from a dingy hotel room. Or back in the day, hiding out in a mosquito infested jungle lookout in full fatigues, waiting for the signal to attack, a signal that could take days.

As he savoured his second cold lager he could feel himself begin to relax. He had two hours before the Englishmen arrived and settling in the opulence of the VIP lounge, sinking into the soft leather armchair, he could wait a lot longer if need be.

The beautiful patterned tiled floor of gold and beige, softened by the dark mahogany of the walls and set against a warmly lit mustard hue of the ceiling provided the perfect backdrop for the Egyptian influenced music that softly ebbed and flowed from the hidden speakers.

The lobby was dotted with idols, pharaoh emblems, portraits, statues and symbols in every space along the walls, providing an absorbing history of Egypt. If you were so inclined, a stroll throughout the lobby could be as satisfying as visiting any museum.

Mitch's mind was on Adam Neill, the youngest in his detail, dead in the Nile Tower Hotel. Found with his guts all over the floor, his moans alerting the security staff. After an attempt by medics to somehow try to help him, he eventually died.

It was reported that he had been alive from when CCTV captured a woman leaving his hotel room, over six hours before he was discovered. The agony that the young man must have gone through during the hours before his death would have been indescribable, which was more than could be said for the woman who left him in that state. Tall, slender figure, blonde hair with distinctive red streaked highlights; Gabrielle.

She was out of control and knowing her as he did, there was no way she would stop until he had suffered. This was personal, and it was clear that it was kill or be killed, but first she was having fun.

He could never forgive himself for what happened to Barbara and he understood the hatred that his ex-wife felt towards him.

But it was an illness, an illness that unless experienced first hand is hard to describe to anyone in a way they would understand.

To see your mother knifed to death by the man you had committed your life to was hard enough. But to be asked to forgive and to see the man who killed your mother exonerated on the grounds of diminished responsibility and the all too easily prescribed PTSD, was enough to send anyone over the edge. What finally pushed her over was Gordon Nightly. The man who provided evidence, convinced the jury and manipulated the courts to clear Mitch, provide him with the means and the know how to forget, to push it away as a simple brain addled fugue, as you would a drunken mistake. A drug infused misdemeanour, a petty crime.

. . .

During his rehabilitation under BioTane's wing, Gabrielle had been thwarted on many occasions to get to him, to make him pay, each time she had failed, finding Nightly's security more than a challenge.

So, she decided to hone her skills. According to the dossier compiled by Nightly, Gabrielle had become a mercenary, a gun for hire. First as a defence force against the pirates of the African trade routes, both land and sea, before being approached by the Russian secret service to train guerilla forces throughout the Baltic states, and as a gun for hire as and when they needed political leverage under the radar.

He had to admit a certain amount of pride that his ex-wife proved to be as proficient an assassin as any man he'd known, but deep down he also feared her.

He didn't notice the two men sitting in the chairs beside him until a jacket was thrown onto the couch opposite, followed by the Middle Eastern man who sat down and looked him in the eye. He was smiling.

"Welcome to Cairo, Mr Dawson. Can I offer you another drink?" Raising his arm he clicked his fingers to no one in particular.

Mitch watched as a swing door opened by the entrance and a waiter made his way towards them.

'No, I'm fine. Thank you." Mitch sat up straight, eyeing both men either side of him.

He took a sip from his glass before lowering it to his lap, holding it loosely with both hands.

"Mr...?" He kept eye contact with the man opposite, ignoring the stares of the men either side.

"Of course, forgive me Mr Dawson. I am Detective Omar

Hamini of the General Intelligence Directorate and these are my colleagues, Seb and Ilie." He indicated the two with a nod of his head, keeping his eyes on Mitch at all times.

The waiter, a young man of no more than nineteen, neatly dressed in a white, gold trimmed waistcoat, crisp white shirt and neatly pressed trousers of deep red, approached with caution. He recognised that he was in the presence of the secret police and other than a slight bow as he arrived, stood in silence waiting for his order.

"Are you sure we can't tempt you, Mr Dawson?" Detective Hamini ordered three Arriha coffees before returning his attention to Mitch.

"No, I'm fine. Thank you."

He nodded to the waiter in thanks and watched him as he whirled and hurried off.

"So, what can I do for you, Detective?"

" Oh, it is just a small matter." The detective leant forward in his seat as if about to whisper.

"We need you to accompany us to the station, Mr Dawson. Just a small matter that we would like to clear up before you continue on your journey."

"A small matter? To do with…?" Mitch began to tense, readying himself just in case.

"I'm sure it is nothing, Mr Dawson. We will take only a moment of your time. We have been contacted by our American counterparts with regards to an incident at your home prior to your flight. We have been asked to detain you, just until we can clear this up. I am sure it is nothing."

The shrug and dismissive grimace from the Detective was there to show that it was a trivial matter. But Mitch knew otherwise.

The authorities will have found two dead men in Taliban shifts and one wounded with indelible ink on his forehead. Had this not been cleared up before he took the flight, he would never have been able to leave the States. This was Gabrielle, or her employer Khan. He was sure of it.

· · ·

As he shattered the glass into the face of the man to his left, Mitch smashed his free hand into the man to his right, catching him perfectly in the temple, knocking him out instantly. He rose to face the man opposite, but was stopped by the barrel of the Colt pistol pushed firmly into his forehead.

"I'd advise you to sit down and collect yourself, Mr Dawson. Otherwise I will leave you here to be collected by the mortician."

24

Watching Professor Faversham struggling to juggle two large suitcases, his rucksack, the size of a small child, and his leather folio, Jack was relieved that LARA personnel on assignments travelled light.

His go bag was waiting for him in whatever hotel he had been assigned, delivered through a network of contacts throughout the globe. A simple pack of weaponry, ammunition and enough clothing and toiletries to last a week.

Should an agent be stationed at one location for any length of time, a workstation was delivered to site, a seemingly ordinary desk with enough electronics and weaponry to support a small army.

Having his Glock, Kabar and his leather jacket, a jacket specially designed with concealment in mind, complete with electronics and RFID insulation to fool most security scans along with his PDA, the eyes and ears of the organisation, he had both hands free to assist the professor with his ridiculous amount of luggage.

"I will have to have a sort through one day. I'm sure I don't need all this, but you can never be too sure."

Grateful for the agent's assistance to traverse the vast baggage hall towards customs and immigration, the professor held on tightly to the leather folio.

His enthusiasm for the expedition had heightened since the flight and his further translation of the scroll. He knew it was genuine, he could feel the power within the words, knew that the discovery could change mankind forever.

Imagine a world of eternal life, where the ageing process is put on hold. To have the ability to watch the Earth age, to see all the advances of both science and nature as man can now seek all of the answers, where advancement becomes a way of life forever.

'Excuse me, Professor Faversham?"

The professor felt a hand grip his arm, not hard, but enough to make him turn.

" Welcome to Cairo, professor. My name is Captain Lasse Najjar of the ENP. We are here to escort you to your accommodation."

The man was dressed entirely in white, the only blemish being the black epaulette on each shoulder decorated with three stars. On his head sloped a blue black beret emblazoned with the Eagle of Saladin, insignia of the Egyptian National Police displayed at its centre.

Behind stood two further police officers, MP14 rifles hanging from their shoulders.

"Under whose authority?" Jack looked the three up and down.

They certainly looked like legitimate police and he wouldn't put it past Abu, Ed or even perhaps Nightly to ensure they had an escort. But he should have been made aware.

"Ah, you must be Commander Case. Welcome to Cairo, Commander. This is a courtesy delivered by the Prime Minister himself. He knows of your vital mission and has offered Egypt's support during these challenging times."

"Did he now. Well it's news to me, Captain. I'm sure that you won't mind if I check, will you?" Jack pulled out his PDA and selected Sara...

. . .

Falling to his knees, Jack felt the floor disappear below him. He looked at the professor, his mouth wide open but moving away from him at an alarming rate until he was no more than a miniature version of the man he'd spent half the day with. Sounds around the terminal building that had been nothing more than a hum now blasted into his ears, a maelstrom of noise. Then everything went black.

～

The professor looked on in horror as one of the police officers pushed the syringe into the neck of the LARA agent, staring open mouthed as Jack Case fell to his knees, his eyes blank, expression devoid of any emotion. He was helpless as his escort fell forward onto the hard tiled surface.

He had a gun but it was in his ruck sack and packed carefully in the centre of his clothing. His only weapon was the leather folio with the scroll secure inside, the scroll that he had been so careful not to crease every time he studied it. But needs must…

Using the spine of the folio as a weapon he sliced it through the air at the captain who had increased the grip on his arm. It glanced across the man's cheek, but aware of the strike, he moved away in anticipation and the leather caused no more than a scratch. He braced himself to have another swing but the butt of a rifle crashed into his head sending him to his knees.

He tried to clear the stars from his eyes and refocus, trying to climb to his feet. He was not going to give up without a fight.

A cloth bag was thrown over his head, his arms pulled roughly behind him. He felt the steel wrap around his wrists, the clasps clicking as they locked in place.

He was hauled to his feet and marched forcibly forward, to where he had no idea, but they were in a hurry.

"Where are you taking me?" He tried pushing back but he was being pulled by two men and he was still in a daze, his efforts were useless.

"Just keep moving, resist and we will make this difficult for you, comply and you will not be harmed. You are an important man professor, our instructions are to keep you safe. Please ensure that we fulfil our duties."

The voice was from the Captain, whether he was real or not he couldn't tell, but from his tone he wasn't playing.

"At least tell me where we are going. What you want? And what you have done to Commander Case?"

He doubled over as the punch caught him squarely in the midriff, air escaped from his lungs and he gasped as he tried to recover. His legs had gone from under him. It made no difference to his captors as they dragged him forward and through a heavy door, before pulling him upright until his feet gained ground.

Again he was pushed forward, this time down a set of stone stairs. Three flights down and he was pushed through another door. The heat hit him immediately, the black of the bag over his head changed to a dark grey as the sun warmed the fabric. It did nothing to improve his vision, he was still blind but the breeze making it billow told him they were outside.

The screech of tyres just in front of them was followed by the scraping of metal as a door was pulled open. Faversham felt himself being lifted up as he was pushed onto a step where he was greeted by a pair of hands, one grabbing him by the arm and the other on the top of his head, pushing it down as he was pulled into the vehicle.

As he settled into the leather seat and strapped into place he was greeted by a new voice, a female voice.

"Just relax professor, we have a journey ahead of us."

The hood was pulled from his head and the sun burnt into his face making him squint and instinctively push back in his seat to move away from the glare.

As his vision returned he was looking at an open bottle of water.

"Here, take a sip or two. You'll be grateful a little later."

He took the proffered water, giving him time to clear his head and take the chance to look around.

After the second swallow all went dark as the hood covered his eyes once again. But not before he caught a glimpse of his blonde captor, a pretty girl with distinctive red highlights.

25

"Move you piece of shit!"
Mitch was pushed through the prison corridors, shoved violently forward every time he slowed. Of the numerous prisons surrounding Cairo he couldn't be sure which one it was but as he was bundled from the car he could see the Nile, which would make it either Tora Leman or Scorpion. Either way he was in trouble.

"In there. Move"
He was pushed into a locker room, rows of tall lockers along each wall with a dividing wooden bench spanning the centre of the floor. At the end of the storage run stood the entrance to the showers.

A tall well built Egyptian came into view carrying a steel cylinder, black, two feet long with a flat silver tip.
He had removed his jacket and rolled up the sleeves of his white shirt, white except for the red stain on his right shoulder. Blood from the gash on his cheek and jaw where Mitch had shattered his glass of lager in the airport lounge.
The door slammed behind him but not before a laugh came from

the guy who pushed him in there. He knew what was was in store for the prisoner.

The guard walked towards him, produced a key from his pocket and held it in front of him.

"Turn around." He spat the words at Mitch with obvious disdain.

"No thanks, I'm fine as I am."

Without notice Mitch flew across the room, his body paralysed by a jolt of electricity that burnt through him, the pulse providing a muscle spasm that propelled him backwards.

The guard smiled, the black cylindrical tube held forward like a sword, a cylinder that sent fifty thousand volts through his prisoner.

"I said turn around, pig!"

With his defences shredded, not really knowing where he was, Mitch staggered to his feet and robotically turned his back, closing his eyes and bracing himself for another shock. Instead, his cuffs fell to the floor, released by the key.

"Now strip!"

It was pointless resisting as he could hardly control his limbs, let alone use them. He slowly removed his clothes letting them fall to the floor as co-ordination was still difficult.

Naked, he knew what was happening next and walked towards the shower room unprompted and unaided.

"Now wash, you stinking piece of shit…get your stench from my nostrils."

He was enjoying this, Mitch could tell. But until he could be confident of all his faculties he would comply, for now. But what goes around comes around and he was determined to be around a while longer.

·   ·   ·

The pressure nearly knocked him over as the freezing water shot from the shower head. The shock shook him awake, invigorated him. Feeling began to return to his muscles.

He grabbed the bar of soap and turning to face his tormentor began to wash, keeping eye contact at all times. He needed to bide his time.

But the guard had other ideas and slowly lowered the cylinder towards the shower floor. Mitch stopped soaping and watched in horror as the reflection of the stick moved closer to the soaked floor. He looked around for somewhere to go, anywhere, but he was in a rectangular tiled cube, no seat, no ledge, nowhere to hide.

The explosion in his feet thrust him into the air and as he landed his body erupted. He felt himself scream, but mercifully, his senses closed down and he fainted.

~

Jack opened his eyes, squinting them closed again as a sharp pain shot through his head.

He lay on his front on a hard spring bed, his face buried into a pillow with a strange aroma. Slight ammonia mixed with a variety of fragrances soaked into the cotton that screamed to be washed.

He could hear metallic crashes and bangs from a distance, echoes filtering through the air, giving the sense he was in a vast building with a lot of open space.

He moved onto his side and stared at the whitewashed brickwork inches from his face. Surveying the paintwork with his improving focus he was able to make out several different scrawls, some in Arabic, some in English, one in particular caught his eye...'If you are reading this you really are screwed!'...scratched into the brickwork.

Rolling onto his back he stared at the filthy ceiling, at the solitary light housed in a rusted steel shade that blended perfectly into the brown stains.

Sitting up on his elbows he waited a moment for his head to stop spinning before he began to take in his surroundings.

On the opposite wall was a bed similar to his own, rusted steel frame, flimsy mattress and off white pillow. The shit brown cover was probably a good description as the aroma in the room began to seep into his nostrils. Or it could have been coming from the stainless steel toilet, the only other item of furniture, no seat, no lid, just an oval bowl. He wasn't surprised to see the steel bars in front of him. He was in a cell.

Where was the professor? He flopped back and closed his eyes again, giving himself some more recovery time. They had been waiting for them as they arrived. It must have been Aruman Technologies, Caelen Khan. Bribing the police in parts of Africa was a daily occurrence and with Khan, money was no object.

Now they had the professor and a head start on discovering the location of the Duat. If it existed, he had only ten days left to find it. He had to get out of here.

Thankfully he had been dumped into the cell fully clothed. He still had his jacket which lifted his spirits a little, he may have the means of escape. Checking through the lining, a cleverly manufactured Kevlar lining with areas of concealment that unless thoroughly inspected will pass a standard pat search.

He found his earwig and pushed it into his ear, there may be a chance that his PDA was in range.

"Sara, do you read?" He kept his voice low just in case there was someone in earshot. No response. He just hoped that it was somewhere in the building.

He checked another pocket and smiled. He could get out of here after all.

Swinging his legs around he sat upright on the edge of the bed and started to survey the room.

The clank of steel doors opening some distance away reverberated through the air. Heavy footsteps echoed through the walls, growing louder as they drew closer.

Spinning around Jack fell back onto the bed and buried his head into the pillow. Recreating the position he was in as he awoke, he waited.

He didn't have to wait too long as the door buzzed loudly and slid away, steel on steel squealing as it moved along the rusted track. Someone entered the cell. Jack braced himself, ready to strike as the captors attempted to wake him. But nothing came. Instead there was a dull thud from across the room as a body was thrown onto the bed. Whoever it was they were still alive as a moan escaped their mouth as they hit the mattress.

"Your companion will be awake soon. You can lick your wounds of failure together."

The professor, what had they done to him? He sounded like he was in considerable pain.

The door buzzed again as it shut with a clank and the lock engaged. Jack waited until he heard the footsteps disappear.

He jumped up and moved to the body on the bed. He had been thrown on his front, his face buried into the pillow.

He was dressed in loose fitting white prison trousers and blue striped shirt, his bare feet were blistered on the sole, some glistening, having already burst.

It wasn't the professor. This guy had short black hair, cut military style.

"Hey buddy, what have they done to you?"

With an effort, the man lifted his head and turned to face Jack.

Both men stared aghast, recognition in their eyes. From their mugshots and from studying their profiles, both Jack Case and Mitch Dawson recognised each other instantly.

26

P rofessor Faversham was glad to be secured in his seat, he was being thrown around like a rag doll as the vehicle dodged and bucked through the terrain. They had traveled for what seemed an age in his darkened fabric filled view of the cloth bag on his head, but he was astute enough to calculate that they were approaching almost an hour's travel and from the rough terrain he could assume that they had entered the desert.

Little was said during the journey, apart from a phone conversation between the woman and who he assumed was her boss:

'Yes we have him… no, no problems…He's gone, no need to worry about him... Yes they have their orders…it will not come back to us in anyway…Yes I'm sure…'

The last part of the conversation was tense, the woman became angry and the cussing that came once the call was cut gave Faversham the impression that she was under pressure or at the very least, facing questions with regards to the validity of her plan.

Did she mean 'he's gone' as a reference to Jack Case? Surely he can't be dead? This was a treasure hunt in a sense, and he knew from the Sheikh that there were others seeking the same as this

Nightly fellow, but he was not expecting this. He had only just stepped foot in the country and he had been kidnapped and his escort could very well be dead.

The game had changed, he needed to be on his guard. There was no way he was going to miss out on a discovery that could very well make the Seven Wonders of the Ancient World nothing more than tourist curios. He needed to get away, but not before he had the scroll. He would bide his time, he was important to them. He could use that to his advantage.

∾

The vehicle finally screeched to a stop although Faversham's body was still undulating inside, his neck muscles ached from the effort of steadying his head over the bumps and crevices.

He could hear commotion outside. Men shouting, some in English American, some in the local dialect of Egyptian Arabic. Each voice seemed to be commanding, barking orders and organising duties and roles. Vehicles passed by, the unmistakeable sputtering of jeeps. The staple desert transport.

The door was yanked open and he was released from his seat and pulled awkwardly from the vehicle. It took two men to hold him upright as his feet sank into the ground causing him to stagger.

The hood was pulled from his head, the burst of the sun's glare forced him to clench his eyes tightly, flashes and sparks illuminated his closed eyelids.

He opened them again carefully, keeping his head down to avoid another glare, staring at the golden sand at his feet. As he raised his eyes he followed the boots a yard away from him, moving up the khaki pants and onto the navy tee shirt, lingering a little more than he should as the material tightened around perfectly rounded breasts, following the line of the large cleavage in the centre of the open collar until he reached the face of the pretty girl who gave him the water, her blonde hair shimmering in the desert heat, red highlights burned irregular lines through it.

.   .   .

"My apologies for the rough passage, professor. It was a necessary inconvenience until we arrived at our destination."

He looked at the row of five large military tents each linked by walkways of plywood. Men in khaki or military camouflage fatigues busied themselves around the camp. Four jeeps moved around each entrance, offloading cargo of various shapes and sizes, wooden crates, steel boxes and canvas sacks. Men moved from unit to unit placing equipment into each.

Each rectangular construction of tan coloured fabric was the size of a small warehouse, at least thirty feet in length, clear acetate windows ran along each side with demountable front panels complete with solid doors.

They were RDS tents, he had used similar, although not as large. The rapid deployment consisting of steel frame and fabric could be assembled in around ten minutes with enough men. He quickly calculated that there were at least fifteen men going about their work, more than enough.

"Come with me, professor."

As the blonde led the way, the man who identified himself as Captain Lasse Najjar back at the airport, unlocked his handcuffs and gently pushed him forward to follow her.

As they entered the first structure Faversham was impressed by the technology that greeted them. The room was cool, the air-conditioning from the portable condensers working overtime to keep the heat at bay. The ground had been levelled with felted floor panelling.

It remained solid underfoot as they passed several server cabinets that powered the impressive workstation on the far wall. Four laptops displaying maps of the area sat on a trapezoidal table construction positioned in front of a fifty inch plasma screen, mirroring the topographical map of the surrounding area.

"Take a seat, professor. There is someone who is keen to speak with you."

Faversham sat at the centre of the table construction in front of a small console, an array of symbols and buttons flashed across the touch screen. The blonde pushed symbols across the console until she found what she was looking for, the blue symbol marked AT.

The maps dissolved on the screen and morphed into the face of a man in his early to mid forties, deep Mediterranean features, jet black shoulder length hair with a shock of silver streaked back from his fringe. His brown eyes burnt back at them, firmly fixed on Faversham.

"Ah, professor. So glad you could join us. I do hope we haven't inconvenienced you too much." The calmness of the man contrasted with his fixed stare, unblinking and fierce.

It made it all the more disconcerting. Faversham returned the stare being careful not to show any nerves.

"Well, you could say that it has been a rather large inconvenience if I may say so, Mr…?"

The man on the screen allowed a wry smile. It altered his entire face, softening his features and creating a warmth that seemed totally natural.

"Forgive me, professor, I should have introduced myself. I am Caelen Khan. My company, Aruman Technologies, is here to assist you in your search. We have unlimited resources and a team of excellent field technicians and experienced monitors. You will have everything you need for your investigation and I will try to make sure that your time with us is made as comfortable as possible."

A balloon cognac glass was placed in front of him and Faversham watched curiously as a man out of nowhere began to pour the golden liquid into the glass, pouring it from the unmistakeable Baccarat designed gothic black crystal decanter of a Remy Martin Black Pearl Louis XIII. The aroma of honey, crisp apples and apricot filled the air as soon as the cognac came to rest in the bowl of the glass.

.   .   .

This Khan fellow had done his homework. He did have a soft spot for a decent liquor, but to be offered a fifty grand bottle in the middle of the desert was a first.

He looked back at the man on the screen, about to announce his displeasure. He was holding a balloon glass similar to the one on the desk in front of him and he guessed, the same cognac. Khan raised the glass and lifted it toward the camera.

"A toast, Professor Faversham…to a successful dig and to the future of a new world."

As the aroma began to fill his senses, now an infusion of pear and saffron, he decided not to let it go to waste. All of his adult life he dreamed of experiencing one of the most expensive cognacs in the world, and to have an opportunity to tick it off his bucket list was one that he was reluctant to miss.

Silently he lifted the glass to the man on the screen and let the smooth liquid enter his mouth. As soon as it touched his tongue the flavours exploded, the fine note of stone fruits balanced with oak, creamy honey, spices, leather, chocolate and lingering acidic minty overtones. He closed his eyes and forgot where he was for just an instant as history, opulence and the fields of the Grande Champagne region of Cognac filled his senses.

Reluctantly returning to the tent in the desert, Faversham collected himself before addressing the man on the screen.

"Thank you for the gesture Mr Khan, but I can assure you that I am not here to lead a dig with Aruman Technologies or anyone else for that matter. I am employed by Sheikh Abdurrahman Rashad Bin Al Sharraff to help save his son's life. So thank you very much for the kind offer, but I fear I must decline."

"No!" Khan screamed at the screen. Faversham turned just as the butt of a rifle held by Captain Najjar stopped inches from his head. Instinctively the professor leapt back off his chair and collapsed to the floor.

The blonde helped him to his feet and assisted him to sit back down. She then turned towards the Captain and pulled a pistol from her waist. The ENP Officer's head exploded as the bullet penetrated his skull, his body fell backwards sending sprays of blood across the tan coloured flooring.

"I must apologise for that professor, and for our over exuberant Miss Millson..." Khan eyed the blonde with an expression of annoyance.

" ...I'm afraid that she can sometimes be a little enthusiastic."

"Enthusiastic...ENTHUSIATIC! Bloody hell, she has just blown that mans head off! What is all this?"

Standing to gain a better position to remonstrate, Faversham felt a strong hand with even stronger nails dig into his shoulder and push him forcibly back to his seat.

"Calm yourself, professor. I can promise you that you will be unharmed as long as you agree to work with us. After all, we have the same goals, to save the Sheikh's son and along with it, the rest of mankind."

"Well, I must say that sounds threatening to me...and if I say no?"

Khan smiled, taking another sip from his glass.

"I am sure that Miss Millson can persuade you if necessary, professor. But I assure you, our intention is not to harm you in any way. Our objective is the same as yours and let me make this a little less...threatening, as you call it.

Once we have identified the location of the Field of Reeds we will allow you to take the scroll back to the Sheikh with a promise of a cure for his son.

This, I assure you, is not the intention of BioTane Pharmaceuticals. Gordon Nightly intends to keep the scroll for himself, does not give a damn about your client's son and furthermore, intends to dispose of everyone once the discovery is made."

Faversham thought for a moment. He was in a predicament and he knew as much about these Aruman people as he did about the others. But for now he had the bargaining chip; his knowledge. For now they wouldn't get anywhere without him.

"So, you are providing all of this, the resources, my safety, your word to save the Sheik's son and cure the world of this disease, because you are a humanitarian?"

"Professor, I believe that you are not as naive as you are pretending to be. The rewards will be astronomical and whoever discovers the secrets, develops a cure, and potentially regenerates the whole of the human race will be seen as the nearest thing to a god. Aruman Technology will go stratospheric, I would fulfil everything my ancestors set out to do and the name of Caelen Khan will be inscribed in the annals of history as the man who gave the people eternal life."

Faversham looked into the man's eyes for any sign of madness, but Khan did a magnificent job of masking it behind his cool exterior. He delivered his speech with the moderation of a politician, believing every word.

"Well at least Mr Khan, you have been honest. I can't say that I am happy with the situation and yet I am in no position to do anything other than accept your terms. But I can do nothing without the scroll and I believe that is now in your possession?"

The Millson woman took over.

"The scroll is safe professor, as are the rest of your possessions. Come, let me take you to your accommodation, you must be tired as you have endured a long journey." She walked over to a side door in the fabric walls to the east and opened it to the heat.

"Yes, Gabrielle is correct. Rest now, professor, and we will meet again at dinner. And thank you for your understanding."

The screen returned to the maps displayed when they first entered.

Faversham followed Gabrielle out of the tent across the ply walkway and directly into an identical construction opposite.

This had been designed as an accommodation block and he was impressed by the sight that greeted him.

He was given perhaps a quarter of the construction. It had been transformed to all intents and purposes into a luxurious apartment.

A lounge area consisting of sofa, armchair, desk and chair all positioned on a plush shag pile carpet dominated the space. Behind the desk an impressive black and glass wall unit included a drinks cabinet, the drop leaf door open with the Black Pearl decanter in position, ready to be sampled.

A dividing wall separated the sleeping quarters, lavishly decorated with a kingsize bed and storage units on a deep pile rug. Two wardrobes stood either side of a door leading to a wet room.

His luggage had been left for him in the centre of the lounge. The folio placed on the desk with the scroll neatly laid out on the surface.

"Dinner will be served in four hours, professor. Take the time to rest until we send for you." Gabrielle left and bolted the door securely behind her.

Faversham opened his rucksack and began to pull items out onto the floor. He needed to work out an escape plan.

27

M itch Dawson woke with a thumping headache. His body ached all over, his shoulders hurting most where he could remember collapsing onto the tiled shower room floor. He remembered the shock from the lightning rod as his body came in contact with the water. After that he only had a vague recollection of being lifted and dragged away, being dried roughly and dressed in some loose garb before being thrown onto a bed.

He laid back staring at the stained ceiling and rusted light shade as he remembered seeing a face before passing out. One he recognised from an image…Jack Case…that was it…Jack Case.

He sat up with a start, forgetting the headache as he recalled that he had a cellmate. He looked directly into the face of the man sitting across from him, watching him carefully.

"How are you feeling, Mr Dawson?"

Jack had been waiting for him to wake, studying the man who was representing Nightly, his Head of Security, the muscle.

He was a powerful man, he could see that from his build, and the short buzz cut to his dark slightly greying hair told him that he was holding on as much as he could to his military grounding. But he was in a state when they brought him in, someone had certainly put him through the mill.

.   .   .

"I'm fine." He lied.

"Had a slight misunderstanding when checking in."

He studied the LARA agent as he tried to lighten the situation. He was every bit the man described to him and he appeared to have been unharmed when brought here, he was even fully dressed in civvies rather than the nightdress he had been lumped with.

His ice blue eyes, shaven head and the strong jaw of blue faced stubble showed a menace that could not be disguised by the concern he was trying to offer him.

The confidence in the way he sat, the way he fixed his gaze, studying him, analysing him, showed his military training. He knew enough to know that Special Forces operatives never lost their edge, however long away from service. He should watch his step.

He noticed that his own feet were wrapped tightly in brown fabric and by the look of the ripped bedsheets beside the agent, he had been busy while he had been out of it.

"Your feet were a mess when you arrived, the blistering would have got worse had they not been covered. I can guarantee that the bandages are far from sterile, but it will help until we get out of here."

Mitch didn't really know what to say. They had a job to do that had put them together and although not on opposite sides, their agenda's were so far apart. Case had been tasked to protect the scroll, which hadn't fared well so far, and he was tasked to obtain the scroll for his boss, which also hadn't fared well, plus he had to dispose of this man once the location was discovered.

He acknowledged the agent with a nod of thanks.

"Didn't you have a companion on your trip?"

He felt that the mission had ended before it started.

.   .   .

The man was supposed to be escorting an archeologist. He could tell he hit a nerve as he watched the agent's head drop and take a deep breath. He knew how he felt. They were both security, the protection, and they were both holed up in a cell having only just stepped foot in Egypt.

"I think we've underestimated this Caelen Khan character."

Jack was used to setbacks, it was part of the job. But even he had to admit that this expedition hadn't got off to the best of starts. Letting Dawson know that he was aware of Caelen Khan helped deflect some of the embarrassment as well as advising him that they had the intel.

Mitch wasn't surprised that the agent knew that others were after the location of the Field of Reeds, but his knowledge of Aruman Technologies CEO surprised him.

"You've done your homework, I'm impressed. But there's nothing we can do stuck in here." He got to his feet, wincing as he put pressure on his right foot, and walked to the bars, pulling at the door.

It came as no surprise that it didn't budge. The electronic design meant that there was no physical lock, so no keyhole to manipulate. It would be activated from a remote location, normally with a guard at every door to escort each inhabitant.

He turned to the LARA agent who was lying back on the bed, eyeing the ceiling.

"Any ideas?"

Jack looked over at Mitch, a resigned look on his face.

"We wouldn't be left here to rot, I'm sure someone will be along at some stage. For the moment I'd rather spend the time getting to know the man working for the madman who is poisoning the world. What's your story, Dawson?"

. . .

Mitch took a seat on the edge of his bed as his right foot began to ache. He had questions of his own, so perhaps Case was right.

"My story, Mr Case…"

"Jack, please…" Jack hated formality.

"My story, Jack… Is that I probably owe Gordon Nightly my life, or should I say, my life as it is now. He brought me out of a very dark place and I felt obliged when he offered me the security role to take it on. The money was more than I had ever known and the role was varied, hunting for rare herbs, plants and chemicals for his research. But I had no idea that he had released the plague until it was too late. Which I guess is what you meant to ask."

"Well it's a start, Mr Dawson…"

"Mitch, please…" He wasn't one for formality either.

"Well, it's a start, Mitch. But what happens when we find out this scroll proves to be the bullshit we all know it is. What happens then? Do you thank your boss for the life you have now? When you start coughing up blood with no way of taking a breath, just spew your guts out until you collapse, an empty shell, and for what? The money? The most money you've ever known won't get you very far then, will it?"

"Now hang on!" Mitch didn't like this, the truth smacking him in the face.

"No, you hang on!…" Jack swung around on the mattress and stood in front of him.

"…Your boss has killed innocent people, every man, woman and child who has died of this has died from one man's hand, at the hand of a nut job who thinks he's a fucking Pharaoh! And as one of his disciples you are as culpable as he is…Ignorance is not an excuse!"

Mitch stood, pushing Jack back once he had reached full height, which was at least four inches below his adversary. They met in the middle of the cell, each gripping each others sleeves ready to throw the other across the room.

A clank from the far end of the block made them release their grip. They stood in silence listening to the approaching footsteps.

Both men lay back on their beds and waited. Better to stick together for now, the other business can wait.

Mitch couldn't remember if it was Seb or Ilie whose face he had smashed with the glass back at the airport. But whichever one it was, he got his revenge back in the shower room.

He had to admit that it was unsettling to see him again, this time staring through the bars.

"So, have you had a chance to catch up? I do hope so." Seb took out his pistol and began screwing on the silencer.

"Hey, hang on, what is this? You had your payback earlier on. You don't have to do this."

Mitch sat up and began to back away. Jack took off his jacket, sitting forward ready to move. The kevlar lining might stop a bullet from some distance but at close range, not a chance. The only hope was to limit the damage if he could. But the Beretta M9A3 had ten rounds as standard and as they were in desert country, could even be seventeen. He could dodge a bullet or two, but ten?

"Oh no, Mr Dawson. I have had my fun, very satisfying. But I have the good fortune of being employed by someone who will pay handsomely if I can do her one last favour."

Her? So Gabrielle had caught up with him. He knew it was inevitable once they began the mission, but she had out-manoeuvred him. She was good.

"Hang on buddy, you need to think about this. The GID would be called into a fight they could never win and you are jeopardising the lives of millions if you prevent us from doing our jobs."

Seb stopped screwing the silencer, turning to the Englishman the ENP had delivered earlier.

"Mr Case, I have no doubt that in your world it is very black and white. But you are in our world now and there is never just one way to solve a problem. They have the professor, they have the scroll. So not only is Mr Dawson a marked man but you are now also surplus to requirements."

He tightened the silencer, racking the slider readying the gun to fire. As he pointed it towards Mitch, Jack gripped his jacket by the shoulders and launched at the bars in an attempt to deflect the shot.

The gunshot was louder than he expected, the normal suppressed whoomp was replaced by a blast that resonated throughout the cell block. It also failed to hit his jacket.

The gunman fell to his knees, blood squirting across the concrete floor from a hole in his temple as the heart used the exit hole to exsanguinate the body.

As both men watched Seb collapse forward, his head wedging between two of the cell rails, a loud buzz and a click sent the door sliding away.

A woman walked into view, a revolver in her hand. She looked to be a local, clear complexion with long black hair that shimmered in the sunlight emanating from the narrow windows high up in the walls. Her deep brown eyes focused on Jack as she approached.

"You're late." Mitch, even though angry was deeply relieved.

Ignoring his rebuke she raised her gun and aimed at Jack's head.

"NO! Don't be stupid." Mitch lunged at the woman, reaching her just in time to push her arm into the air.

The air was filled with a cloud of dust as the bullet shattered into the ancient concrete of the stained ceiling.

"Aya, what the fuck are you doing?" He stood in front of her to stop her from releasing another shot.

"*We have our orders.*" She whispered into Mitch's face.

"*Not before we get there*" He mouthed back

"Jesus Aya, this is Jack Case. He is with us." Mitch hoped he'd covered the awkward silence.

.   .   .

Looking over Mitch's shoulder, Aya nodded at Jack. It was part apology, part acceptance and part greeting. Jack found it alluring as her lips formed into a pout that extenuated her cheek bones and narrowed her teardrop eyes, the kohl eyeliner bringing out the brilliance of the whites surrounding her dark brown irises.

"Here..." Aya moved along the corridor and retrieved a brown paper package and a pair of lightweight military boots.

"Don't waste time, we need to leave before we are discovered." Aya handed Mitch his clothes and walked away to check the exit.

"Seems a nice girl." Jack watched her as she walked away, checking her handgun racking it, ready to fire.

She was slim, athletically built and confident. She moved provocatively in figure hugging jeans and tight tan leather jacket, although it failed to disguise the slight swagger in her gait.

"Nice is not something I would use to describe Aya. Let's just say she is better onside than not." Mitch laced up his boots and stamped a few times to test the balls of his feet. The right one stung a little but he'd live.

"Right, let's get out of here. We have your professor to rescue."

28

P rofessor Faversham studied himself in the full length mirror on the wardrobe door. His tan chinos, although a little creased, had washed up nicely. The oil stains from the last expedition were hardly visible, which pleased him as these were his favourite pair. He covered his creased shirt with his trusty leather jacket, scuffed, ripped and repaired in several places, but comfortable and with the added advantage of discreet inner pockets to hold his gun, knife and the means of his escape.

He toyed with his fedora, pushing his hair into the hat didn't feel right as it had just been washed. It was a little flyaway which made it sit on top of the hair rather than on his head. He tried letting the shoulder length blonde locks fall naturally which made him look like a scarecrow. So be pushed his fringe back and trapped it under, letting the hair fall naturally at the back. That seemed to work.

The king size bed had proved to be effective, allowing him an hour of restful sleep. And after showering in the wet room he felt refreshed and focused on getting out of here.

Caelen Khan had thought of everything and had he not known better, he could very well have been housed in a five star hotel, remarkable. But, as with all of the mega rich he felt entitled, and as he had lavished him with this outrageous luxury he assumed he had bought his services. How wrong could he be.

The Sheik, albeit mega rich himself, proved that he was more concerned about the health of his son and the return of his ancestors right. Yes, he was well compensated, but Abu was more focused on a successful result than the wealth it may bring in this instance.

Success was eluding him however. He tried to translate a little more of the scroll but the words just didn't show themselves. The Eritrean mixed into the Egyptian script was hard enough, but this, it just would not come to him. It meant that he had only part of the key to the Duat, without the rest it would be near impossible to complete the journey.

The door opened in the lounge.

"Dinner is served, professor. If you would care to join us?" It was more a command than a request.

Gabrielle was standing in the doorway, waiting for him as he left the bedroom. She had changed for dinner, replacing desert fatigues for a figure hugging evening dress, low at the front with a split in the skirt that finished at the top of her left thigh. The floral print and short cap sleeves gave her a Mediterranean allure which although contrasted with her blonde hair, took nothing away from her beauty. She required very little make up, a little mascara and lip balm dissolved the hard exterior into a vision of feminine grace.

"I say, Miss Millson, you look ravishing." He smiled his best model smile as he took off his fedora and threw it onto the couch. He would retrieve that for his journey later.

"Well, thank you, sir." Gabrielle curtsied, genuinely pleased with the compliment.

As the door locked behind them Faversham offered his arm which Gabrielle accepted.

He could see men working, feverishly loading equipment onto the Jeeps and transporters, it looked like they were packing away.

Gabrielle knew what he was thinking.

"We will be leaving at first light. Your accommodation will be the last to be dismantled professor, you will get the rest you need. In the meantime our chef has created a splendid table for this evening…Shall we?"

The door to the communication tent opened and a guard walked through, holding it for them to pass.

29

A ya was in the anteroom having cleared the observation area to the jail. Two police officers lay unconscious at their posts, both with head wounds that would hurt like hell once they woke.

She opened a storage unit and retrieved Jack's Glock, Kabar knife and PDA, handing them to him reluctantly, staring at Mitch as she did so. Mitch followed her glare with a nod of his head.

Jack mulled over the relationship between the two, it wasn't clear who trusted who, but it was certainly a cool one. He knew he would need to watch his back with these two and he wasn't sure yet who was the most dangerous.

Checking his Glock he holstered it and pushed his earwig.

"Sara, do you read?" He waited for the response…wishing he had a way of controlling the volume.

"JACK!…Oh my God…what the hell has been going on?"

"Ambushed I'm afraid. Lost the professor but don't tell the old man yet, give us a chance to catch up."

"He'll know soon enough. You'll get a few hours at most."

She could cover her tracks for a short while, but Ed Ryker had an uncanny way of finding these things out.

"OK, that will have to do. Can you gather as much intel as you can? See what chatter is doing the rounds in Cairo, and scan the outskirts...see if anything shows up."

"Ok, Jack. Shall I give you the egg back when I've finished sucking it?" She had been doing this long enough to know what she was doing.

She knew Jack was pissed that he'd dropped his guard, but she wasn't prepared to take the brunt of his embarrassment.

"Fair comment, Sara. I'll leave it with you...out."

Occasionally he screwed up and when he did it angered him, galled him, really pissed him off. Sara knew that, so although he realised he had been a little short with her, they knew it would be forgotten the next time they communicated.

They came to a set of stairs leading up to the station house. Aya had reported light numbers due to the pandemic, but there was still enough to make it difficult. As they climbed towards the single steel door with one small barred port window, Aya turned and beckoned for the two men to get down. They crouched behind her as she walked up to the window.

Suddenly out of nowhere, Aya screamed.

"ilHa'ni! ilHa'ni! Sebnie iwahdie! ilHa'ni!..." Over and over again

"Help! Help! Leave me alone! Help!...

"What the fuck!..." It was Mitch who reacted first, leaping to his feet, only to be pushed back down by the screaming girl.

Shouts could be heard from behind the door and a bleep from an electronic keypad. The door buzzed and flew open.

Aya pushed the heel of her hand into the chin of the first police officer on the scene, he collapsed back into a colleague sending them both crashing to the floor. Once clear of the door she wheeled around and high kicked a third officer in the throat before he had time to reach for his gun. The last officer in the room held his hands up in submission.

Aya barked an instruction to him in Egyptian Arabic and caught the bunch of keys that he threw at her.

Mitch and Jack walked into the station house and looked at each other. Jack raised his eyebrows, Mitch just shrugged.

"Come on, let's go!" Aya ran to a door and pushed through into the open air. Mitch and Jack followed…

They leapt down the steps into the sun towards a group of SUV's complete with blue emergency light bars and police insignia. Aya pushed the remote and watched for the lights to flash. They followed the sound of the single high pitched bleep.

"Get in!" She entered via the driver's door and fired the engine as the two men bolted into the rear through the automatic sliding door. The car lurched forward as the door began to close.

"Hold on to something" She shouted behind as she headed for the chained gates.

The car lurched as it smashed through steel, bouncing several times before it straightened as it hit the highway. Both men scrambled into a seat, instinctively grabbing the seatbelts and securing themselves in.

Neither spoke as they travelled along the highway, they just stared through the windscreen and watched the SUV eat the road.

30

G abrielle was right to recommend the chef, the evening meal had been exquisite.

Starting with a Foie Gras lightly seasoned with Jurancon wine and Juniper berries with a slice of light toast and fig chutney, followed by a succulent Lobster Thermidor with a crisp cheese crust and a delightfully fluffy mound of Jasmine rice.

After finishing a decadent ice cream dish that Faversham could not pronounce, he sipped his coffee.

"My compliments to the chef." Professor Faversham held his cup up to the screen where the gesture was returned by Caelan Khan, who preferred to continue with the Dom Pérignon.

"Gianni is one of the best. What he can't make to perfection has not been invented yet. I am glad you approve, professor. Perhaps once we finish our business we will dine together at my home. I will show you what he can conjure with a proper kitchen." That wasn't likely to happen, but he offered an appreciative nod to the screen.

"Now, professor. I understand you are having difficulty with the final passages of the scroll. What appears to be the problem?"

. . .

Faversham knew that they didn't have his current translation so he held all the cards. But he needed to be careful so as not to jeopardise the whole expedition with a false trail that was too obvious.

"Yes, the scroll has Egyptian and Eritrean script for the majority, but the last part seems to be a code, a cipher of some sort."

"But you have enough to know which direction we are heading, I assume?"

"Yes, as you can see from my work." Faversham gestured at the screen as Khan lowered his head to read what he had received earlier.

"Yes…so far…"

'*To the Northwest of the Nile Delta,*
Where the Palms hold the moon,
At the top of the noon sun,
on the 19th day of Thuthi.
After the night of the full moon,
when the blind shall see…'

"…And do we know where to start looking?"

This was it… his one chance to divert before he set his plan in motion.

"Well it has to be west of Alexandria, I'd say near to the Libyan border. Palms are plentiful towards Sidi Barrani. That is all I have, without the rest of the scribe I can't be certain, but it's a reasonable guess and as I am sure you are aware Mr Khan, archeology is eighty percent guess work, ten percent fact and ten percent luck."

Khan stared from the screen, his eyes looking him over, scrutinising his words, trying to psych him out. Faversham had experienced many mind games in his career, he also loved chess and poker, each relying on a cool head. He will get away with this, he could feel it.

"Well then professor, I hope you are suitably refreshed as we have a long journey ahead of us tomorrow. I will bid you a good night."

The screen went blank.

"Time to go." Gabrielle stood behind him and gently pulled the chair back, forcing him to stand.

"Well that was altogether marvellous, I must say." He smiled at her as he turned.

She returned his smile with a blank expression, back to the steel that seemed to be her preferred stance.

"Make the most of the experience, professor. Gianni won't be coming along for the ride."

Nothing more was said as they left the communication tent and walked to the accommodation block.

As he entered she locked the door behind him.

"We'll come for you at first light." Not a goodnight, sleep well. Nothing. But then again, he should have said goodbye. Better left as it was.

Carefully drying the parchment, Faversham put the decoy on the desk. It was a good copy as far as he could see, although some of the Anubis symbols looked more like Snoopy. But it would give him an extra ten minutes at least.

He carefully rerolled the scroll and placed it back in his jacket. Taking two bottles of water from the drinks cabinet and putting them in his small shoulder bag, he grabbed his fedora and headed to the wet room.

Using his knife, he jammed the blade in between two tiles towards the edge of the raised floor. They both popped away from the housing, he had guessed right...There was a gap between the wet room floor and the sand below, more than enough of a crawl space to take a man.

Pulling away four more tiles he was able to lever himself into the space and lie on his front. The frame underneath the wet room was exposed to the elements to allow room for the pump and pipework, leaving airspace to take away any steam through the vents in the floor.

Looking out from his vantage point he watched as the torch passed and the guard's boots continued around the side of the tent. He waited for a further pass which took a good five minutes, proving that the guard completed a full circuit of the block. More than enough time.

He crawled from underneath the frame and ran. He had noticed a set of dunes around twenty yards from the rear of the tent and he made it in good time, laying on his back and holding his breath as best as he could.

He waited for the shouts of discovery, the jeeps firing up, lights shining all around, but none came.

He set off heading West and after half an hour or so he came to a small clearing surrounded by ryegrass. He risked lighting his maglite, shining it across a small pool of water overlooked by three palms. A tiny oasis.

He shone the torch around him to ensure that he wasn't sharing the spot with sleeping snakes, inquisitive scorpions or any other creepy crawly as he sat down. He unscrewed the bottle of water, taking a small sip.

It would be at least four hours before they would notice him missing, and with any luck a fruitless hunt Northwest in search of him. By that time he should be a good few miles away to the West.

It was a clear night and the chill had started to surround him, not bitter, but he would have felt it more had he not had his leather jacket.

Thoughts of his jacket made him turn his attention to his escort, Jack Case. He had left him flat out in the airport and he was hauled away before having a chance to see if he had survived. By all accounts Jack was one of the best according to Abu, so he hoped that he got away somehow, perhaps already looking for him. Faversham had to admit he could do with some support, it was likely to get hairy the closer he got to the destination.

He needed to keep going through the night and hope things would look a little clearer in the daylight. But for the moment he felt very much alone.

A rustle to his right made him start and shining the torch he expected to see Gabrielle striding towards him, gun in hand.

Instead, standing still as the beam shone over it was the tiny face and oversized pointed ears of a Fennec fox. Its eyes wide and sparkling in the small beam, pointed snout twitching nervously as it tried to gather a scent from the stranger in its back yard.

They stared at each other for a few moments before the fox took one step towards him, stared for a few moments more, then bolted away into the darkness.

"Don't worry little one." He whispered after it. " I'm leaving now, it's all yours."

Putting his bottle back in the bag, he switched off the light and sat for a little while longer allowing his eyes to adjust to the moonlit surroundings of shadows.

A hand clasped around his mouth and he felt the cold steel of a blade pressed against his neck. He could smell the stale stench of alcohol and cigarettes as warm breath enveloped his ear.

"Make one sound and I will slit your throat from ear to ear."

Faversham nodded slowly in understanding. He kept quiet as strong arms yanked him to his feet and pulled him away from his hiding place.

31

The car slowed as they entered the outskirts of 6th of October City, the last urban town to the west of Cairo before they hit the desert.

Nearing Liberty Square they came across Cityscape Mall. Parking the police issue SUV within customer parking they entered Starbucks, the emptier of the surrounding cafes, with a rear seating area well away from prying eyes.

"Jack, we have some activity twenty miles west of your location…"

Jack joined the others and putting his latte down to add sugar, popped the top as Sara continued.

"We found a temporary camp made up of half dozen RDS instal-lations erected three days ago. They broke camp this morning at first light. Three transporters left heading northwest while five jeeps stayed behind circling the zone. By the way they are manoeuvring it looks like they are searching the area."

"More like looking for someone, like an escapee perhaps?" Jack filled the others in as he stirred the froth around his cup.

"…And you think the professor is out there?" Mitch was already in Jack's mindset.

"Could be… Sara, send over the co-ordinates of the area the

jeeps are looking in and keep an eye on the transporters. Let us know if anything changes."

Taking a mouthful of the milky coffee Jack headed for the exit. Mitch and Aya followed close behind. They were thirty minutes away, with any luck they could intercept one of the jeeps. He hoped that his hunch was right.

"How do we know that this is where your professor is?" Aya had spoken very little throughout the journey so far.

She explained how by posing as a GID officer she was able to get into the prison, but no explanation as to why she hadn't been at the original rendezvous. After that nothing, until now.

"Well it's all we have to go on at the moment and the professor confirmed the scroll pointed to the west of the Nile Delta. So whatever happens we are going in the right direction,"

Jack followed Mitch in belting up again as the SUV cleared the end of Al Dabaa Corridor and began the off road journey west.

Mitch answered a call on his mobile. Looking over at Jack he passed the phone to Aya who connected it to a cable stretching out from the dash.

"Someone wants a word with you." Mitch nodded towards the front of the car.

"Mr Case." The voice boomed from the speakers.

"It is a pleasure to make your acquaintance. My name is Gordon Nightly of BioTane Pharmaceuticals."

Jack sat up straight. The American accent had a smoothness about it. He enunciated every word clearly and succinctly, with a confidence in his tone that sounded all too arrogant.

"Well I can't say it's a pleasure from where I'm sitting. We're all trying to sort out your fuck up…"

.   .   .

"…Now, Mr. Case, I was hoping that we could see some form of collaboration as we are fighting the same enemy. You have experienced first hand the extent of Caelen Khan's determination to gain an advantage to the discovery. It appears all too clear that he is now in possession of the scroll along with your charge, Professor Faversham.

I can't imagine the pain Sheikh Abdurrahman Rashad Bin Al Sharraff is going through right now. He put all his faith in LARA, and had it not been for my team you would still be in a cell."

"Listen you sonofabitch, you have jeopardised every life on this planet for your own narcissistic greed and an obsession for a fucking fairy tale! You will be made to pay Nightly, that I can guarantee." Jack was having none of it.

He knew that the scientist had a point, they alone had been tasked to protect the scroll. The professor had been an afterthought, an additional complication that no one accounted for at the start. But he will do everything in his power to get back on track. He wasn't about to let the Sheikh down, or his son.

But this fruitcake had created a moral paradox that put him in an impossible position. To succeed in his task he had to work with Nightly to find the scroll, rescue the professor and stop the disease.

The SUV bounced along the desert tracks kicking dust all around the vehicle. The sun, clear of any cloud, had begun to whiten the horizon as they continued west.

Nightly had gone quiet, Mitch looked over at the LARA agent. The scientist would be having kittens by now as nobody spoke to him like that. His instructions were to get rid of Case once the entrance to the Field of Reeds was discovered. Nightly will be mulling over the notion of doing it right now. It was a rash decision, but he knew the man well enough to know that he often acted first and thought later. Even he had to admit that releasing a disease with a mind of its own had been one of those times. He had delivered a death sentence to many and was relying on the faith of a race that has been eradicated for thousands of years.

Nightly's voice came over the speaker, the confidence had gone.

His smooth tones replaced by a matter of fact, almost reluctant overtone that clearly indicated he was hurting, probably angry and most definitely on the verge of a tantrum.

" Mitch, your team will be with you on the ground by the time you reach your destination. Provide Mr. Case with whatever support he needs to get the professor and the scroll back to him. I will meet you all at the entrance to the Field of Reeds, until then I will be monitoring the situation.

One other thing…Aya, you know what to do."

Jack instinctively felt for his Glock as Aya reached into her jacket.

He relaxed as she passed a small container to Mitch. Mitch opened the hinged box and withdrew an aluminium syringe.

"You need a shot of this." He passed the instrument to Jack who looked at the small vacuum delivery valve.

"And this is?" He was not about to take anything without a full explanation.

"It's an antigen to help prevent you from contracting the disease. It will protect against any airborne risk or contracting through the skin. No guarantees on total exposure of diseased saliva or blood but it gives some protection, better than nothing.

"…And I'm expected to take your word for it? "

Jack stared at Mitch and caught Aya's eye as she peered at them through the rear view mirror. He expected to see a pistol trained on him until he agreed to take the shot. But no one made a move, just waited for him.

Mitch tutted and held out his hand for Jack to pass it back. Once it was in his hand he held it to his arm and the hiss and click confirmed that he had injected himself. He then took another vial from the case and handed it over.

.   .   .

"It could very well save your life. There is one in here for the professor when we find him."

Jack studied the vial again, turning it over in his hand. He knew that if he became infected it would hit within twenty four hours. They had four days to find this Field of Reeds and it was anyone's guess as to what they may come up against during the search.

He pressed the vial to his skin and pushed the button. The hiss and click confirmed delivery.

He had a feeling that over the next few days there will be more questions than answers. But the current question on everyone's lips as they drove further into the desert was …. 'Where is the scroll?'

32

F aversham sat on the decorative rug and buried his head in his knees as he hugged them for comfort. Being captive is a demoralising experience, to happen twice is embarrassing.

After being pushed around for several miles his captor had thrown him in the goat hair tent, gave him a wineskin full of water and left him there for what seemed like hours.

He had counted the forty multicoloured cushions spread out on the crude orange and green striped covered couch several times and paced the thirty foot square construction more than once. He even contemplated setting fire to the tent using one of the burning lamps hanging from the ceiling. But the way his luck was going he would probably be the only one to perish and that would not do at all.

He'd been relieved of his satchel, gun, knife and scroll and by the way the bedouins began arguing in crude Arabic, he was unlikely to see any of them again. This annoyed him as the knife in particular had been a gift from a charming young lady who had spent many months as his chief field technician on several expeditions. Charlotte was a lovely girl but her maternal clock began to tick too loudly and she eventually succumbed to the challenge of motherhood. It was a parting gift that he cherished for two reasons; a precious gift as a momento of their time together and relief that he had been presented with a knife and not a son or daughter. That honour was bestowed on Chappers, one of his site monitors. Which begged the question, how did she find the time?

The flap was thrown open and his captor strode into the tent. He was dressed in a striking royal blue and gold robe with a loose fitting turban, the tail of which wrapped around his neck like a scarf.

"I apologise for keeping you for so long, but you have proved to be quite a prize."

He was a good looking man with eastern features, his black beard carefully crafted to follow the contours of his chin. His English was good but heavily accented with the dialect of a Berber, which made sense as he could hardly make out some of the words he heard from outside. The language was a mix of Egyptian Arabic and the Afroasiatic tongue used by many North Africans, originating as far back as the Ottoman Empire.

It was unsettling however as the name Berber is a variation of the Greek original word barbaros or barbarian and they had a formidable reputation, particularly around the Libyan borders, to which they were now a lot closer than he would have liked.

"You travel light for a man who was being treated like a king." The Berber handed him his satchel, it still contained his water and more surprisingly his knife and gun, the bullets had been removed but lay in the bottom of the bag.

" I believe it is because of this…'

He held the scroll in front of Faversham. It had been taken from the cellophane sleeve which made the professor nervous. In some circumstances, heat and the sun's rays can deteriorate papyrus in a matter of minutes.

Turning it over and scanning the designs of the script, it was obvious that it meant nothing to him. But to Faversham it suddenly meant more to him than ever before.

"That's it…by God! Of course."

He shot to his feet and grabbing the scroll looked into the Berber's eyes…Time stood still for a moment as both men held the scroll at either end, eyes locked together in a meeting of minds.

"May I?" Faversham pulled the scroll gently towards him, the Berber's hands moved with it.

Releasing the scroll he watched as the professor held it up, searching the back of the parchment as the light shone through the papyrus. The last lines of the scroll appeared through, along with a jagged etching that could have been taken for a stain without the benefit of the flickering light.

"Yes, yes! Very clever, very clever indeed." He could see the last lines clearly now.

They were written in reverse and as Hieroglyphics are read either left to right or right to left depending on which way the symbol faced, and as the upper symbols are read before the lower, it was a complicated translation that still needed work. But now he had the key he could complete it.

The only thing left to do was to decipher the etching. It looked like a crude drawing of a dragon or a bird of some sort, but with just an outline and no detail, he couldn't make it out.

"So you know where to go?" The Berber watched as the professor held the scroll to the light. He felt excited as the discovery was made and smiled as he realised that his life was going to change. He was about to become a very rich man.

"Well, I wouldn't say that I know where we are going. But I think I now know how to find it."

The Berber clapped twice and shouted towards the entrance of the tent. The flap was thrown back allowing several men to enter, all dressed in robes of varying colours, each bright and vibrant, a distinct characteristic of these particular nomads. Music began to fill the tent as men with reed flutes and Mizwids, the Arabic version of a bagpipe, accompanied by rhythmic drummers began to dance around the floor. They were followed by several women, as brightly adorned as the men, carrying meats, fruit and several rices on serving dishes that they placed on low crudely crafted tables around the tent's edge.

"Here, take this." Faversham was presented with another wine skin, this time filled with what the name suggested.

"I am Malik of Qara and this is my brother, Ishmael..." The Berber pointed to the man walking towards him with a woman on each arm.

"...this is Talia." He stroked her thick auburn curls and pulled her towards him kissing her forcibly on the lips. She accepted him subserviently.

"… and this is Ula." He stroked her flaming red hair, she pulled his hand away and kissed it.

"Two of my wives and the most lively of lovers. They are yours my friend, a gift in appreciation for leading us to Aaru."

He looked at the two young girls, they must have been twenty years of age, no more. They followed the Berber tradition of bright garments, a flourish of yellow, red, purple and green and adorned with gold chains, bracelets and headpieces filled with jewels. They swayed rhythmically to the music, keeping their eyes on their husband's captive.

Faversham looked at each in turn and smiled, bowing his head in greeting.

"Your gift is very kind Malik of Qara, but I would like an opportunity to translate the rest of the scroll. We have four days to find the path and I fear I will need two days to complete my work."

Malik and Ishmael stared at the professor in such a way that he felt they were waiting for him to grow a second head. He had a feeling that he may have offended them by not accepting their women. But in truth, he really did want to complete the translation and even though he was in no doubt that the ladies would have given him a pleasurable welcome, he was not planning to stay.

He stared back at the two Berbers, anticipating their next move. Malik, a broad grin on his face, walked over to him and slapped him on the back.

"Ha ha! You are indeed a strange man. You shall have the time you need to finish your translation, my friend. We will leave before dusk. In the meantime drink, eat and enjoy the hospitality of the people of Qara."

The wineskin was pulled from his grasp and Malik uncorked the pointed neck and tipped the wine into Faversham's mouth. He managed to open it just as the heady liquid poured out.

Slapping him on the back again, Malik thrust the skin back into his arms and strode off with his brother and wives in tow.

Spotting what looked like chicken on a tray close by, he realised that he hadn't eaten yet today. As he had no way of escape for the moment, he took the opportunity to build his strength. He had a feeling he would need it.

33

With no landmarks they travelled far enough into the desert to see nothing but sand all around them. One dune, hillock, rift, looked like all the others and with the sun reflecting a pulsing haze off of the surface, it was easy to confuse an undulation with a mirage, which worked wonders on the stomach as it lurched when it shouldn't, causing nausea that Jack hadn't felt since he was last on a boat.

"How are we doing, Sara?" He pressed his finger to his ear to cover the earpiece from the screaming jeep engine.

"You have movement less than a mile from your location to the north, two vehicles. The other three are a mile to your east. The transporter is ten miles from Alexandria, there has been no deviation from its route."

Jack checked his Glock and spare clips, resting the gun in his lap, ready.

"Looks like they are still searching. Although where he has found to hide is anyone's guess, it's just sand and more sand."

"We are close to several oases including Qara and Siwa. There are rock formations and some fertile areas giving a few places that could provide cover."

Aya was familiar with the landscape which explained how she was able to keep them on course.

"Well, we'll soon see for ourselves." Mitch nodded towards a plume of dust that smoked across the horizon.

"Jack, you have more company. Moving towards you at speed...Aircraft."

Whether through instinct or an uncanny link with Sara, Jack saw two black shapes appear a distance away through his window, the blades flickering through the blue sky.

"Two choppers Sara, any intel available?"

"They are my men, Jack. Twelve in all...good men. I think we might need them." Mitch was relieved that they still had a fix on their position.

As they flew closer Jack recognised the distinctive shape of the Black Hawk, a formidable attack helicopter.

"Nightly has a fleet of Black Hawks?"

This took Jack by surprise, it appeared that the mad scientist had impressive resources for a maker of medicines.

"You would be surprised what he has up his sleeve." Mitch knew that this was a lifelong obsession of Nightly's.

Nothing was out of his reach when it came to the Field of Reeds.

"Sara, keep an eye on the three vehicles to the east. I've a feeling they may be joining us soon."

"Will do, Jack. Be careful."

She couldn't resist. She had been saying the same thing ever since she had taken the post in tactical. But now after seeing him again after such a long time, her feelings surfaced far more than they should. Inwardly she berated herself for letting her guard down again, but it was momentary as she was well aware that if she didn't do her job she may very well put Jack in more danger. She focussed her attention on the other vehicles, ready to react at a moments notice.

The first jeep came into view heading straight towards them, ruining the element of surprise. Bullets clattered into the SUV as Aya swung the wheel to avoid a head on collision. Glass exploded into the vehicle covering them in sharp fragments. Jack swung open his door, diving onto the sand followed closely by Mitch. As their vehicle moved away from them, they were both fully exposed to the elements. Sand spray filled the air as bullets clattered all around them.

Both men scrambled back, franticly scrabbling for footholds as the sand moved under their feet giving no hope of traction. Jack managed to get two shots away, one flew harmlessly skyward, one clattered off the front bumper.

The jeep suddenly exploded, flipping several times, sending men flying through the air. One of the gunmen ignited and screamed as fuel and flame ate into his body with no hope of extinguishing. He landed in the soft sand and tried to scramble to feet that had melted away in the molten heat, sending him to his knees. The screaming stopped but he remained kneeling as bone, skin and fabric fused into one, leaving him as a smouldering statue on the scorching sand.

The Black Hawk that unleashed the mortar at the jeep released six cables from its open sides. One soldier rappelled on each line, all six men landing in a running motion, firing at the second jeep that appeared from over the horizon.

Mitch stood awkwardly, trying to stand straight as sand fell away from under him. He looked for Jack who found it a little easier to get to his feet. He had no time to react as the LARA agent shot at him.

The scream made him turn just in time to see a survivor from the exploding jeep fly backwards, a neat hole in his head and the gun aimed at Mitch land harmlessly on the ground.

Mitch nodded in appreciation as both turned to assist the men take out the second jeep.

Two more vehicles appeared in support, two soldiers went down in a hail of bullets before one jeep was disabled as the driver took several hits to his body, followed by two passengers who were felled as they tried to disembark,

Above them the second Black Hawk released six cables sending six more soldiers rappelling towards the ground.

The chopper exploded losing its tail, causing it to spin uncontrollably overhead. Four soldiers fell to the ground landing safely, two became caught in the lines and swung precariously in the air as the body of the shattered Black Hawk fell to the desert floor exploding in a plume of black smoke. The tangled soldiers fell into the smouldering wreck, dying instantly.

Jack and Mitch took cover behind a stricken jeep, joined by Aya who abandoned the SUV as it succumbed to a barrage of lead.

The soldiers flattened into the sand making themselves a difficult target, picking off the jeep riders easily, every bullet hitting its target with military precision.

An explosion sent sand and three mutilated soldiers into the air. A hail of bullets cut through the dust cloud, followed by the final jeep, the passenger at the rear reloading the rocket launcher as the others sent automatic fire into the prostrate soldiers. Jack, Mitch and Aya all had the same idea, each puncturing the reloading passenger several times, the bazooka flying harmlessly away. The remaining riders stood no chance as they were felled from all directions by Nightly's remaining team, they emptied their clips into the bodies of the attackers until the last bullet left its chamber. Overkill, but necessary to avenge the death of their fallen comrades.

·   ·   ·

Moving away from the protection of the jeep, Jack surveyed the devastation. The golden sand was stained with blood, black scorch marks sent swirls of smoke lazily into the still warm air and bodies lay scattered everywhere.

"Jesus Christ!" Mitch saw his men, good men, lying motionless among the ruins of four vehicles. The Black Hawk helicopter still smouldered a few yards to the east, a fiery grave for three more.

Jack stayed behind as Nightly's team looked through the carnage, checked on their colleagues and made the fruitless search for any casualties that may still be alive.

As he briefed Sara on the current situation he was hoping that strategical had come up with something for them. But he was disappointed.

"Sorry Jack, we have no further activity in your area. The transporter, however, was west of Alexandria heading towards the Libyan border. They reached El Salloum, stopped for a while and are now heading back your way. They have added several vehicles to their convoy out of Tobruk so they must have received word of your last encounter. I'm guessing that you have less than four hours before they reach you. You need to get away from there." Sara was as frustrated as she knew Jack would be, but with no signals being received via the airwaves, through transmitter nodes or satellite spikes, they had no way of pinpointing an individual if they had no access to technology.

If the professor was still alive he was well hidden, and at the moment completely invisible.

"We can't really do a lot without Faversham. I'm looking all around Sara, there is nothing, not a lot of places to hide. Don't forget the jeeps had over an hour's head start on us, even on wheels they found nothing. Where's the nearest place from here? Perhaps he has taken refuge?"

Sara could see a few possibilities and one stood out more than the rest.

"Well, you are a few miles east of the Qara Oasis. A population of three hundred, it's the closest for someone on foot to reach safely. If the professor is familiar with the area then it seems a likely destination. There are a number of ruins along a mountainous area and the village itself is made up of a maze of narrow streets."

"Sounds good to me. Send me the co-ordinates although I think we have someone with us who may know the way. I'll let you know when we find him...out!" He remembered Aya mention two Oases, Qara being one of them.

Mitch gathered his team around him. They were checking their weapons, reloading, checking their sights, cleaning them down and preparing them for further use.

As Jack neared them he heard Mitch encouraging them, referring to the men they had lost, vowing to succeed for the sake of them. It was a morale boosting speech that each man seemed to take on board as the five remaining squad members were nodding in unison.

They all turned to watch him as he approached. Mitch stopped talking as he could see that the LARA agent wanted to add his own input.

"We need to move. We have company on its way to us and I have a feeling they will want to avenge their comrades. We need to find the professor if he is still alive and Qara Oasis seems a good place to start. Aya, I assume you know it from here?..." The girl nodded, pointing south west from their position.

"...Good. We have a four hour head start. So I suggest we make a move."

He didn't wait for an answer as he turned south west and started walking.

Gabrielle Millson pushed herself further into the sand, the rye grass cut into her stomach as she dug in behind the rock outcrop she had come across after leaving the jeep. Once the Black Hawks arrived they should have left, but Khan's thugs thought they could be heroes. She wasn't going to hang around for them to be proven wrong.

She studied the guy as he walked away from the group, Jack Case, the LARA agent tasked with escorting the professor. Even through the lens of the binoculars she could tell from his expression that he was not happy. By rights he should be dead had Mido and his cronies carried out the instructions for which they were paid handsomely.

It could now work in her favour as they were all searching for the professor and until reinforcements arrived she was in the best position to observe, watch how things developed and strike when the time was right.

Once she had calmed him down, and having the advantage of him being five thousand miles away, Khan had agreed to bide his time. But he was pissed and made it very clear that he was going for payback. He had amassed a small army from Tobruk and he would make sure that Nightly paid for what he had done.

The professor will also pay for his subterfuge. Khan was a generous man, but cross him or throw it back in his face and there was nowhere to hide.

She caught sight of her nemesis following Case, hurrying after him to catch him up; Mitch.

She could feel her blood begin to heat up, her face reddening, her neck burning and sweat run down her back. Through gritted teeth she pulled the revolver from the back of her fatigues and resting her hands on the rocks to steady her aim, pointed at her target. Without the help of the binoculars the target was small, so her aim needed to be true. She closed one eye to focus on the tiny sight marker at the end of the barrel, following the target until she was sure that she was focussed on Mitch's temple. She pulled the trigger.

There was a sense of exhilaration as the hammer clicked home. Had the gun been loaded she would have nailed him.

Even though she wanted him dead she was never quite sure if she could pull the trigger when the opportunity arose.

Now she knew that she could... easily.

34

C amels stink. They have no etiquette even with the grand title of ships of the desert. Farting, belching, sneezing, chewing and snorting with whoever they had in the saddle.

Faversham rolled around in the leather seat as he tried to match the sway of the beast, smacking his groin several times against the wooden handle at the front of the hard leather saddle.

He was a couple of paces behind Malik and Ishmael with two other Berbers bringing up the rear.

Even though he was in no doubt that he was their captive, they could not have been more hospitable. They had left the tent with the festivities still in full flow once Malik realised that his prisoner was not in the mood to party.

"Come, let us provide a more suitable location for you to continue your work." It wasn't a request, more an instruction. Within ten minutes they were on their way.

Travelling through the dry track of a mountainous rock formation they came across a grove of date palms, scattered in no particular formation and in full bloom. Many had weave baskets at their base full of harvested dates. As they thinned a little, the fertility of the land became quite clear as rye grass, small reed beds and small clumps of papyrus grasses began to sprout more regularly, particularly when they entered the low walled village of Qara.

Labelled as an oasis, it was dry apart from a strange structure of pipework that sat on a mound at the centre of the low rectangular sandstone buildings. Three pipes connected to an oil powered pump turned a crude metallic waterwheel. Water was then forced through a fourth pipe that filled the well at the centre of the mound. It appeared that they were dredging an underground water source to service the three hundred inhabitants.

Faversham was surprised to see street lamps and overhead cables serving electricity to the houses.

"Our generators provide our electricity through solar panels." Malik had stopped to allow the professor to join them and noticed the focus of his attention.

Faversham's camel started to produce bubbles from its mouth as it became bored, the rasping noise that accompanied them drowned out any further conversation until it had finished its performance.

Malik dismounted and encouraged the professor to follow suit. He then slapped both camels on their flanks. The beasts trotted away to a set of rails in one corner of the yard where food and water was waiting for them.

"Lianna is a loyal servant to the people of Qara, but she has the temperament of a child."

Faversham straightened up and tried to make himself a little more comfortable by pulling the fabric of his trousers away from his groin in the hope that feeling would return soon.

"Well, she is a comfortable ride." Faversham offered, hoping not to show that he was lying through his back teeth. He felt at the moment that he wouldn't be able to sit comfortably for a week.

"I do have one question for you however, Malik. We are less than a mile from the village. Why would you build camp so close?"

. . .

Malik's smile vanished and he could see that the Berber was struggling to find the right words. He looked at the professor, concern etched across his face. There even appeared to be a tear pooling in the corner of his eye.

"We have the scourge…"

Nothing more was said but a nod from the Berber beckoned him to follow.

The sun was still burning in the west, not yet ready to leave daylight behind. The heat was radiating off the low buildings as they passed through the narrow streets, crudely made by bordering rocks of sandstone either side of the dusty track to act as kerbs winding around the entire town. Faversham moved the satchel from his shoulders and removed his leather jacket. Draping it over the bag he hung it back around his neck.

The warmth in the air carried with it an acrid smell of disinfection, harsh and with enough ammonia to bring tears to the eye.

The professor fumbled into his satchel pocket drawing out his face mask from the flight. It was the first time he had thought of the need for protection as he hadn't been required to use it at any time throughout the journey.

It was thought the pathogen was only at its deadliest through direct saliva transference or aerosolised. But it was clear now that perhaps it was deadlier than first thought.

Watching the Berber wrap the tail of his turban around his nose and mouth several times and seeing what they were walking towards, he wasn't about to take any chances.

After the first row of houses they reached a barrier of oil barrels, wood and wire. Several houses sat beyond the barrier but Malik's focus was on the first one. Carefully manoeuvring past the obstacles he signalled for Faversham to follow. Ishmael, who had remained quiet throughout, stayed where he was.

.   .   .

There were no doors, only curtains shrouded across the stone door-
ways. Once they entered, Faversham was amazed at how cool it
was. They arrived in what looked like a kitchen, a large table with
eight handmade stools positioned on a traditional angular pattered
rug dominating the centre of the room.

By a hole in the wall that acted as a window there was a stone
trough like sink, a spout with a curved handle fixed to its edge to
pump water. Slots had been carved into the sandstone walls that
housed plates, cups and bowls. Slots on the other wall contained
bags of grain and foodstuffs. Meat hung drying above a large fire-
place, a crude bowl shape cut out in the rear wall, a gully hollowed
out at the top to act as a chimney.

    Two curtains hung at the corners of the room, entrances to
further rooms of the accommodation. Malik escorted Faversham
through the left doorway.

They entered a bedroom. Light was restricted by the cover over the
window. Laying in a bed in the centre of the room was an old man,
his head buried deep in the pillow, his eyes fixed on nothing on the
ceiling above. His white hair and beard were congealed in blood, his
mouth slightly open, a rasping breath escaped occasionally followed
by a coughing fit that brought more blood from his nose and mouth
to blend with the rest.

A woman sat by his bedside, she looked older, dressed in a shawl of
black covering most of her frail frame. She dabbed the old man's
mouth with a damp cloth taken from a bowl on her lap, the bowl full
of bloodied water.

"Mother…"
    Malik walked to the old lady and took the bowl and cloth away

from her. As he left the room he looked at the professor saying nothing, but the pleading in his eyes said all that was needed.

The room felt heavy with grieving, the smell of death trying to suffocate the atmosphere that was struggling to keep it at bay.

Malik returned with a clean bowl and cloth, he bent over his father and tried to clean him as best he could. He choked back tears as the old man struggled to breathe, tried to speak and coughed some more.

Handing the bowl back to the old woman, he stroked her cheek and spoke words of comfort in a tongue unfamiliar to Faversham. Leading the professor from the room, they met with Ishmael who was waiting in the kitchen.

Malik squeezed his brother's arm as they passed, Ishmael nodded in understanding.

"My father has the scourge, as does most of the village. If the gods are not willing, we will have no one left. I needed to get the healthy away, but we all have family and they have the right to be close."

They walked back over the barricades and headed away from the quarantined area.

"You are our only chance, professor. Please take the scroll to Aaru, allow the gods to give us back the gift of life."

As the sun began to redden and move towards the horizon, Malik entered another house and switched on the light. They were in a similar kitchen to the last building although this seemed altogether brighter, coffee steamed from a pot on an iron stove. Fruit, fresh and ripe, sat in a bowl in the centre of the table and cold meats were laid out on a plate with a loaf of bread.

Although not as oppressive, the smell of disinfectant was evidence the property had been recently cleaned. Following Malik's lead, Faversham removed his mask.

. . .

"This will be your home for a while, professor. We have provided you with food, water and some American coffee…you have clean linen and fresh blankets for your stay…" He sat at the table and bit into an apple, juice dripped off his chin. He invited the professor to sit by a note pad and several pens at the end of the table.

"…All I ask of you, professor, is that you find Aaru, discover the secret and save our village. I will leave you now and will return in the morning. I need to help Ishmael with my parents. Two of my men are outside…should you need anything at all to assist you, please let them know. I will be with you in an instant."

He stood, bowed and left Faversham staring at the swaying curtain. He sat there for a while wondering what he had got himself into and hoping against hope that he could aid his captor, the village and the rest of the world.

~

The coffee pot was low and most of the fruit had been eaten. How long he had been poring over the scroll he couldn't tell. He was interrupted about an hour ago by a lot of shouting and commotion but was reassured by his guard that it was nothing and asked to return to his work.

With a feeling of triumph he stretched and with his fifth coffee he toasted the notepad that carried the translation. It was easier than he thought, apart from two areas where he was sure his knowledge and some guesswork had come through.

He studied it once again just to make sure, but he was happy:

' *To the west of the Nile Delta, where the palms hold the moon.*
  At the top of the noon sun, on the 19th day of Thuthi.
  After the night of the full moon, when the blind shall see
  The eyes of Ra will show the way, let light shed upon oneself
  For the ripe and the righteous to shine'

．　．　．

Now it was just a case of finding the area, he was pretty sure he knew what the etching meant, but he had no idea where to test it.

He could really do with a computer, or his chaperone if he was still alive. Jack Case would know less than he did about the scroll obviously, but LARA had the resources to help with the translation. At least he could throw some ideas at them and wait for their research to give him the answers. He wanted to find Aaru for his own curiosity, for his employer Abu, but more importantly for the moment, for Malik and his family.

He should report his findings immediately, but the thought of travelling any further on Lianna made his balls hurt. He was tired and could do with freshening up a little before he left. Behind one of the two curtains was a wet room. The toilet left a lot to be desired and the shower consisted of a pump that after pumping furiously for thirty seconds gave one minute of water, cold water.

Ten minutes later he had washed clean and although forced to put on the same clothes he originally arrived in, felt a lot better.

Packing his satchel, carefully folding the scroll and pocketing his notes, he entered the bedroom and lay on the bed. Fifteen minutes shut eye should be enough to recharge his batteries, or at least bring his groin back to life to tackle Lianna.

He closed his eyes and began to drift.

∽

It was a strange dream.

He was in the desert, the scroll in his hands and signposts showing the way. Looking behind he could see Jack Case and Abu, they were both sitting on Lianna...He shouted at them, but he couldn't open his mouth. He tried again...nothing...it was as if his lips were stuck together. He tried to scream... but only a muffled wail came humming from behind closed lips....

He awoke with a start, a hand over his mouth. He couldn't move with the weight that was on him, pinning down his arms. He couldn't see a thing. He began to struggle...

. . .

"Shh, professor. You need to come with me if you want to find Aaru…" He recognised the female voice.

Not again!

35

"*Still nothing showing on the grid, Jack. You have what looks like an encampment in front of you and Qara about half a mile from there.*" Sara could see the shapes through the satellite images but no electronic signals.

She was able to make out movement around the encampment and limited activity within the structural layout of Qara, but she couldn't be sure if any were of the professor.

"*What I can tell you though, is that you have an army coming at you from the North. The transporter with several vehicles plus those out of Tobruk are making good time. They will be with you in less than three hours. You need to get out of there, Jack.*"

"Not until we get the professor. With any luck we'll find him at our next stop and then we can get out of here. Do we have a team of our own nearby? Perhaps if we do they can slow down our pursuers."

"*Ed has scrambled a team from Morocco, but they won't be with you for at least four hours even with the fastest aircraft. You'll be safer holing up at the Siwa Oasis, it's a major town with a decent police force. Their Chief of Police, Maloof, has agreed to help if you can get there before they arrive from the North.*" Sara knew it was pointless giving Jack a time constraint.

He would get there when he had found the professor, either dead or alive. She could tell from his tone that he was not in the best of moods, he hated complications, particularly when things were taken out of his hands. No one could blame him for losing sight of Faversham, but she knew that he will be beating himself up inside for allowing it to happen.

"Then we had best get a move on. Let me know the progress of the convoy, we'll worry about it when they're a mile away. Out" Briefing the others as Mitch and his team were in earshot, the ground began to vibrate around them.

Looking ahead the sand became interrupted, fogging the horizon. As it covered the waning sun in a thickening haze it was impossible to make out any shapes until the horses burst into view thirty yards from them.

They seemed to come from all directions carrying riders armed with rifles trained on each of them. Two camels ambled between the horses and headed straight for them, the riders handled the creatures expertly as they focussed on Jack and his team. Stopping a yard in front of them the leader removed the white sash from his mouth as he studied them for a moment.

He was dressed in a vibrant blue robe and matching Keffiyeh, with a white sash draped around his shoulders.

A good looking man with Eastern features, his black beard carefully crafted to follow the contours of his chin. He spoke slowly, his English good but heavily accented with the local dialect.

"Why have you brought destruction to Qara?" He focused on Jack, deciding that the well built stranger was the leader of the group.

"We were ambushed while looking for a friend of ours." Jack watched the man, keeping his arms loose by his side, ready to grab the Glock he'd pushed into the back of his jeans.

"But you were the ones with the helicopters, were you not?"

Although the question was meant as a challenge, Jack sensed that it wasn't accusatory. The man's smile seemed genuine, his relaxed pose meant to alleviate any threat.

"A search party." Jack responded. He wasn't sure if the disease had reached the area, but he hoped that the people of Qara had received news from Cairo where many had already been infected.

"The man we are looking for has the knowledge to cure an illness that is killing millions of people."

Jack had never thought of himself as a diplomat and as soon as it left his lips he wished it hadn't. Mitch looked at him and shrugged. He couldn't have put it any better himself, although he was glad that he hadn't delivered it.

"So…you are looking for a God?"

And there it was, exactly the reaction he expected. The sniggers from the horsemen who had an understanding of English, just made it more of an embarrassment.

"I am, of course, playing with you, my friend. He sounds an important man. Come let us discuss your predicament over wine. I am Malik of Qara and this is my brother Ishmael…" Malik pointed towards the other camel rider.

"…You will be our guests while we discuss ways of finding your companion."

Turning the camel around in a wide ark, Malik set a slow pace and led the group westward. The horsemen, their guns lowered, waited for them to pass before closing ranks and in formation, followed behind.

Whether they liked it or not they were heading for Qara.

36

"Now, I am going to take my hand away. Please don't scream out professor, you know it will do neither one of us any favours."

Faversham nodded to indicate his agreement, he wasn't about to give her away anyway, so he played along for now. She was good at a lot of things, but kidnapping wasn't one of them.

As the hand moved away from his mouth Faversham lifted his right knee, smashing into the back of the body on top of him. As the body lurched forward he freed his right arm and caught the wrist of the hand that was smothering him. As the momentum was in his favour he turned to his right and felt the mattress fall away as they both fell to the floor, Faversham landing on top. Even blindfolded, he managed to straddle his adversary and pin both arms to the floor. He was positioned on her pelvis so she had no chance of lifting her knees as he had done.

"So, I guess you didn't take as much notice in kidnapping school as you did in my classes. Always ensure that your captive is immobilised, put all your pressure on the pelvis, kneel on it if you have to. Oh, and never let your captive know that you know them…"

He heard and felt the deep sigh of resignation as she had to admit he was right. Taking his hand away from restraining her left arm he pulled away the blindfold and looked into her emerald eyes.

"Hello Tia. It's been a while." He moved off her, grasping her arm and helping her to her feet.

"Hello Iggy. Sorry about all this, but I need to get you away from the brothers. They are nothing more than common thieves and would betray you for a profit at a moment's notice."

Faversham watched as she dusted herself down, patting the dust from her khaki shorts. She had developed into a fine looking woman, her high cheek bones and voluptuous lips had always turned many male heads. But now, five years on, she had filled out, both in curves and muscle, each complimenting the other. She had let her jet black hair grow to an extraordinary length, which she formed into a plait that hung just past her waist. She tied the bottom of her loose fitting blouse just below her ribcage, leaving a small section of her midriff exposed. The tiny jewel stud in her navel flickered in the low light as she moved towards him.

Putting her arms around his neck she pulled him towards her. Being six inches taller, Faversham stooped to accept her waiting lips. Holding her close he let the movement of her mouth envelope him and the warmth of her tongue bring an urge that he hadn't felt for a number of years. Five years to be exact, the last night they had spent together. The night he put a stop to the affair.

The ten year age gap wasn't the reason; the student, teacher dilemma was. It would have ruined both of their careers and it started to affect their daily lives. Faversham began to cover his tracks, felt as if he was living a lie and taking advantage of the trust of his colleagues. Tia, on the other hand, had started to lapse in her studies, her marks were down, she lost concentration.

. . .

He took an assignment in the Yemen for twelve months, a simple dig, one that was more suited to an intern than one of the University's eminent archaeologists. But it got him away, allowed him to take stock, to recharge and to forget her.

It wasn't easy for either of them. Calls were ignored, messages deleted and emails blocked, but written correspondence upon his return managed to draw a line under the whole affair, allowing them to remain friends.

Tia had excelled in her course work, achieving a Bachelors Degree in anthropology before opting to work with her father, a legend in his own right in global salvage, and she was flourishing in her new found career.

The first call between them had been awkward at first, but as their enthusiasm for the ancient world dominated the conversations, thoughts of their lost romance was soon nothing more than a brief moment in time. They used to speak regularly, with Tia using Faversham to help with analysis of her latest quest or for a second opinion of her own theories.

But after she left her father to go it alone her calls became more infrequent. He had not heard from her for nearly two years, until now.

"How did you get past the guys at the door?" Faversham pulled away before things went too far. The question had been burning in him as soon as he realised it was her.

Tia nodded to the robes on the floor behind them.

"Malik has more wives than any man on camp can count. If he was to send one to your room, something that he has been known to do to soften up his targets, he'd ensure they were hidden from any prying eyes."

Smiling, Faversham shook his head. He admired her ingenuity although it didn't surprise him. He had seen as a student how astute and streetwise she was. She never suffered fools and could definitely handle herself.

He remembered many of the male students attending classes with bruises and weals across their faces, some even limping for a few days. Not one offered valid explanations as to the cause. But the women were all too quick to spread the rumours of Tia's prowess in handling unwanted attention, particularly drunken advances.

"So, you have cracked it?"

Tia had moved over to the table and was studying the scroll. Holding it up to the light she turned it over and smiled.

"Yes! I knew I was right. Excellent. Let's get a move on, Iggy. It's a full moon tomorrow night. We need to be in place so that we know where we are going."

"And where are we going?"

"My dear Iggy, would I be here, risking my life…Oh, ok… pretending to be your whore for the night…If I wasn't sure of my convictions. Of course I know where we are going."

"Right. Stop right there."

She had a way of niggling him, only a little, but enough to make him want to stop playing games. Most of the time her playful ways were endearing, in a funny way very sexy, but then she just took it a little too far. Far enough to niggle.

"I think you need to explain yourself, young lady. How on earth do you know about the scroll? And more importantly, how come you've managed to translate the thing? It had a cipher."

Tia filled him in. Starting with the initial find, the auction, through to the sale to Abu and her run in with Mitch Dawson. She included her knowledge of the contents of the scroll and the mad scientist, Nightly. She finished with admitting that she had taken a copy and had spent the past weeks translating it.

"…and as far as the cipher is concerned, it was pretty basic. A double mirror. Something that was used more often by the Spartans than the Egyptians, but a simple one all the same."

She inspected her fingernails before gently buffing them on her chest, showing off as usual.

. . .

Faversham was taken aback and a little annoyed that he was unaware of all this. Neither the Sheikh or Jack Case mentioned her involvement... but then again why would they. Their concern was in the translation, the location and the destination of Aaru. Nevertheless, he couldn't help feel a little let down. The excitement he felt at meeting Tia again was tainted by her smart arse attitude. He had forgotten how much of a pain she could be.

"Had I had the time I'm sure I'd have got there. But it has been out of my possession for far too long since I arrived. I caught the first mirror through a flame...Once I saw it, I could see that simply reading the script backwards gave the answer. But I'm still a little behind when it comes to the location, I will admit."

"Look, let me show you." She moved the scroll along the table until it was under the direct light of the lamp.

"...'To the west of the Nile Delta, where the palms hold the moon'...Well, when you think about it...there is nothing west of the Nile Delta with palms other than the oases...

'At the top of the noon sun, on the 19th day of Thuthi'...refers to the 6th August, the day after tomorrow...

'After the night of the full moon, when the blind shall see'... The full moon is tomorrow night and when the blind shall see... I'll come to that after the next line...

'The eyes of Ra will show the way'.... It's the Siwa Oasis, Iggy. Think about it..."

Faversham thought hard.

Siwa he knew was the largest town in the middle of nowhere, housing over twenty thousand citizens, mainly Berbers. It has vast groves of date palms that surround the region and many historical sites dotted throughout the town...that was it!

. . .

"Of course…" Realisation came to him.

"…The Temple of Amun!"

"Exactly!" Tia knew that it wouldn't take long for the professor to catch up.

"The Temple of Amun is nothing but ruins, and it would have been known as the Temple of Amun Ra by the time the scroll was formulated. Said to have been built over the Solar Well of the God Amun, many of the disciples of Amun named it the Temple of the Oracle; the all seeing eye. It overlooks the main palm grove facing the Nile Delta…"

Faversham finished the thesis…

"So by standing within the Temple of the Oracle on the night of the full moon…" He held the scroll up to the light and looked at the etching inscribed on its reverse.

"…It will show the moon held within the silhouette of the palms and when lined up with this etching, it will show us the direction of Aaru."

They both stared at each other for a moment, letting their find sink in. They had discovered a secret that had remained hidden for three thousand years.

"Well I guess we should make a move." Faversham broke the silence.

"We need horses, Siwa is at least thirty miles away." He knew they had camels and he was fairly positive they will have horses too.

"Not a chance…" Tia knew a little more about the trip they were about to make.

"There is only one road to Siwa and although as the crow flies it is thirty miles, by road it is a ten hour journey and we wouldn't last an hour before being caught. We have to go through the mountains…It will take close to a day…but we will be hard to find. A camel could take us half of the way and cut down the journey a little, but forget a horse. Too treacherous."

Faversham thought of a trip through the mountains on the back of Lianna, the rocky undulations, the belching and farting; and the smell.

"I think we'd be better on foot." He offered, without much hesitation.

"Let me get my bag."

Jack recognised the goatskin tents of the bedouin as soon as they came into view. Four multicoloured marquee sized constructions that looked like they had been thrown up in a hurry. The undulations made by the haphazard placement of tent poles made the material look as if they were ready to collapse at any moment. He knew, however, that they were stronger than some houses, able to cope with regular sandstorms some of which would put a typhoon to shame. The skins would also tighten in a rainstorm creating a solid mass that water simply bounced off.

It was a strange place to set up camp considering that on the horizon he could see the walls and square stone buildings of what he assumed was Qara Oasis. Why was the town under siege?

"We will take wine here." Malik and his brother dismounted their camels and gave them to handlers to stable. He walked though the flap of the largest of the tents, followed by Ismail who held the door open gesturing for the group to follow.

Jack moved first, eyeing Mitch and Aya with a 'be on your guard' glance that they appeared to understand and followed. Mitch looked back at the horsemen as they dismounted and herded the rest of his team forward.

The interior was a kaleidoscope of colour. Carpets of every known Pantone covered the floor, vibrant, rich reds, blues and orange dominating the decor of what seemed to be piles of bean bags. Low crudely carved tables dotted around the room contained dishes of fruit, meats and cheeses with large earthenware jugs full of wine in the centre.

"Come, join us." Malik took his seat behind the longest of the tables and beckoned for them to sit.

Jack sat first, followed by Mitch and Aya either side of him. Aya noticeably stiffened, watching the shrouded figures of the females as they flitted around serving plates of delicacies to the table, filling the goblets as they went. Finished with the main table, they served Mitch's five remaining crew members before returning to sit amongst the other women congregated at the back of the room.

Malik noticed Aya staring at them as they performed their duties.

"My wives." He offered as an explanation.

"Your servants, you mean." Aya glared at him, her clenched mouth twisted as if holding back on more that she wanted to throw at the man.

His sardonic smile indicated that he wasn't about to let this slide. He liked strong women, and this was his domain.

"My, you are a feisty one. Perhaps we could come to some arrangement?"

Aya leapt to her feet, pulling the gun from her belt and pointing it at Malik's head. The tent was filled with the clicks of rifles racking as all of Malik's riders advanced from their positions and aimed at the visitors, at least three rifles to each target.

Jack put his hand on Aya's gun arm to lower the revolver, but she was having none of it and held her aim firm.

"Aya, you need to put the gun down." Jack spoke softly, feeling her arm tremble as she fought with her decision. Her finger rested on the trigger, ready to punch a hole in the pig's face.

Being of Middle Eastern blood she was used to fighting prejudices and inequalities all her life. However hard she wished for change, she knew they would never be fully eradicated.

She admitted that she used her sexuality to gain advantage, but all it proved was that however advanced the world became, however determined all nations demonstrated a commitment to change, there will always be a faction that would refuse to leave the dark ages. This Neanderthal was one of them.

"Aya! Look around you. Let it go, put the gun down." Mitch had two rifles aimed at him, and it was clear that they would shoot without hesitation. He would never reach his gun in time, and neither would anyone else in the group.

Aya took her eyes off of Malik for just an instant, but she saw enough to know that if she got her shot away, she and all the others wouldn't stand a chance.

Jack felt her arm relax as she began to lower her revolver.

Malik smiled and held out his hand to take the gun from her. He would not allow a woman any amount of control in his presence, particularly when surrounded by his people. He needed to teach this bitch a lesson.

Jack leaned forward before the gun reached him and pushed a small metallic ball into Malik's hand, curling his fingers around it before he had time to react. The three riflemen turned their attention away from Mitch and trained their sites on the other man. Malik raised his hand to stop any of his men reacting.

. . .

"I think we need to calm down a little, don't you?" Jack stared at the Berber chief as he produced his PDA from his jacket with his other hand and held it in the air, his thumb on the screen.

"In your hand is a pearl grenade, blast radius of five metres. It will kill us all around this table and destroy this structure, the casualty radius is fifteen metres, killing or maiming all of your wives along with everyone else in here. My thumb is on a dead mans switch, kill me and the grenade explodes…immediately."

Several gasps filled the tent, one of the wives screamed and several began to babble some form of prayer recital. Malik looked at his hand and then back to Jack. He smiled.

"Very good, my friend. But do you really think that you can keep your thumb pressed on there forever? I am happy to sit here and wait for you to tire, however long it takes. I doubt very much that you would detonate and kill all of your colleagues. You don't appear to be a man who craves martyrdom." Malik looked over at the man in front of him.

The rugged features, the battle-hardened look and the piercing eyes. He could see military, but something more, a look of resignation. The more he studied him the more uncertain he felt.

He played poker; he was a good player, could read people well. But this man had an inscrutable countenance that gave nothing away.

Jack moved his hand away, Malik's heart skipped a beat as the weight of the grenade forced his hand to the table. He caught himself and steadied his hand, lowering his elbow to the table to steady his arm.

Removing another pearl grenade from his jacket, Jack rose slowly to his feet. Many of the riflemen began to shuffle back slightly, their sights still on the madman.

"Let me show you something."

Jack waited for Malik to nod, although his expression showed that he wasn't about to like what he was about to be shown.

Moving to the door, two of the horsemen blocked his way; he felt the nozzles of the rifles push into his body. He just stood and stared at them. Malik barked an order and they parted reluctantly, allowing him to push the flap aside, exposing the desert as dusk began to form in the sky.

Pulling his arm back, he threw the grenade as far as he could. The size and weight made it easy to throw it at least two hundred feet into the sand. Turning back to the table, he made his way back to his bean bag and casually crossed his legs, making himself comfortable.

Malik stared at the man quizzically. What was this?

"Sara." Jack pushed his ear twice, setting the earwig to broadcast.

"Yes Jack, I'm here." Sara's voice came out of the PDA.

"West of my position Sara, about fifty yards. When you're ready."

The explosion caused a commotion as women screamed, men shouted curses in different dialects and four of the horsemen fled through the door. Malik sat frozen to his seat; his eyes fixed on his hand. Fear spread across his face, pursing his lips as he nervously ground his teeth.

He lowered his hand slowly, and turning it over gently rested the grenade onto the table.

" Don't!"

Jack closed Malik's hand shut over the grenade again just as he was about to release it. The beep coming from the sphere made him flinch, causing him to pull his hand away, but Jack held firm.

"What is this? What have you done?"

Beads of sweat began to appear from beneath the Berber's head-wear, one escaped and ran down his cheek, soaking into his beard.

"The grenade in your hand now has an imprint of your biometric signature, your fingers are part of the bomb. Let it go and it detonates, harm anyone of us, and it detonates. Sara, show him."

The sphere beeped again. Malik physically jumped in his seat.

"Ok, ok, take it away, you are perfectly safe. No harm will come to you, I swear."

Jack studied the Berber, pleased that he had got his attention.

"Not a chance, Malik. We need a little chat, and I would prefer to do it without a gun pointed at my face. Mitch, collect the rifles from those men and put them in the middle of the room. Take two of your men and post them at the entrance."

Mitch rose from his seat and after an affirmative nod moved to the three men closest to them. One barked an order and backed away, his gun raised, pointing at Mitch's head.

Malik went through a convoluted exchange with his men, many shouting and cursing in response. The tent filled with a cacophony of guttural cursing, screamed obscenities and wailing grew from the huddled group of women as the wives began to voice their own displeasure.

A high pitched whistle filled the air, piercing enough to stop the noise in an instant. It was Ishmael, the brother.

"Enough! We are not a people who disobey the commands of our Leader. Look, take a good look, my brothers and sisters, is this not a time when Malik needs us most. Our time will come, and when it does, we will rip the throats from these infidels and leave for the Nasir to strip them of flesh to the bone."

Jack looked to Aya to see if they had an agreement.

"He says that they will feed us to the vultures once they rip out our throats…"

Moving from her position alongside Jack, she approached Ishmael and stood nose to nose with him. She whispered something inaudible, which made him take a step back. But not far enough, the slap around his face sounded like the crack of a whip in the tense silence.

. . .

The man erupted in anger, screaming a guttural roar as he glared at the bitch who dared degrade him in front of his people. He drew his gun intent on blowing a hole in her pretty face.

The pistol flew in the air as Aya planted a well-timed kick at Ishmael's wrist. Before he had time to collect himself, she stooped, and with her leg outstretched, spun a hundred and eighty degrees catching him in the shins, sending him sprawling to his knees. With momentum on her side, Aya leapt onto his back and pulling a wire from her pocket placed the garot across his throat pulling him back-wards sharply until he was upright on his knees. Ishmael scratched at his neck as he tried to pull the wire away, but Aya just pulled tighter, his choking gasps began to subside as she blocked his airways.

She felt his body go limp as he was about to pass out and released the garot letting him collapse gasping to the floor.

Picking up his discarded pistol, she returned to the table and placing it in front of Malik, stared at him in silence.

Two of the gunmen in front of Mitch dropped their rifles at his feet, the third turned his side on and passed it into his arms. Like falling dominos, the rest followed suit each handing their rifles to the men from Mitch's crew, or laying them on the floor.

Once they had all been disarmed, the crew piled them into the centre of the floor. The two who chose to guard the entrance took a rifle each as they made their way through the tent flap, taking their position outside.

It took Malik a few moments to compose himself. He had been humiliated in front of his people and his family, his men had been forced to disarm and now his brother was left broken in front of him. He would make his captors suffer in ways they could not imagine. The bitch last, once his men had ruined her, defiled her, made her beg for death.

But for now, he will bide his time.

. . .

"Please forgive my brother; he was only trying to assist me and appeal to our people."

"By promising to kill us? Good job, Malik. In that case, forgive our female colleague. She was only standing up for herself and didn't fancy being fed to the vultures."

"Now let's get down to business. Where have you taken the professor? Let him go, and we will be on our way."

Jack knew they had Faversham as he had met people like Malik before. They were thieves, opportunists. They would see a ransom, a finders fee and knowing Faversham and his passion for his trade, he would bet the professor had used the importance of the scroll to try and appeal to their religious beliefs and heritage. Something that Jack knew would mean nothing to the Berbers without the dollar sign.

Mitch helped himself to the wine and a selection of cheeses as they watched Malik struggle to respond appropriately.

How difficult it was for him was anyone's guess, but he was trying to decide whether to deny any knowledge of the professor, try to deflect the question with some clever misdirection, or try to regain the respect of his people by fighting back. But with a grenade stuck to his hand, it would prove difficult.

He thought about grabbing Jack and holding on until they surrendered, using the fear of a violent death his only ammunition.

But he had the impression that his adversary was not afraid to die and that scared him. He had met many military men throughout his forty three years, but he had never come across one with such confidence, focus and a ruthlessness bordering on psychotic. It was the eyes, those steel blue orbs that showed no emotion, but perhaps a touch of madness.

Scouring the room he saw his riflemen devoid of weapons standing with their heads bowed awaiting their fate, his wives huddled together like frightened children shaking and mumbling prayer chants to ward away the demons. And there was his brother lying panting on the floor, a weird croaking interspersed with strangled sobs.

He had no choice. He sighed, admitted defeat and looked over the table to his waiting guests.

"He is in Qara, safe. We gave him accommodation so that he could translate the scroll. We have the scourge, it came to us just a month ago and we have lost many. The town is not safe; we will lose many more, my parents included. All we hoped was to use the secret to save our village."

It was a genuine answer and one that Jack realised had finally made Malik see some sense.

"Then why didn't you say that at the beginning. You have not only caused us a delay that we could do without, you have also endangered your people more than you know. There is an army intent on taking the scroll for themselves and they will go to any length to get it, including destroying anything in their path. You need to get the professor and start packing away. You need to move away from this place. Take the settlement towards Siwa, we have been offered support."

Malik thought for a moment. He could use this to his advantage, at least to gain favour back with his people.

He ordered one of his men to fetch the professor, escorted by two of Mitch's men under Jack's orders.

"Siwa is a journey that we are unable to take. It is a treacherous one and at least ten hours by road, a road guarded by pirates and nomadic murderers. The quickest route across the mountains is even more dangerous and without a hundred camels, we would never be able to cross it. We will stay and stop the army. This is our land and we will not allow it to be taken."

"Not a hope Malik, you don't have the men or the firepower. You saw what they did earlier today. You would be wiped out."

Jack could see what he was doing. The bravado was for his men, his wives, his own self-esteem. But it was madness.

"Then we will die trying." Malik stood firm. He will not abandon his people or the town he had been raised in. A town that has stood for thousands of years, beginning as an oasis to refresh travellers until settlers took it for their own. Settlers that were his ancestors, his family.

"We are only three hundred and fifty strong, but one hundred have the scourge, one hundred care for the sick. They have no protection other than what we provide. We will not abandon our people."

'Shit!' This changed everything. They had been brought into a fight that was nothing to do with them. A fight they could never win. Hundreds of innocent lives were about to be decimated unless he could do something.

"Sara. Can you read?" He needed to act fast.

"I'm here, Jack." She had been there all along, listening to everything that had happened since she set off the grenade. She was also aware of what Jack was about to ask.

"How far away are the Moroccan team. We need them asap."

"Yes Jack, I know. They are an hour away. Adams is aware of the situation, they will be ready."

Josh Adams was a good agent, straight out of Special Air Service. Ed had done his homework. But he knew that an hour was too late.

Sara could read Jack's silence.

"The convoy is forty-five minutes away, Jack. You'll need to start without them."

"Great, I hate being early to a party. Talk later…out!" Jack cut the call and turned to Mitch.

"We need to organise ourselves. Once we get the professor, we need to keep him safe and that means Siwa. We need to commandeer one of the vehicles from the convoy and get him away from here. Even though I don't particularly like it, I trust we have the best interests at heart for the conclusion of this thing, so I suggest Aya escorts Faversham. She knows the terrain and I have no doubt she will keep the professor safe from harm."

Mitch received a nod from Aya to confirm her acceptance. After all, she would be holding the jewel in the crown. Something Nightly would be delighted with.

. . .

"That leaves us to work on the perimeter. We have around thirty minutes to dig in and I want a few surprises up our sleeves for when they get close."

Malik's rider returned, flanked by Mitch's men.

"He has gone! The professor has disappeared." He all but screamed at Malik in his native tongue.

Jack looked to Aya for the translation.

"We're fucked!" She thought it better to get straight to the point.

38

A s the light began to fade to black, the shadows made by the waxing gibbous moon moved menacingly across the rocky passage between the mountainous area of the Siwa Mountains. They had made good time and Faversham was finding the pace exhilarating.

The current phase of the moon, the night before a full moon, caused ocean waves to swell and the atmosphere to become heavy, which when inland can create an ominous sense of the foreboding. Night creatures quieten, the air carries any sound away into the night and senses become paranoid to any movement, whether real or imaginary as they force their way into the peripheral vision.

Faversham followed the tiny beam of Tia's headlamp as they traversed the rubble of fallen sandstone through the narrow mountain passage. At no more than a yard wide with walls that disappeared far above them, they needed to be aware of their footing, careful to keep sound to a minimum for fear of a rockfall. In the tiny confines they would be buried with no hope of survival. Neither spoke for the last hour, they were beginning to think that the passage went on forever.

. . .

From his position to the rear, Faversham's beam gave him enough light to see where he was stepping as well as illuminating the shapely form of his female companion.

Her preferred adventuring outfit was a loose fitting blouse, cargo shorts which hugged her figure, widening slightly at the thighs to aid movement, and hiking boots. The tools of the trade were packed in a backpack hung across her shoulder blades. Her long plait swung erratically across her back as she stepped over, jumped and scrambled past obstacles. He found it quite mesmerising and gave him focus as they struggled on. She must have had a feeling that there was going to be trouble on this trip however, as strapped to her thigh was her ever reliable Heckler & Koch pistol. He must remember to ask her who she was expecting when they were able to talk again.

Finally the passage widened and they were soon out into the clear night sky. But instead of the desert floor they were expecting to find, they stepped out onto a ledge on the side of the mountain, hundreds of feet in the air.

"I don't remember climbing?" Faversham took off his headlamp and shone it over the edge and into the darkness below, he couldn't see any ground.

"We didn't climb. It's a depression. There are a few in this area. We just had to pick a particularly large one as our destination. We should have studied the map a little longer."

"Well, as you were out of the window before I grabbed my bag, we had very little chance to check anything." That was another thing he remembered; she was impatient.

"Never mind, where there's a will." She began fumbling through her pack.

"Look over there…" Tia nodded out from the ledge towards the horizon.

Tiny lights flickered in the distance, little pin pricks of amber that as his eyes adjusted, grew to a faint glow in the distance.

"Siwa." Tia offered as she found what she was looking for.

"At a guess I would say at least a day away on foot."

Faversham felt the rush of exhilaration as he thought of the scroll and its translation. This time tomorrow they will know the location of the Duat, the entrance to Aaru, and the Field of Reeds.

"Voila!" Tia announced as her headlamp shone on the items taken from her pack.

"You have to be kidding me!" The professor began to regret their decision to run for it.

39

"How the bloody hell could you lose him?"

Jack could not believe this was happening. He knew he couldn't blame himself as circumstance had played a part. But the professor should not have been snatched at the airport. He should have been more diligent, he was military and had always been thorough in building strategies. It was a matter of life or death.

Faversham had now eluded him twice and each time he should have prevented it. He needed to up his game or the whole mission would be a disaster; a disaster that could mean certain death.

Malik continued to question his man. The conversation gained momentum and became more heated after each sentence.

With a look of disgust he waved the riflemen away.

"Apparently a woman posing as one of my wives visited the professor. The guard would not have suspected that she was an imposter as they have known me to gift my guests on several occasions."

Malik glanced at Aya and noting her look of disgust, moved the bomb still grasped in his hand to his lap just in case. Realising what he had done he hastily moved his hand away from his groin and back to the table.

"How much longer do you intend to torture me with this item?" Malik offered his hand to Jack, showing the metal orb through his fingers.

"You'll know when it's time." Jack offered.

"For now you need to safeguard your people. I suggest you move the women back to the town and protect them as best you can. We need to work a way to resist the threat for as long as possible until the LARA team arrive."

Mitch had some ideas of his own and set his plan in motion.

"Glen, Rick, get yourselves out there and recce the area to the North. Dig in and let us know when you get a sighting. Aya, escort the women with one of Malik's guys and make sure they know what is happening, I don't trust this lot. Collect any able men on the way and send them back to us, the women can take over if any are looking after the sick. Tell them by order of Malik. Mac, go with her as back up."

Aya gave him the glare, she didn't need back up. Mitch ignored it, he wasn't about to take any chances.

"I am having none of this, they need to leave. Now!" Ishmael got gingerly to his feet, one hand grasped to his throat, his fingers feeling the deep line imprinted across his larynx.

"They are coming for you, not us. This is not our fight, although I would watch with pleasure as they tear you apart." He made a point of staring at Aya as he spat the last few words.

"Ishmael, don't be a fool. This is for all of us, for the scourge, for our Father! We have to fight for the sake of Qara." Malik had suffered the tantrums of his hot-head of a brother for some years now.

Once their father relinquished control in favour of working the olive and date groves, Malik as the eldest was given the role of chief of the Qara people. Ishmael couldn't come to terms with the fact that age was the deciding factor and began to create factions amongst the men, believing he should be the one to lead his people. People who, as a majority, saw the youngest son as nothing more than a belligerent fool.

It made running a town with only three hundred inhabitants a democratic nightmare.

. . .

"Then you help them Malik, I'm going to get mother and leave this place. One of us needs to think of our family and our people." He stared at his brother for a moment, letting the words hang in the air, hoping that it would register. Seeing nothing, he turned his back on them all and barged past the Americans posted at the entrance. Throwing back the tent flap his anger was clearly evident.

Ishmael writhed and danced back into the room, synchronising perfectly with the bullets that smashed into his torso. His robe exploded into fragments of fabric, blood and flesh, his body spinning several times before crashing to the floor.

Jack dived over the table pushing Malik to the floor with him. He kicked the table onto its side, catching sight of Mitch who had done the same, pulling Aya with him.

The tent began to fray as bullets cut through it. Panic ensued as Malik's men dived for cover, some taking direct hits. Mitch's men instinctively hit the floor and overturning tables, took cover behind them, pulling as many of the Berbers with them who were close enough. Two of the wives ran towards Malik and were cut down instantly. The rest of the women screamed, the wisest of the group pushing themselves into the ground, pulling the rest with them.

"Ishmael! No!" Malik fought to struggle free of Jack in an effort to be with his brother. The grenade fell from his hand as he grabbed at the agent's lapels.

Both men looked at it as it rolled between them, releasing the other's grip instantly.

Jack grabbed the bleeping sphere and prayed for a Hail Mary as he launched it towards the doorway. A man's strength increases tenfold when in the grip of fear and he felt as if he had unleashed an almighty throw as it headed for the exit, clipping the fabric slightly as it passed through. They felt the explosion as it sent a tremor along the floor and seconds later the thunderous blast, loud enough to cause a man to flinch, but far enough away to cause no harm to the tent's inhabitants. It did however, stop the gunfire.

The sounds of battle were replaced by the whimper and moans of the injured and terrified. None more so than Malik, who was incanting either a curse or a prayer as he rocked on his knees in front of Jack.

"Malik, I'm sorry, this should never have happened. We need to get you and your people away from here."

The Berber raised his head and stared at Jack through reddened eyes, his pupils constricted as anger coursed through his veins.

"My brother spoke the truth. This is your war and you have brought it to our people. I should have listened. Now my brother is dead."

Jack thought for a moment. He could argue but it would get them nowhere, he could lay the blame back in the Berber's lap, again with no satisfactory conclusion. He wasn't known for his tact but he had to think fast or no-one will leave here alive.

"Sometimes we can't be blamed for actions if we believe them to be well intentioned. You saw the professor as the man who could cure your village and save your parents.

As their leader your role is to protect Qara and he must have seemed like a gift from the gods. But you weren't to know about the others who will stop at nothing to take the professor's secrets for themselves. We are here to protect him, to ensure that he succeeds in finding a cure for every man, woman and child throughout the world."

He wasn't sure if it would work, but he had to keep him onside. He waited and watched the Berber, his focus unwavering, his unblinking eyes shedding floods of tears. His mouth trembling, opening as if to speak and then closing to tremble some more, holding back the anguish.

"We will make them pay…" It came out as no more than a strangled sob, but enough to understand.

He sat still for a moment as he composed himself, his pupils dilated as the anger waned.

"Bring out the professor and we will let you live!"

The woman's voice echoed through the tent flap, enhanced by the loudspeaker. Jack couldn't tell how far away she was, but he was encouraged. The grenade had given them food for thought. They weren't sure how many were inside and what firepower they had. He hoped they would continue to remain cautious.

"Oh shit! She's here."

"You know her?' Jack called over to Mitch who was sitting with his back against the upturned table, staring up at the ceiling.

"You could say that…Ex wife!"

"I'm guessing not an amicable break up?"

"Long story…but I killed her mother."

As Jack looked at him he could think of nothing to say.

Every mission is different, most could be resolved through careful strategies and controlled actions. Sure, there was the unexpected as it is impossible to cover every base and outside influences can sometimes change events. But this mission just ripped the rulebook into tiny pieces and threw it away.

"You have two minutes to comply…" The female voice hardened, it was not a request.

"…Hand over the professor or we will blow this structure into smithereens and after that we will flatten Qara."

"I will go to them." Malik got to his feet. His legs buckled as he caught sight of his brother, his corpse a misshapen mound of bloodied robe. Jack caught him and supported him upright, he could feel the man shaking uncontrollably.

"You can't, Malik. They will cut you down. We have to think of another way."

"Well we need to be quick, we only have a minute left." Mitch dusted himself down and moved to join them.

"Wait, your hat. Give me your hat." Jack held out his hand and gestured for Mitch to pass the fedora he was using to dust the sand from his trousers.

"I have an idea."

40

A s Tia unrolled the fabric and began spreading it across the floor, Faversham was trying to work out where this was going.

"So I assume this is a wingsuit for one?" She took a small chute from the backpack, giving it the once over in the beam of her head light.

"Of course. I was hoping to take a flight over Luxor from the horn in the Theban Hills once we'd finished here. I thought you would have yours with you. You were always so well prepared."

He watched as she began to pull on the ripstop nylon suit, jumping several times while pulling at the waist to ensure a snug fit.

"I did have it with me, but had to leave it with the Millson woman along with everything else I couldn't fit into my satchel. But why use it now?"

Tia sighed as she finished zipping and fastening herself into the suit.

"My dear Iggy…you are funny! You haven't taken a blind bit of notice of what I have been saying, have you? We are a day away from Siwa…at least, and that is without whatever could be waiting out there for us on the way. We need to work as a team."

He thought for a moment but every thought he had he didn't like. This trip was proving to be more challenging by the minute and he had a feeling that it was about to take a turn for the worse.

"It is vital that we are in position at midnight for the scroll to provide the route we need to take. If we miss it then we will have to wait another year. The way the bacterium is spreading, there will be no one left to save."

The news from home had shown that the world was in the thrall of a pandemic that was showing no signs of slowing down. Every city was facing more and more deaths as the disease attacked indiscriminately. The World Health Organisation were struggling to broadcast any encouraging news. There was no cure.

Tia had no idea that the scroll she was selling to the highest bidder could be the key to finding one.

She might have assisted sooner had she taken that Mitch character seriously back in Cairo. But whether it was the thrill of the find, the millions at stake or her genuine mistrust of any man, she refused to listen. It wasn't until she arrived home, saw the devastation, saw first hand, friends and family dying that she decided her next expedition was to assist in saving the earth.

Thanks to the Sheikh she was excited to know that Professor Faversham had been assigned to the expedition and couldn't wait to surprise him at the airport as he arrived. But she could only watch in horror as he was ambushed and led away, leaving his companion unconscious.

It took a while to pick up the trail after the lengthy process of hiring a quad bike, but knowing that Siwa was the final destination she was hopeful of catching up with him.

. . .

Heading from 6th October City she came across an impressive campus where she caught sight of the car used to take Iggy from the airport. But by the time she was in a position to begin her search the camp erupted as they realised Iggy had escaped. She was lucky to escape detection herself as they sent jeeps in all directions, bright searchlights scouring the sands for any sign.

Sinking back into the dunes she continued to head west but apart from frightening a Fennec fox, she was beginning to feel that she had lost her way.

Just as she was about to rethink she came across a small oasis. She decided it was a good time to take a rest and plan her next move.

Catching sight of two men in the distance and using her mono-scope, she could tell that one was being forced to move as he was being pushed every few feet. Even through the scope she couldn't fail to recognise the trademark fedora and leather jacket of her mentor and friend, Ignatious Faversham.

Realising he had been captured by the thief and his brother, she had to step up her efforts to get him away from there.

Looking at him now, she wished she'd had a little more time before they left Qara to explain her plan to him. But once she had something in her head it was difficult to shrug off and her priority was to leave quickly.

From the look on his face however, it would appear he wasn't going to like what she was about to say.

"I guess you will need this." Faversham pulled the scroll from his satchel.

He never failed to surprise her. He was analytical, more thought than action, and rarely wrong.

"Just like that? You are just going to hand it to me?"

She held her hand out.

"No I'm not! What the hell Tia...you planned this!"

He was angry, but she could tell, not furious.

'Of course not! Iggy It's me...you know me." She realised that in the dark her fluttering lashes really had no effect.

"Yes, that's the problem Tia, I know you. You take me through the mountains to a place where we are what, twelve hundred, two thousand feet in the air? You just happen to have a wing suit with you and we are a day away from our destination. You have to take the scroll to ensure that it reaches Siwa by midnight. From there you will know the destination and you will be able to reach it in time to activate the scroll. How am I doing so far?"

Tia couldn't hide her regret and her head naturally dropped, as it always did when she was in trouble.

This time her intentions were genuine. It dropped because Iggy thought she had let him down and that was the furthest from the truth. She wanted to help, needed to help, after all it was hers to begin with. Had she had her time again, had known what she had in her hands, she would have done the right thing. Searched for The Field of Reeds.

"Here…" Faversham handed her the scroll, he was smiling.

"You are right. It's the only way, and if I am right the destination is somewhere between here and Siwa. Which means that once you have the location you can point me in the right direction and meet me there."

She couldn't help herself as she rushed into his arms, smothering him in a blanket of nylon as the suit's webbing shrouded them both.

"Steady old girl…You'll have me over the edge. Which reminds me, I assume you have a way of getting me down from here?"

Counting the cables, checking the harness and collating the anchors, Faversham had to admit that he couldn't have come better prepared himself.

Tia checked the altimeter as she secured it to her wrist.

"I'm reading two two four five, so at twelve hundred above sea level, I make that around twelve hundred feet to the bottom. Shouldn't take you too long."

She positioned her night vision goggles and switched on the three halogen lights, shining them out into the void. They gave a hundred foot of vision which was all she needed. Switching them off she turned to the professor who was still rummaging through her rucksack.

"Look after it for me, it has my spare ammunition, some provisions and my make up."

Faversham pulled out a belt and holster equipped with a Heckler & Koch pistol.

"Oh yes, and a spare just in case. You take it, it might come in useful."

"What were you expecting, Tia? You have a small arsenal here." He pulled out several boxes of 9mm shells.

"Homework…" Was all she said as she moved past him and pulled out a satchel.

"You take one of these and pop this in." She passed a sat phone to him and a tiny receiver that Faversham placed into his ear.

"We'll stay in contact constantly. I need to know you are ok and it's important that we can see where we both are…just in case."

Faversham studied the readout on the miniature green screen, two small red icons flashed on the topographic image of the mountain range. It gave him a strange sense of comfort that they were linked in some way.

He was in no doubt that Tia was there to assist in the discovery of the Field of Reeds. She was too much like her father, and like him, would rather seek to know the truth than just take the money and run. He was sure that had she known the true scale of the scroll's worth she would have set out to find the secret. And although he couldn't be sure, it wouldn't have surprised him if she had sought out his assistance.

"Right, we should get on then."

Faversham needed to move before he gave up on the whole thing. She had got to him again, similar to their University days and he couldn't afford the distraction, nor could she. More importantly nor could the world.

Fitting the harness, he hammered the anchor into the ledge and fitted the carabiner in place ready to link the first line. Adjusting the rucksack to fit his shoulders comfortably and jumping a few times to let everything settle he signalled he was ready with a thumbs up.

Tia held him again, this time pressing her lips against his. They kissed tenderly, an affirmation that they would see each other in more comfortable surroundings once this was all over.

"Take it easy, Iggy. See you tomorrow."

Without lingering any longer, Tia switched on the halogens surrounding her goggles and leapt from the ledge.

Faversham watched the lights fall forward and plummet down, he heard the whoof of fabric as it caught the breeze. Holding his breath he watched and waited...for far longer than he should have...had she misjudged the depth? Had the suit failed?

Thirty feet away in the distance three tiny lights lifted into view and as they rose the light from the moon cast a silhouette of a wavering, fluttering line of fabric. It could have been mistaken for the fluttering of a bat in the night sky, but he knew it was his partner, making her way to Siwa.

"Oh well. This won't do." Faversham spread his legs wide, his back to the open air, leaning out he kept his eye on the descender and ensured the cable moved smoothly in a figure of eight through the device.

Happy with what he saw, he leapt into darkness.

41

M itch handed Jack his fedora thinking there was no way it was going to fit on the big man's head.

"What are you planning to do with my hat?" It was part of him and he hoped that he would see it again.

Jack ignored him and searching the floor found a small sack of apples. The fruit bounced and rolled across the floor as he tipped them out and threw the empty hessian bag to Malik.

Finding some excess rope on a tent pole he cut the length he needed and creating a loop at one end, placed it over his head letting it fall around his neck.

Approaching Malik he produced two pearl grenades from his jacket and offered one to the Berber Chief.

"Malik, you need to trust me or nobody will leave here alive." He handed one of the grenades to him.

Malik narrowed his eyes and stared at the silver ball, then back at the agent who returned his gaze with a steely determination, as explosive as the sphere being offered to him.

· · ·

"Malik. Now!" Before he had time to object he was once again holding a grenade. He flinched as it beeped in his hand.

"Jack, what are you up to?" Mitch had no idea and being military himself, he hated being unprepared. He needed to know the plan.

"They are expecting us to hand them the professor, so we will give him to them. Faversham dresses similar to me or at least wears the same jacket and that damned fedora. It's a style thing apparently..." He eyed Mitch questioningly. Mitch just shrugged, he liked the look.

"...So, you will cover my head and lead me outside by the rope. They will expect you to be hostile so hold the gun to my head..." Jack scooped up one of the rifles and threw it at Malik.

"...It should give us the time we need and an advantage to familiarise ourselves with the surroundings. They won't hurt us for fear of you shooting me..."

"And who is to say I won't?" Malik had a reason, and now the ammunition.

'You won't." Jack took the bag and put it over his head. He was pleased that, as he thought, he could see through the fabric. It was hazy, but enough to make out shapes.

"Once we are out there, stay close and I'll talk you through this..."

"Jack! Do you read?" His ear crackled into life. It was Sara.

Pulling off the bag he pressed his ear.

"Hi Sara, I'm a bit tied up at the moment. Is it quick?"

'Is it quick?' Sara could feel her blood boil...

"No Jack, I thought I'd just check in, tell you about the weather and see if you could help with the crossword I've been doing while I was bored...Fucking Hell!"

'Touché' He thought. Jack realised that he could be insensitive sometimes and during missions could forget how important the team were, in particular Sara. She had saved his life more than once and he knew that this would probably be another instance.

"I'm sorry, Sara...we have a situation. What have you got?"

The silence, even for only a few seconds spoke a thousand words. He had a situation translated to Sara that he was in extreme danger. She knew she needed to be fast.

"I've just picked up readings in the mountains southwest of your position. Two signals heading towards Siwa Oasis. It has to be our man."

"Two signals, so he has company. What makes you so sure it's the professor?"

"It has to be, Jack. The first part of the scroll that we know is…'To the West of the Nile Delta, where the palms hold the moon'. It has to be an oasis and there are only two significant locations, Qara and Siwa. The signal is moving towards Siwa, one quicker than the other and as it is mountainous terrain I'm guessing a light aircraft of some sort."

It made sense and he was used to following Sara's assumptions as she was rarely wrong.

"Ok Sara, keep an eye on them and I'll let you know when I'm on my way. Radio silence until then…"

"What, radio silence? What can I do to help, Jack?" She checked her screen moving to his position.

"Oh, shit! Jack, I see five of you in an enclosure and at least thirty surrounding you."

"There are only five with receivers Sara, count fourteen able to fight out of here. But we have eight women, some casualties and our enclosure is just a tent. I could really do with Adams getting here sooner rather than later."

"He's heading your way, Jack. Just hole up for another ten minutes or so."

"No time, we have to give them the professor or they will destroy this place and everyone in it…"

"The professor…but…"

"Yes, Sara I know, that's why we need to go… keep your eyes peeled, I'll let you know when I'm done."

Sara stared at the screen, at the blue dot that flashed rhythmically, the vital signs on the pop up panel showed a strong heartbeat, although a little faster than normal. She had his back, he knew that, but it was times like this when she wished she was still there alongside, to cover his back. They were a good team, the best. That was until emotions began to cloud their judgment and they became a danger to each other. Now all she could do was to keep the dot flashing blue, ensuring the pop up stayed blue…keep away from the amber warning signs and heaven forbid, red.

She kept her eyes on the blue dot as it moved slowly across the screen and felt her heart begin to accelerate as it left the enclosure.

∼

"Stop! Stay exactly where you are."

The female voice bellowed from behind the spotlight fixed to the jeep directly ahead of them. Jack could make out four sets of headlights from the vehicles in front and to their left a larger vehicle, a six wheeled transporter. From the shadow cast by the vehicles he could see the figure standing behind what he could only assume in the haze, was a fixed machine gun.

He could feel the barrel of the rifle begin to shake as Malik faced the threat in front of him. It was bad enough that he had the rifle pointed at him in the first place, but to make this work it had to be convincing. He would prefer to keep his head intact throughout.

"Calm down, Malik…We'll be fine as long as you keep it together. How many can you see in front of you."

Thankfully the vehicle engines were running which helped to keep his voice undetected. Malik, doing his best ventriloquist impression, spoke through the side of his mouth trying as best as he could to keep his lips from moving.

"Twenty thaw…" was the best he could manage.

That left six unaccounted for. He could only assume they were covering the rear.

"Just stay firm and don't let me go. You need me to safeguard your people…"

. . .

"Over here professor, we have a job to do." The silhouette of a the female moved to the side of the spotlight, he couldn't make her out in full detail, but he saw enough by the way she moved and her stance that she was fully in control.

"No! You can take the professor once I guarantee the safety of my people. I need to ensure they are safely back in their homes."

Starting hesitantly, Malik became more confident as he completed his sentence. The gun stopped shaking and Jack hoped that his other hand was ready with the pearl grenade.

It appeared to have worked and they assumed he was the professor. They were of a similar height and in this light it was difficult to gain a clear indication of body size. Wearing the leather jacket and holding the fedora at his waist was enough to convince those looking on that he was their man. It also gave Jack the space to conceal a sphere of his own in one hand and his Glock in the other.

"You are in no position to give us demands. We will cut you down before you have time to pull your trigger."

The sound of guns racking and safeties being released filled the air as soldiers prepared their guns to fire.

"I think not." Malik, with an element of panache held the pearl grenade in the air so that all could see the metallic sphere glimmer in the fluorescent light. He pushed his hand into Jack's pocket, being careful not to let go.

Nobody saw Jack's eyes open wide with surprise and a reasonable amount of panic as the Berber thrust the grenade into his jacket.

'What the hell was he up to? This was NOT part of the plan.'

"If you shoot me, the grenade will blow your professor into tiny little pieces. We will all lose. Let my people go."

Jack had to admit it was a good plan. But he would liked to have been in on it and more importantly, he hoped he was prepared to take it back out again.

"I hope you know what you are doing, Malik. Don't let go of it or none of us will survive."

"Well, let's hope I want to survive." Malik's tone, even through the side of his mouth, sounded ominous.

There are some in the world who see martyrdom as an honour, a victory for their people. He just hoped Malik wasn't one of them.

"Well played…" The woman applauded.

"Very well. You have a deal. We will let your people go…on one condition." She let the words settle for a moment or two.

Her way of gaining the initiative and bringing back control.

"Mitch! I know you are in there. Show yourself."

Time stood still as the majority of those present tried to digest Gabrielle's last command. Many then looked on in surprise as another man emerged from the tent and stood alongside the hooded man and the Berber.

"Hello Gabrielle." He knew that somewhere along this expedition their paths would cross. He had hoped they would get a little further before they did.

Gabrielle ignored his pleasantries and drew her gun.

"As part of the agreement to release your people, you will give the scroll to this man and he will hand it to me. Don't worry professor, it will be perfectly safe, just an insurance for us both."

Jack closed his eyes, he hadn't thought of that. He felt the rifle barrel shake against his cheek. Neither had Malik.

"Where is the scroll, professor?" It was more a command than a question, but he thought he sensed the first signs of doubt in her voice.

Keeping the fedora in place with his right hand, a tricky manoeuvre as he could only hold it with his forefinger and thumb while keeping hold of the grip of his gun, he concealed the grenade in the palm of his left as he moved it out into the open and pointed at the pocket still containing Malik's hand.

Mitch moved in front of Jack so that his body concealed the

moment Jack handed the grenade to him, the beeps were drowned by the rumble of the engines. As he turned to Gabrielle he put his hand into the inside pocket of his jacket feigning the placement of the scroll while keeping hold of the sphere. Facing her, he put both hands in his pockets.

"What now?" Mitch was twelve yards away and unable to make out her features clearly, but he could feel her stare penetrating the gap between them, could feel the hatred reaching out towards him.

"Bring it to me." Plain and simple, an order devoid of emotion.

He took a step, removing his hands from his pockets, another step, he turned to look at his two companions, a silent goodbye. Taking another step he stopped and looked at his ex-wife.

From eight yards away he could see that she had looked after herself, she looked healthy, toned and she had kept her hair long, something he always favoured. But she had her ugly face on, which ruined it.

Not that she wasn't beautiful, some would even say stunning. When she smiled the room would light up, sparkling eyes, perfect teeth and a cute wrinkle in her nose to melt any heart.

But when she was pissed, her features changed so much, ripping it all away. A malevolence filled her features with such hatred it made maintaining eye contact almost impossible.

"How do we know you will keep your promise? After all, you have just murdered that man's brother." He pointed back at Malik.

"Unfortunate, but necessary. Which is more than I can say for the fate that will befall you all if you delay ANY LONGER! Give me the fucking scroll!"

Now that was a scream he had heard before, one of pure hatred and anger. But the gun pointed directly at his head was new, and by the look of it, she was ready to pull the trigger.

"Ok, ok…calm down…if you want it, here…catch."

He threw the grenade at her feet and dived for cover.

. . .

Four explosions erupted before he hit the ground, bullets ripped through the air and the earth heaved beneath him. He risked a look and saw bodies lying all around. Above, the dark shape of a helicopter hovered overhead, the backdrop of the moon casting ominous shadows. The guns burst into life from it's fuselage, flashing brightly as it released shells into the surrounding troops. The cavalry had arrived.

He was grabbed by the shoulders and pulled to his feet.

"Come on, move!..." Jack pushed him towards the tent, firing behind them as they ran. Malik, having already disappeared was rounding everybody up as they entered through the bullet ridden flap.

Jack moved to the furthest west facing wall and using his Kabar sliced it from top to bottom, his knife cutting through the goatskin easily. Pulling it apart he leaned out, gun in hand. He blasted two soldiers who were covering the area, they collapsed before they realised they had been hit.

With the area cleared he prized the skin apart wide enough to take a body and moved aside to let Mitch through. They both pulled again, this time large enough for two of his men to pass through followed by the women and the remainder of Malik's menfolk. The rest of Mitch's team exited at the rear and Mitch poked his head through to verify that the tent was empty.

"Where's Aya?" He had to shout over the din of gunfire and explosions.

"No idea. She was with you before you were asked to join us I assume.?"

"Yes, she was looking after the women. I left her to it when Gabrielle called for me."

"She has gone." Malik stood between them after making sure that his people were safe to return to Qara.

"My wives say that she assured them that she would cure the world of the evil and cut her way out before the explosions."

"Shit!" Jack wasn't surprised, she was Nightly's puppet. She knew after his briefing from Sara that the professor was heading to Siwa. She didn't need them any more.

"We have to get after them. Malik, your people will be safe. Commander Adams will clear the area and leave a team behind to protect your town. You need to be with them, assure them that we will be back with a cure if there is one. You have my word."

Malik looked Jack up and down before fixing him with swollen, reddened eyes.

His life had changed, his brother was gone, his father will die and his people will continue to suffer unless a cure is found.

He tried to imagine what his father would do right now, what action to take in this time of crisis. Had Ishmael been right, was he the wrong choice to lead his people? He had so many doubts, no one to share the burden. Could he be the one to fail his people after thousands of years of eminent rule?

"You are fundamentally a good man, Malik. You do everything for the sake of Qara. You will make this work. Your people need you, respect you. We will keep you safe."

Jack could see what Malik was going through, feelings of self doubt were not lost on him. He suffered from self doubt at times, to the extent that he could just walk away and give up on everything. But it solves nothing, eventually you have to confront your fears and be strong enough to cope with the consequences. Better to realise that at the start as it destroys lingering doubt and creates a new energy, an energy that provides the direction you need to take.

"Thank you. I can see that you are a man true of heart. If there is a cure, I can see that you will help us. I will pray for safe passage for you and your friends."

He placed his hand around the back of Jack's neck and pulling him forward kissed both cheeks. He turned to Mitch and did the same.

"There is however, one last thing I need to do."

Malik opened his hand to reveal the smooth sphere of the pearl grenade. With one smooth movement he tossed it through the slit and pulled both Jack and Mitch to their knees.

The explosion ripped half of the tent apart leaving the rest ablaze. They moved away in unison as the heat began to penetrate the skin next to them. Watching in silence as the fire grew, accompanied by tiny explosions as bullets exploded from the discarded rifles.

Malik walked away towards Qara, keeping his back to them, his head bowed as he thought of his task ahead.

Nothing was said by either man as they watched him until he disappeared from sight. In grudging respect for a thief with one thing on his mind. The welfare of his people.

"Well, what now?" Mitch shouldered his rifle as he was joined by four of his men.

"Siwa…"

Jack slid down the bank into the darkness beyond. Mitch and his team followed, leaving the battle behind that had died down to occasional bursts of gunfire to fizzle out without them.

42

T ia pulled the canopy towards her, wrapping it uniformly to be stowed for reuse, just in case. As she peeled away the wing suit she calculated the twenty miles or so she still needed to travel. With any luck she will reach Siwa by lunchtime as long as the route remained fairly straight.

She had landed in a dry gorge which not only helped to add more travel distance, it was also filled with depressions and rock falls which provided ample cover to store her suit.

Clipping a GPS tag onto the chute and wrapping the equipment as tightly as possible she wedged the bundle into a small outcropping, forcing sandstone rocks on top to fill the gap.

Removing the sat phone from her pouch she marked the location and waited for the tag to activate. Once the green dot flashed registering the chip she pinched her fingers on the screen and opened the map to show greater coverage. She was relieved to see the red beacon of Iggy flashing brightly.

"Iggy, I'm down. How are you faring?"

"Well, I would prefer abseiling in better light, but apart from a bruised knee and a devil of a headache, I'm at ground level. Those blasted lights reflect wonderfully off sandstone."

She smiled, a bruised knee and a little glare headache would wear off in no time. She knew him well enough to know that nothing ever went perfectly. He had to find something to moan about.

"I've set a marker in a dry gorge, my suit and canopy are there. Be a dear and collect it for me. I'll set another when I get closer to Siwa. According to my reckoning I should be there by lunchtime, all things considered."

"Well by the looks of the terrain in front of me, it will take me an hour or two to traverse the next five hundred yards." He was surrounded by a series of gnarled rock outcrops, each at least twelve foot high, he would need to climb each one as circumnavigating them will take twice as long.

The topography on the screen was so busy it looked as if someone had scribbled aimlessly just to fill it.

"You should have packed two suits. Flying away from this area was a stroke of genius."

"Ooh, have I earned a gold star, Mr Faversham?"

Her giggling made him smile. She had a playful nature, almost childish, which was one of the reasons he was enamoured of her. She was strong, hot headed and impetuous, but there was a vulnerability that was either borne from fear of failure, of letting down her father or an underlying need to be accepted, liked, even loved.

Whether it was because he was alone in the middle of a dark uncompromising desert and she was his companion for the journey, or his feelings were revived from their time in the past, he couldn't be sure. But he was determined to explore the possibilities once this adventure had reached its conclusion.

"I'm sure I can come up with something."

"Oh I'm sure you can Mr.... Hello....what the?....no....wait... no...NO!...Mmmmm....."

"Tia!..." His shout filled the air, echoing through the rocks and into the distance.

"Tia...talk to me...Are you ok?" He stopped and cupped his

hand over his ear as he strained to listen into his earpiece for any sound.

What he heard filled him with dread. Panic shot through him as he tried to steady his heart beat, to hear more clearly over the thudding in his chest.

"She's a pretty thing. We can have some fun...no."

It was a male voice speaking English with a heavily accented local dialect.

"You touch her and you'll pay with your life. You know that already... He gave strict instructions and I will ensure they are carried out to the letter."

This male was distinctly American and commanding.

Faversham felt helpless. He could hear through the receiver in her earpiece but he couldn't communicate with her. He just hoped that it stayed live during her ordeal, it may give him a clue as to where they were taking her.

" Hang on...what's this?" The American had made a discovery. Faversham could hear a crackling and popping through his earpiece, as if it was being jostled.

"You won't need this where you're going, girl."

Faversham screamed in anger and frustration as communication died, leaving him alone, without the scroll and without a hope of finding it.

43

Viewing the cotton fields of pristine white clouds below from the panoramic windows of the Gulfstream, was the perfect way to relax before the high pressure meetings that Gordon Nightly normally attended. But today he couldn't contain his excitement or his anger in equal measure.

He was ten hours from Cairo and for the past six hours of flight he had heard nothing from Mitch.

Aya's reports had spoken of the ambush and enabled him to provide support before the battle with Khan's troops overwhelmed them. Her last report was of the disappearance of the professor. But nothing from his Head of Security.

She had left Mitch with the LARA agent to follow a hunch that Faversham had escaped into the mountains on his way to Siwa.

He thought he knew Mitch as well as he knew anybody, but he was beginning to question his judgement.

Aya told how he stopped her from killing Jack Case when she had the chance. He was of no use to them, they only required the professor and the scroll.

. . .

She was of the opinion that he had a connection with Case, some military camaraderie, a mutual respect of some sort. She had lost patience with him, with his orders. He knew that he was pairing a most unlikely couple, but they were needed for the operation. Mitch for his muscle because if he was right, the twelve trials of the Duat would be challenging. Once they reached the Field of Reeds he required Aya for her heritage.

He was meticulous in his planning from the beginning. The plague had produced the panic he had hoped for, had brought the medical world to its knees, left them reliant on BioTane. He had them where he wanted them and by tomorrow he would be the saviour. He hadn't expected the bacterium to gain a mind of its own and its virulence surprised them all. But he will eradicate it, defeat all illness, create a better world, a perpetual world where life meant life.

His anger grew as he thought of the professor and Caelen Khan.

Khan had been one step ahead of him, managed to outwit him, disable his operation. The professor was out of their grasp, somewhere in the desert, and they were less than a day from destiny.

He stared at the large screen TV protruding from the mahogany cabinet, preferring to monitor his journey than watch a movie. The tiny aircraft slowly crawled across the map, a red arc protruded from its tail changing to green as it passed the nose cone before settling in Cairo. Underneath the craft showed they were at 40,000 feet with a clock counting down from nine hours forty three minutes. He just wanted the clock to register zero as he needed to resume control. He was sure the numbers counted down slower and slower as he watched them.

Stacy placed the headphones on the arm and swinging the TV away from her, left the plush leather seat. Taking the pouch from the side table she moved along the cabin to sit alongside Nightly on the sofa.

. . .

"This will be the last one, Gordon." She unrolled the pouch and as she waited for him to roll up his sleeve, prepared the syringe.

" But, before I give you this you need to know something."

She had been steeling herself for this moment, going over and over in her head how to tell him. Should she provide the medical version? The blunt, straight to the point version or the sympathetic optimistic version?

He paused mid roll, his sleeve still two turns short of revealing the vein. She could feel his eyes on her, trying to second guess her, attempting to break into her head to read her thoughts.

To hell with it.

"This will serve you for seven days at the most. The genome has become unstable, it has started adding chromosomes and reorganising them. It has worked a way to attack the immune system before making its way to the brain. It's out of control."

Nightly just stared at her. He remained calm, his breathing normal. He continued to roll up his sleeve, offering his arm to her as he finished.

"This vial is at an accelerated state as we increased the testing specifically for you. But those on the stabilising drug have less than two months after their next shot before the morphing starts to take place. Even then we are only guessing, we could be talking months, weeks, even days. If this Field of Reeds doesn't exist or proves to be nothing but a myth, we will not be able to stop the disease from wiping out the human race."

"It is real. My faith is not based on myth or legend, I am here to carry out the wishes of my people and serve the will of Ra. We will not fail. Now inject the damn thing and let's get this party started."

He had to admit to himself the treatment he'd been taking to stave of the disease had taken its toll on him. He was constantly tired, exhausted, at times unable to keep his eyes open. Now there was blood, occasional clots, first thing in the morning…sometimes from his nose, at other times after a tickly cough that persisted until he spat the bloody globule into the sink.

He had also developed a slight wheeze, normally when lying down, not debilitating but noticeable. He was aware more than anyone that the disease was fighting hard to take over his body. But, it would not win. He had fought battles all his life and he had overcome them all. He would not let it take away the very reason for him being on this earth in the first place. He will fulfil his destiny.

As Stacy left him to return to her seat, Nightly sat back and closed his eyes. He was confident they would find a route to the Duat, the underworld, where he will be judged, the heart weighed and given passage through to the Field of Reeds and eternal life.

44

The pain was excruciating, Her cheekbone was exposed, skin melted away by the grenade as it sent a molten shard into her face.

She was unaware that the shard had stuck to the skin as she fell away from the carnage and managed to crawl under one of the jeeps. The smell came first, a sickly burning, oddly familiar and nauseating. She was aware of her vision being impaired by smoke covering her left eye, she moved her head to clear her vision, the smoke followed.

Then searing pain, a pain like nothing she had felt before, like a bolt of electricity jolting through her skull. She grabbed at her face and pulled away a small plate of metal, yanking it away from her melted elasticated flesh that protested as it let go, ripping skin away as it came.

She tried to examine it, but had to let go as it burned her fingertips.

In an attempt to get away from the pain she crawled from underneath the vehicle and ran. The pain came with her, but her mind told her to run, run as fast as you can, beat the pain, get away from it, just don't stop or it will return. But it didn't stop, the pain kept with her, she couldn't get away from it and it was getting worse. She remembered screaming before her legs gave way and everything went dark.

~

"This will need surgery, Miss Millson. You are in a bad way, I can't do any more than this. You have third degree burns from your jaw up to your cheekbone and most has gone as far as the subcutaneous tissue, with fourth degree from your cheekbone to your temple."

As a former medic Falmer had seen many wounds in the field of battle, some that still haunted him in quieter moments. But the severity of the head wound on this woman was on par with the worst burn victims he had ever treated.

He had found her as they began to retreat away from the surprise attack at the bedouin encampment. They had regrouped in a depression a mile away. There was enough cover to keep them hidden, with enough rye grass to keep the two jeeps away from prying eyes. The camp was made under a rocky outcrop large enough to fit the five of them, deep enough to hide a fire and wide enough to allow them to stretch out to sleep.

He had limited equipment to treat any severe wounds and nowhere sterile enough to treat such a serious burn victim.

But the woman was built of sterner stuff.

"I'll be fine. My face hurts around the jaw but the rest I can hardly feel. You have worked wonders, doc." Gabrielle was putting a brave face on things.

It hurt like hell and she was using every ounce of her strength to avoid collapsing in a sobbing mess.

"No, Miss Millson. The burns on the upper part of your face won't hurt but they are the worst injuries. They are fourth degree, you will feel no pain, the nerve endings have been destroyed. But if left untreated, the whole area is open to infection. We need to get you to a hospital as soon as possible."

He had cleaned the wound as best he could while she was still out cold and managed enough sterile bandage to cover the worst affected area, doubling up the gauze to cover the exposed cheek-bone. But without immediate surgery she would be disfigured and the risk of infection was extremely high in this climate, he couldn't rule out sepsis.

His sat phone buzzed in his pocket. Moving away from the patient he took the call. Gabrielle strained to hear the conversation as she knew who it was.

"Yes, sir. She needs immediate medical attention…No sir, I would not suggest it…Yes, sir of course…Yes, I would suggest Cairo, it's the nearest with adequate theatres… "

"Falmer!…" The medic turned at Gabrielle's shout…

"Give me the fucking phone…NOW!"

It was loud enough for the caller to hear her. Nodding to the phone several times, Falmer handed her the receiver.

"Gabrielle, seems you've had a bit of trouble." Caelen Khan's sardonic tone didn't go unnoticed.

"I'm fine Caelen, it's just a setback. We will regroup and get the professor for you. We were ambushed. But I'm confident that we can still get him."

"My dear Gabrielle, it wasn't a setback. You had the setback when you let him escape in the first place. You have let me down, cost the lives of many good men and you are intent on grabbing a professor who is of no use to us now."

She had to think for a moment. Had she missed something? Why wouldn't the professor be of use?

"We have the Stirling girl in Siwa, she has the scroll and will lead us to the Duat. She found the scroll in the first place and her relationship with the professor is, shall we say, close. Marcus has her, he will discover the location."

"No, you can't! This is my mission and I will get it for you. Caelen, you know Marcus as well as I do, he will go too far and we will lose everything."

·   ·   ·

Marcus Villin was Aruman's former head of security, a hot head, thug and an ex con. She had replaced him after uncovering his connection to the mob. A connection that threatened Aruman's reputation and finances.

Alhough he couldn't be trusted, he had built such a relationship with Khan that even after his sacking he managed to remain on friendly terms. He even provided some services beneficial to Aruman that he sold to the CEO as 'making amends for his discretions'. Somehow he had wormed his way back in.

"Remember who you are speaking to, Gabrielle. I can and I will do what is best for Aruman. You have messed up three times now and I can't afford any more mistakes. We have one more day before the secret of the scroll is revealed to us and I will not allow Nightly to get there first. Now we have the upper hand, I intend to keep it.

I have a helicopter on its way to take you to hospital. Make sure you are on it and let's meet when you have made a full recovery."

"Caelen, no…"

"Enough! Gabrielle I am so close to ordering Falmer to put a bullet in your head, putting us all out of our misery. You will board the aircraft and you will do as you are told…do I make myself clear?"

Gabrielle sat in stunned silence, letting the receiver drop to the floor. Falmer picked it up and put it to his ear.

"…Yes, sir, understood…Yes I have something for her. I'll make sure…Yes sir…Understood." Falmer put his phone back into his pocket and rifled through his kit bag.

Pulling out a small aluminium case he knelt in front of Gabrielle.

"Here, let me give you something to help while we wait for transport." He opened the case to reveal six full syringes.

"Morphine. One of these will last you for the next eight hours, enough for you to feel a little more comfortable at least."

He gave her the box to hold as he prepared the syringe and turned her arm to receive the dose.

The box, smooth brushed aluminium on the outside was highly polished and clear inside. Clear enough to see the reflection staring back at her.

Half of her face was heavily bandaged, her hair pushed back or singed away by the heat. But it was her eye…what had they done to her eye?

It didn't line up with her other eye, it had drooped further down her face. The reason was probably because her bottom eyelid had melted away, there was nothing to hide the bottom of her eye, all that was left was the wet bloody mush of a socket and the perfect dome of the sclera, the white of her eye.

She couldn't help it as she heard the tiny mewl escape from her mouth, and was helpless still as the mewl became a howl, until she was wailing at the top of her voice filling the enclosure with the sound of utter despair.

"Oh, I'm sorry Miss Millson. I didn't think it would hurt that much." Falmer had misread her emotional state, wiping the insertion area with the alcohol wipe as gently as he could.

"Oh move away, you fool!" She pushed him hard enough to cause him to tip backward and land on his backside.

When he looked back at her she was pointing her gun at his face.

"I'll take these syringes. What else do you have to help with the pain?"

Her face, already contorted, was filled with venom. Falmer sat rooted to the spot, he had no doubt she would hurt him if she had to. Pain can cause many emotions, self pity, anguish, desperation and anger probably the most common. He could see that her wounds had brought all of them to the fore.

"Now, Miss Millson, we don't want to do anything silly, do we?"

The three other soldiers began to stir as they saw everything unfold, one reaching for his gun. Gabrielle put a bullet in each one and before waiting for them to collapse to the floor, swung the gun back to face Falmer.

"You condescending prick! What else do you have to help with the pain? I need whatever you have to last me a few days."

Scrambling back from her he reached his kitbag and pulled it in front of him, sitting with it between his legs, hoping it might deflect a bullet if she fired. He pushed the flap open and looking inside began to rummage.

"One false move…" Gabrielle had the gun trained on his forehead.

Falmer closed his eyes as he searched, opening them with relief when he came across what he was after. Taking out a bottle of pills he threw them at her…they bounced across the floor, sliding to a stop beside her. She turned the bottle over in her hands looking for a label.

" Hydrocodone. It will help with the pain and help prevent infection. Take two every twelve hours."

She popped the top and took a swig allowing two, maybe three, even four tablets enter her mouth. She swallowed all with one gulp.

"Jesus…" Falmer looked at her, seeing a desperate, dangerous woman. Volatile, unforgiving and scary as hell.

She rose to her feet, waiting a few seconds for the dizziness to pass. She checked the pockets of the dead men, taking a knife, some ammunition and a hip flask. The scotch burnt her throat on the first swig, but welcoming. The second went down smoothly.

In the distance the sound of blades chopping through the air signified that her ride was about to arrive.

She took the kitbag from Falmer and tipped its contents onto the floor. She put back the bandages, gauze, swabs and a box of alcohol wipes, collected a handgun from one of the dead soldiers and placed it inside along with the spare ammunition, securing the flap once she was satisfied.

.   .   .

"I know you won't mind if I borrow this."

Falmer had no time to answer as the bullet shattered his skull. The morphine began to kick in and she felt alive again.

With renewed strength she dragged Falmer's body deep into the outcrop and positioned him against the other three cadavers. Taking the sat phone from his pocket she grabbed one of the bedrolls and, spreading it out, covered the bodies to ensure they were well hidden.

Dusting herself down she tidied her hair as best she could. Collecting her kitbag Gabrielle left to meet the helicopter.

The rotors sent sand swirling into the air as the Sikorsky touched down in the enclosure yards away from her. The side door slid open and a crewman signalled her to come on board. They knew they only had minutes before they would be intercepted by the troops guarding Qara.

As she stooped to take the force of the downdraft from the blades, she noticed that the crew consisted of the pilot and the crewman holding the door open for her.

She shouted as she neared the door to the cabin.

"What!" The crewman shouted at her.

"I need you to get out…" She shouted as she held her hand out for him to help her up.

As he took her weight and pulled her into the cabin, she pushed him out and shot three times before he hit the ground.

Sliding the door shut she clambered into the cockpit and pointed the gun at the pilot.

"Hi.." She smiled at the man staring back at her, his eyes wide, mouth moving but nothing really tangible escaping.

"Slight change of plan. I need you to take me to Siwa."

She was feeling exhilarated, almost high with the excitement of it all as the helicopter rose majestically into the air. She was going to prove Khan wrong, complete the mission and at the same time ensure that Mitch Dawson rued the day he ever met her.

45

As the morning began to push the darkness of night behind, the sky created a panorama of reds, purples and neon blues. The hue made the craggy desert in front of him resemble the surface of Mars. Faversham began to feel as if he really was the lone survivor in an alien land.

For hours he traversed rocks and crevices, wondering if it would ever end. Jagged outcrops and hillocks several feet high made him glad that he had the equipment left by Tia. He was now becoming dangerously low on anchors and the thought of free climbing in his current state did not appeal. He was knackered.

He checked his receiver several times at the start, calling her name in the hope of an answer. But he knew her earpiece had been removed and whether the receiver was being monitored or not, he had a feeling that Tia wasn't the one monitoring it. So he made a conscious effort to remain silent until he could get to Siwa. If he could get there.

Checking the screen he could see his own green marker and the small blue tag flashing to show where Tia had left her gear a few hundred yards ahead of him. He had to scroll up three complete revolutions before he could make out any building structures. He was still miles away.

.   .   .

Sitting on one of a million rocks he sipped slowly at the water, still cold within its flask. Nibbling on an energy bar he tried to figure out how he had managed to get into this situation.

He was ninety percent certain that the scroll was genuine and he was just as certain that it showed the location of something. He doubted himself that it would open a gate to the underworld, but as has been proven, many myths and legends were based on fact at the very beginning of their tale. It was also widely known that the Egyptians were incredible architects, engineers and scientists. They were so close, but it all seemed to be at an end now.

A rattle of loose rocks behind him made him start. It sounded all the more menacing in the silence of his surroundings as it echoed around the rocky terrain.

He instinctively drew his gun and followed the sound.

"I wouldn't do that if I were you"

He was faced by five robed men brandishing rifles. He couldn't make out any features as they all wore their Keffiyehs with head-scarves covering their faces. They wore the traditional dress of the bedouin although even in the poor light he could tell that they weren't the cleanest bunch.

One moved away from the group, his robes darker than the rest. Across his shoulders he wore a bandolier, a sash full of bullets, each pocket occupied by a rifle shell. His tunic was belted across his waist supporting two handguns, a knife and what looked like a short bladed scimitar sword. He was definitely the leader.

Faversham put his gun away to show that he meant no harm, standing as still as he could as the dark man approached. He faced forward as the man circled him several times, slowly looking him up and down as he moved. He could smell the stale smell of ciga-rettes, alcohol and fish.

.   .   .

"You are a long way from home, are you not?" His English was passable, deep and hoarse, probably from years of smoking.

"Yes, I am trying to get to Siwa to find my friend."

"A friend? This friend is a good friend? A friend that will leave you in the Siwa desert all alone? Tell me about your friend."

Faversham could tell that he was being toyed with and he knew they were bandits. He was also without anything of value, which could cause him a problem when it came to bartering for his life.

"Come now. It is a simple question. Tell me about your friend? Is she a good friend...a close friend perhaps?"

Faversham looked through the fabric to the dark eyes staring back at him. He knew...he knew about Tia.

"What do you want?" Faversham thought it best to approach the situation head on. It couldn't get any worse for him.

" Sixteen million Egyptian will offer you safe passage, I would say." He unwound his scarf so that Faversham could see him clearly, see the smile and the five stained teeth grinning back at him.

His face was coarse, pock marked and scarred. His beard was patchy where scarring had stopped any growth and his nose had been broken many times. He looked a brute of a man. If it was meant to intimidate him, it worked.

"I'm afraid I don't have that kind of money on me." He couldn't help himself, even though he tried not to make light of the situation, his mouth often became the first thing that operated.

Sixteen million Egyptian equated to a million pounds. He had nowhere near that amount anyway.

"Maloof will find that acceptable, I am sure."

He had no idea who Maloof was, but it appeared that he was the one with the money.

"They have her, your friend...Maloof and the American took her to Siwa. They searched for you but could not find you. It appears that you are important to them."

.   .   .

He was relieved to hear that Tia was alive and by all accounts they were seen as a team. It made sense that if they were searching for him, they would keep Tia safe until he was found.

"Then lead the way Mr…?"

"You can call me Barak…but we are not here as your tour guides you fool. If they are not prepared to pay for you, we will put your head on a pole at the edge of our encampment. You can be our lookout."

The laughter from the others made him chuckle along, but he couldn't be sure if they were fooling or not. He was bound to find out.

He was escorted along a winding pathway through a break in the rocks where six quad bikes were waiting for them. A single rider watched them arrive, kicking his engine into life.

" Ah…so our bounty is here…" He shouted to the group as they joined him.

"We'll see…" The leader, Barak, replied.

"He could yet be our latest lookout"

Faversham decided not to join in with the joviality this time. He was feeling nervous.

"Sit behind me and hold on tight. Don't fall off…where we are going you will not survive the landing."

Faversham fell backwards as the bike jolted forward. He grasped at the robed rider, grabbing a fistful of cotton with both hands and pulling himself back into the seat.

"Hold tight, fool! You will kill us both."

Barak felt behind and grabbing the professor's arm, pulled it around his waist. Faversham followed with his other arm and linking his fingers, pressed his face into the rider's back. Thankfully the wind blew into his face as they hurtled along the dusty track. It helped to dilute the stench of body odour, filth, cigarettes and alcohol.

He thought it was best to keep his eyes shut as the quad bike tore up the side of the mountain. He held on for dear life as Barak threw the four wheels all over the place. Speeding around blind curves, bouncing over rockfalls and power sliding into tight bends.

Thankfully they levelled off and the bike slowed as they came to a group of caves, a bizarre sight of three cavern openings at ground level and three above, connected by rudimentary cane ladders. They had been roughly hewn into the face of a mountain wall that stretched at least a hundred feet above their position.

Faversham stared at the pole ahead of him, it rose fifteen feet in the air in front of the central cave. Perched on top was a human skull; the lookout.

"I think you would like the view from there." Barak cut the engine and shaking the professor's arms from his waist, climbed off and pointed to the open landscape, a rocky vista complimented by the orange streaked blue sky of dawn.

He chose to ignore the laughter, keeping his eyes focused on the horizon and wishing he had kept moving.

"Come, we have work to do."

As Barak walked to the central cave, Faversham was led by the arm to the cavern on the right.

Light was provided by bulbs wired along the centre of the rough chiseled ceiling, a gentle hum emanated from deep within the recesses from the generator providing power.

Along each wall were cages, crafted from palm wood. The professor recognised the lattice construction tied together with reeds from old Egyptian research. Traditional handcrafted cages large enough to hold a human being.

He was taken aback when he saw each cage was occupied by young women, all moving into the light, grabbing the bars to look at the new arrival. They were dressed in light cotton shifts covered in grime and all in their late teens, early twenties. Their haunted features a mixture of fear and exhaustion.

"What is this?" Faversham was appalled, which seemed to please his captor as he grinned back at him.

"You need not worry about them, they are nothing to do with you. We have one of our special suites for you over here and one of your companions for company."

Tia? Did he mean Tia? He was sure Barak told him that she had been taken.

They passed another dozen cages when the cavern opened out to a storage area filled with brown paper packages about the size of a large envelope, tightly wrapped and stacked to the ceiling. A much larger cage sat alongside and it was occupied by a woman. Sitting with her arms resting on her knees, dressed in jeans and tan leather jacket, she watched them as they approached.

"This is your new home for a while, food will be sent soon. Let us hope that Maloof values your worth or that meal might be your last."

He unlocked the fist sized padlock and shoved him roughly into the pen, keeping his eyes on them both as he locked up. He checked the lock several times to ensure that it was secure. Happy, he shouldered his rifle and disappeared.

The woman said nothing as she watched him survey the surroundings. She was of Middle Eastern origin, clear complexion with long black hair that fell to her shoulders. Her deep brown eyes showed a defiance that disguised any fear.

Seeing a blanket close to her he gestured in his best English way for permission to sit.

·   ·   ·

"May I?" He produced his best smile as she nodded, trying not to object too much to his back tweaking as he sat cross legged across from her.

"I'm sorry but do I know you?" She was definitely someone he had never met before. He would certainly have remembered if he had.

"No, you don't." Her response wasn't altogether friendly, but not aggressive.

"I didn't think so. Professor Ignatious Faversham. Pleased to meet you." He extended his hand and tried to produce the best smile he could in the current circumstances.

She stared at his hand, choosing against shaking it before looking back at him for an uncomfortably long time, eyeing him up and down. He felt a little awkward as she kept going back to his ramshackle hair. He found himself pushing it back several times, trying to get the bounce back into his fringe, but failing miserably.

"I am Aya. Dr Gordon Nightly has tasked me to get you to the Field of Reeds."

46

A s dawn hit the valley Jack tried to calculate timescales. By midnight tonight the scroll should reveal the location of the Field of Reeds. Twelve hours on would be the time that the cure, or whatever was going to stop the plague, would reveal itself. According to the professor, there were traps or challenges to be defeated before they reached their goal.

He was no expert on Ancient Egypt, or particularly knowledgeable on riddles or any other form of cryptic clue. But he was conscious of time, strategies and preparation, all of which were distinctly lacking on this mission.

Time was running out, the professor had disappeared, Aya had disappeared and whoever had been with Faversham at the time of Sara's report had also vanished and they had little to go on. Sara had come up with nothing since.

They stopped at a steep depression, finding the anchors that had been used to abseil the rocks. Being unprepared, they had been forced to find an alternative route, losing several hours. Even Jack was beginning to lose faith that they would ever recover a trail.

His ear crackled to life.

. . .

"Jack, I've found something. Two hundred yards southwest of your position. A beacon of some sort...tiny as it only showed once I zeroed in. I've tagged it so you'll be directed straight to it."

"Great, I was starting to run out of ideas. We need to step up our game, we are beginning to lose track of what is happening here."

Sara knew it was a generalisation, but as Jack's eyes and ears she took it personally. Desert assignments were tricky due to the topography, wide expanses of underground and undiscovered routes and the distinct lack of technology. Even though LARA had access to any satellite circling the earth and the resources of all the latest released and yet to be released tech, without a signal to latch on to, they were blind.

"It's light on the ground, Jack. I've scanned most of the surrounding area but all I'm getting are sporadic signal bursts, hardly anything to set a trace.....Oh....Hang on a minute..."

Jack held back, letting the others pass to continue trudging West. After Aya had used the information to her own advantage he wasn't about to pass on any further intel. He hadn't yet worked Mitch out. On one hand he was ex military and seemed to be focused on the task at hand, on the other, he was keeping something back, an agenda that he wasn't party to. Jack would provide intel on a need to know from now on, he was uncomfortable and had to regain control otherwise they would fail. That was not going to happen on his watch.

"...There's an aircraft heading directly for Siwa, a helicopter. There's no chatter so I'm assuming it's not supposed to be there."

"Military?" Jack's first thought was that Khan had mobilised more troops.

"No...that's the thing. It's an EC135 from Cairo, a medical chopper. Give me a minute, I'll do some digging. Out."

～

Mitch was stooped, scanning the ground as Jack caught up to them.

. . .

"Look at this, tyre tracks." He was feeling the ridges with his fingers, following the treads as they weaved patterns in the sand.

"ATV's and quite a few of them."

The tracks led away northwards, meandering through the undulating terrain until they disappeared into the granite of a mountain trail.

"I've sent Peel and Stratton to follow it and report their findings. What have you got?"

Finally it appeared they had something to go on. Sara had uncovered activity near Siwa, their current destination, and now tyre tracks next to the beacon she had locked into his PDA. More than just a coincidence.

Checking the handheld screen he moved past Mitch to a small outcrop of rock. Studying the formation he could see a uniformed mound that seemed out of place amongst the natural spread of fallen sandstone and granite.

Jack brushed aside some of the smaller rocks and pulled away a fist sized piece of granite that appeared to have been wedged in place.

Pulling the fabric free from its hiding place he yanked it open watching the orange chute tumble into the sand as the blue wing suit unfurled in his hands.

"What have you got there?" Mitch moved away from the tyre tracks, joining him at the rocks.

"Looks like we have found Faversham's mystery companion." Jack explained Sara's report of the two travellers from earlier, one moving swiftly across the landscape, the flying suit providing the answer.

He found the tracker clipped to the discarded chute, a simple battery operated GPS locater. Tucked within the clasp was a small folded sheet of paper.

'See you in the Duat, Iggy xx TS'

· · ·

"So at least we know his companion was female... and she knows him well."

Two of Mitch's men jogged towards them. They slowed to a walk giving them a chance to catch their breath as they approached. They had ditched their heavy jackets, favouring their military issue vests which were now drenched in sweat as the morning sun began to warm the air.

"The trail leads up the mountain, sir. Peel and Stratton are following. We've swept the area, there is nothing else to see for miles."

"Then I guess we should join them." Jack handed the slip of paper over to Mitch, letting the suit fall to the floor. It was too small to be of use to any of them.

"Sara, what do you have? We have a TS to track down and a trip up a mountain. I could do with some eyes."

"I can give you a little more than that, Jack. Hold on to your hat..."

Jack switched from his earwig to his PDA putting Sara on loudspeaker for them all to hear.

" Ok, here goes. The helicopter was sent from As-Salam International Hospital to recover a serious burn victim by the name of Gabrielle Millson. They have been unable to contact the pilot and they have no way of knowing the whereabouts of the helicopter. But we can confirm it has just landed in Siwa.

The mountainous region to the north of you has a plateau a hundred feet up and satellite images show a camp of some sort. Several vehicles have entered the area and although it is not wholly clear, it looks like there are a network of caves. There are smuggler networks operating in the area, smuggling anything from drugs, weapons, even people. This is likely to be one of them."

They all listened intently, apart from Mitch who was pacing up and down, rubbing his head and massaging his neck after the mention of his ex wife.

. . .

"So I guess the Millson woman has gone in search of this TS friend of Faversham's?"

"You could be right, Jack. And I have that name too...The Sheik was on earlier looking for an update. He mentioned that he had been contacted by the seller of the scroll, she made an offer to help with the search. Her name is Tia Stirling. She is an ex student of the professor's and has quite a reputation as a treasure hunter."

"...And has a mean throw on her...We have met. She can definitely look after herself." Mitch stopped pacing to listen to the rest.

"Ok Sara, but why Siwa? Do we have any ideas?"

"Sorry Jack, no idea. I guess the professor is the one to ask. But, whatever it is, let's hope that it leads to a cure...It's bad Jack, thousands are dying daily. The whole world is in lockdown and the BioTane drug is failing to halt the disease."

That didn't surprise him. They were up against it from the start, with a manufactured disease that was unpredictable at best. Nightly's decision to play with humanity for financial gain and a twisted commitment to cure the world after the fact was nothing short of premeditated omnicide.

"How's Abu...any news on his son?" The billionaire had been on his mind recently.

A year ago he was offered a name your price position as part of the Sheikh's security detail. It was something he had to turn down as a matter of protocol. He had just rescued his daughter from kidnappers and he couldn't afford to accept gratitude or misguided sentiment when emotions were running so high.

But there was something about Abu that appealed to him. He was a ruthless businessman, an entrepreneur and did not suffer fools lightly. As Head of his Security Jack would be afforded the total running of the detail and paid handsomely for his trouble. He could work in an environment that wouldn't be fraught with danger at every turn. He could retire a very rich man.

. . .

"His son is dying, Jack. His body is beginning to reject the stabil-ising drug. We don't know how long he will last..."

Had he accepted the Sheikh's offer he would be by his side to add support or no doubt be on this very assignment with the life of his son solely in his hands. He would also be without the resources of LARA, an operation he already controlled, and forced to work alongside his successor. He was better off staying right where he was.

Yet again, when taking stock of his own life, his role and duties, his own moral compass, he came to the same conclusion. He was going nowhere.

"We are getting closer, Sara. Should he call back tell him not to give up hope. We will know if we can obtain a cure in the next twenty four hours. Just keep your fingers crossed that this thing is real."

47

T ia awoke with a slight headache and a mouth that tasted as if she'd been chewing dirt through the night. She swallowed a few times and ran her tongue around her mouth to try and clear it, but it just made her grimace at each swallow.

She could smell pancakes, a nice sweet smell and an underlying aroma of coffee that blended perfectly to remind her that she hadn't eaten for a while.

Sitting up, she looked around for breakfast...Then it all came back to her...

Jumping to her feet she backed away, coming to a stop at the padded wall. She was in a single room, a mattress lay against one wall next to a small set of shelves with a recorder unit positioned on the top shelf. In the centre of the room was a plate of pancakes, a jug of maple syrup and a pot of steaming coffee on a square steel table surrounded by four battered plastic chairs. The white soft panelled walls on three sides of the room ran from floor to ceiling separated in part by a rusted steel door, three steel bars within the small window showed the grey walls of the corridor outside. The main wall was panelled only a quarter the way from the hard vinyl floor. The rest was mirrored, spanning the length of the room.

. . .

"Ah, Miss Stirling you are awake. Please help yourself to breakfast, the pancakes are delicious." The American voice from the tiny speakers high in the corners sounded assured, almost arrogant.

To make matters worse, she knew that he was watching her from behind the two way mirror.

"Who are you?" She didn't expect an answer but as she began to recall her abduction, the fear and uncertainty that had gripped her quickly turned to anger as she realised that she was trapped.

She had to get to Siwa before midnight and although she was unaware of how long she had been out, she was sure that the day had moved on considerably.

"What time is it?" She had to know.

"Still time for a late breakfast, my dear. We can discuss your translation of the scroll once you are fully refreshed."

It was matter of fact, knowledgable…He knew enough to realise that the scroll had been translated.

"Well without my colleague, Professor Faversham, I'm afraid you will be disappointed. I cannot translate the document without him." It was a test to see how much he knew.

Unfortunately he passed with flying colours.

"Come now, Miss Stirling. We know you left Faversham waiting for you to do whatever it is you need to do here in Siwa. We are aware he is awaiting your instructions."

Siwa? They had brought her to Siwa. She began to feel a little more encouraged. Now she just has to work out how to get out of here. She assumed, by the look of the decor, that she was in an interview room, so logically in a Police station. Were the Police involved in this?

. . .

"Am I under arrest?" She needed to think and it helped if she could keep him talking.

She took advantage of the short amount of silence to pour coffee into a mug, taking a sip of the dark heady brew.

The caffeine hit almost immediately, wiping any tiredness away. She decided to confront things head on. Walking around to the mirrored wall and cupping her hands over her face she leant onto the glass, trying to block out the light to see if she could see any signs of life. Straining her eyes she thought she could see slight movement but couldn't be sure.

"You are not under arrest, Miss Stirling. Calm yourself, we are just holding you momentarily. We need you, and as you will soon find out, you need us. In a short while you will be famous and incredibly rich. Our employer is very much looking forward to meeting you."

She remembered the American she'd met in Cairo, the Head of Security for Gordon Nightly. Mitch, he said his name was. This man did not sound like Mitch. He was more brash, New Yorkish, and even though he tried to soften it with a structured vocabulary, the underlying brutishness in his tone was still evident. It has to be the other group who were after the scroll, the ones who had taken Iggy from the airport…

"Well, you can tell your employer that I have no interest in his offer. Have you not seen what is happening to the world? People are dying, the human race is on the verge of extinction. We need to put our cheque books down and stop this from happening. The longer you keep me in here the less time we have to prepare…"

The blast of gunfire made Tia leap back from the glass, she hit her back on the tabletop and collapsed to the floor. She instinctively scrabbled underneath to take cover.

The glass escaped damage even though she felt the impact of at least one shell hitting the surface. She had heard at least five shots, but now only silence. She daren't shout out in case she alerted them, or had they come to rescue her? But why the guns?

She was in a locked room, one exit and a solitary table for protection. One of the first rules for any explorer was to always have an alternate escape route. She was at a distinct disadvantage as she was drugged and placed in here while unconscious, but she should never have allowed herself to be caught in the first place.

A door slammed outside, she could hear a commotion, a lot of shouts and screams getting closer. They were coming for her.

She moved out from the table and grabbed one of the chairs, gripping a leg in each hand. Standing in front of the glass wall she swung with all her might, closing her eyes to protect herself from the broken glass.

The chair flew out of her hand, bouncing harmlessly off the mirror, clattering across the room and coming to a rest on the floor, a buckled frame of metal. With a strength that surprised her she turned the table upside down and grabbed at one of the legs, pulling with all her might to try and break it free. The metal frame held fast, she couldn't even bend the thing.

The door flew open. Steel crashing against the outer wall, the open doorway filled with the figure of a uniformed officer. His white bush jacket was splattered in blood around his chest, dripping from his red soaked beard. One of his three starred epaulettes hung from his shoulder as he stooped forward unsteadily on his feet.

Raising his head, his brown eyes locked onto hers for a few seconds before he tumbled into the room, catching hold of the back of a chair to stop himself from falling headlong onto a table leg.

His momentum was helped by a shove from the woman who entered behind him. She didn't look in any better condition than the man. In fact she appeared far worse. The left side of her face was covered in gauze, bandaged around her head like a headband. Her blonde hair hung on one side, barely covering an eye that looked as if it was ready to come loose. She couldn't be sure if the hair was streaked with blood or dye as it clung to her wet flesh.

"Sit down Maloof, we have more to discuss after I have dealt with this young lady." The woman looked over to Tia, her revolver pointing at her chest.

"Miss Stirling, I presume?"

Tia slowly backed away, a natural reaction although she had nowhere to go. The panelled wall stopped her from moving further.

"What do you want with me?"

With a gun pointed directly at her by a woman who looked like an extra that George Romero would be proud of, it was all she could think to say.

She could feel herself stiffen as the anticipation of a shot to the heart began to register in her brain. She began to shake as her options were either to dive for cover where there was none or launch at the woman, knowing that the bullet would beat her to her goal.

"This is for you." The woman pulled something from her jean pocket and shook it open. It was the scroll.

Tia just stood and stared at the ancient parchment in the woman's hand. Was it a trick?

"Here, take it." The woman waved it in the air and held it forward once again.

Her heart was racing as she edged forward, waiting for the bang, the punch in her chest as she was flung backwards by the blast. A foot away and she raised her hand, grasping at the corner of the parchment. As soon as she had it in her fingers the woman released it.

"Now leave us. Maloof and I have things to discuss."

Tia didn't need to be told twice. Giving the woman a wide berth, she walked around the policeman who remained in the chair, head bowed. As soon as she left through the door she ran along the corridor, not sure where she was going but for the moment, anywhere else would do.

The station was deserted. Once she left the interview rooms she entered the main office. Most of the desks were covered in files and unfinished paperwork with chairs neatly pushed into them. It seemed as if they had closed for the day.

The reception desk that served as a booking counter also stood empty. In the walls behind were four cells, their doors open and devoid of people.

Making her way to the exit, Tia tried the doors. Locked.

Panic came across her briefly, until a green button caught her eye on the wall. With a press, the doors hummed and let her out into the late afternoon air of Siwa.

Descending the stairs she broke into a run. She wasn't sure which direction she needed, she knew only that she had to get as far away from the building as she could.

"So, Maloof, how long have you been under Khan's employ?"

Gabrielle stood behind the chair looking at the back of the Chief of Police's head. A tactic that helped to increase the sense of dread, particularly when you had already experienced a beating from the questioner.

"I would not concern yourself with me. I'd be more fearful for your own skin when Caelen finds out that you have disposed of his Head of Security." It was painful to speak, he suspected that the woman had broken his jaw.

But he refused to show her any degree of deference, whatever power she thought she had over him.

He had no time to reach for his gun before being pistol whipped to the ground. He feared he'd been shot as gunfire filled the room, but as Marcus Villin's ruined face appeared alongside him, eye blasted clean away and half of his forehead missing, even though he was in pain, he realised he had escaped a bullet as he was roughly pulled to his feet.

"Head of Security? That idiot Villin couldn't even protect himself."

. . .

With the handcuffs she'd ripped from Maloof's belt she pulled his wrists roughly behind the chair and weaving the chain around the rear strut of the seat secured his hands tightly, ratcheting them until the cuffs bit into his skin.

She moved around the chair to face him, staring in silence at his bowed head, waiting for it to rise, which didn't take long.

As their eyes met she could see the determination in him. It was hard enough for him to accept that his station had been compromised, even harder to accept that it was by a woman.

Whether it was because of his damaged jaw or a natural inclination, his mouth drooped to show half of his clenched teeth. Had he been a dog he would be growling at her. His brown eyes glared unmoving, eyelids narrowed with pure hatred.

Gabrielle pulled a small aluminium case from her pocket. Lifting the hinged lid she showed him the five full syringes held inside.

The exertion of the past few minutes had taken its toll and her face was on fire. She could feel herself begin to shake as pain coursed through her body.

"See these…" She tried to keep her emotions in check even though she wanted to scream in agony.

"…Morphine. A wonderful thing…makes me feel so alive." Peeling a syringe from its housing, she pocketed the case.

Pulling the plunger out to its full extent, she pushed it back in until a tiny spray emitted from the lumen. Without hesitation she pushed it into her bicep and emptied the liquid into herself. She closed her eyes and sighed deeply as she pulled it out.

"Ahh…Just a few more minutes for the trip of a lifetime. Now Maloof…would you like to try some?"

Before Maloof could react Gabrielle rushed to his side and pulling his forehead back, jabbed the empty syringe into his jugular vein. With the plunger extended she forced the air through the tube. Maloof struggled, kicking his feet into the floor trying for purchase, trying to force the woman away, but she held on tight until the plunger had fully pushed home.

Breathing heavily as adrenaline began to speed the effects of the morphine through her body, Gabrielle returned to face Maloof. His head was still back, his bearded chin facing her, his breathing appeared normal…for now. She waited for the convulsions to start, the shortness of breath, the brain embolism to bring on the stroke.

Maloof's chest began to shudder, he choked a little, then a little more. It then became rhythmic as the wheeze turned to laughter, subtle at first but as he brought his head forward he began to laugh openly, his hysterics filling the room, travelling through the open door and into the corridor.

"You have been watching too many movies, stupid girl. Did you really think air from that tiny tube would harm me? You need something twenty times the size, even then, one hundred milligrams may still not be enough. Now uncuff me and let's get after the girl; Khan needs her."

"Khan needs her…"

Gabrielle could feel her senses increasing, her heart began to flutter, a renewed strength pulsing through her muscles, her focus pin sharp, her anger unfettered.

"…Well why didn't you say that before. We mustn't disappoint must we."

She sauntered towards the Chief of Police, straddling him and ripping his shirt open to expose his off white cotton vest.

"What are you doing, girl?…Get off right now." Maloof was sure he made her see sense, particularly as Caelen Khan would be in a fury once he knew of the murder of Villin and the girl's escape. He just needed to stop her from playing her silly games.

"Now get off me girl, we have no time for…"

. . .

The syringe thumped through his vest, passed the ribs, nicking part of his lung and jammed into his heart. He gulped as the pain filled his head, like the shock of a thousand volts. He stared at the girl as she removed the syringe, lifted it back over her shoulder and thrust it into his chest again…and again…the snap of the needle made him jump as it echoed in his chest, sharp surgical steel stuck in his right ventricle. There was no pain, he needed to close his eyes, his last sight before his eyelids gave way was that of a woman with half a face, and she was smiling.

Gabrielle watched life leave Maloof's body, staring at the blood as it soaked through his vest, the small spot of red growing in size until it covered most of the white cotton. She patted the dead man's cheek as she moved off him.

"You know what they say, Maloof. If at first you don't succeed…"

She checked her gun clip, five bullets left. Maloof's was still full. Taking his gun and placing it into the back of her jeans, she holstered her own under her jacket and left the room. She had a scroll to decipher.

48

From Jack's vantage point he studied the six cavern entrances and watched as the robed occupants transported containers from trucks, spreading them throughout the complex.

Some of the containers were cracked open and the contents inspected. Sara was right, they had found a smuggler ring. He watched men inspect several machine guns, manipulating their mechanisms and checking the scopes. Some contained packages that were cut into and contents tasted, the taster nodding his satisfaction as to the quality of the contraband.

As they worked diligently they failed to notice intruders spreading around the perimeter. Jack took a direct route along the outcrop from the mountain trail, bedding in amongst the rocks closest to one of the cavern entrances. Mitch took position behind a boulder directly in front of a pole that bore a human skull.

Peel, Stratton, Hunt and Bower spread out to the West, each finding suitable cover to observe the smugglers undetected.

As crates were hoisted by pulleys into the upper caves and the last of the weapon crates were placed into the lower caverns, the doors were pulled open from the last truck. A smuggler held his hand up for support as he guided a young woman from the container. She was shackled to another who gingerly dropped to the floor, followed by another. Each female squinted at the sun as their eyes reacted to the sudden influx of light.

Fourteen girls, each dressed in flimsy shifts were led into the cave nearest to Jack's position. As hard as it was for Jack to watch the young womens fear as they were led back into darkness, he was encouraged to have a better idea of where they may be holding the professor.

Signalling to the others to hold their positions, Jack edged his way forward, shuffling on his front, careful to disrupt as little of the dust laden floor as he could.

He froze as one of the smugglers emerged from the central cavern, his voice loud and urgent as he barked into the sat phone. He grew angrier the longer the call progressed.

"Sara, can you track a call signal close to my location?" Jack risked a whisper loud enough to carry to his earpiece hoping that the frantic shouts covered him.

"On it, Jack. It's connected to Siwa... the Police Headquarters?"

The Police Headquarters? That was unexpected. As far as he was concerned they were offering support.

"Jack, the line to the station is dead and Maloof isn't responding on his mobile...I'll need more time, but I have a feeling they have been compromised."

Or in on it more like, Jack thought as he watched the smuggler finish the call and follow the women as the last of them disappeared into darkness.

Jack signalled to Mitch and his team to advance as he got to his feet and ran to the edge of the cave entrance, pressing his back into the mountain wall. He risked a glance into the darkness, catching a glimpse of a wooden cage. Traffickers, this just got better and better.

Mitch and his men kept their eyes on the LARA agent as he peered into the cave for a second time.

The raised hand with two fingers thrust into the darkness three times signalled for them advance and take the smugglers down.

As Jack disappeared from view, Bower joined Mitch at the central cave while Stratton, Peel and Hunt entered the third.

~

The crude lighting of the bulbs suspended from the cavern ceiling helped Jack's eyes adjust almost immediately. It took him a little longer to take in the sight before him.

Rows and rows of bamboo cages lined the walls, stacked two high, each containing a woman dressed in the same garb as the females he had seen taken from the truck. Light cotton shifts, the stains and fraying on some showed they had been here a while. They all had the same expression, that of abject despair. As he moved silently from one to the other, not one of the girls lifted their head to look at him, preferring to keep their eyes lowered. Some even chose to close them as he passed. He could only assume they thought he was a buyer.

He drew his Glock as he moved further into the cave. Two men had entered before him and he could see no sign of them.

As he came to the end of the cages, the cavern opened out into an expanse full of cartons stacked irregularly, an ideal hiding place to catch someone unaware.

Stooping low, Jack shuffled around the first stack and headed towards the wall, better to keep a solid surface on one side at least.

Sure that the area in front was clear, he edged past another stack of cartons, scanning ahead to his left and then behind, before resting against the wall behind a solitary carton. It unnerved him that there were no signs of the men and apart from the steady hum from what was likely a generator, he could hear no voices. They must know he was here.

.   .   .

What he saw as he risked a glance over the wooden crate however, made him break cover and rise to his full height.

He was facing a room sized cage with two occupants, Faversham and Aya. Sprawled out on the craggy floor in front of them was the body of a robed figure.

As he sidled around the crate, putting his gun away, he raised his hand in greeting in response to the professor's frantic waves in his direction.

Only he wasn't waving in greeting, he was waving a warning.

As soon as Jack had cleared the crate he felt the cold steel of a blade pushed into his throat as he was grabbed from behind, a firm hand pulling back on his forehead.

"Stay perfectly still and you will not be harmed."

The voice, perfect English with a Middle Eastern tone, was controlled, soft and at the same time, menacing.

Jack remained rigid, his eyes concentrated on Faversham, watching as he slumped to the floor shaking his head, frustrated that he hadn't been able to prevent his capture.

It helped Jack to focus, concentrate on his next move, he could feel the tension rise inside as the frustration at being duped turned to anger.

There was only one move he could make as the knife was tight to his throat and his forehead pulled back by a strong hand. The attacker was pressed into his back, the only way to gather the strength needed to hold Jack firmly. His arms were free, but he wouldn't have time to grab the knife before it sliced into his throat.

The only option he did have was still a risk, but one he had to take. It meant he would need to make his move at exactly the right time. He had to get the guy talking.

"What do you want?" Jack didn't care, he just needed the answer.

As he felt the attacker breathe in to speak, Jack braced himself…

"I am…"

Jack flicked his head up catching his adversary on the nose, at the same time pushing backwards with all the strength he had. He had guessed right as they crashed into the solitary crate, its edge smashing into the man's kidney, winding him. The knife loosened giving him time to grab the attacker's wrist and twisting hard he threw the man aside, kicking his legs from under him as he fell away. In one movement Jack was able to wrench the knife away and slam into the attacker as he fell.

Roles reversed, Jack held the knife at the man's throat. He stared into the dark eyes poking through the navy tagelmust covering his head and face.

"So, shall we start again?"

Jack's heart sank as he heard the distinct click of a hammer being retracted, feeling the hard steel of the pistol's barrel as it pushed into his stomach.

"As I said once before. Stay perfectly still and you will not be harmed."

The calmness, mixed with a touch of self satisfaction in his voice forced Jack to move the knife away and hold his arms out in surrender. He was good, he grudgingly accepted as he released the man and got to his feet, stepping back a pace, allowing the gunman to rise, the barrel still pointing at his midriff.

As he removed the scarf from his nose and mouth, Jack was surprised to see the clean shaven features of a man much younger than he appeared. He was definitely from the region but his demeanour as well as his cleanliness belied the perception of a smuggler.

"I am Hakim Sewell...Mossad... and you are?"

"Case...Jack Case ..."

"LARA..." The Mossad agent finished the introductions. He was well informed.

"We knew you were in the area, but I didn't expect to have you interfering in our operation."

Jack took umbrage to that. He had no idea that Israeli intelligence were operating in the area. Of all of the world's agencies, Mossad were one of the worst for disseminating information. They would even go to the extent of denying the existence of any operatives in Egypt, let alone a specific location.

"Well, we weren't planning on being here, believe me. We were supposed to be in Siwa."

"Ah yes. You are following a fairy tale."

The wry smile showed Jack that agent Sewell was going to enjoy this. LARA had many run ins with one agency or another and they were able to take precedence most of the time. Many held their hands up, more than willing to relinquish control; Mossad weren't one of them.

"We are following a lead…"

"…A lead!" The Israeli's laughter echoed through the cavern.

"A lead from an ancient God or zealot Pharaoh. As I say…You are chasing a fairy tale of demons and demigods."

Jack was forced to concede that a quest to find the underworld of Ancient Egypt to uncover the secret of eternal life was more than a little far fetched. Even more so nowadays with the advancement of science proving that creation was more Big Bang than big man.

But what choice did they have? If their mission succeeded, they found the secret to eternal life and a cure was discovered, he was willing to believe in fairies.

"It is what it is, Hakim. Now, if you can let these two go, we can get on with our quest and you can continue with your operation."

Time was pressing and he certainly wasn't going to stand here trading unpleasantries for much longer.

Hakim studied the captives for a moment as if pondering his next move. Facing the LARA agent he stared into the ice blue eyes fixed on his own, cold orbs searing into his skull, powerful, emotionless, dangerous.

"It is not that simple. I cannot just set you free without blowing my cover. It would ruin two years of surveillance which has brought us closer than ever to shutting down the trafficking operation from Gaza. These girls are the last piece of the puzzle, once we make the drop we will have them. I will not jeopardise this whole mission for the sake of a few fanatics and a fairy story."

There he goes again…he just couldn't resist the cheap shot. Jack had had enough, he needed to put an end to this…It helped that somebody else had the same idea…

He caught the keys just before they hit his midriff as the Mossad agent tossed them at him.

" You will find all of the ATV's ready to go with enough fuel to reach Siwa. Take the track to the north of the encampment. It is a straighter route down to ground level. I trust that you will leave me alive in exchange?"

Jack looked to the body of the smuggler on the floor in front of him, the congealed blood that had seeped from his temple had began to dry into the sandstone surrounding his head like a dark halo.

"There are always casualties as a result of a surprise attack." Hakim shrugged, his tone matter of fact, devoid of emotion as if explaining an everyday occurrence, but his eyes expressed the need for Jack to understand his motives.

They were, after all, soldiers with a job to do.

Jack nodded his understanding and using the keys, unlocked the cage releasing Faversham and Aya from their confinement.

.   .   .

"I say Jack, you are a sight for sore eyes." The professor raised his hands and moved in for a hug.

"Let's just get out of here, shall we?" Jack moved several steps back until Faversham's arms lowered.

Aya greeted him with nothing more than a nod, her eyes gave away her anger and frustration. To allow herself to be captured was bad enough, but to be caged along with the other women was a degradation that she could not accept. She will make them pay.

Hakim placed his gun by his feet.

"Make it convincing but allow me to tell the tale."

Admiration replaced the distrust of his Mossad counterpart as he walked up to him. Many sacrifices are made for the success of a mission, this was something Jack would never allow to happen. This took the trust of a stranger further than most who valued their lives ever would.

"Ok, after three…"

The Mossad agent nodded in agreement…Jack smashed his fist into Hakim's temple before he had the time to complete his acknowledgment.

The Israeli's legs went from under him and he crashed to the ground in a heap.

"Hang on, Jack…That wasn't three…you hadn't even started to count. That was bad form, I must say." Faversham was horrified.

"Shock, professor. He would have blacked out with no recollection of the pain. The surprise will register in the brain in a different way. He'll have a slight headache when he comes round, but he won't have felt what put it there. Now let's make it worth his while and get out of here, shall we?"

. . .

Both men turned to face the commotion from the direction of the cavern entrance, shouts, screams and further in the distance, gunfire.

Jack wheeled around

"Where's Aya….Oh no…you have got to be kidding… Come on!"

Pulling Faversham with him he weaved past storage crates and came to the first of the empty cages that had once contained a young woman.

"Damn! That bloody woman"

Jack could see several open cages, doors flung open, some hanging off hinges. Ahead of them several women in light shifts were ripping doors apart with crowbars, shovels and anything else that was at hand, assisted by the distinct figure of Aya, shouting instructions and organising the breakout.

One young girl, no more than twenty years of age, her dirty blonde hair knotted and stuck to her face with the sweat of exertion and grime, spotted the two men watching their break for freedom. Gritting her teeth she squealed in anger and ran headlong at them, a steel bar held tightly above her head ready to bear down on them.

"Bloody hell!" Faversham backed away as the banshee approached. He was sure she was looking straight at him, her face twisted in a rage that chilled him to the bone.

Jack stooped just as she reached them, her thighs crashed into his shoulder and as he rose, her body weight flipped her into a somersault, the steel bar flew from her hands, clattering away in the distance. She landed just behind him on her back, winded, breathing heavily but unharmed. Before she could scramble to her feet Jack was on her, his forearm bore down on her shoulders, pinning her where she lay.

"Friend!" He shouted at her as he stared into her angry eyes…It had no effect.

"Comrade!" He shouted, trying again to get her to understand.

Language was never one of Jack's fortes and he always thought at times like these that it might be a good idea to try and learn another language.

The blonde spat into his face, a massive gloop of hatred that covered his eyes, dripping down his cheek. He wiped what he could away with his free hand.

"For fuck's sake! Say something to her." Jack looked up at the professor who was watching the exchange with a morbid fascination.

"Oh yes..sorry...Of course." Bending over so that the girl's eyes flicked to his own, Faversham tried his winning smile, flashing his perfect veneers.

"Friend!" He shouted, slightly louder than Jack had at the start.

"What was that?..." Jack stared at the professor incredulously.

"... Talk to her in a language she'd understand...Jesus!"

The blonde began to struggle, trying to shake Jack off her. He needed both hands to keep her from striking him.

"Ah...I'm afraid I am not as fluent in their language as I'd like to be..."

The explosion ripped through the cavern, filling the air with a thick cloud of sand, dust and smoke.

Jack let the woman go and pushed Faversham towards the exit as he scrambled to his feet. Screams surrounded them as they ran past several women, some frozen to the spot, some hunched together, holding each other while others jumped back into the cages for protection.

The source of the blast became clear as the heat from the flaming truck just feet from the cavern entrance forced them to stay low and shuffle along the outer wall until clear of the gasoline fuelled furnace.

Battle raged across the plateau as Mitch and two of his men returned fire from behind the cover of rocks as machine gun fire penned them in. Volleys of bullets from the Kalashnikovs flashed from the upper caverns as the smugglers dug in to repel the invaders.

It took a while for his eyes to adjust from the dim light of the cavern to the midday sun as it burnt into the mountain, but once the pops and swirls cleared from his vision he was greeted with the sight of several bodies strewn across the ground, two of Mitch's crew amongst them, their blood soaked torsos showing they had been cut down as they ran for cover.

Across the plateau to the North West stood five quad bikes, the ATV's the Mossad agent had confirmed as their source of escape.

"Jack, do you read…For god's sake answer your goddam radio…" Sara's shouts bellowed into his ear causing him to wince.

"Ok, Sara, no need to shout…"

"Jesus fucking Christ! Jack…Where have you been?" Sara breathed a sigh of relief as she heard his deep voice berating her.

It may have only been a short time of radio silence, but several attempts at reaching him with no success had started to panic her.

"Stuck in a cavern…probably out of range. What's up?"

'What's up?' That was all he could say? What's up! She knew that they had encountered hostiles even without the gunfire that exploded through the speaker. But to Jack it was as if she had just called for a chat.

Her job was to serve and protect the field agents, but Jack was more than that, everyone knew it, apart from the man himself. She hated being girly, hated caring for him so much.

He was focused, she got that and as a former field agent herself she should know better. But it was impossible, even more so now they had met again, even for only a short while, it hit her harder than ever.

"Sara? Are you reading me?"

"Sorry Jack…Yes, I read you. I was thinking you might need a little help? It's getting lively down there by the looks of it." Sara's

screen was alive with green pips flashing randomly in a concentrated cluster.

She could make out Jack's blue pip flashing rhythmically to the eastern edge of the mountain range. His vital signs were strong which was encouraging, but he was static for far too long which was a sign that he had encountered a problem.

"You could say that, Sara. We have come across a smuggling ring with a cache of weapons large enough to equip a small army. We need to get to our transport but they have us pinned down. What do you have?"

"I can make out two at the edge of the plateau and you and one other to the East with a group of ten or so to the North East. Does that compute?"

Looking over to the North of his position he could see the young women congregating at the cavern's edge with Aya at the head trying to keep some form of control. One broke away from the group and ran towards the ATV's, seeing her chance to make a break for it. She was cut down as soon as she cleared the burning remnants of the truck. Several bullets pounded into her, lifting her off her feet, her lifeless body rolled and bumped back to the flames, igniting the corpse instantly.

"Whatever you have Sara, do it fast. Hostiles are in the North wall twenty foot or so up…coordinates are tricky from here…But we are all clear."

"Ok, Jack. Just remain in position for a few more minutes"

He knew he could rely on Sara. She would already have a contingency in place just in case.

From the plateau's edge the view seemed to fluctuate as the heat shimmered through the air, blurring the scenery as it flickered like a translucent flame. It then ripped apart as a black form came into view, propellors sending sand, dust and rock around the plateau floor.

.   .   .

The Sikorsky Black Hawk hovered above them, its nose facing North towards the cluster of caverns. The machine guns exploded into life sending .50 calibre shells into the stone and granite. The entrance to the upper caverns disintegrated sending chunks of granite, stone and mutilated smugglers into the ground below.

It was over in seconds, all sounds of gunfire replaced by the roar of the rotor blades as the sixty five foot helicopter moved onto the plateau, manoeuvring into position to land.

The side door opened allowing armed troops to leap out. Running with heads down until clear of the downforce, each soldier knelt in position with muzzles of their M16s trained on the cloud and debris to the north. As the last of the eight knelt, two peeled away and ran to the entrance of the lower caverns throwing stun grenades into the void. As they entered through the shield of smoke, two more soldiers ran to the edge of the cavern entrance, guns raised in support awaiting any escapees.

Jack pulled Faversham by the arm and approached the helicopter as the blades began to slow, the rhythmic whine filled the air as the engines slowed to a stop.

As the pilot exited the cockpit he removed his helmet, smoothing his red hair as best he could. After several sweeps he realised that the tufts were not about to be tamed, he would find a mirror on his return. Placing the helmet under his left arm he strode towards the two men.

"Jack Case, still causing trouble I see."

The handshake, hug and back slap showed Faversham the strong bond. He brightened up, this might work out after all.

"Josh, nice shooting. How are things back at Qara? Malik behaving himself?"

"It's as good as it can be. Malik has his village working together, but more have been quarantined. We have medics providing the vaccine, but the older villagers, particularly his father, are in a bad way. If something isn't done soon, I don't hold much hope."

"Well, we will know by tomorrow. Thanks for the assistance. Let me introduce Professor Faversham, our expert plague killer. Professor, this is Captain Josh Adams, one of the good guys."

Faversham looked at Jack quizzically as he shook the hand of the pilot. He wasn't too happy with the label of a plague killer. He was taking no responsibility for the success or failure of the quest.

"Ah, the elusive professor…You've had us running around all over the place. Hopefully you'll try and evade capture from now on."

Faversham was impressed by the Captain's smile. Perfect veneers, and dimples that appeared as he grinned. He would love them.

"I assure you Captain, I intend to remain glued to this man beside me."

"Good move professor, you are exhausting our resources. Come on, let's get everyone together and we'll drop you at Siwa."

"What…No…You can't. We need to head west from here. What we are looking for is not in Siwa."

The two LARA operatives looked at each other.

"But your…er…companion is in Siwa and she has the scroll." Adams was sure that his next flight was to the oasis.

"She has what!…What is she doing with the scroll?" This was news to Jack, and not good.

"I gave it to her." Faversham stood to his full height to try to show these military types the conviction of his action was justified.

The glare from Jack's ice blue eyes took inches off him instantly, he could feel himself shrinking by the minute.

"Oh, I'm so glad you have joined us on this trip, professor. Are there any more ways to screw up a mission or have you something else up your sleeve? Not only have we lost the scroll to whoever has kidnapped your girlfriend, but we now know that Mitch's demented ex is on her way to find her…"

"We need to get to Siwa." Mitch joined the group along with his two remaining men.

"We have to stop her getting her hands on the scroll. If I have this right, Nightly has to be at this Field of Reeds with the scroll to activate this cure, or something like that. All I know is that he has something that either triggers this thing or has to be with him at the right time…Without it we have no chance."

They all stared at Nightly's Head of Security in silence.

"Look, don't shoot the messenger…It's all I know. Listen, it's mumbo jumbo to me but we can't let the scroll get into the hands of my ex… That will screw it all up."

"Siwa it is then." Jack knew they had no choice.

"No!…We can't. We need to go west…That is where we need to be. I assure you."

Faversham was not having it. He knew where he needed to go, or at least had an idea of where they should go. He would not be turned.

"What are you talking about, professor? Without the scroll we are guessing and it's a hell of a landscape to guess in. Also your girl-friend could be in danger and the scroll could fall into the wrong hands. We need to go to Siwa…enough said."

"No Jack…Trust me. Tia will be fine, she will find the location and she will let me know..and she's not my…well not really…no she's not….she's not my girlfriend. But I trust she will find a way. I will take one of the quad bikes and head West….I will then be somewhere close to the area we should be at. Jack…trust me…if this is real and I think it is…we only have one chance to find it. And with or without your help…I will find it."

Jack was taken aback. The professor had finally shown some balls, although not in the way he thought.

He pictured the man relishing the role as knight in shining

armour, grinning with pride and perfect teeth as he rescued the damsel in distress. But it appeared that he was focused on the task ahead. He could see that he was sure the cure was in reach. Whether it was the archeologist in him or the fantasist wishing to discover the mystic world of the ancients, he couldn't be sure. But there was enough in the professor's conviction to give Jack food for thought.

"Well, I'm not letting you out of my sight. I can't trust that you won't disappear again…"

"I'll go with him."

Aya had left the group of women in the safe hands of the troops. She was more concerned with making sure the Field of Reeds was found for Gordon Nightly and would remain with the professor until it was uncovered.

"Well that's decided then. Mitch, you go to Siwa, find your ex and stop her from causing any more trouble. Find Tia Stirling and let us know where we should be heading. Here take this."

Jack passed an earpiece to Mitch.

"Keep it in at all times. Sara can keep an eye out for you if you need her assistance."

He had grown to believe that Mitch was similar to him, ex military with a job to do and they all shared a common goal, to rid the world of the plague. Anything else at this late stage would jeopardise the whole operation. No, Mitch was fine, he was sure that he would follow the plan.

Aya, however, was a different story. She had an agenda of her own and he needed her close.

"Siwa it is then. We'll drop you on the outskirts and return to sort this mess. Jack, take care my friend and good luck, all of you."

Captain Adams put on his helmet and turned to the Black Hawk, signalling for Mitch and his team to follow.

"Right, I guess we should make our way West."

Reaching the ATV's Jack chose one of the two seater buggies and packing a small bag of supplies, bread, fruit and water collected by Aya, beckoned for Faversham to get into the passenger seat. The professor accepted gratefully, he didn't fancy another trip on a quad bike.

Aya preferred a bike, which she mounted expertly, fired it up and headed West without a word. Reversing the buggy Jack took one last look at the destruction left behind. The truck was now just a black hulk of twisted metal, smoke billowing from the body, black shifting to grey before disappearing as it mixed with the blue of the cloudless sky.

The Black Hawk crew were assisting the captured women to leave the caverns, reassuring them that they were being transported to freedom. All of the remaining smugglers left alive were rounded up and made to sit in a circle guarded by the M16 rifles held by two vigilant soldiers alert to any false movement.

One of the smugglers kept his eye fixed on the buggy, watching intently as Jack manoeuvred the vehicle towards the exit.

He recognised him instantly as the Mossad agent Hakim... and he looked severely pissed off.

49

Gordon Nightly examined the tiny ceramic sun disc in the palm of his hand. The amulet stolen by Aya in the Manchester Museum, the puzzle piece to unlock his future. Running his fingers over the blue green disc, toying with the tiny hole in its centre, tracing his forefinger around the rectangular base feeling the tiny chips and blemishes, marvelling in the fact that for an artefact crafted over three thousand years ago, it was in remarkable condition. A condition that enabled it to be used as intended, perhaps preserved just for this very moment. He was to become the saviour, a new messiah. The man who saved the world.

The Gulfstream taxied into the hangar, the fuselage shimmering under the fluorescent lighting, leaving behind the diminishing light of Cairo International Airport as night began to close in.

Stacy finished her report on Nightly's meds as she pondered over whether to tell him the news from the lab. There was nothing she could do from here and the news wouldn't help his condition as it would worsen anyway over the coming days. Unless, of course, there really was a cure to be found somewhere in the desert.

All of the test cases had now died and the pathogen had altered to a level of robustness that produced too many multipliers within the PAMPs. It made recognising the innate immunity to create any form of treatment impossible. They had created a monster and it was taking over the world.

They expected the stabilising vaccine supplied world-wide would keep the bacterium at bay for at least two months. It would provide a small window to create a vaccine once Nightly had made his discovery at the Field of Reeds.

But it had already begun to claim lives within a week of the final vaccine, and the death rate was increasing daily.

As the door was set aside for them to disembark she watched Nightly walk slowly along the aisle. He was slow, deliberate and concentrating far too much in ensuring both feet propelled him forward. Had she not known better she would have thought he was under the influence.

"Are you feeling alright, Gordon? You don't look so good."

"Just tired, Stacy. It's been a hell of a task, but we will see the fruits of all our labours tomorrow. It will all be worth it."

She watched the thin line of blood trickle from his nostril and fumbled in her bag for a tissue.

"Oh dear." Nightly studied the red stain on the handkerchief, staring at it as if waiting for answers.

"Here, take a seat for a minute." Stacy cleared her files and offered him a seat next to her.

"My dear Stacy. I am dying, we know that. We also know that I am going to get worse as the night progresses into tomorrow. That does not mean that I am to be treated like an invalid, do you understand? You just need to ensure that I reach the Field of Reeds, from there I will do the rest. Now, get me off this damn plane and let's get on with our program."

～

Mel Blindt watched as Nightly descended from the Gulfstream. The scientist had aged considerably since the last time he saw him in

Boston. It was unsettling to see him with a handkerchief pressed against his nose and mouth, even more so when he began to cough sporadically.

It was last minute when he was asked to report to Cairo, apparently Mitch Dawson was causing concern according to Nightly's bitch, Aya. She was his favourite, an exotic beauty, but boy did she play on it. She was also a manipulator and it appeared that her influence was at play again. Her reports began to question Mitch's loyalty, his motives and his ability to lead the mission.

Utter bullshit! They served together in Afghanistan on several tours of duty and there is no-one you would rather have fighting by your side than Mitch Dawson. He was more concerned for the well being of his crew over and above his own, always leading from the front, never shirking responsibility.

Mel took the Khan assignment while Mitch took Egypt. It made sense as Mitch was head of the security team from the start of this mad adventure.

When he was brought in originally and told exactly what the job was, he would have run a million miles from it had it not been for Mitch. Who in their right mind would want to be associated with a madman who had unleashed a plague on the world without a cure, and all for personal gain?

He did it for his Sergeant, a loyalty that will last a lifetime, and also for his friend, a friend who was asking for his help.

Blindt became wary as Nightly approached, he could see the blood splatters on the handkerchief covering his mouth.

"Holy shit!" Mendez, part of his tactical team was by his side and instinctively crossed himself.

"Mendez, cut that out." It was only a whisper, but Blindt was horrified to hear it resonate clearly in the silence of the hangar.

"No…That's fine, Sergeant Blindt. I don't look myself at the moment as is quite obvious to all that know. I have the plague, I am dying, but I assure you that it is all but temporary. This time tomorrow evening we will be celebrating a new world, a world eradicated of disease and decay. A world that will thrive forever."

Nightly stood several feet away from his security detail but he could see the fear and uncertainty in the eyes of all six.

"Your role is to protect me until we reach Aaru, the Field of Reeds. Caelen Khan is a dangerous man, he has already tried to hinder us and I know he will not stop in his attempts to prevent me uncovering the secrets which will save our world from this terrible disease."

"One you started, you insane prick!" This time Mel kept his thoughts to himself.

Even though it galled him to assist this man, they really had no choice. By all accounts this nutter, through some hereditary anomaly, was the only person to activate whatever it was to create a cure. He had to do it for the sake of his men, his friend Mitch and more importantly for the sake of humanity.

"Now, there is one thing that I need to make you aware of that you may or may not agree with, but for the sake of everything we have worked so hard to achieve…It is imperative…" Standing before Mel, Nightly's eyes reddened with tiredness and disease, his pupils, flicking uncontrollably, focused as best they could on the Sergeant.

"It appears that Sergeant Dawson has become distracted and is making too many mistakes. I need you to remove him once we reach our destination, before any mistakes prove fatal to our cause…"

"…Whoa! Hang on. You want us to take out Mitch? Not gonna happen, Mr. Nightly…He's one of us." He thought they had been assigned to provide additional support, not this.

"Calm yourself, Sergeant. I am a reasonable man and Mitch has served me well from the beginning. I can only surmise that ghosts from his past have taken their toll. No, I just require you to keep him under guard until the end, keep him away from the Field of Reeds. As I have said, I am a reasonable man. You keep him under guard, he will be kept safe…If however you fail to restrain him then I will have no choice. Aya will be tasked with his execution."

"You deranged piece of shit...That's Mitch you're talking about... You won't..."

" Fisher...No! Get back." Mel grabbed the young soldier by the arm, forcing the pistol from his hand.

He pushed him back and mouthed 'leave it' directly into his face. Fisher was one of the new recruits Mitch had taken under his wing during early drills and exercises at the start of the recruitment process. He was already a capable soldier, but his aptitude and speed of delivery was way and above that of the others.

Fisher obviously felt he owed a loyalty to Mitch that included protecting his honour.

The click clack of rifles being racked echoed menacingly around the hangar as engineers, cleaners and other staff, who had been going about their business seemingly oblivious to the discussions, suddenly produced semi automatic machine guns, each trained on Mel's team.

"Gentlemen, gentlemen. There is no need for all of this when we are so close. My only interest is the safety and well being of every man, woman and child, which includes Mitch. I just need to take measures to ensure that nothing gets in our way, to ensure that destiny is in our own hands."

Nightly waved his hands in a shooing motion to his armed personnel, keeping his eyes on them as they lowered their weapons and slowly returned to their duties. His show of strength was more than enough to persuade his protection detail that he would not take kindly to dissent in the ranks.

"Now we have everything settled, can I suggest that we get some rest until we hear from Aya? I trust you will find the accommodation to your satisfaction. I have arranged for entertainment, food and refreshments. Please take the time to relax and consider your role in this life or death mission and the rewards that it will bring to us all."

. . .

As the limousine pulled away with Nightly and his nurse safely out of earshot, Mel turned to Fisher and the rest of his team.

"Come on lads, lets get some R and R, it's going to be a long day tomorrow. And don't take any notice of the boss's bullshit. We won't let Mitch down, if anything we need to neutralise that bitch, Aya."

50

F adi had yet again proved his worth.

Tia spent a little while composing herself after the encounter with the corrupt Siwa police and the crazy woman with the face. She replayed it over and over again in her mind and still made no sense of it.

Why had the woman given her the scroll when the whole reason for her abduction was to take it from her?

She knew there was another group looking for the scroll and wasn't surprised that they were likely to come up with some obstacles during their quest, but to have enough power to influence the police terrified her, she couldn't trust anybody.

After a call to the Grand Hyatt, the ever reliable Fadi just happened to have a cousin who worked at the Siwa Paradise Hotel and after some careful negotiation, which involved another several thousand Egyptian pounds, she was given a room and an account that more than covered her short stay.

Showered and refreshed she attempted to grab a few hours sleep before venturing out to the Temple of Amun. But every time she closed her eyes it wasn't long before the ravaged features of the woman who handed her the scroll came into her head. That ruined face with one eye barely fixed in its socket, drooping as if melting before her eyes.

. . .

"Your drink, madam." Tia jumped as Jelena placed the rum and coke on the table beside her lounger.

"Thank you, Jelena. Call me Tia, please. I have known your cousin Fadi for years now."

"Thank you, madam. But I am no relation of Fadi's. He calls everyone his cousin, brother, sister or any relation that fits the person he wants us to be. He thinks it helps in his business and gives comfort to the client by being embraced by his family. Fadi is a rogue, but as honest a rogue you will find in the whole of Egypt."

Tia had to agree with the description. He was a rogue and he was out for Fadi first and foremost. But with everything he did he tried his best to please and she definitely had no complaints so far, just an emptier purse.

"Here's the information you need to gain entrance into the Oracle." Jelena gave her a hand drawn map written on the hotel's headed paper.

In the lamplight of the pool area Tia was able to make out a meandering path leading to a plan view of an L shaped building.

"This will take you through the lower barriers at the southwest of the temple. There are only two guards but you are not likely to come across them as you will be shielded by the foliage that covers most of the abandoned village of Aghurmi." The waitress ran her finger around the map until stopping at the upper left square of the plan view of the building.

"This is the Temple of the Oracle, or what's left of it as it has crumbled and continues to suffer rock slides. You will need to be careful of your footing as most of the interior is full of rubble. You will need this as there are no lights." Jelena handed her a small halogen torch, not quite a maglite, but better than nothing. She was hampered by having all of her equipment confiscated during her capture, so was more than grateful for any assistance Fadi could provide.

. . .

It was a warm night and she had spent the last three hours by the hotel pool, an area enclosed by palms thick enough to provide total privacy. The blue lit pool along with the bright lamplights surrounding the paved courtyard illuminated the whole area. The full moon drifting along the dark skies, the only indication to the lateness of the hour.

She thought about Iggy, hoping that the professor had kept out of trouble and found a place to wait for her. She knew he wouldn't give up hope that she would be in contact. Similarly, she was sure that he was alive and waiting for her to communicate somehow.

But how to make contact would have to wait until she knew where they were headed.

She finished her drink, checked the scroll one last time, pocketed the map and torch and headed out towards Aghurmi and the Temple of Amun.

$\sim$

The palm groves were extremely dense, obliterating any light emanating from the full moon as it began to travel across the clear sky.

Mitch led the way with the help of the beam from the maglite held by Stratton as he and Hunt followed on behind.

Studying his watch to check the co-ordinates to Aghurmi given by LARA, the time read 23:40. They had less than twenty minutes to reach the temple if the professor was right and the Stirling girl had escaped.

If she hadn't then whoever had the scroll was in for a surprise as they would not be leaving the temple alive.

Peel and Bower had been old Afghan vets along with most of his carefully picked crew. Although he was their commander they were all comrades, brothers in arms, and irrespective of the circumstances of how they lost their lives, had Khan and his cronies not taken the professor from the airport in the first place, all of the men who started this mission would be alive today.

Once clear of the palms, the light from the moon lit the ground a ghostly white and the building's structures shone like grey statues in the foreground, rising on mounds of grey boulders, rocks and stones until the definition of the ruins of the Temple of Arun dominated the black skyline.

From a distance it appeared that a number of walls were missing and some of the few still standing had eroded to irregular shaped blocks. A tower stood to the North, the top tilting slightly as weather erosion and excavation had taken its toll.

Some of the rocks fell away as their boots tried to gain purchase during the climb. As each man stumbled, they held their positions for a minute or so, listening out for any activity before pushing on.

After what seemed an age, they reached the base of the temple walls. To the west a stepped pathway came into view leading to a wrought iron gate set within the stone walls.

Mitch spotted the light first, the flicker of a flash light fifty yards below the pathway. He signalled for his men to get down as he watched the beam get ever nearer, it then turned away from the path, heading north. Before the figure disappeared from view he caught the shine of a distinctly long pony tail as it swayed and bobbed, caught in a shaft of moonlight. It was Tia Stirling. The professor was right, she had managed to escape.

As they moved towards the path to follow, Mitch waved a warning and each man froze on the spot. Straining to see in the distance he scanned the foot of the pathway, sure that he saw another figure move north following the beam. It may have been a trick of the light, a shadow perhaps. Whatever it was, it disappeared as quickly as it appeared.

They descended the stepped pathway, being careful not to scrape sand and stone under their boots, as they followed Tia to the Temple of the Oracle.

51

J ack had to admit that Aya had proven her worth as he sipped the aromatic coffee. Before they left the smugglers camp she had ensured that there were enough supplies to sustain them during the wait. A period that would last for at least the next few hours.

The fire had been simple, there were enough dried shrubs, reeds and lichen to keep a flame burning for months.

But the coffee pot, water supply, fruit and sourdough was a stroke of genius. They found a small spring by a solitary palm tree surrounded by a rock formation that provided adequate seating. Not quite an oasis, but paradise in the circumstances.

"So professor, what are we likely to come up against when we find this Field of Reeds?"

He waited for Faversham to finish chewing a mouthful of dough which he washed down with a swig of coffee. The professor's face shimmered orange in the light of the fire, his blonde hair matching the licks of the flames as it swayed in the warm night breeze. Remarkably he had managed to keep his fedora which rested on one knee, the brim slightly dented and a crumpled crown, but still wearable.

. . .

"Well by all accounts, the Field of Reeds, or Aaru as it is called in the ancient tongue, is waiting at the end of the journey…"

As he began his explanation, Faversham returned the hat to his head, pinched the crown into a manageable shape and rubbed his thumb and forefinger around the brim to iron out any kinks. He then leant forward, rested his hands on his knees and like a teacher on a night away at camp, he continued his story…

"…The ancient Egyptians saw death not as the end, but rather a continuation of existence. They believed that the soul resided in the heart and if found worthy, you were allowed to enter the Field of Reeds, or the afterlife. You would be rewarded with a house by a lake, a field of eternal crops to harvest and be reunited with your loved ones, pets and any livestock that were in your possession or had died prior to your own death."

"Eternal life." Jack chipped in.

"Exactly. But before any of this, you would need to travel through Duat or the underworld, through a series of gates. It is said up to twenty one in some stories. Each gate is guarded by evil demons armed with knives, each guard has to be defeated before moving on to the next gate.

Should you survive the perils of Duat your heart would then be weighed on a giant scale against a feather. Souls that balanced the scales were allowed to enter the Field of Reeds and eternal life. Those whose hearts proved heavier than the feather were said to be heavy with evil and would fall into the crocodilian jaws of the demon Ammit and sent back to roam Duat for all eternity."

Jack sat for a moment looking at the professor who returned his gaze with a decided twinkle in his eye. Jack took another deep swig of the dark brew, swallowing loudly.

"And you believe this is what we are looking for?" Jack couldn't believe he was even asking the question.

"It is, and the scroll will show us the way." Aya joined the conversation.

Both men turned to her, partly because it was the first thing she had said since they arrived.

. . .

"The scroll is a genuine artefact of the Egyptians, said to be written at the time of the Book of Gates, The book of Caverns, The Amduat, the coffin texts and the Book of the Dead. It is a roadmap to Aaru, hidden for three thousand years, waiting for the purest of hearts to venture forth, waiting for Gordon Nightly."

Only the crackle of the fire broke through the silence that lasted a while as each digested what they'd heard.

Jack Case looked into the dark night sky, at the glowing full moon looking down on them as they contemplated the journey ahead.

With a deep sigh he returned his attention to the fire, watching as the tendrils of flame danced fiercely in front of him. He had never been a religious man and was indifferent to the hocus pocus of the scriptures that seemed designed to addle the brain. But after all he had heard, the reason they were here, and the saviour according to Aya, he could think of only one man to confide in.

"God help us."

52

The beam of the torch found the opening to the temple. Tia felt the exhilaration flow through her as she passed through a pile of rubble and according to her map, entered the second hall of the Temple of Amun.

She stood in awe as she shone the beam around the dilapidated structure, the crumbling floor and derelict, roofless hall.

A hall that was once in the presence of Alexander the Great in 331 BC, a temple he visited to consult the Oracle in order to seek confirmation that he was the son of Zeus, legitimate ruler of both Egypt and every other land he conquered. He needed to confirm that he was in fact, the god Amun.

Moving across the rubble she entered a larger area marked on the map, Sanctuary. Again the roof had long since disappeared, but some of the walls still intact caused her heart to beat a little faster. Two of the walls either side of her carried inscriptions highlighted by the light of the moon that cast its rays through the various rock slides and excavations, illuminating the intricate designs in every detail.

. . .

The first carving, that of King Amasis, in whose reign the temple was built and decorated in his honour, stood proudly to the right of the entrance. Although his head and part of his body had been chiselled out, the crown of the North still remained intact. The King's name was written inside a cartouche that still remained in every detail. On the east wall sat the god Amun along with the other gods, Amenre, Mut, Khonsu and Mahesa.

Tia followed each line of detail, sucking in the history of thousands of years. She smiled to herself as she realised that she was born to this life of adventure and treasure hunting. To her it was an addiction, more toxic than any drug. It fed on her need for more information, the need to know, to find out, the pleasure of discovery.

The Maglite exploded in front of her, the beam piercing her eyes causing her to instinctively duck to escape the light. She grabbed a fist sized rock and threw it in the direction of the torch.

"Ow! Jesus, Miss Stirling, do you always have to resort to violence whenever we meet?"

She recognised the voice of the American, the same voice from La Pacha back in Cairo.

"Mitch?" Tia shone her torch at the three armed men in front of her.

She recognised the stocky figure and rugged face of the American. He was flanked by two other military men each wielding a rifle.

She tried not to show the relief she felt that it wasn't the woman with the face, or anyone from the other side. She knew his connection to Nightly and Iggy's allegiance, which meant that they were on the same side.

"Are you with the professor?" She tried to look behind the three men but could only see a wall of darkness.

"No, but he is safe. In fact they are waiting for you to give them the co-ordinates. You still have the scroll I hope?"

"They? Who are they?" She was either missing something or being set up. She began to feel on edge.

"He's with Jack Case of LARA and one of our client's assistants. He's fine and looking forward to hearing from you. He had every faith that you had escaped."

She knew of Jack Case as he was at the airport when Iggy had been snatched and Mitch confirmed his client to be Gordon Nightly. But she was in the middle of an ancient ruin in the dead of night facing three armed men. She was unarmed and feeling particularly vulnerable.

Mitch's ear crackled into life…

"Sergeant Dawson, this is Sara. Pass me to the young lady would you. It might sound better coming from a woman."

Mitch instinctively put his finger to his ear as Sara's voice came through the earpiece. He had all but forgotten he was wearing it.

Taking it from his ear he wiped it on his shirt, being gentlemanly in his own way, before passing it to Tia.

"Someone wants to talk to you." He wasn't making introductions. Sara didn't sound like someone to argue with and he had given up being in charge a long time ago.

Tia held the tiny earpiece between her finger and thumb and placed it in her ear.

"Hello?"

"Miss Stirling, I am Sara Moon of LARA, Land and Air Reconnaissance Agency. We have been appointed by Sheikh Abdurrahman Rashid Bin Al Sharaf to escort the scroll in your possession to its destination and return it safely at the end of the mission. Jack Case, our lead agent, is tasked with this mission and is currently with Professor Ignatious Faversham to assist him and ensure the project's completion. I can assure you that the professor is perfectly safe and as Sergeant Dawson confirmed, he is waiting for your co-

*ordinates so that he can meet you at the location once it is revealed.
I can also help you with that."*

This was all too strange. While it was comforting to be offered
help and it all sounded legitimate, she was still aware of what had
gone before. She had learnt to be cautious over the years, particularly when dealing with priceless treasures and the avarice they
bring with them. She just needed to be sure.

"Sara, you may very well be who you say you are but you can't
blame me for asking for some proof. I'd like to ask you one question, a question that only the professor will know the answer to. Are
you able to do that for me?"

"Sure, fire away." Sara didn't hesitate. She would have done the
same thing, this girl was smart.

"Ok. What are the last two lines translated from the scroll?" It
was a question that only her and the professor knew, she was sure
of it.

*"Got it. Give me a minute and I'll get back to you. In the mean-
time Miss Stirling, please stay where you are. I can assure you that
Sergeant Dawson is there for your protection."*

The earpiece clicked as the call ended and Tia was left with the
three armed men for company.

"So, Mitch. Are you my knight in shining armour?"

She was beginning to feel more confident. Sara Moon sounded
convincing and she was willing to give her the benefit of the doubt
for now. It was clear that if Mitch wanted the scroll, he and his two
cohorts would have no difficulty in taking it from her.

"I wouldn't go that far. But we are here for your protection. As you
know, there are others after the scroll and they will stop at nothing
to get hold of it."

"Yes, I know what you mean. Like that crazy woman..."

"Gabrielle, you've come across her?"

Tia was surprised at how loud Mitch's question left his mouth.
His words echoed around the ancient halls.

. . .

"Oh, you know her?"

"Know her...He married her!" The guy to Mitch's right said snickering. His colleague tried to surpress his amusement and only succeeded in snorting loudly.

" Stratton! Zip it." Mitch turned to the comedian while punching the snorter in the arm.

"She's your wife? Wow, tell me more..." Tia always had time for a little intrigue, even in the most unusual circumstances.

"Ex wife and a long story. All I'll say is that behind all that beauty and charm lies a dangerous woman."

"Well, I'm afraid that she is now just extremely dangerous. I'm sorry Mitch but I think something has happened to her as she is heavily bandaged and part of her face has been severely damaged, possibly by a fire. But the weirdest thing of all is that she gave me the scroll which she took from the men who snatched me."

Mitch felt something in the pit of his stomach, as if he had just hurtled over the top of a rollercoaster, a jolt of pity perhaps, or something else?

He wondered how she had escaped the explosion back at the Bedouin camp. It now appeared that she hadn't. He wasn't sure how he was supposed to feel as they had been apart for so long now and for most of that time there was no love lost. But she was beautiful, there was no denying that, and she knew it. To lose her looks would be worse than death to her, and he had caused it. Again, he had ruined her life.

The silence that followed felt awkward to everyone in the sanctuary. Nobody spoke as they were at an impasse and no-one dared to say anymore.

To Tia's relief her ear crackled and Sara's voice broke the silence.

"OK, Miss Stirling. The last two lines of the translation are... 'The eyes of Ra will show the way, let light shed upon oneself...For the ripe and the righteous to shine.' Is that enough for you to trust us?"

Tia was relieved, it was all but impossible to gather that information without communicating with Iggy in such a short time…

"Oh, and Miss Stirling. Professor Faversham says that he hasn't forgotten the gold star he owes you. I assume that means something?"

Tia smiled and tried to stop the lump in her throat escape from her mouth as a gasp of relief.

"Yes…Thank you Sara. Tell him I will hold him to it. "

"Well I'm staying with you now Tia, so you will soon be able to tell him yourself. Now once you know the location I should be able to set co-ordinates for Mitch and pass them to Jack and the professor so that you can all lock on to the same position. I am ready when you are."

This is it. Tia could feel the exhilaration flow through her as she took the scroll from her pocket. A mystery kept safe for three thousand years and she was going to be the one to uncover it.

"We need to move into the temple next door and if we are right, the scroll will do its stuff."

Tia moved past Mitch and his team. Leaving the Sanctuary and turning right they entered the last room of the building, the Temple of the Oracle.

∿

The temple would have at one stage contained a roof, and had it not been for disintegration of the surrounding rock face, four walls.

Tia moved carefully over the rubble, reaching the centre of the room before the floor fell away and sloped precariously towards the edge of the hillside. Mitch followed behind.

"Stratton, stay outside and cover this room. Hunt, move back to the main hall and cover the entrances. If Gabrielle is out there, now is the time to ensure she gets nowhere near us."

Both men disappeared, leaving him alone with Tia.

"If you could do your thing as quickly as you can, Tia. Trust me when I say that Gabrielle is extremely dangerous and knows every trick in the book."

Looking through the northern wall, which had been all but destroyed apart from four rows of stone brick supported by crude buttresses to preserve it a while longer, she was faced with a sea of palms across the horizon, their dark fronds sharply pointed shadows in front of an indigo sky illuminated by the full moon.

The ghostly sphere hovered above the trees waiting as if for this very moment. Tia unfurled the scroll and holding it directly in front of her at arm's length, looked at the reverse side seeing the strange etching that resembled a stain, blacken and sharpen the edge as the illuminating rays flooded onto the parchment.

"What do you see?" Mitch's thoughts were on Gabrielle and he felt vulnerable, he needed to get away from the ruins and into more cover. She was close, he could tell. She would never have given the scroll to Tia had she not expected to receive the location. He was in no doubt that she had to be here.

"Wait…" Tia was deep in concentration.

She aligned the top edge of the etching with the tops of the palms, but however much she tried there seemed to be no match. Sweeping slowly from left to right, then from right to left slower still, she could not find a match.

"Shit…It doesn't work."

She turned the scroll around and read the words again, just to see if she had read it correctly, being careful to ensure the Hieroglyph was facing in the intended direction. The beam moved slowly from symbol to symbol.

. . .

' To the west of the Nile Delta, where the palms hold the moon.
    At the top of the noon sun, on the 19th day of Thuthi.
    After the night of the full moon, when the blind shall see.
    The eyes of Ra will show the way, let light shed upon oneself.
    For the ripe and the righteous to shine.'

What was she missing... Think girl! She was sure it was the right place...it had to be. They were at the Temple of Amun Ra, inside the Temple of the Oracle... 'Let light shed upon oneself?' That was the key.... It was the moon that shone the light.

She turned to Mitch to see if new eyes could help with the answer...Then she saw it...Luck was on their side. Had the Temple been totally destroyed they would never have solved the puzzle.

With no wall to the North it was impossible to know that the Temple of the Oracle had been on two levels. Above the American's head, against the wall leading into the Temple, was the line and remnants of the ceiling and a second level. The wall above the line was bathed in moonlight.

"Give me a leg up, I need your shoulders."

Mitch followed her gaze and realisation registered immediately. Cupping his hands he supported her weight as she climbed the wall with her hands. She planted her feet onto Mitch's shoulders and he backed into the wall until they were both resting their backs against the sand and stone. Tia held the reverse of the scroll in front of her.

Almost immediately she could see exactly what she had to do. The additional height had brought the moon closer to the top of the palms and the landscape of the horizon had altered to more of a wave that closely resembled the etching on the parchment. But the most significant find was something that neither she nor Iggy had noticed under normal light. The image of the eye of Ra appeared on the right of the page, perfectly detailed with a pupil that glimmered at its centre. It was a marker.

Tia's heart began to flutter as she carefully moved the parchment from right to left across the horizon. Half way along, the shaded lines joined as one, the horizon disappeared replaced by the parchment's image. The Eye of Ra glimmered as if pulsing on the scroll just below the top of the palms to the east.

"Found it!" She felt breathless as she called down to Mitch, her hands shaking as she struggled to keep the scroll still.

"Great. Point it out if you can and I'll try and get a reading."

It proved easier than she thought, as her arms were already extended, and the scroll held open as she released her right hand and aimed her forefinger at the eye. She moved the scroll away holding her arm still and looking down watched Mitch turn the outer ring on his watch face, twisting one of the dials. Happy, he pressed a button to set it.

"Got it... OK I've got 29° 45' N 25° 49' E. Can you see if Sara is able to narrow it down a little."

"I'm on it Tia...Give me a moment." Tia took hold of Mitch's raised hands and bending her knees, leapt from his shoulders. He caught her by the waist to prevent her falling into the rock strewn floor.

"Good job. Now let's get out of here. We can get a start and be away from here before we get a pinpoint."

They moved back into the second hall where Stratton was waiting for them.

"Go and get Hunt. We'll leave in the east corner, plenty of foliage and not such a steep incline."

Tia's ear crackled to life.

"Tia, I have the co-ordinates or as close as I can to pinpoint an area that seems most likely. The only significant brush anywhere along both axis that contains enough vegetation to show any signs of life is 29° 45' 3" N 25° 45' 12" E."

"I'm not sure that we are looking for vegetation, Sara. The Field of Reeds is at the end of the search. What makes you think this is where we should be heading?"

"Well, I got as close as the satellite image would allow and I

think you might want to check out the area anyway. As I said, there is enough vegetation surrounding a small body of water with what appears to be a pathway leading into its centre.

But more interesting is the shape.The foliage creates an almond with a circular body of water in its centre. The pathway curves away from the centre to the southwest. I've done a quick search and the closest image matching the shape is a hieroglyph.

It's in the shape of the Eye of Ra."

Tia could not contain her excitement as she gave the co-ordinates to Mitch, blurting them out in such a rush that it took her three attempts before he was able to program his watch to the correct setting.

"Mitch, over here." Stratton shouted through the darkness to the south. He headed towards the flicker of the Maglite in the distance.

Staying close behind, Tia had a distinct feeling that someone or something was in the hall with them. The crunch of their boots as they traversed the rubble reverberated around the walls making it difficult to separate sound. .

She stopped for an instant, but the sound of two sets of boots continued crunching over rocks only this time, as well as Mitch's ahead, she heard footfalls behind her.

As the hand covered her mouth she watched, eyes wide, as Mitch disappeared from view into the first hall through the crumpled doorway. She grabbed the hand trying to pull free, but her arm erupted in pain as she felt the blade slice into her forearm. She was held with such force that she could hardly breathe, let alone shout for help as she was dragged back into the darkness.

∽

Stratton greeted Mitch with nothing but a sombre stare. He didn't need to say anything, the beam from the Maglite spoke volumes.

Hunt's head, or what was left of it, was pressed into the blood soaked rubble at Stratton's feet. The crown was missing as if sliced apart, a slate tile resting only a foot away, its sharp edge stained red. The obvious culprit.

· · ·

"His gun, ammo and knife have gone." Was all Stratton could offer.

It was difficult for them as they both knew who had done this, but neither uttered a word.

Mitch closed his eyes. It was beginning to get to him, she was tormenting him and she was targeting everyone around him. She had to be stopped.

"Leave him Stratton, there is nothing we can do for him now. Tia, tell LARA to make sure he is cared for will you?"

He looked back at his fallen comrade...wondering if it was worth saying something, anything...but decided it was better to move him from here.

"Tia, get on to Sara would you."

He had expected, like him, she was unable to speak on finding Hunt in such a state. But she wasn't there, nowhere to be seen.

"Where's Tia?"

Stratton just shrugged. He only saw Mitch enter the room.

"Oh...Shit!"

Stratton watched as Mitch ran back to the north east quadrant vanishing through the hole in the wall. He looked back at Hunt. Twenty six years of age and the rest of his life to look forward to, until Nightly got his claws into them and his cheque book began to spew millions. First Peel and Bower back at the smugglers, now Hunt. When you knew the enemy it felt as if you were fighting and dying for the cause. This was different. Men were dying for the greed of a corporation, a long lost secret that may or may not exist and certain death if they failed. Looking back, he wished they had never heard of Gordon Nightly. He would have his bar in New York by now, watching the Nics, master of his own destiny. He crossed himself and followed Mitch into the darkness.

· · ·

Tia had disappeared. The second hall wasn't large and the only other two rooms, the Sanctuary and the Temple of the Oracle were even smaller. They searched, each sweeping their lights throughout. Nothing.

Stratton and Mitch met at the northeast corner by the exit down the hillside.

"Tia?"

It was loud enough for anyone in the vicinity to hear. Stratton swept the light behind them following the contours of the rectangular room, stopping at every hole, gap and doorway. The place was empty.

"Now what?" He held his gun at the ready, just in case.

Both men stood in silence, listening for the smallest sound, shining their torches throughout the hall yet again. Looking for the tiniest detail, straining their eyes to catch any movement. Crickets began their night calls creating a loud rhythmic chirrup that was difficult to mask out.

"Where the hell is she? She has the scroll and our only communication. She has…"

"Wait…Listen." Stratton gripped Mitch's shoulder to stop him speaking.

They listened again. In between the chirrups they could hear something, faint at first but as they got used to the crickets, clear enough to hear the name 'Mitch' in shrill tones.

Instinctively they moved to the hole in the wall that led out of the temple and down the dense hillside. Halfway down, the hill plateaued to form a ridge before it continued down to the palm grove. Tia was waving furiously at them, flicking her torch on and off. If she was trying morse code she had failed as neither man could translate. Mitch caught what he thought was 'bun' but other than that it was just a light flashing.

"How the hell did she get down there so quickly?"

Mitch cupped his hands around his mouth and shouted at the top of his voice.

"Hang on! We are on our way."

The three hundred foot scramble down the hillside wasn't as hard as they first thought, apart from a sore knee and a bruised elbow, but Tia hadn't fared so well. She had blood seeping from a cut on her forehead and her arm had three slice marks just below the elbow that covered her forearm in blood. She was wearing khaki shorts but her legs seemed to be unscathed. Her injuries hadn't impaired her too much on her descent.

"Jesus, what happened to you?" Mitch shone the beam over her head to look at the cut. Blood was seeping from a dark weal that had begun to swell. She winced as he pressed his thumb below it to stem the bleed. It seemed to help.

"It was Gabrielle. She came at me with a knife, caught me off balance and hit me with a rock. Next thing I know I'm slaloming down this hill."

Pulling out his shirt, Mitch used his knife to cut a four inch strip of fabric from the bottom. Ripping it clear he wove it around her arm, tightening it to stop the bleeding.

"It's temporary until we get to some water to bathe your arm, but it should stem the bleeding. We also need to get that head looked at..."

"I'm fine, let's get out of here before she comes after us." Tia looked back up towards the temple. She had the sense that they were being watched.

"I'd be surprised if she tried anything until we get nearer the location. That'll be her next strategy. She would have heard the co-ordinates when you gave them to me earlier, she's got a head start on us."

Tia's ear crackled.

"Tia get out of there. I have a heat signal in motion fifty feet above you and it's descending towards you."

"Come on, quickly! She's coming after us."

Mitch helped Tia over the plateau until her feet hit the steady gradient of the hillside that would take them to ground level.

"Stratton, get a move on."

Stratton was surveying the foliage above them, shining his Maglite over every scrub and bush. If he could catch any movement he will get the bitch before she got any closer.

The first blast from the M16 caught him just above the right knee, shattering bone, causing him to collapse on his good knee. The second shot thumped into his chest; blood, flesh and bullet exploded from his back and into the night air. The third smashed into his skull blowing the left side of his head clean from his shoulders. Stratton's lifeless body slumped forward, sand and dirt billowed all around it as it crashed into the ground.

"No!" Mitch screamed in anger and frustration as he watched the carnage unfold before his eyes.

Rooted to the spot, his brain failed to register his next move. Stratton was dead, but should he just leave him? Should he follow Tia? Make sure she gets to their destination safely? Or should he climb and take Gabrielle out, once and for all?

As the bullet ricocheted off a rock just a foot above his head, he made up his mind and turned to follow Tia down the shallow incline, first at a run until he was at a speed that allowed him to slide on his back and then using his boots as brakes, scrabbled downwards towards the palm grove below.

53

He felt like he was riding a jet ski as he hurtled down another dune and bounced at the bottom sending an explosion of sand into the air around them.

The halogen headlights seemed to transform the grey dunes into huge waves surrounding them in an endless sea.

As Faversham coughed deep raucous, grit filled splutters, Jack slowed a little to allow the buggy's four wheels to remain in contact with the desert floor.

"Sorry about that, professor. Won't be long now." He was actually enjoying himself. If he ever got any decent time at home in Marazion, he might have to look into getting one of these. The sand of Cornwall with an ideal stretch of beach would be exhilarating, and some of the dunes as well as Prussia Cove would prove a decent challenge.

"Don't worry, dear boy. Although we may need to go back for my stomach."

Faversham was holding his Fedora tightly on his head with one hand while gripping the seatbelt for dear life with the other.

. . .

Jack's PDA showed the location was no more than ten minutes away, they had made good time. He was relieved that they had made it, or at least the first part. During the past few days he was beginning to wonder if they would ever get here.

Sara filled him in on the trouble at the temple and that Mitch and Tia were heading this way, with Gabrielle in hot pursuit. He decided to let the professor know that Tia was on her way in the company of Mitch and that she was in good health. But he thought it best to leave their pursuer out of it, for now.

"So what exactly are we looking for, professor?"

Now he had slowed, the buggy's throaty roar dulled considerably allowing a reasonable, if slightly loud conversation.

"I haven't the slightest idea, Jack. If Duat exists then I would suspect an entrance of some kind and if it is indeed the underworld, one that is below ground."

As the ground began to rise, rocks appeared more frequently causing Jack to concentrate as he manoeuvred around them. He caught sight of Aya who, having chosen a trail bike, was having no trouble at all as she weaved in and out with perfect grace and balance.

As the terrain altered to just rock and vegetation, the climb became more treacherous. The buggy bumped and jostled along a trail of rubble, a natural path made from landslide and erosion. The deep tread of the tyres made short work of the climb and as they levelled off, the ground smoothed to a fine dust and brush.

Overhead the sky had turned a deep purple as night struggled to maintain control, the moon began to disappear to the northwest leaving the light coming from the east to cast an orange stain across their path.

Jack's PDA showed their vehicle as a green flashing light honing in on a flickering orange marker, positioned by Sara to indicate their target. They were getting close as the dots were all but merged. A red dot showed Aya, pulsing just behind them.

. . .

"Jack, you have company." Sara's voice came over his earpiece.

She was carefully monitoring the scene from the skies during this key part of the operation.

Checking the PDA he saw it immediately, a yellow dot entering from the southern edge. It was moving towards them at quite a pace.

"Brace yourself, professor. Things might get a little hairy."

He pumped the accelerator to the floor and aimed for the mountainous area ahead of them. Faversham just managed to grab the Fedora as it began to fly from his head, jamming it back in place and holding on for dear life.

Jack needed to find some cover, or at least have a mountain behind him. They had climbed two hundred feet above sea level onto a flat plain with a mountain range to the north and east. Massive boulders and scattered rock fragments smothered their bases, ideal protection if he could cover the few hundred yards before their visitors caught up with them.

They crashed through heavy brush and several reed clusters, one of which took Faversham's attention. He turned to face it, his body squirming to keep his eyes fixed on the area as Jack pulled away from it.

"Jack, stop! That's it…"

The buggy continued on, the engine screaming in protest as the tyres cut through the surface with ease.

"Jack…STOP!"

Faversham pulled on the handbrake, sending the vehicle into a slide. Jack cursed as he pushed the wheel into the skid and wrestled with it as the right side protested, he couldn't hit the foot brake for fear of the buggy toppling over and sending them somersaulting across the sand and gravel.

The boulders at the base of the mountainous backdrop came rushing towards them as Jack continued to ease the vehicle out of the slide. Feeling the tyres levelling out he risked a tap on the foot-brake. The buggy spun to the right, its rear wheels losing grip and beginning to lock up. He released the handbrake and thrust the foot-brake to the floor. Skidding to a stop the vehicle rocked from side to side as gravity and momentum took hold. Both men were jostled to a stop as their bucket seats rocked in sync with the buggy. They stared in silence as they faced back from where they came.

"What was that, you fucking idiot!" Jack bellowed at the professor.

"It's there…We've bloody found it." Faversham was oblivious to Jack's curses as he pulled his seat belt loose and began to lift himself from his seat.

Jack pulled him back down, holding his arm tighter than he should.

"Stay exactly where you are."

Faversham looked over to protest, but Jack wasn't looking at him. His eyes were facing forward.

The Airbus H175 Helicopter hovered over the clusters of brush and reeds sending the vegetation into a frenzy. Sand leapt from the floor transforming into a swirling dust cloud as the aircraft began to descend.

Aya still straddling the trail bike, sat in the downdraft watching patiently as it came in to land.

Checking his magazine, happy that it was full, Jack slid it back into his Glock. Engaging drive he let the buggy crawl forward in the direction of the chopper. He knew who they were about to meet, he just wasn't in any rush.

As the giant propellors of the forty six foot transporter slowed to a rhythmic whine, the side door glided effortlessly aside.

Ten black clad military personnel leapt from the aircraft and lined up, five on each side of the door, like a guard of honour.

Who was this guy? Jack quickly scanned the guards to get a heads up as the buggy moved into gun range.

They were a fully prepared tactical team. Each had an M16 assault rifle held across their chest and Beretta M9 pistols strapped to their legs. Their open stance showed that they were ready to move at a moments notice. For now they concentrated on the open cabin door.

First to exit was a woman in her thirties. Not really dressed for the desert, her neat black trousers and perfectly pressed white blouse, along with her slightly austere manner gave the impression of a PA who was not to be messed with. Jack gave a wry smile as he watched her glare at the unfortunate soldier who broke rank to offer help her disembark.

She turned and waited as the wizened old man slowly eased himself in a seated position, being careful to keep the handkerchief firmly against his mouth.

He was dressed from head to toe in khaki, a dress code suited to the wild life reserves of Africa. But the resemblance to a big game hunter stopped once past the clothing, he looked as if he was at death's door.

"Well I guess our Mr Nightly has become a victim of his own failure."

The guy had given himself the plague that was decimating the human race, a plague manufactured to ensure there was no cure. By looking at the madman as he eased himself to the floor supported by his PA, it didn't look as if he would last long if a cure wasn't found soon.

Aya dismounted and walked through the line of guards to greet Nightly with a hug. She kissed both cheeks before stepping back and nodding slightly in respect.

Then Jack remembered something. Not everyone was immune like Aya, some needed to take other precautions.

"How do you feel, professor?"

Faversham was watching the scene unfold in front of him. He couldn't take his eyes away from the man in khaki. The guys dark hair, although slightly thin at the front, belied the wizened, drawn, ageing face of the man it adorned.

"Better than him, that's for sure."

Jack took the box from his pocket, opened the clasp and offered the contents to Faversham.

"You should have taken this when I first found you back at the mountain. Let's just hope that you haven't been exposed to anything and this thing acts quickly."

It was the vial given to him by Mitch to provide a barrier to infection. Jack explained it to Faversham who took the vacuum delivery valve and injected himself without question. Jack was pleased that the professor had that amount of trust in him, because there would be occasions without a doubt over the next few hours that he will need to obey orders to the letter.

Jack parked twenty yards from the helicopter, now just a silent shadow against the lightening skies. Nightly began to walk towards them followed by his PA, flanked by his ten security guards. This guy thought a lot of himself obviously as it looked like a presidential procession or more likely, someone playing at Pharaoh. Jack felt he had it right with the latter.

Aya arrived by the buggy almost unnoticed, which was unnerving as he should have seen her peel off from the group and circle around to reach them. He needed to be more careful as she could have a knife to his throat before he even knew it.

"I need your vehicle." No please or may I? This girl needed to learn manners.

"Sorry, was that a request or an order?" Jack stared into her brown eyes, almost black in the light of dawn. She returned his glare unmoving.

"Forgive me, Mr Case. I asked Aya to find Mitch and Miss Stirling, and of course the scroll as without it we cannot continue. I assume we have your permission?"

It was said in a way that was clearly not a request. Aya had obviously briefed him on the current situation and he wasn't about to have a wasted journey. In fact, nobody could afford any mistakes.

"Sure, knock yourself out." Jack looked over to Nightly.

He was in range to put a bullet perfectly between his eyes and the more he looked at the man, the more his finger twitched.

"Do any of your goons have a radio?"

He watched as the prickle ran through Nightly's henchmen, some noticeably stiffened at the shoulder, a clear sign that he had hit a nerve.

One, the one closest to Nightly, threw the radio at him. He caught it one handed before it hit him on the chin. Good shot he had to admit.

"Sara, take this reading and program Mitch in for me would you." He turned a dial on the army issue handheld and pressed receive.

Sara got to work fast and by the time Jack handed the radio to Aya, an American preprogrammed voice came over the airwaves.

"Travel one mile south southwest…"

"There you go…you now have SatNav."

Aya gave him a suitably derogatory glance before jumping into the buggy, sending it skidding south southwest. Making short work of the flat plain, she disappeared into a large expanse of reeds, the engine protesting as it sped away.

"It's here."

Professor Faversham had been scanning the crop in front of them. Clusters of love grass, its small white flowers in full bloom dominated most of the vegetation in between numerous cacti and ryegrass, along with the dead looking Tamarisk shrubs that were as old as the desert itself. But it was the vast expanse of reeds that caught his attention.

"Jack, I think what you are looking for is one hundred yards to the west. There appears to be a line of brick or stonework, you can't miss it as it is surrounded by water."

Sara could see the grey line but the grainy satellite image wasn't sharp enough to distinguish the material, the fact it was a pathway however was undeniable. It had to be what they were looking for.

"Right, west it is. Come on." Jack moved through the love grass, heading towards the reeds to the west, with Faversham close behind.

Looking back at Nightly he beckoned for him to follow.

"You're not going to save the world standing there blowing your nose. Are you coming?"

Nightly removed the handkerchief from his mouth, ensuring the flow of blood had receded, wiping several times to clear any specks before replacing it in his pocket.

He didn't like Case, he was trouble. He would let Aya take care of him on her return.

With Stacy supporting him they moved gingerly amongst the vegetation and followed the trail to the cluster of reeds ahead of them.

54

She had taken the Hydrocone before the chase through the palm groves. Two or three tablets, she wasn't sure how many, but for now she didn't care. The pill bottle still rattled, so she had enough for more doses.

Gabrielle leant against a tree and sighed deeply as she withdrew the syringe. She needed a morphine top up as her face was on fire. The exertion of the chase had caused her heart to race at an alarming rate, the pulsing seared into her face at every beat.

Damn that pretty little bitch, she was stronger than her petite frame portrayed. She had her in the temple, had her firmly in her hands. The morphine gave her the strength of a superwoman, it should have been so easy. Once the location had been found she knew that the dead soldier would grab their attention, and Mitch being Mitch would be distracted enough for her to snatch the girl. It worked perfectly, she had her. All she needed to do was slit the girl's throat and grab the scroll. Three times she sliced and each time the girl's arm got in the way, even the hilt of her dagger across the temple didn't bring her down. She just ran and leapt through the hole in the wall, sliding down the hillside as if she was on skis.

. . .

Now she was knee deep in palm fronds and her quarry was getting away from her. After disposing of Mitch's other comrade, the coward decided to run for it and disappear with the girl into the grove.

She kept with them for a good while, but they always seemed to be one step ahead of her. The girl was hurting, not only from the cuts to her arm, she had caught her hard around the temple. There was sure to be an element of concussion or a serious headache at least.

They were heading on a steady path north north east so she had a good idea that if she stayed on route she will eventually catch them.

As the drugs began to flow through her bloodstream she felt invigorated both physically and mentally. She would catch them before the drugs wore off, she could feel it.

Leaping to her feet she held the M16 close to her chest as she powered through the trees.

~

Tia felt nauseous again for the third time, she was going to have to stop. Wrapping herself around the nearest tree she wretched, nothing came. Her head span and she could feel her stomach protesting yet again.

Had it not been for Sara in her ear she would have stopped for a while and perhaps slept. She was exhausted.

"Tia, you have to keep moving. She is closing in on you and any more delays will shorten the distance as she is moving fast. A vehicle is coming for you and is less than half a mile away, just ten more minutes and we should be able to get you away from there."

Mitch stood far enough away from her to avoid the straight arm smash he received the last time he tried to help her when she took ill. He was only trying to give support but soon realised that there are those who would rather barf unassisted.

. . .

"I think we should put a bit more space between us and Gabrielle. Shall we give it a go?"

Tia, head down, focused on a dead frond, its two points moving together slowly, she kept staring as she watched the leaf become one as her dizziness receded. Once she was sure the frond was staying in focus she looked over to Mitch. The concern on his face was probably a mix of her concussion and Gabrielle's pursuit.

She still found it hard to believe that he had been pitched against his ex wife in a life or death mission. She could tell that he was struggling with the concept himself, she really would like to learn more. If they survive this she would definitely arrange the drink they never quite shared in Cairo.

With hands on her hips she took several deep breaths, happy that the nausea had passed. She could feel the cuts on her arm which began to throb a little more than before.

"Guess we should get on our way then."

The light purple sky overhead made vision a little clearer, they could now make out the gaps in between the trees without the aide of a torch, less of a moving target. They could finally see an advantage, perhaps they would get away after all.

"Sara confirms that the vehicle they're sending is less than half a mile. We just need to keep on course."

She began to feel a little better as she controlled her breathing. In through the nose, out through the mouth in rhythm with her pace, which she was surprised to see had increased from last time.

Mitch checked his watch, they were there or thereabout on course...Then he heard it. It sounded like the buzz of a fly, until the gear change and as it neared it became the undeniable sound of an ATV.

He picked up the pace, overtaking Tia as he could see the welcome site of an open expanse of sand as the palm grove began to thin out.

. . .

Tia caught up with him as he stood at the edge of the grove looking at the halogen headlights of the buggy as they drew nearer.

It took a minute or two for the vehicle to reach them, causing some uneasiness as they both looked back warily into the darkness of the palms. Mitch held his gun at the ready just in case he caught any sign of movement.

Aya spun the wheel putting the buggy into a drift and slid expertly to a stop in front of them both.

"Come, we need to leave." Mitch hadn't missed her blunt matter of fact manner, but he had never been so happy and relieved to see her none the less.

The buggy was only a two seater and being a gentleman, he assisted Tia to sit next to Aya, providing a formal introduction as he helped buckle her in as she struggled with her injured arm. Aya barely nodded her head in greeting, choosing instead to look at the horizon, fixing the route in her head.

Mitch climbed in between the two seats to sit on the frame at the rear that housed the engine, the fuel tank pressed into his groin. Holding onto the roll bars for support he braced himself ready for the propulsion.

"Right, let's get outta here!"

The initial jolt nearly sent him back into the engine, but as the buggy picked up speed he settled a foot behind each seat and straightened to get ready to ride the bumps and crevices that he was sure Aya will fail to avoid. He just hoped the journey wouldn't be too long as his groin had already begun to numb.

Warm water splashed into his face from nowhere, he nearly lost his grip in surprise. The buggy noticeably slowed for a few seconds before picking up speed again giving him time to settle and wipe the moisture from his face.

. . .

"AYA, STOP!" He had to shout over the noise of the screaming engine.

She took no notice, instead choosing to floor the accelerator and speed on to their destination.

Aya's head bobbed slightly from side to side as she fought to keep it upright. She also struggled to hold the buggy straight as with only one hand on the wheel, the lack of power steering caused every bump and crevice to impact the direction and send them veering off course.

Tia, seeing the problem, grabbed the wheel with her good hand and helped to keep it from turning.

The buggy began to slow again, this time it continued to reduce speed. As they were almost at a dead stop Aya slumped forward onto the steering wheel, her feet free of the pedals as she drifted into unconsciousness.

The liquid that hit Mitch in the face wasn't water at all, it was blood. Blood from the shattered shoulder of Aya, part blown away by an M16.

"Holy crap. Aya!"

Mitch jumped from the rear and ran to the driver's seat. Aya was out cold, blood poured from her shoulder wound. Without a thought he ripped away his shirt and tearing it into three, rolled one piece into a ball and pressed it into Aya's shoulder. He wrapped the second strip over the ball of fabric and winding it around her underarm tied it off as tight as he could to stem the bleeding. The third strip he made into a sling to hold her arm to her chest to prevent movement as best he could.

"Can you drive this thing?" Tia nodded, leaving the vehicle and running around to help Mitch pull Aya free.

Carrying her to the passenger seat Mitch secured her with the belt, the blood had slowed to a trickle but they needed to get help quickly.

As he went to jump in the rear, a bullet pinged off of the steel roll bars. Looking back at the palm grove, Gabrielle was racking the rifle for another shot and began running towards them leaving the cover of the trees behind. She was no more than two hundred yards away.

"Drive!" Mitch screamed as he jumped on the back.

The buggy lurched, its wheels spinning as they fought for traction, dust spraying in their wake until treads filled with sand and gripping hungrily, accelerated away. Mitch leant forward, held on tight and closed his eyes, praying that he was not about to feel a bullet puncture his back.

The scream of the engine obliterated the scream of rage from Gabrielle as she pumped her legs at a sprint, watching in frustration as the buggy moved away, growing smaller and smaller, until it passed a mound of rocks and disappeared from sight.

55

Ignatious Faversham stood for a moment and studied the sight before him.

"Magnificent."

After walking through the shrub and love grass, the ground began to soften as moisture infiltrated the soil. The further they walked the damper it became until the ground became sodden and the vegetation began to thicken and thrive. They were soon facing a wall of reeds at least six feet high.

With the help of Nightly's men to clear the path to ease passage for their sick boss, they came to a meandering body of water. Large granite flagstones weaved through the water's centre, an elongated S of stone.

Faversham walked the length and back again, counting fifteen slabs in all.

"Well professor, is this what we are looking for?"

Jack watched as Faversham walked the path again, stopping occasionally to look into the water either side of the stone pathway, squinting into the thickets of reeds that ran along each edge, scratching his head and mumbling to himself as he thought of several theories.

He returned to the bank and turning back, looked at the meandering pathway a little more.

"Magnificent."

"Yes, I get that professor, but what does it mean? Is this what we are looking for?"

"I have no idea." And he meant it. Jack told him through Sara, that the satellite image resembled the Eye of Ra, which would have only been noticeable once the love grass had bloomed, so it made sense that it was designed to direct them to this point. But what they should do now was beyond him.

Gordon Nightly was watching intently, he had perked up a little since he first left the helicopter, the illness bearable for now.

"So, professor. What do we have here?" He was standing unaided a yard or two away. Both Faversham and Jack stepped back as they turned to face him, just to give themselves an additional foot or two of distance.

"I was just about to ask you the same thing, Mr. Nightly. I have no doubt we are supposed to be here, but I have no idea what comes next. Perhaps the scroll will help when Tia gets here. All fifteen stones appear the same, granite, rough hewn and no noticeable markings."

Jack had more pressing things on his mind after cutting the latest call from Sara.

"I assume we have medical supplies on the chopper?"

They all turned to the LARA agent, he didn't appear to be unwell.

"Aya has been wounded along with Tia and they both need medical attention. Aya is in a bad way apparently."

"NO! Not my Aya!" Nightly had to be held up as he seemed to lose it.

"We have to go…get the supplies..Stacy..you need to save her… save my Aya!"

Silence greeted his outburst. Stacy took him by the arm and helped him back through the reeds, although support was the last thing he needed as he was more leading her.

"What was all that about?" Faversham watched them disappear from view.

"No idea, but then again, what's new? Best to just go with the flow." Jack followed Nightly's crew who were all just as perplexed.

No one spoke another word as they made their way back to the helicopter.

$\approx$

Aya's shoulder was a mess. Once they removed her garments the true extent of the damage was clear to see. The deltoid muscle had been ripped away revealing the head of the humerus, the rotator cuff shattered rendering the arm useless.

All Jenson could do was to attach as much muscle as he could to the subscapularis to prevent movement, sewing as much of the skin that was left around the shoulder as tight as he could to immobilise the arm.

As a medic he had seen many wounds, conducted many repairs and operated in some of the most hazardous areas of Afghanistan to ensure that the mission was a success. Working in the back of the Helo within the confines of a hastily erected surgical tent was new even for him. But although it was as sterile as they could hope in the circumstances, she needed a hospital urgently.

.   .   .

"Out of the question. She needs to be with me. I will save her."
Nightly rejected the offer of transport to the nearest hospital.

"She may not last seven hours without treatment, sir." Jenson
may be part of Nightly's security team but he was a doctor first and
foremost.

"We have enough here to keep her alive for a few more hours.
Once we enter the field of reeds she will have no need for treatment,
she will be made whole again."

Aya was laid on a gurney, the only furniture in the helo available to
double as an operation table. Her right arm was strapped to her side
to avoid any movement from the shoulder. She was still under
general anaesthetic with tubes attached to her good arm to replenish
her system and help fight infection.

Jack could see that she was in a bad way and need more than a few
hours to recover.

"She needs better treatment than we can offer here. She's of no use
to anyone in this state and if you're right, that we have no more than
six and a half hours to find this reed field, we don't need anyone
who will slow us down."

With a strength that belied his illness Nightly pushed Stacy to
one side, grabbed an assault rifle from the hands of Beckett, who
like everyone else was subconsciously agreeing with the LARA
agent, and aimed the muzzle at Jack.

"NO! She goes with us, goes with me…she has to be by my side.
Do you understand? Nobody here is essential to the completion of
our quest more than myself and Aya. We are destined…you will
take us there…"

"Whoa, hold on a minute, Nightly. Put that gun down…this
won't solve a thing."

Jack took in his surroundings, the cabin of the H175 can
comfortably house eighteen people, but with a makeshift operating

theatre and nine rifles pointing in his direction, the cabin seemed surprisingly cramped.

"Stand easy men. Put those fucking guns down and remember who your commanding officer is." Mitch was angered at the way his team reacted.

Nightly may be the paymaster, but this was his team. Four of them lowered their guns almost immediately, the others hesitated as if undecided on the chain of command.

"You were their commanding officer Mitch, not anymore."

Mitch looked over to Mel Blindt, his second in command. Did he know about this? He was the only man not to raise his rifle. But by the look on his face and his struggle to avoid eye contact, there was more to this than met the eye.

"You are relieved of your duties, Mitch. I have instructed Mel to take command and you will be under house arrest until we return with the cure. I cannot have this ruined, we have come too far. I need to know that I have my people with me."

"You sonofabitch! You can't do this…" Mitch took a step towards Nightly.

This time Mel did raise his gun, but instead of pointing at his commanding officer he aimed it at Nightly.

"Not going to happen, Mr Nightly. Drop the gun, Mitch is our chief, not you." Everyone looked at each other as if waiting for the next move. The air was thick with tension as all eyes flicked around the group. The only one to try to shrink away from the situation was Beckett, who after letting Nightly take his rifle away from him, just wanted the ground to swallow him whole.

"Oh for goodness sake! Give me that…"

Stacy pulled the rifle from Nightly's hand with ease and threw it at Beckett, who caught it awkwardly, thankful that the safety was still on.

"…Look at us all. We have six hours to find what we are looking for and we are fighting over who's in charge. Pathetic!"

Nightly turned to Stacy ready to scream at her for countermanding him when a trickle of blood seeped from his nose. Scrabbling for his handkerchief he pushed it into his face to prevent any further embarrassment. All eyes were on him and his resolve crumbled. Backing away he slumped onto one of the passenger seats and bowed his head, pinching on his nose to help stem the blood.

" Come on Gordon, let's try and take it a little easier. You need to keep your strength for when we find the Field of Reeds, you know that."Stacy knelt in front of him and gently rubbed his leg as she spoke, trying to soothe him as best she could.

The disease was taking hold and she knew that any further treatment would have no effect. All she could do was to try and keep him as calm as she could to avoid any acceleration of the bacterium.

"I think they are right. Aya should be taken to a hospital, she needs specialist medical attention."

Nightly shook his head as he moved the fabric from his mouth.

"She has to come, Stacy. She is part of the ritual, part of me."

As their eyes met he could see the quizzical look in the young scientist's eyes. He had confided in her a lot over the past few years, particularly as the bacterium began to become unstable. But some things he kept within, even to his closest confidantes, and that included Aya.

"Aya is my daughter."

56

T he vibrant blue sky of the early morning brought with it a heat that foretold of a hot day ahead. Even though the sun hadn't risen to its fullest, Gabrielle could feel it warming the back of her neck as she trudged across the barren expanse of sand.

She focused on the rock strewn horizon, particularly on the cluster the jeep had driven behind, she was determined to catch up with them.

Had it not been for the reflection of steel flashing into her vision to the east, she would never have seen the distant blur of the vehicles kicking dust into the air as they sped towards her.

She didn't have time to mess around with pirates and she was certainly no tour guide, so whoever it was would be given short shrift. With any luck they would pass her by as her patience was at a level that was not worth testing.

She would all but explode if she felt she was being pursued. Nope, couldn't abide that.

She faced the vehicles as they drew nearer and sat cross legged with the M16 rested on her lap waiting for them to arrive.

· · ·

They were large SUV's, jet black with an expanse of chrome that glimmered in the morning sun. Two of them, identical blacked out windows, highly polished and apart from the crackle of the tyres as they ripped through the sand, silent except for a slight whoosh as the electrically powered engines carried the enormous chassis' toward her.

As the first approached and slowed feet away, the rear doors slid aside and two soldiers leapt from the vehicle. They wore tactical black, their heads covered by balaclavas with slits for eyes. They were heavily armed with bullet and M67 baseball grenade belts criss crossing their torsos. They trained black kalashnikovs on her as they approached.

If they were expecting her to panic, show fear or grovel in front of them in surrender they would be sorely disappointed. She looked at the men as they approached and started to laugh.

" I can't see your dicks from here but I guess they are tiny if you need all that ammo to impress the ladies." She remained seated with her gun still rested in her lap, her finger close to the trigger.

"On your feet." One of them barked at her, his muzzle pointed at her head.

"Fuck you! You drop your weapon or your comrade will never have children."

His comrade looked at the muzzle of Gabrielle's M16 pointing directly at his crutch and took a step back.

"One more step and it's bye bye pee wee." He froze and looked at his colleague.

"Now now Gabrielle, play nice..." Caelen Khan had exited the second vehicle and stood a yard or two in front of her, two more of his tactical team by his side, their rifles trained on her body.

" Wow Caelen, even in the desert you dress to impress."

He wore an open necked short sleeved black tee shirt, perfectly tailored and untucked over expensive dark blue jeans, boot cut over sand coloured combat boots. His immaculately styled black hair against his light coffee skin along with the carefully crafted stubble made it look as if he'd just walked from a photo shoot.

His brown eyes had an element of sadness in them as he looked down at her.

"Oh my goodness, Gabrielle. What have they done to you?" He tried to disguise his revulsion at the mess of the face of a woman he had always found stunning in both looks and demeanour.

But now, apart from the section of blonde hair with the distinctive red flash, her disfigurement made her unrecognisable.

"Well this…" She pointed at her face.

"…was from a grenade. Made a right mess as you can see. But it was in my face, not behind my back where I had no chance to defend myself. But I'm resilient, Caelen and I'll finish the job, however many people you send to bring me down."

Her good eye focussed on Khan. The other one still worked, but she found it a strain to keep it focused on one spot.

He shook his head slowly and clasped his hands together, holding them in front of his groin. A stance he tended to prefer when he liked to make a point. His thumbs pointed outwards, moving in time with his voice.

"That was not the case, Gabrielle. I was providing you with some support as it was running away from us. You were in need of back up…they destroyed us at the Qara camp…"

"And I was doing something about it. Villin and that fool Maloof were screwing it up for you…They hadn't a clue. The girl needed to have the scroll to find the location and once she had it, I would be there to take it from her…"

"…and how did that go?" She had fallen into his trap, his voice said as much, full of condescension, making the most of her slip.

"Fuck you, Caelen. Had you not done the big production at the beginning and just forced the professor to show us the location we wouldn't be in this situation…"

She could feel her temperature rise and the venom course

through her veins, her finger tightened on the trigger, she was not going to be taken for a fool, not after everything she had suffered.

"Look, Gabrielle. Let us discuss this on the way. We now know where they are, thanks to you. Nightly has landed a helicopter just over the ridge a mile away, let's get this finished shall we?"

Gabrielle put her rifle in the sand alongside her and held both arms towards the two gunmen.

"Help me up, boys....As you can see. I am in need of support."

As the two men helped her up, a third moved behind and swept up the rifle, pulling the magazine free and racking the active shell away from the chamber. He nodded to Khan once it was empty.

"You travel in the first vehicle, Gabrielle and we will meet you there."

Khan and his two guards moved past the first vehicle as one of the two gunmen tasked with escorting Gabrielle climbed into the SUV and held a hand out to help her.

"No thank you. I think I'll be safer where I am...In fact..."

She paced backwards and rotated her forefingers in the air...smiling.

Spinning around her fingers were two large rings, safety pins from a grenade she had taken from each man as they helped support her.

Six seconds was hardly enough time for the gunman to look down at his torso to see if one of the safeties were missing from his cache.

The vehicle erupted, lifting off the floor as the explosion ripped through the interior, tearing the unfortunate man's body to smithereens and with it igniting the other five grenades strapped to him. More explosions erupted inside as each occupant already seated in the SUV had their own ammunition explode on them.

Engulfed in flames the burning vehicle began to roll, a misshapen ball as each explosion propelled it further away.

The second gunman just burst apart in a red puff of smoke taking with him the man tasked with collecting her weapon. The air filled with a damp spray of blood which felt to those in its path like a fine mist of rain with a slight metallic smell.

Khan and his men looked on aghast at the scene in front of them which gave Gabrielle ample time to take the pistol tucked behind her and send a bullet into the heads of each balaclava clad guard. Keeping her pistol arm extended she strode purposely towards Caelen, pushing the barrel into his temple.

"Shall we go?"

Pushing the barrel harder into his skin, Khan stumbled towards the remaining SUV clambering awkwardly into one of the bench seats followed closely by Gabrielle who looked around at the bemused faces of the eight military personnel staring at her misshapen face.

"If any of you have any ideas of preventing us from reaching our destination, I'd be very careful before you make any moves." In her other hand she held up the M67 grenade for all to see. The safety clip had been removed.

"Shall we get a move on, driver?"

The SUV moved on, being careful to avoid any lumps or bumps in the terrain. Just in case.

‘ To the west of the Nile Delta, where the palms hold the moon.
        At the top of the noon sun, on the 19th day of Thuthi.
    After the night of the full moon, when the blind shall see
    The eyes of Ra will show the way, let light shed upon oneself
    For the ripe and the righteous to shine’

Tia read and reread, out loud, in her head and out loud again and again.

"What are we missing?" She sat by the bank near the flagstones after she, Iggy and Jack Case left the others to digest Nightly's revelation back at the helicopter.

She had escaped with minor lacerations, only requiring five stitches on the worst of Gabrielle's knife attacks to her arm. She felt guilty as Jenson took a lot of care in treating her minor wounds before tackling Aya's catastrophic injury. Thankfully it took little more than ten minutes to stitch, dress and administer a painkiller.

Jack sat alone looking at the water as a slight breeze rippled through its surface. He was still trying to work out how Nightly had been able to keep his paternity away from Aya all her life. According to Sara, hospital records showed that she was born of Egyptian parents Anipe and Cepos in the coastal town of Idku. Although according to record, the father, Cepos, died shortly after her birth. But that was where the records ended, no death certificate, no place of rest, nothing.

"But listen to this, Jack..." Sara was nothing if not thorough.

"...the name Anipe means 'daughter of the Nile River' and Cepos literally means 'Pharaoh'. Quite a coincidence, huh?"

More than a coincidence. Carefully planned, a lifetime to get to this moment in time. To this exact location, with the people who were supposed to be here. He couldn't imagine a world where just one moment in time could dictate a life, could possess someone to endanger the world for a dream, a myth where your whole life and the life of everyone on the earth relied on that myth becoming a reality. Utter madness.

"Any ideas, Jack?" Faversham slapped his foot to bring him into the conversation.

"This is your area of expertise I'm afraid, prof. I struggle on Sudoku from the start. Can you not break it down like a puzzle. You know, start at the corners and work from there, or something like that?"

"Tried that..." Faversham could tell that Jack's thoughts were elsewhere, so he decided to recount their musings. It might help them to include a third perspective, however inexperienced.

"We are to the West of the Nile and the palms holding the moon directed us to this location. Today is the 19th Day of Thuthi and we know that we need to be in position at midday. Last night was the full moon and the eyes of Ra, or the oracle enabled us to see the path to this location. So it just needs us to understand the last two sections... 'Let light shine upon oneself' and 'for the ripe and right-eous to shine'. It is here right in front of us but I can't see it."

"Ok...so for something to shine could mean to succeed...does that mean something?" Jack tried his best to participate but he wasn't sure if his brain was as highly tuned to ancient riddles as the two archaeologists in front of him.

"Probably. Being ripe and righteous also means something but it all seems out of our reach. We are missing something, something obvious...But what?"

Jack looked at the line of flagstones winding its way through the water.

"And this path leads nowhere? Is there any relevance to the stone used? The size of them? Or the way they are laid?"

Faversham again shook his head as he continued to study the scroll.

"What about fifteen? The number of stones in the water...is fifteen relevant?" He was beginning to feel as if there were no answers as he watched Tia shake her head.

"No. Numerology was part of the Egyptian way of life...either sacred, holy or magical but there were only four significant numbers. The numbers Two, Three, Four and..."

Both Faversham and Tia looked at each other before shouting in unison...

"...SEVEN!"

Faversham jumped to his feet and looked Jack up and down.

"Yes, perfect...Come with me."

The professor jumped onto the first of the flagstones and counting forward reached the ninth slab. He turned to face Jack who was still standing on the edge of the bank, staring at him. What had just happened?

Tia explained as Jack began to follow Faversham along the path.

"Seven is the symbol of perfection, effectiveness and completeness. The symbol for water is seven zigzag lines, similar to the shape made by these stones. Ripe is the completion of a process and right-eous is seen as religious perfection. In other words, for the complete and perfect to shine. Seven is the key to this little puzzle. You need to stand on the seventh flagstone from the south and Iggy is on the seventh from the north. If we are right, we should find what we are looking for."

Tia walked behind Jack as they stepped onto each stone. Once

Jack reached the sixth, Tia remained where she was and waited for Jack to step onto the seventh flagstone.

"Come on old boy. Let's see what this is all about, shall we?"

Faversham smiled as the LARA agent stepped onto the seventh stone, but inwardly he held his breath. He had no idea what to expect.

Both men stood still, looking at each other either for support or for answers. No one spoke as time seemed to freeze. Nothing happened.

Jack looked at the professor, awaiting instructions. What should they do next? Should he jump up and down? Stamp on the stone? Incant some form of ritual spell?

He heard Tia gasp behind him at the same time as he felt the cold rush of water fill his boots. He was sinking.

"You've done it!" Tia's shout of excitement sounded above his head and to his surprise the eighth flagstone in front of him had moved up to just below his knees.

In fact Jack and Faversham were both sinking into the earth, so smoothly that they hardly noticed the movement. As all of the other stones remained in place, their stones slowly began to descend into the earth. The surrounding water began to reduce as they slowly sank, sucking through a void beneath the eighth stone as more granite became exposed, it was as if they were lifting it.

Within minutes the water disappeared leaving a bog containing fifteen tall pillars.

"Very clever."

The professor was studying the stones he and Jack were perched on. The bases of each were wedged, carefully crafted to cut into the eighth stone in front of them. As the two stones were depressed in unison they lifted the eighth, levering a section of it up, which had acted as a stopper for the stream.

As both men moved from their flagstones and dropped into the sodden earth, the stones held fast, interlocked into the base of the eighth stone.

"Here give me a hand, would you?" Faversham put both hands onto the supported stone and gestured for Jack to stand alongside him to do the same.

"After three…One…Two…Three!"

Both men pushed, putting all of their weight against the granite just above where all three stones interlocked, beyond a thick line that appeared to be cut into the stone, a line that allowed the water to seep through. It moved slightly as they pushed, putting their shoulders through immense strain as they continued to add pressure. Digging their heels into the earth to gain traction, it started to move freely. The top of the stone fell away and thumped into the mud.

"Oh my god!" Tia gasped as she looked into a perfect square hole left in the stone. It was at least a metre square, the interior wall smooth and highly polished like marble. Descending into the darkness was a smooth set of marble stairs.

"Duat." Professor Faversham could barely believe what he was seeing. They had found it.

58

Ignatious Faversham couldn't take his eyes from the walls of the elongated chamber they entered once they descended the polished marble steps.

Markings, hieratic text, etchings and paintings adorned every inch of the walls that stretched forty yards before them.

Amber light illuminated from the ceiling as the sun pierced through the base of each flagstone pillar above them. It created a fiery iridescence that flickered with bursts of orange, red and yellow as they caught rays from different angles.

Two wide gullies at the base of each wall glimmered with water from the stream released by the eighth stone above ground and finishing at a small pool at the end of the corridor. Jack was knee deep in water, running his fingers around the bottom of a vast circular engraving, convinced that it was a door of some kind. It had to be a door otherwise the underworld comprised of a fifty metre hallway full of pictures.

"My, my..." Faversham pulled off his glasses, pushed them back on again, pulling them off once again as he studied the various inscriptions.

"As should be expected, a lot of depictions of Osiris and the weighing of the heart. Bearing in mind he was the Lord of the

Underworld and Judge of the Dead, it's no surprise. But the depiction of Set usurping the throne, Isis restoring her husband's body and the birth of their son Horus, here in such detail, makes it the more remarkable."

Jack was pushing his Kabar through the groove surrounding the circle in the sandstone wall, the blade passed into it with no resistance, there was definitely something on the other side.

"So what makes it so remarkable, prof? I thought this was supposed to be what it was all about?"

"Yes it is..." Tia was looking at other portions of the walls that were full of similar depictions.

"But I also have images of Anubis, the Egyptian death god wearing the head of the jackal, preparing a mummified corpse for its journey. What makes this all the more remarkable is that there is no official Egyptian source to give a full account of the story of Osiris. It was only ever translated from Greek and Roman writings..."

"...and this is very much Egyptian text." Jack was feeling like a student of Archeology as Faversham continued from where Tia left off. They jointly relished their discovery.

"Which means that this is either an elaborate hoax..."

"It is most definitely real..." Jack was cut off mid sentence... Gordon Nightly appeared on the marble steps supported by Stacy on one side and Mitch on the other.

"This is what we have been looking for, Duat. The underworld of the Pharaohs."

The ancient chamber began to fill up as Nightly, Mitch and Stacy were joined by Mel Blindt and three of his men, followed closely by the medic Jenson carefully negotiating the steps with a colleague as they retracted the wheels of the gurney to push Aya onto the marble floor.

. . .

"Welcome to the party. But I think it unwise for us all to go on this trip, don't you?" Jack was looking at Aya first and foremost, but Nightly wasn't looking too clever either.

"You are talking about the trials, Mr Case. Twelve perhaps fifteen in all and I agree with you, we can't all participate in the trials as we do not know what they are, or what they entail. But I need to be there with Aya once we uncover the Field of Reeds, or all will be lost."

Before Nightly could continue, Jack's ear crackled into life.

"Ja...Do y...ead. Jac...c...oo...hear...e..over" Sara's voice crackled before crumbling into static.

The signal was failing and he knew that as they progressed it would die completely.

Leaving his inspection of the circular doorway he climbed the stairs, leaving Nightly and his entourage to look at the blue sky above in silence as he disappeared from view.

"Sara, what have you got?" The static disappeared as Sara came through loud and clear.

"You have activity to the southwest. Two explosions and an SUV on its way to your location. I have a feeling the Millson woman is still on your trail and has collected some back up on the way."

Damn! They will need to concentrate on the task ahead as time was racing toward midday. He had to mobilise some help or they could be in trouble.

"Where's Adams, Sara? He must have finished with the smugglers by now." Captain Josh Adams was the closest to them and if he could get a team together they could at least cover their backs for a while.

"I'll sort it, Jack. But I'm not sure how to let you know, I can't get a fix on you. As soon as you move underground you disappear."

"It'll be tricky for the next couple of hours I can see that. But keep an eye over the area Sara, I'll try and get a signal to you somehow."

She had no idea how, but he would think of something, he always did.

"I'll monitor the square mile around you and we'll have support on the ground by the time you are ready to re surface. This has to work, Jack, deaths are escalating at an alarming rate, the World Health Organisation have no answers, everyone has all but given up hope."

"If the cure's here we'll find it. I'll catch you on the other side, just make sure Adams is briefed and ready when we need him."

"Will do...and Jack...Be careful, you are dealing with the unknown and that's not just the Field of Reeds thing. Nightly is not one to be trusted, watch your back." God, she hated saying goodbye.

One day it could be forever and every time she thought it, she hoped upon hope, this wasn't that time.

59

I t wasted twenty minutes, but hopefully offered an hour's delay to any pursuers.

Jack, Mitch and Mel pushed the top of the eighth stone back into place trapping them inside the chamber. The rest of Nightly's security team working from the surface, ensured that the seams matched to disguise the entrance as best they could, adding mud from the damp ground to weather the stone, hiding any cracks. Scoring the other surrounding pillars with picks and shovels uncovered from the maintenance cupboard of the Helo, ensured the rest of the pillars looked identical. They were unable to do anything with the recessed stones, but were hopeful that it would add enough confusion to add further delays.

"Right, I guess we need to get a move on." Jack checked his watch as he descended the marble stairs. 7:50AM, just over four hours to go.

There were now nine of them trapped inside the chamber. It was decided that Jenson remained with Aya to continue to treat her as best he could with the equipment retrieved from the Helo. The small PP-50 generator gave enough from its fifty watts to power the monitors, intravenous pumps and lighting, and with seventy two hours of power from one gas canister, there was more than enough to ensure Aya remained alive at least.

Nightly remained behind with Stacy until the rest had cleared a path to their destination, if one existed. It was obvious he would not make any arduous journey and with the current mood amongst the group, it was best if he kept away until absolutely necessary. Stacy had several vials of the temporary vaccine in a portacase, which each person administered, even Nightly. It was felt that he had received the maximum dose but for the next few hours it would do no harm.

"Ok. Any ideas? We need to get through that wall. That is definitely a doorway of some kind but I haven't been able to locate an opening or any mechanism or handle to open it."

"It's the water…" Faversham spoke in such a way that everyone should have known that already.

"…Pharaohs were crafted boats when laid to rest and positioned in their burial chamber for the journey through the underworld. It is said that the ferryman of the gods, a creature with eyes on the back of his head, was the only person allowed to pass through the twelve gates of hell, either by being asked or being threatened."

"And we are supposed to believe this bullshit?" Mel looked at the group waiting for someone to concur, no one did.

"Well, by all accounts the underworld or to be true to the texts, the netherworld, was said to be a great river in the sky. But I must surmise that as our own bible has proven, by being written by thousands of people of learning throughout the centuries, things can be open to interpretation. So, as I said from the beginning, we need to look to the water."

Faversham moved to the end of the chamber and dropped into the shallow pool that ebbed slowly from the wall containing the circular door. Bending forward to look through its surface he tried to find anything that could act as a latch, or any imperfection that could be manipulated or poked. But he found nothing.

Jack and Mitch went to the gullies either side of the pool, not really knowing what they were looking for, hands submerged feeling around for something that might help.

"Is this anything, professor?" Mitch's hand was still in the gully feeling a slight circular indent on the bottom, close to the wall.

Jack positioned himself opposite Mitch and placed his hand in a similar position and felt a circular indent at the base of his gully.

"I have one too...a small circular disc on the base. Give it a push."

Both Jack and Mitch straightened their arms and with their hands clenched in a fist, pushed down hard. The theory was that similar to uncovering the entrance above, they could activate something in unison.

Nothing happened.

"Ah, I see...of course..." Faversham moved to the pool's centre as he grasped the intricacies of the door's secret.

"The Egyptians were master engineers as most of the architecture they left behind proves. It is thought that they used water in a number of their constructions, in particular the pyramids, and created several mechanisms using water as a source of power. They also created the first pin-tumbler locks, fascinating deadbolts, but rather cumbersome at two feet in length. Only really useful for gigantic doors."

He looked up at the vast disc cut into the wall in front of them. Looking down, he moved a foot from his current position and waited for the water to settle around him, giving him a clearer view of his feet.

"Ok chaps. Try again, would you."

Both men straightened their arms, clenched their fists and pushed into the discs. Faversham's body dropped a further foot into the pool as the disc he was standing on sank into the ground. At the same time, Jack and Mitch's fists sank further into the gully as their discs sank a few inches.

Water began to pour through the openings made through the depressed discs, the floor vibrated as the walls began to shudder. All three men leapt away from the water, moving back onto the solid floor of the chamber and watching as the monstrous disc sank into the wall in front of them. As the last of the water sucked away through the sink holes, the disc rolled away from sight leaving behind a large dark circular hole.

"Well, it appears that it was a door after all."

The professor left the rest of the group staring in awe. He made his way through the empty pool and onto the lip of the opening to look inside.

~

The strange blue luminescence that greeted them as they stepped into the chamber was an ominous sight. The water had escaped through the first chamber into three gullies, two at the base of each wall to the west and east and one directly along its centre. The sound of rushing water filled the chamber as it raced along each gully, bubbling with energy as it was propelled along.

"Why is this glowing?" Mitch was on a ledge just inside the chamber, surveying the empty room and the bright blue sheen that emanated around the walls.

"Well it appears that the waterways are made of some form of crystal. Maybe calcite although that is normally clear. But depending on the mineral deposits within the compound it could very well glow blue, yes. The water also adds to the colouration and by the way that its moving it looks like it is serving a purpose to activate or propel something. As I said before, the Egyptians often used water for mechanisation."

. . .

Faversham was studying the images on the walls, more indications of the trip through the underworld. One wall was solely focused on the weighing of the heart, with Osiris seated on the throne with the other deites Anubis, Ammut, Henefer, Maat, and Thoth greeting a subject in the afterlife, the heart being weighed against the feather of Maat.

Even in the weird fluorescent glow, the detail was remarkable.

"Can you see anything?" Jack was surveying the three gullies to see if he could see any more submerged discs, but from where he stood he couldn't see past the blue ripples of the water's surface as it continued to flow along the tracks.

"We need to be careful, these empty caverns are never what they seem. And don't forget the underworld is a land full of gods, demons and monsters, many of which were out to kill the soul that tried to pass through each chamber. It will try and stop us every step of the way."

Tia was alongside the professor, studying the flagstones crossing the floor to a ledge on the other side, obviously the ledge with the exit awaiting them.

"And you believe all of that bollocks do you?" Mel was already off of the ledge and standing on the flagstone floor of the chamber. His M16 cocked and ready to go.

"Hang on, Mel. Let's wait for our experts to come up with something. We have no idea what's in here."

Mitch was way out of his depth and more than happy to wait for the archeologists to provide their thoughts before moving on.

"Wait for what? There is nothing here. We just need to find a way out at the other end like the last door."

Racking his M16 again, just for effect, he turned and ran across the floor, zig zagging as he went, skipping over the central stream until he reached the ledge twenty yards away. He lifted both arms in triumph, a big grin spread across his face.

"See, what did I tell you?"

Mitch lowered himself to leave the ledge and follow his colleague. Jack grabbed his underarm preventing him from going any further.

"Wait...Listen."

Over the torrent of constant running water, there was another sound. It lasted only a few seconds, a flurry like a gust of wind, although the air was still. It returned and again there was no evidence of a breeze, just the sound.

All on the ledge could hear it and began scanning the walls and ceilings looking for any tunnels or openings that could generate the sound. The walls were smooth and complete and the ceiling, although roughly hewn to a curve, showed no signs of a chimney or any holes large enough to create the sound.

Mel, on the far ledge, checked the wall in front of him to see if he could work out how to get out of there. Its surface was covered in finely etched lattice work, each linked diamond shape perfectly formed and in perfect symmetry, like a giant sandstone net. There were no other markings or images and no sign of a door of any kind.

He stamped on the ledge to see if there were any loose pavings or any protuberances that he could push or pull. He found nothing.

Looking back at the entrance he was surprised to see everyone still standing where he'd left them. Why the delay?

"Come on guys, are we moving on or what?" He was fired up after the run across the chamber and was itching for the next challenge.

.   .   .

"What have you got over there?" Faversham shouted louder than he thought, hearing his voice reverberate around the walls.

"Come and see for yourself, there's nothing here. No doors, buttons, handles; Nothing apart from some fancy design on the wall."

Tia shone a torch across the floor, over the three channels of fluorescent water, around the base of the walls and slowly across the flagstones. She moved along the ledge a little further away from the group and shone the torch again. She saw something that concerned her, something that may provide the answer to the noises. She moved back to the group, deep in thought.

"We need to find the exit from here. There's something about the floor that I don't like. Look for something on this side, a switch, a depression, something that we can manipulate. We need to stop the water flowing and get it out of this chamber."

Tia checked the walls while Faversham and Mitch examined the floor of the ledge leaving Jack to focus on the chamber floor, in particular the water. It was recycling somehow as if on a conveyor, moving rapidly through the gully across the chamber.

Laying on his front he managed to stretch his arm over the edge to place his hand in the water, the force was so strong it whipped at his fingers, blowing his hand clear of the gully. What the hell was propelling it?

He followed the stream as it cascaded across the floor, as far as the other ledge containing Mel, where it disappeared into the flagstones.

He was still trying to figure out how the water was being propelled when two booted feet appeared. Mel had left the ledge for some reason.

"NO! Get back on the ledge. NOW!" Jack screamed across the chamber, jumping to his feet, his eyes fixed on the military man as he strode towards them.

"You need more eyes. I can't help much from here." Mel walked deliberately towards them, surveying the floor for clues as he went.

"No Mel, get back on the ledge, man! We don't know what's in here…"

The sound came again, the rush of wind with no substance. Mel was half way across the chamber when he stopped. His rifle flew into the air, ripped from his grasp, landing with a clatter onto the flagstones.

"Mel?" Mitch stared at his second in command, at the man staring back at him.

Dark stripes appeared vertically on Mel's face as he stood transfixed in the centre of the chamber floor, the same vertical stripes ran down his body, appearing to widen. As they all watched in horror Mel fell apart, he began to split into thin strips, fanning out as his body peeled apart inch by inch.

The sound came again and the M16 flew into the air once more. Before it landed, Mel's body exploded into tiny shreds of flesh and bone, falling to the floor with a sickening splash as it spread across the flagstones, blood glistening black in the blue light of the rushing water. Drips of blood fell from the ceiling, echoing around the room as it spattered across the ground, like rain dripping from high surfaces after a heavy storm.

Tia was the first to react, screaming until she ran out of breath. The men stood aghast, unable to move, unsure about what they had just seen.

Mitch was the first to react.

"He…he just fucking exploded! What is this?" It was more of a wail as his voice wanted to scream like a banshee.

Jack jumped into the water along the east wall and drawing his Kabar smashed it into the gully. It resonated like glass, a loud clink as the steel of the blade made contact. But it held firm as it continued to propel water around his knees. He had to lean back and support himself with one hand wedged in between two flagstones to stop from being hurled forward along the glass track.

Drawing his Glock he fired into the gully, he felt the shudder as the bullet smashed into the crystal but the water kept flowing. He fired again, another shudder only this time he could feel movement underneath him. He felt the gully pop, then it shattered.

The water disappeared along with the crystal gully and he fell sharply into the void. He grabbed the flagstones, leaping as far as he could, managing to grip the edge of a stone slab, his fingers tearing at the join to gain purchase.

"Shoot the water!" He shouted up at Mitch who had already seen Jack shoot through the water and he fired into the central stream.

It took three shots to explode the crystal gully. The chamber darkened as the crystal shattered. He moved past Faversham who was comforting Tia and shot at the last gully running along the west wall. As it shattered the chamber was plunged into darkness and the noise from the running water disappeared leaving only silence.

Jack pulled himself up onto the chamber floor and rolled onto his back, he could feel a vibration through the stone. It was slight at first, but it soon strengthened and with it a rumbling sounded to the north. Now what?

Without warning the entire wall to the north slammed into the floor, bathing the chamber in the light of torches that burst into flame in unison showing them the way to the next task.

"What on earth has happened here?"

Gordon Nightly stood with the help of Stacy at the entrance. He grimaced as he looked down at the pool of flesh and blood in the centre of the chamber floor.

60

"So what actually happened to Mel?"

Mitch picked up the blood soaked M16, wiping as much of Mel off it as he could. It was a gruesome job but after what he had just seen there was no way he was leaving it behind.

"It was the floor…" Tia and Faversham helped Stacy pull Nightly onto the ledge towards the torch lit exit from the first chamber. Tia tried as best she could to explain what happened now that she had composed herself after the horror they had just experienced.

"…the floor had tracks similar to the lattice marks on the wall. It was either highly crafted calcite crystal, some form of glass or razor sharp steel or wire that was activated by pressure points in the floor. Once Mel stood on one of the active flagstones the water pressure pushed the razor through the floor at tremendous speed. Check the bottom of the rifle, I'm sure you will see some evidence of the sharpness."

Mitch could feel the lesions on the steel body of the M16. A strip of two millimetre deep slots ran the length of the under body and along one side, which would have occurred when it was lifted for a second time. The damage this caused to the metal would have cut through skin and bone like a hot knife through butter. Mel didn't stand a chance.

. . .

"Well from now on we stay together as a group. Nobody does anything without the rest of us agreeing."

Jack came up behind with Jenson, carrying the gurney and Aya through the chamber, lifting it onto the ledge ready to join the rest.

He had seen many things during his tours of duty and some of the weirder LARA missions, but this scared him. If Nightly was right they were about to uncover something that man could only dream of, even though in his own mind it just didn't register.

The thought of discovering the secret to immortality was a fantasy dreamed up by philosophers, theorists and zealots in the same way Armageddon was always just around the corner. He still found it hard to believe, but after what he had just seen from something apparently designed over three thousand years ago, he was beginning to think that there may be more out there than just simple logic.

∼

Jenson sighed as he saw the flight of stairs they would need to carry Aya down. After releasing the frame to activate the wheels and negotiating through the exit, they would need to start all over again. He was a medic, second to his main role as a soldier, he was trained to keep men fighting alongside him, not an orderly wheeling around the sick and wounded. He would need to work harder to get her to move by her own steam.

As they descended the stone flight of stairs taking them deeper into the earth, it was noticeable that the marble had been replaced by rough hewn sandstone. The heat was building as they continued to move down towards the bare wall awaiting them.

Mitch took to the rear, helping Jenson with Aya while Jack took the generator and support equipment.

. . .

Faversham studied the new pictures, which under the torches gave the impression of movement as flames licked the air.

It was a portrait of Ani and his wife Tutu entering the assemblage of gods while Anubis weighs Ani's heart against the feather of Maat. The monster Ammut is standing by, ready to devour Ani's soul should he prove unworthy and finally the image of the god Thoth standing with his papyrus to record the event. The scene stretched the length of the stairwell on both sides using striking colours that still looked as perfect as if they had just been painted. Robes of brilliant white, trimmed with reds, yellows and greens and the scaled green of the crocodile Ammut, perfectly rendered with some of his scales glowing wet in the light.

Mitch was way out if his depth and couldn't pretend to understand what was happening. Razor sharp blades cutting a man apart was enough to tell him that this was unknown territory, but he had always been inquisitive and there was one question that needed to be answered. A simple one, but one that would nag at him until it was answered.

"How did the torches light all by themselves? I mean we all saw them burst into flames as the wall collapsed. How is that possible if this place has been hidden for thousands of years?"

He heard theories as he was growing up that the Egyptians might have been an alien race, particularly when it came to the construction of the pyramids and sphinx's, a seemingly impossible task. The torches lighting themselves seemed other worldly to him, even in this day and age.

"Can you smell the faint scent of garlic?...

There was a distinct smell in the stairwell and through the smell of burning wood there was a garlic undertone. Mitch nodded in agreement to Faversham's observation.

"...It's white phosphorous. The chemical ignites when exposed to warm air of at least thirty degrees centigrade. I can only assume the stairwell was air sealed after the torches were soaked in phosphorous and as soon as they were exposed to the air from the chamber it reacted, setting fire to the wadding. There is also a slight smell of sulphur so I'd imagine other chemicals were included. Clever lot those Egyptians."

Tia and Faversham reached the base of the stairs first. As soon as they left the last step the wall in front of them fell away and torches exploded into life illuminating another chamber. The sound of running water filled the air.

61

Aya opened her eyes and looked into the face of Jenson as he moved in with a torch to check her responses. She went for his throat, but her arms wouldn't move. She saw the straps wrapped around her chest and began to struggle.

"Aya, you are awake."

The recognisable face of Gordon Nightly came into view, he began smoothing her hair away from her eyes, his hands gentle and kind. His smile was sweet, fatherly, she felt comfortable in his presence…What was this?

She began to recall the trip in the buggy, the pain in her shoulder, Mitch shouting at her. Then nothing.

But it wasn't nothing…she remembered little snippets, the pain as she was lifted from the car, waking on a gurney in a surgical tent, waking and not being able to move, Nightly announcing he was her father…

She began to scream, kicking at the gurney, fighting to release herself from the straps. She wanted to rip the throat out of the man who had ruined her life, had lied to her, had killed her…

Then it all went dark, the last thing she saw was the man pushing the needle into her arm.

. . .

"That'll hold her for a while. But she won't be out for long." Jenson put the syringe in the waste bag and ran a ticket from the monitor.

The vitals were good as her blood pressure began to drop.

"But if I were you Mr Nightly, I would prepare yourself for hell when she comes round."

"Just do your job and leave your opinions to yourself." Nightly glared at the medic and started to shake.

Stacy moved in and held him by the arm. He pushed her away, nearly knocking her to the floor.

Needing no excuse Jack grabbed Nightly by his lapels and shoved him against the wall. After realising that there was some truth in this Field of Reeds story and seeing the demolition of Mel, he knew they were dealing in the unknown, something that never registered well with him. Inwardly he was terrified and without a plan they were at a severe disadvantage. A disadvantage that the man, now wide eyed in front of him was culpable. He had been the instigator of a clock that had now become a ticking time bomb.

"Now let's get this straight. This fuck up is down to you, all of it. We are here to find a cure for your screw up. We are here to make sure that we succeed and you have convinced us that you are the only one that can get this for us. That is the only reason I haven't put a bullet in your head. You do not give orders, you do not dictate, you let us do our jobs and you do your thing when we get there. Got it?"

Nightly looked the LARA agent in the eye and then turned to Mitch, hoping that their relationship meant something. He had looked after him after all.

Mitch moved toward them and stood alongside his employer, leaning toward his ear.

. . .

"The man asked you a question. I'd answer if I were you, Gordon. Because he isn't the only one who has a bullet with your name on it if we fail."

Nightly turned to his Head of Security open mouthed. How dare he!

"Gentlemen, shall we? Come on Gordon, let's move over here." Stacy could see that things were getting out of hand yet again.

She pushed in between the three of them and grabbing Nightly by the arm, pulled him away to join Jenson as he tended to Aya.

It was never her intention to be his carer during this trip, but if she didn't keep him separated from the others the mission would fail, without question.

Peering into the chamber Faversham was surprised to see foliage spreading across the floor and creeping across the walls. There was no ledge to start from as the floor was level with the corridor, a floor of sand mixed with earth and moss instead of the expected flagstones.

The sound of water was an indicator as to how the vegetation had propagated, although there were no signs of the source.

As they stepped onto the soft floor, the aroma and oppressive heat reminded Tia of her last trip into the Amazon. Apart from the lack of bird sound, she was transported back to the rainforest.

"Now what?"

Jack entered next, looking around at the weird scene in front of him. He had no sooner placed his trailing foot into the chamber when the wall thrust from the floor and smashed into the ceiling locking them in.

"Jack!" Mitch's shout sounded distant as it weakly penetrated the stone seal. He managed to jump back just in time to miss the wall crushing him as it rose suddenly just as he was about to follow the others.

"I think we have to work out the exit to unlock the door. Use your earwig, we can communicate as we work through this." Jack pushed his ear to connect and was greeted by a female voice.

"Uh hum." Tia pulled the earpiece from her ear and waved it in the air.

Jack shook his head, Mitch had given it to her for some reason. He signalled for Tia to put it back in her ear just in case.

"Mitch! Never mind, just keep everyone safe. We'll get this open for you." As he shouted at the stone seal, he hoped that his voice permeated through enough for him to understand.

Tia and Faversham studied the images etched onto the smooth walls a few feet above the top of the swirling vines that stretched across both sides of the chamber.

They were basic shapes, a circle with a horizontal line through its centre followed by three blue wavy lines one above the other, finished with a circle with a vertical line through it. Directly underneath was the same set of symbols in a different format, a circle with a vertical line through it, three red wavy lines one above the other, finished with a circle with a horizontal line through it.

"Any ideas, Iggy?" Tia was trying to see anything that may resemble the shapes amongst the foliage but apart from a few piles of leaves and what looked like mangled tree bark, she struck out.

"Well it could be a code of some form. We know the waves are water, but I can't think what the circles mean."

"I think we have more to think about for the moment guys. Look!"

Following Jack's gaze toward a cluster of leaf mounds they saw the lines weaving towards them. They glistened in the light of the flaming torches, lines of golden, some copper red and some undulating shades of brown.

. . .

"Oh dear…" Faversham took his glasses off and folded them away in his pocket.

"…Cobras."

Jack looked over at the professor whose eyes were flitting all around the cavern, looking for something.

"You have got to be kidding me." Looking at the lines as they continued to slither towards them, he realised that he wasn't.

"We need to find higher ground…" Tia began to walk across the floor, checking for anything that could give them a lift.

She found an old tree bark that looked solid enough to support them, kicking it hard to ensure that it was rigid enough.

In front of her, its cervical ribs expanding to create a hood around its scaled neck, rose an Egyptian cobra awoken from its slumber within the confines of the stump. Reaching a height of three feet, its golden body began to sway to and fro, black eyes fixed on its prey, tongue flicking in and out as it prepared to strike.

Tia held her arms in front of her, palms facing the reptile, and followed the sway with her hands, moving in unison with the cobra's death dance. She put one foot behind the other and backed away in a smooth minute motion, movement hardly noticeable, repeating it with her other foot, edging further away without taking her eyes off of the dark globes and pointed tongue that continually licked the air as it savoured the scent of the prey in front of it.

The bullet sent shattered splinters of bark into the air as it struck the stump. Tia instinctively fell to her knees and watched the cobra slither away at frightening speed as it retreated to the base of the west wall and disappear into a clump of vegetation.

"NO! Jack, no bullets." Faversham ran to him flapping his hand towards the ground as if bouncing an invisible basketball.

Several hooded cobras rose to their full height across the floor and the hiss of warning drowned out the sound of the water.

"The vibration has spooked them. Now they are angry and will come for us."

"They're angry? I'm fucking livid." Jack looked over to the rising hooded beasts as more of the cobras rose majestically, rhythmically swaying as their tongues tasted the tension in the air.

"Quick, over here." Tia beckoned for them to join her at the petrified trunk.

"Give me a hand."

She held one end while Faversham grabbed the other and they lifted the bark and placed it a few inches away from the west wall. Jack joined them on the trunk which was just long enough to hold them all comfortably, their backs resting against the wall.

"How can they be here if this hasn't been found for thousands of years?"

Jack watched the cobras weave their way towards them, knowing that the height advantage of a few feet would do nothing to prevent the snakes from reaching them. He hunted around for anywhere else to hole up, but it was limited.

"This is a nesting site. They will have access into the chamber from the outside somewhere. The site would have been prepared thousands of years ago for this very purpose, but these creatures have evolved several thousands of times since then. We have invaded their home and they aren't about to give it up any time soon."

The wall moved, slightly at first, just a nudge, then smoothly into their backs until it rolled the bark and threw them from their perch.

"The walls are moving!" Faversham shouted the obvious as they stumbled onto the sand.

The walls to the east and west began to move into the room pushing some of the vegetation along with it. Many of the cobras turned tail and disappeared under two inch open vents dotted along the base of the walls, but at least a dozen continued weaving their way toward their prey.

"We need to get up there. Look!" Jack pointed to the top of the walls moving across the domed ceiling.

A gap began to appear twenty feet above them creating a platform underneath the curve.

"Great, how do we get up there?"

Faversham found it difficult to take his eyes away from the advancing cobras. One thing he hated more than anything were snakes, they terrified him and he could feel his heart palpitations become more frequent. He was on the verge of panic.

"Here, get on my shoulders." Jack pushed his back into the wall and setting himself held his hands in front of him,

linking his fingers to assist in giving Faversham a leg up. Moving his feet forward slowly in time with the moving stonework he nodded to the professor.

Faversham climbed onto Jack's shoulders, realising what he was to do and grateful that he was six feet away from the advancing reptiles. Careful to avoid falling he managed to reverse himself so that he also had his back against the wall. He positioned his hands in front of him and linked his fingers.

Tia came next, climbing nimbly over Jack and after being pulled up, she managed to kiss the professor softly on the lips as she passed, stretching as far as she could once she positioned herself onto his shoulders.

"I'm short by about three feet." She shouted, panic beginning to register in her voice as she realised that the walls were closing in faster than she thought. They were less than thirty feet from closing in on each other.

"Bend your knees…" Faversham bent his own as he shouted up to Tia.

"…And we'll jump up. Are you good with that Jack?" He shouted down to the man he was standing on, feeling his feet move as the LARA agent braced himself.

"Go for it…" Jack pushed hard into the wall to provide as much of a solid foundation as he could.

"…After three, ready? One…Two…Three!"

Tia was propelled into the air grabbing the ledge with both hands and pulling herself up with ease.

Faversham didn't fare as well. Jack tried to catch the professor's shins as he landed back down onto his shoulders but the movement of the wall put them out of line and Faversham crashed to the ground.

The sand wasn't as soft as expected, blowing the wind out of him as he landed in a heap. He closed his eyes in pain, trying to breathe air into his lungs through bruised ribs, taking several deep breaths until he was sure his lungs were functioning as they should.

Opening his eyes he stared into the hooded face of a copper red cobra, its tiny black eyes stared in anger as its blackened forked tongue flickered, spitting venom into the air. Faversham could only stare as if in a trance as the snake moved its head back, striped hood quivering in anticipation as it rose to its full height…then the cobra struck.

Reptilian blood covered the professor's face as the cobra's hood exploded in front of his eyes, the rest of the snake's body slapped him in the face as it passed by his head, landing harmlessly feet away.

Jack put his Glock away and helped the professor to his feet, letting him dust himself down as he checked the area he had fallen on. Sand had blown clear from the impact point exposing stone flagstones, placing his hand flat he could feel the water pressure below. It must be where the water source ran through the chamber.

· · ·

"Iggy! Up here…" Tia shouted down from her vantage point, the walls were now only twenty feet apart.

"…I have one of the symbols here. It's a bowl with a rod through its centre. It appears to be a dial of some sort but I can't turn it."

Jack thrust his Kabar around the joints of the flagstone, the blade slicing through the brittle grouting which he pulled away with his fingers.

Faversham stared up at Tia's face, her black pony tail hung down the side of the wall, jiggling as she spoke.

"Can you see a second dial?" It was obviously related to the diagram on the wall which was growing larger by the minute. It was no more than fifteen feet away.

Tia shone her Maglite around the surface but could see only the one, she had little time to find it as she looked across at the east wall which was moving closer. Then she saw it.

"There's one on the other wall in the same position as the one I have. The dial is set ninety degrees to mine."

"Ah, so this matches the diagram…the only thing missing is the water." Faversham could see it now as clear as day.

"The dials must control the flow of the water and with it the direction of the walls. We need to move the dials to match the diagram with the red water symbol, that would reverse the direction."

The wall was now a little less than ten feet away and someone had to be by the other dial to reverse it. They had no time.

"Well, I've found the water."

The chamber filled with blue light as Jack pulled a flagstone out of the floor. Water rushed by in a gulley of blue calcite. As one had been removed it was easier to pull another stone away revealing more of the channel as it travelled north.

"We need to get up there somehow Jack…" Faversham pointed to the east wall which was now only eight feet away.

"…Any ideas?" They both looked up as the ceiling began to disappear.

"How's your ribs?"

Faversham looked at Jack.

"My ribs? Sore…why?"

"Get in the water…Now!"

Before Faversham had time to protest Jack pushed him into the gulley. He struggled as he tried to protest and pushed Jack's hands away as he tried to scramble out.

"Stay there you idiot…you will never make it. Wait here, submerged. We need to reverse the direction."

Before he could protest Jack was climbing the walls. They were no more than three feet away and using his left hand and foot on the west wall and his right hand and foot on the east wall he pushed himself up, ascending in small star jumps. Faversham lay back in the water and watched the LARA agent move further and further away from him.

Jack's arms and legs burnt in protest as he ascended in small jumps, all the time feeling the walls close in on him. By the time he reached the top he had to squeeze his hips through the tight gap which was now less than two feet wide.

Knowing he had no time to lose, he pulled his protesting body forward and reached the small bowl shaped indent. He grabbed the vertical bar, looking over at Tia who was now only a few feet away from him.

She shouted across at him, panic clearly in her voice as she thought of Iggy below.

"Right, together turn clockwise…One…two…three."

They both twisted the bars in each bowl. The handles turned

ninety degrees and came to rest with a satisfying click. But the walls kept moving, closing with a clump that vibrated through their bodies.

"IGGY!" Tia screamed at the seam as east and west walls met. She looked to Jack for reassurance, but he could only stare at her. He had nothing to say.

62

Faversham lay in the darkness after he watched the walls close completely over him. His face was just above the surface of the water enabling him to breathe, but as he moved his head a little further his forehead touched the base of the walls.

Apart from the splash of the water as it rushed over him he heard nothing else. To avoid panic, he decided to embrace the sound and closed his eyes as he tried to imagine that he was laying in a rock pool in the Bahamas.

He thought of white sand, clear blue sea, the gentle waves as they washed over him. Sounds of the exotic birds as they sang their songs of summer, the gentle piano music that filled the air from the bar where his cocktail was waiting for him once he had finished his swim.

It lasted less than a minute as he began to wonder what would happen to him in this watery grave. Would he go mad? Would he drown before he starved? Should he move under the flagstones, move further down the gulley, get it over with?

He began to shake as the water chilled his body, filled every crevice as it began to embrace him, pull him into its world, provide a blanket to shroud him in death.

. . .

He opened his eyes as he felt something on his leg, moving up to his groin and onto his stomach.

The water stopped moving, the sound changed to gentle splashing as it brushed against the gulley walls, ebbing and flowing as it came to rest.

He could feel the pressure on his stomach move to his chest. He remained still, not daring to move his hands.

Water covered his face as it began to move again, but it had reversed, moving over him rather than passing him. A thin strip of light appeared above his head, as it grew wider he could see the rough hewn detail of the curved ceiling of the chamber. As his eyes adjusted he could make out the surface of the smooth walls as they moved away from the gulley.

With relief he lifted his head ready to leap free, but moved slowly back into the water as he faced the bronzed head and tiny black eyes of a cobra looking up at him as it settled onto his chest. He knew that the Egyptian cobra could swim, they could be seen weaving through the Nile on a regular basis. But he didn't expect to be sharing space with one in these circumstances.

The water began to speed up as it propelled the walls further back to their original position and he could feel the pressure on his feet as it pushed forceably into him. If he didn't move soon he would be forced back under the flagstones behind him. He felt the forked tongue flicker against his chin, the cobra was moving towards his face.

Bracing his feet and arms against the walls of the gulley to wedge himself in as best he could he took a deep breath and ducked under the water. The cobra shot across his face and disappeared as the pressure pushed him away.

Faversham leapt out of the gulley rolling clear of the water and stood on the solid floor covered in sand. He brushed himself down and shuddered as he thought of the snake climbing up his body.

"Iggy...Thank God." Tia ran into his arms, nearly knocking him to the ground in her enthusiasm. She had descended along with Jack as the walls began to move, an easy descent as they were supported all the way to ground level.

"Sorry about that…" Jack apologised as he waited for him to be released from Tia's grip.

"…But I needed to make sure you were safe."

"Oh don't mention it, old chap. Good strategy." He shook his hand furiously, which unsettled Jack a little, especially as he had to use his other hand to prize himself away from the grateful academic.

"We need to get out of here." Jack moved away and started to look for an exit.

As soon as the walls settled back in place, the south wall collapsed and a section of the north wall rose out of sight revealing the exit.

Mitch burst in from the south, gun raised, and stared at the three of them in the centre of the room. The professor was soaked and covered in sand. He assumed he had been in the water he could see flowing through the glowing blue gulley in the floor.

"What's happened here then? Been having fun without me?"

63

G abrielle was aware that she was on the edge of madness and she didn't care. It was exhilarating sharing the experience with the voice in her head.

'Not long now and we'll have it all. But it's only for us, you know that don't you, Gabi?'

Mum was more like a sister, they were so alike. She had missed her big time. Missed the laughter, the camaraderie, the synergy. Now she was back they would prove a formidable pair to anyone who got in their way.

"Yes, mum I know. Don't worry, I have it all under control."

Caelen Khan looked at his Head of Security and wondered how she was still able to function. Her face was a mess, she must be in pain surely. The burns that were clear of any bandages were weeping yellow fluid onto her top, and her eye socket was struggling to keep the eyeball in place. She had begun to talk to herself in between barking orders to his team as they entered the reed fields under heavy fire.

She stayed behind with a gun still aimed at his head and a live grenade primed in her other hand as she sent the rest of his team to secure the area.

It had been easier than they thought after coming across the helicopter bordering the tall vegetation.

Faced with resistance from eight gunmen guarding a site of stone pillars, Gabrielle had proven her skills as a strategist and although taking three casualties of their own, it was over in minutes.

One of the pillar guards had been left alive, shot in both legs and propped against the centre pillar. He was breathing heavily as Gabrielle approached.

This was only Beckett's second full blown mission and his day wasn't going well. As he watched the hideous woman approach, in between shards of pain shooting through his legs, he knew it was about to get worse.

She approached on the arm of a well groomed Middle Eastern man. Holding a gun across her chest, she held a grenade in the other.

"You will tell us what these stones mean." Her voice was steady, forthright and it was not a request.

"I don't know what they mean, lady. We were just told to hold our positions here by the stones."

He was unarmed, unable to walk and knew that he would not escape from the five armed gunmen and the crazy woman, but he wasn't about to fail in his duties as he knew the importance of the mission. Not just for the sake of the group underneath their feet but for the sake of mankind, for his mum, his dad and Julia. To give them the chance to lead normal lives again.

Anger began to fight its way through the pain at the realisation he would never father the child he and Julia had tried so hard for over the past couple of years.

He would be leaving her a widow at thirty two and worse still, forced to move on. Perhaps he wasn't ready to let go, perhaps there was a way to get out of this.

As the woman approached he shifted his weight onto his right side, a bullet had lodged into his thigh but he could move his leg with a pain he felt he could withstand. His left knee was shattered which rendered his other side useless.

She was holding the gun across her chest aimed at the man on her left side, which being his right gave him a chance to leap forward and wrestle it free. She was three paces away, her eyes on his as she approached. Pain wracked his thigh as he prepared the muscle to push him forward, his fingers pushed into the ground to gather as much purchase as he could, his biceps taut, trembling as they reached their peak.

As the crazy woman was a pace in front of him he leapt forward and grabbed for the gun.

The smash across the temple sent him crashing to the ground. She had been prepared for him to try his luck and had the gun ready to crack across his head.

"Don't be a fool." She signalled to Caelen's men to assist.

"Get him up and make sure he doesn't move."

Caelen nodded his agreement as they looked to him for permission even though he had no choice in the matter.

Two of his team helped Beckett back into a seated position. Resting him back against the central stone they stood either side of him, ready to move should he try anything else.

"You've let them do it again, Gabi. Why do you keep giving men the chance to hurt you. Look at the state of you, Mitch did that and now this man has tried to cause you more harm."

"I've got this mum, don't worry."

Gabrielle stepped back a couple of paces pulling Khan with her. She focused on the wounded man as he began to come round.

He wiped blood from his eyes and after several blinks returned her gaze.

"So why are the stones either side of you lower than the rest? Is that the entrance, a doorway of some kind?" She smiled as she caught the surprise in his face that she knew the secret of the stones.

It gave her the upper hand, this would please mother.

"Look, I know nothing about any of this. We were told to hold the area, that is it. These stones were how we found them. That's all I can tell you." Beckett knew that he had lost his chance to escape from this.

His only hope was to ride out the situation with ignorance and hoped it was enough to keep him alive.

"I promise you, lady, if I knew anything I would tell you, I swear."

Gabrielle stared at him for a moment longer, satisfied that she could see the fear in his eyes.

She studied the faces of the two men either side of him, the insecurity in their eyes pleased her. Their boss was being held at gunpoint by a woman who had just torched many of their comrades. They were trying to work out who was in charge and they feared her.

The same could be said for the other three standing at the edge of the bank, guns at the ready but unsure where to point them. She was enjoying the power she had over them all, mother would be pleased.

But she needed to get a move on, time was of the essence, mother wouldn't wait for her forever.

She focused on the wounded man once again and smiled.

"My apologies, my dear. I know you are only doing your job. It's a nasty business when you are ordered to do something without reason and look at you, badly wounded. We need to do something about that."

She saw the relief in his face, the silent but evident exhale of breath coincided with the relaxation of his muscles as he noticeably calmed.

"Here take this. It will help with the pain."

The grenade exploded as soon as it hit his chest, blowing him apart and tearing into the two standing guard alongside him. She put a bullet in each of the three bystanders killing them instantly as they stood transfixed at the horror in front of them. Caelen Khan fell backwards, rolling onto his front and covering his head as blood soaked mud and stone showered over him.

Gabrielle stood and watched as the dust began to settle around the stones. There were body parts strewn all around including a head that had come to rest on one of the lower stones but it was too misshapen to see who it had once belonged to.

The stone where the unfortunate guard had been resting was now a little shorter, part of it had blown away, a dull light emanated from its top.

She caught her breath as she gazed at the marble stairs descending into a dimly lit chamber, she had found it. She knew she would, she had proved them all wrong and now she could show Caelen how foolish he had been to doubt her.

She turned to call him over but he wasn't where she left him, cowering in the mud in fear of his life.

He was over by the bank, bent over one of his dead soldiers, picking up a discarded rifle.

"What do you think you are doing, Caelen? You have to see this."

She reached him before he had time to rack the rifle, kicking it out of his grasp and shoving him to the ground, pushing her gun into his cheek. He felt his teeth cave in as she thrust the barrel deep into his skin.

. . .

"Get up!" Pulling him to his feet she dragged him towards the stones. He couldn't believe the strength she possessed as he was pulled along like a rag doll.

"Look, I told you I'd deliver. Look!" She forced his head over the lip of the stone, his chin scraping against the rough granite, peeling off a slice of skin.

"Gabrielle, yes I can see. For god's sake stop all this. What do you want me to say? I'm sorry, ok?"

Feeling the weight of her hand relax he eased from her grasp and turned to face her. The cold tip of a blade pressed under his chin pushing his head back, forcing him to look down his nose to gain eye contact with her.

"Now don't be stupid, Gabrielle. You were right, I can see that now, I should never have doubted you. Let's stop all this and finish what we started."

"Oh I plan to finish this, Caelen, as I promised I would from the start. It's just a pity that I had to prove it in such a way. But finish it I will...on my own."

Caelen Khan's eyes moved up into his head as the blade pushed through his mandible, sliced through his tongue, past the roof of his mouth and dragged an optical nerve upwards until it severed as steel passed through the brain before coming to rest at the roof of his skull.

Watching the body of her former employer slump to the floor, she wiped the blade on her jeans and pushed it back into her belt.

Taking a deep breath as the weight of responsibility fell from her shoulders, she climbed into the stone and descended the smooth flight of stairs.

"Wait for me mum. I'm coming."

"I'm here my, darling, don't worry I'm waiting for you. I am so proud of you, Gabi."

64

J ack looked at his PDA, staring at a blank screen. No map, no coordinates and no sign of a signal of any kind. He wasn't sure how far underground they had travelled, but they were well out of sight of any satellite. The only communication was the earpiece that he now shared with Mitch.

It was agreed that he shadowed the professor and Tia while Mitch ensured Nightly and Aya were kept safe. With their combined military experience it meant they had someone looking after their six, which in an alien environment could make all the difference.

After the last chamber there was a sense of foreboding amongst the group.

Jack had never come across anything like it and he was effectively flying by the seat of his pants. Without the support of Sara's eyes and the technical support of his PDA he was back in a war zone with only his wits as company, something he was comfortable with but hoped was all behind him.

Faversham, already feeling uncomfortable in his drenched clothing, had begun to doubt his own credentials. He liked the thrill of the adventure but he realised that he preferred studying the findings of others rather than being part of the discovery itself. He was scared.

Tia was relishing the challenge but was far more comfortable looking after herself without the need to look out for others. She had a history with Iggy and as the mission progressed, so too had her feelings, which was dangerous for both of them. They were both experiencing it and sooner or later they could take one risk too many, which would mean the end for both of them.

After descending a further flight of stairs they congregated in a wide corridor twelve feet away from a stone door engraved with the image of a woman kneeling with her arms outstretched, each arm possessed a wing of flowing feathers.

"That's Maat..." The beam of Tia's Maglite cut through the gloom, bringing clarity to the fine details.

"...Goddess of truth, justice, wisdom, order and harmony."

They moved forward in unison, Jack taking the lead with Tia and Faversham, followed by a decidedly shaky Gordon Nightly clinging on desperately to Stacy. Mitch walked behind keeping distance between Aya and Jenson and her newly discovered father.

Aya walked unsteadily, having woken to insist that she would complete the journey on foot. No one could persuade her otherwise and save for knocking her out again, she would have none of it.

Heavily strapped, her left arm immobilised and her pain controlled, she said little on the descent. But her eyes remained fixed on the back of Nightly's head, the grimace that remained on her face a mix of pain and pure hatred. There was more she needed to know and once they were free of this place she will seek the answers.

Halfway across the corridor the image of Maat disappeared as the door slid away to reveal their next chamber. The flickering glow emanating from the opening confirmed that phosphorous was still igniting to show the way.

Jack turned to face the group and waited until Aya came to a stop a few yards behind them all.

"I'll do this with the two archeologists. Better to give us another option should we fail to get through."

Mitch nodded, he was right. If they failed at least Nightly was still around to continue on.

Tia looked at Jack. Fail? That wasn't an option. She hadn't gone through this to see it all go to waste.

"The door will open again when we succeed..." She emphasised the 'when'.

"...The gods allowed the dead a choice at each gate. Move on and seek immortality or return to rest for all eternity surrounded with the wealth you were left with. A reward of sorts by always giving the choice to go back."

"Nice to have a choice." Jack turned towards the flickering light and walked through the doorway.

∽

They were in a thirty foot square chamber with a burning brazier in each corner. Glowing embers floated from the bowls like glowing fireflies illuminating the upper walls until extinguishing as they reached the ceiling.

The walls were roughly hewn apart from the far wall that contained a stone stairwell leading to an exit of black marble. A larger image of Maat had been inscribed on the wall bordered by five heart shaped symbols above her head and four weighing scale symbols ascending in line with the steps below her kneeling frame.

As Faversham moved towards the stairs, the door behind them slammed shut leaving the rest of the group behind.

"Mitch, can you read?" Jack tested communications, relieved that at least part of the 21st Century had followed them below.

"Loud and clear, Jack. What have you got in there?"

"Not a lot, a few burning fires and a picture of Maat, similar to the image on the doorway, some pictures of some scales and hearts and a set of stairs leading to the exit. I'll let you know more as we go along. Out."

Encouraged that they had communication, Jack followed Tia and Faversham to the stairs.

It began to rain…

"What the hell?" He wiped the water from his head feeling the slimy texture as it clung to his fingers.

It smelt organic, industrial…Oil.

"Quickly get to the stairs, I don't like this."

Running across the mosaic floor as the oil continued to spray over them made it increasingly difficult to remain upright. Tia slipped and tried to get back onto her feet, scrabbling on all fours as the floor turned to slime. Jack managed to lift her up, but couldn't let go as they needed each other for support as they crossed the floor like a pair of amateur skaters, all four feet trying, but failing, to move in the same direction.

Faversham reached the stairs easily having crossed half of the floor before the oily rain began. He held out his arms in anticipation as Jack and Tia slid towards him. It would have been a comical sight had it been at an ice rink, but it had suddenly become a life and death struggle.

"Quick as you can, come on now! You really must get a move on" He shouted at them in a panic as they struggled towards him. Something caught his eye.

The braziers were tilting forward in unison moving slowly towards the floor, embers shifting within the bowls, rolling over and over as they moved towards the edge.

Tia held her arms outstretched, fingers inches from Faversham's hands. Jack saw the first of the flaming sparks leave the bowl, sprinkling towards the oil soaked floor. Pushing with all his strength he shoved her forward into the professor sending them both crashing onto the stairs. They held on to each other for support and to ensure neither fell from the steps.

Jack leapt after them, his boots landing either side of Faversham's head as he embraced his former student.

The floor erupted in waves of fire and heat as the oil ignited, flames leaping feet into the air as tendrils grabbed at the drips still falling from above.

"Up the stairs, quick!"

Jack cleared the crumpled bodies of the archeologists and ran the stairs, reaching the platform leading to the exit. It was only ten feet in length but enough to fit the three of them.

Faversham joined him, brushing dust and gravel from his leather jacket. Tia came up the rear, no worse for wear after using the professor as a crash mat.

"Now what?" Jack had to shout over the roar of the flames.

"This is the river of fire…" Faversham shouted in return.

"…said to be guarded by the swallower of sinners. The flames are said to burn the bodies of those who have sinned and allow the innocents to pass."

"Great, so are we toast or is there a way out of here?"

The heat was beginning to draw clean air from the chamber making breathing difficult. Any deep breath burnt the throat, clear evidence that they had to work fast.

Tia shone her Maglite over the images etched into the wall.

"It has to be Maat, she is the goddess of law and morality so it makes sense that she could be seen to be the swallower of sinners. She is the key to getting out of here."

Jack recalled the previous history lessons given by the two at certain stages of their journey here and he began to feel an element of relief. Was this what they were looking for?

"Isn't Maat where the heart is weighed against a feather or something like that?"

"Something like that…" Tia continued to study the image, passing the beam over each detail.

"But this is not the hall of two truths where the heart is weighed, there is however something about the images…Look!" She shone her torch over the scale and heart symbols, in particular one of the hearts above the head of Maat.

"Ah, I see…" Faversham followed the beam, squinting to focus through the flickering light.

"…There is a heart that shouldn't be there. For us to leave here we need to be innocent, so one heart has to be removed."

The flames reached the stairs, savouring each step as it licked at the oil stained stone, it had devoured the third and began to attack the fourth as a five foot wall of flame slowly crept towards them.

"Well we need to move fast or it won't matter anymore. How do you plan to lose a heart?"

"That one." Tia shone the beam over the centre symbol directly above the head of Maat.

The hearts either side were smooth and shimmered as the beam moved across them, the central symbol was a dull flat image, seemingly added as an afterthought.

"So what's the plan?"

The flames moved to the fifth step leaving only eight more before reaching their platform. They were twenty feet above the chamber floor which was now a burning inferno. The air thin and acrid as the smoke overpowered any clean oxygen. They all began to cough sporadically in between laboured gasps.

. . .

"We need to destroy it somehow, remove it from the image." Faversham coughed as he breathed in deeply after shouting a little too much.

The heart was at least twelve feet away and directly above the sixth step which was now alight, the flames beginning to gain pace.

Jack aimed his Glock and fired. Stone chippings burst from the wall into the flames, flaring with a flash as they came into contact.

"Look, it's combustable. We need a flame to burn the rest away."

Both Tia and Jack stared at the professor as they stood surrounded by a growing inferno. Then looked at each other.

"Any particular flame or will one in here do?" Jack had to stop to cough the smoke from his lungs, bending low to stop from gagging as he forced his diaphragm to work overtime.

"Give me your knife." Tia held out her hand.

Having no ideas of his own Jack handed her his Kabar.

She held it comfortably testing its weight, spinning it several times as she judged its suitability.

Satisfied, she unwound the bandaging that Jenson used to cover her knife wounds and wrapped the knife covering the hilt, winding it along the length of the shaft leaving only a small section of the tip exposed.

Crouching, she wiped the covered blade across the floor soaking the bandage in oil before moving steadily down the steps toward the flame. Holding the Kabar by the exposed tip she moved the blade towards the burning steps.

The bandages caught immediately, flames covering the hilt and running up the shaft as Tia rushed back to the platform.

Turning towards the image of Maat she held the tip aloft, flames fluttered above the hilt helping to assist her line of sight.

All but three of the stairs were now alight, seconds away from reaching the platform and engulfing them.

Tia threw the blade, all three watched as the flaming missile spiralled towards its target. The tip landed and pushed into the misshapen heart, the stone and clay loosened by the impact of the bullet.

. . .

The flash that exploded from the heart filled the room with a light so bright it temporarily blinded them.

A square slab of stone shot from the opening, protruding a foot from the image. Suddenly the platform dropped a foot, sending Tia off balance and over the edge.

Jack saw her stumble and dived towards her, catching her wrist as it flailed in front of her, her fingers grabbing at nothing. He gripped her tightly, not feeling her nails as they cut into his forearm as her fingers held on gratefully.

The entire chamber floor had dropped along with their platform and water flooded in, rushing over the flames as it burst through, filling the chamber with thick white smoke. As the water rose it crept along the steps meeting water that cascaded down the body of Maat, clearing the last of the flames.

A vibration of stone on stone told them that the exit had opened, but it took a while for the smoke to thin before they could see the void in front of them.

The water disappeared beneath the chamber floor as quickly as it had entered, forced along by a damp but clean rush of air.

Jack pulled Tia back onto the platform, both laying there for a moment as they caught their breath.

"This is yours I believe." Faversham stood over them, handing the Kabar back to the LARA agent after finding it on the steps below.

He waited, his arm still outstretched as Jack put away the knife and grabbed his hand, pulling him to his feet.

"Shall we go?"

65

As the door fell away allowing the rest of the group to enter from the passage, Mitch had no idea what he was about to see.

Listening through the earpiece and hearing the tumultuous roars, the shouts and the final eruption from inside it sounded more like a war zone. Looking around at the scorched walls, the wet, slightly slippy floor and Jack and the archeologists sitting on the top of a set of blackened stairs on the far wall, there were more questions than answers.

He crossed the floor slowly, remaining in between Nightly and Aya, the tension still hung in the air and getting this far, he would make sure they finished the mission and found the cure. After that Aya could do whatever she needed to do and he would not stand in her way.

Although it wouldn't take much as Nightly was looking worse by the minute as he stumbled across the flagstones supported by Stacy, who was finding it just as difficult to hold him upright. Aya on the other hand, even after being in an induced coma for the past few hours, was in much better shape. She was being escorted by Jenson, walking alongside her carrying a well stocked medipac of morphine just in case, staying close enough to support her if needed, which she assured him many times that she didn't.

. . .

"How many more of these things do we have to get through?" Mitch was sure that with Nightly on the way out and Aya in a medicated fugue, they may not last the three hours they had left before midday without a decent rest to recharge.

"According to the Book of the Dead there are twelve to fifteen gates to pass."

Tia met Stacy at the base of the stairs and helped her with Nightly to negotiate the steps.

"We have no chance of another nine or more of this."

"WE HAVE TO!" Nightly spun to face Mitch as he spat out the words. Stacy nearly lost her footing as he fell towards her. Pushing him upright she forced him up the stairs. She for one will be glad when this was all over.

"Well, I think we may have come to the end of our journey." Faversham emerged from the entrance to the next chamber, his normal optimism a thing of the past.

This was one task too many and without some form of miracle, this is where it will end.

"This next one is impossible. There is no way we can pass this one."

66

J ack shone the Maglite into the darkness below. Thin stripes of orange flashed into view for a few seconds followed by tiny puffs of smoke, but it was so far down it was difficult to work out what he was seeing. There was also a distinct scent of sulphur, a metallic scorched smell that irritated his nose as he breathed in.

"Well it looks like we've found the centre of the earth. I think that might be lava down there."

His voice echoed all around them, reverberating through the darkness.

They had entered a vast cavern of natural rock, even the flaming torches bursting into life as they entered failed to light the whole expanse, disappearing into deepening shadows to the left and right of them.

Above, the torches reach was just high enough to illuminate the tips of stalactites pointing at them from several feet away.

But it was what was in front that was causing them so much concern. They were faced with a canyon stretching over fifty feet across and dropping several hundred feet into an abyss.

Two cables stretched across the gap spaced five feet apart, one above the other. Each cable disappeared into slots cut deep into the wall.

"I doubt that we have travelled far enough to be anywhere near the centre of the earth." Faversham stood back from the void and removed his glasses, putting them safely away.

"Well, I can cross this." Tia pulled at the top cable, lifting her feet to ensure that it would take her weight.

An audible click and a sudden rush of air filled the cavern. Scanning the walls with the three Maglites available found nothing amiss.

Jack checked the ceiling just in case the stalactites had begun to descend towards them, the beam returned a glimpse of the pointed tips as before. He left the beam in place for several seconds as he didn't trust what he was seeing anymore.

They remained stationary.

"Any idea what that was?" Mitch was still scanning the wall across the ravine when he came upon a tunnel that he hadn't noticed before, just to the right of the tethered cables.

"I guess that must have been it, there's the exit. We just need to work out how to get across."

Easier said than done Jack thought as he looked at a near dead Gordon Nightly and the heavily bandaged Aya. He had to agree with Faversham, this was near impossible.

"Let's see if there is anything to help on the other side. I'll do a recce and report back."

Tia walked the ten yards to the edge and stood on the cable, grabbing hold of the other above her head with both hands. This will be a doddle, she was proud of her athleticism, something she had to use on all of her expeditions.

Jack agreed that it was a start but he was nervous, they needed their wits about them as anything could happen.

. . .

In sequence, Tia eased her left foot along the bottom while simultaneously moving her arm along the top, her hand gripping the cable loosely but ready to clench if needed. She then slid her right foot and arm to join the left.

Her weight made the line sag as she continued to shuffle out over the canyon keeping her eyes fixed on the tunnel entrance as well as the end of the cables, preparing herself just in case they broke away.

She felt the click through her feet and stopped for a second as a rush of air passed by her left ear, then another passed by her right ear, a whoosh like the soft hum of a mosquito. She felt something brush against her bare leg but daren't look down to see what it was. Instead, she moved steadily on, smaller strides but faster than before. It made the cables swing a little but she soon found a rhythm that allowed her to glide along.

The pain in her right arm caused her to lose her grip, her limb flailing behind her causing her left hand to pull her forward and with it, the cable backwards. She felt her legs swing forward as the line under her feet took most of her weight. Something sharp nicked the back of her thigh.

Using all the strength in her legs, she forced her feet against the line and bending her knees pulled back and managed to bring her feet underneath her again. She released her left hand and dropped onto the line leaning forward as the cable hit her groin.

Reaching out and grabbing with both hands while wrapping her legs around the line, her weight caused her to rotate until she was suspended with her back facing the deep ravine. Hugging the cable she closed her eyes as she waited for the line to stop swinging.

"TIA! Are you ok?" Jack saw her fall, his torch catching the moment she managed to wrap herself around the line. Tiny flashes flew above her in both directions, too fast to register but arrow straight, like tiny cluster laser beams, luminous dashes crossing the ravine.

"Yeah, I got this." Tia called back as she felt the line settle to a gentle sway.

Her arm was hurting like hell, she put it down to the four inch rod that was protruding from her forearm.

She could still see them as they shot across her eyes, the steel illuminated by Jack's torch beam, the rush of air humming as they sliced through the darkness. Hundreds of them filling the space between the two cables, a metallic swarm of death.

Thankfully it lodged into muscle inches below her elbow and came out easily as she yanked it free, letting it fall into the abyss. The pain eased a little and although she could feel the warm flow of blood run down her skin, dripping off her elbow, she had full motion of her arm as she shuffled along the line, using her knees and ankles to push herself along, pulling gently with her hands to avoid any sudden jolts of pain.

As she felt the welcome scrape of stone below her back she released the cable and lay on the canyons edge for a moment to catch her breath and feel around the wound to survey the damage. She could feel a small hole, far smaller than it felt. The blood began to congeal, its flow slowing. It was more a flesh wound which would hurt for a while, but she would live.

The rush of air had ceased and shining her Maglite over the ravine showed only clear space. The steel swarm had stopped.

The beam caught sight of the other six members of her party, all unmoving, staring across the void.

"I'm safe guys..." She slowly got to her feet and scoured the area around her.

"...But we need to do something about the cables. They seem to be controlling these little missiles. I don't see anything to help over here."

She shone the torch along the wall, over the rough crevices, scanning the floor as she went. She risked stepping into the passage cut into the cavern, being careful not to go too far in case she became trapped. There was nothing but darkness.

Checking the area one more time Jack finished with the cables, running his torch along the rope and into the holes, following the line until it disappeared from the reach of the beam.

They were connected so far into the wall that it was impossible to reach whatever contraption they were connected to. There was only one way for it, but was there anything to help?

Stepping back he scanned the wall again…looking for an obtrusion, a lip, anything strong enough to hold a rope. He stopped at the burning torch, the light flickering from the phosphorus soaked reeds, tightly woven to create a cone held aloft by a steel ring fixed into the stone.

"Here Prof, give me a leg up." Faversham obliged by linking his hands and resting his back against the wall. Jack lifted himself and pulled the torch free from its housing, sparks flew across the cavern floor as he threw it down.

Faversham, realising that Jack had finished with his assistance, stooped to pick up the torch and held it up to help light the wall where he was holding onto the fixed ring, both feet digging into the wall, pulling with all his might.

"That will do nicely." Jack dropped, landing comfortably on his feet and beckoned Jenson and Faversham over, taking the torch from the professor and handing it to Stacy.

"I'm going to cut this line. I need you two to keep hold of it as I think it may be heavy and we can't afford to lose it."

They had ten yards of floor before the ravine, plenty of space to stop the line falling over the edge, but to be on the safe side Faversham stood a yard from Jack as he pushed the Kabar into the hole to cut the longest section of cable he could, as Jenson dug in five yards from the edge.

Jack began to saw at the rope.

"OK, ready?" He looked back at his two man tug of war team, both hands on the rope, feet positioned to take the weight.

They both nodded.

· · ·

After three strokes the rope came free. A thud echoed through the walls as whatever the line had been connected to fell away. Faversham's feet crackled against loose stone, sounding a lot worse as it rasped around the cavern but stopped after a few inches.

Jack took the weight and pulled the excess from the hole. Happy that the other two had hold of it, he let it drop to the floor.

Leaving them holding the line he walked to the edge of the ravine and cut away the bottom cable, letting it fall away into the void. Another thud resonated from the wall. At least they had stopped the mechanism and if he got this right, he had stopped it for good.

Cutting the remaining piece of cable from the wall Jack thrust his Kabar into the thick strand two feet from the end, the blade pierced easily. He then wrapped the remaining twenty four inches in a 'V' shape, alternating between the handle and blade until the knife was covered, tucking the last few inches into itself and pulling it tight, tugging several times to ensure that it was secure.

"Tia, keep your light facing me. When you get the knife I need you to follow this in sequence.

First, pull up the bottom rope and leave it on the floor. Second , leaving the bottom rope attached in the hole, cut a ten foot length from the wall. Next, cut the top cable and keeping hold of it, tie it to the attached ten foot section on the floor in a double fisherman making sure it's tight. Then connect the remaining cable on the floor to the line around the knife and throw it back to me…Got it?"

Being a climber Tia was well aware of the various knots used to secure lines on a climb, Jack was aware of that too.

"Got it." She acknowledged.

Jack gathered in the line and letting the weight of the tethered knife fall through his hands until it was just below his knees, he began to swing it back and forth. It was only fifty feet so it should easily reach, at least he hoped it would.

Tia's shelf was ten feet below their own giving an advantage in the elevation he was hoping for. He swung back one last time and on its return launched it high above the canyon.

All eyes followed the Kabar as it arced over the ravine, a tail of rope slithering behind it. As it descended it wasn't clear if it would reach its target, they all held their breath as they knew the implications if it failed.

It hit the wall with a dull thud and clattered to the floor yards away from Tia's position. She gathered it up and unwrapping the blade, set to work.

Following Jack's instructions Tia finished tying the top cable to the bottom and pulled several times to ensure the double fisherman knot was secured.

Pushing the Kabar into the rope as Jack had done before, she wrapped it in preparation to throw it back across to him. She laid out the rope retrieved from the ravine, ensuring that there were no snags and connected one end to the knife using a square reef to ensure it could be undone once Jack received it. She tied the other end to her wrist, just in case it failed the first time as the new weight may affect the trajectory and plummet into the ravine.

She needn't have worried as, using her good hand with a strength she knew she possessed, the covered blade flew easily through the air at a height that sent it crashing into the wall close enough for Jack to grab hold of it before the trailing rope could drag it over the edge.

"Good Job, Tia. Now we can join you."

Taking the cable from Jenson who had been holding it safe throughout, he used Faversham's cupped hands again to reach the torch ring and tied the rope off, pulling down with all his weight to ensure it held secure.

"I think it best you join Tia first, professor. If you have no objection." Jack cut two lengths of cable, twisting them together, doubling their strength, then using a slipknot formed a loop at each end.

"Absolutely, Jack. More than happy to oblige."

Finishing the makeshift pulley by tying the remaining fifty foot of rope at its centre, Jack ensured that it would return once the professor had crossed. He then moved to the edge and shouted to Tia.

"I'm sending the professor to you first. Make sure you take the weight of the rope…just in case."

Understanding fully, Tia moved to the chasm wall and forming a loop stood in its centre, pulling it up until it rested under her armpits. Grabbing hold of the cable she set her feet to take the weight, raising her hand to let Jack know she was ready.

Throwing the looped pulley over the fixed line, he turned to Faversham.

"Ready?"

Faversham placed a hand into each loop and pulled until the rope tightened around his wrists, grasping just above to ensure that they didn't tighten too much, cutting off any circulation. He followed the cable with his eyes until it finished on the distant image of Tia, her hands grasping the rope in front of her.

As he moved towards the edge, his hands sliding the pulley along with him, he looked at Jack.

"You said just in case earlier. What were you referring to. Just in case what?"

Jack smiled back at him.

"Oh, I wouldn't worry too much, I am sure that we have disabled the booby trap. But the lever that Tia is standing in front of is still connected to the mechanism behind the wall. She's just holding on in case your weight happens to pull the switch and start the metal flying again."

"Hang o..o..o..o n! …"

Jack pushed Faversham off the edge before he had chance to

argue and watched as he hurtled over the ravine. He was holding the excess rope in his hands, letting it smoothly pass through, hoping there was enough left once Faversham reached the other side. He watched the roll at his feet wind away, growing small and smaller.

As he saw the shelf and Tia get ever closer, Faversham raised his feet to make sure that he cleared the edge. He was travelling at such a speed that if he didn't do something soon he would crash into her and crush her against the wall. He began to lower his feet, hoping that the soles of his boots would survive the ravages of the stone floor as he used them as brakes.

He was yanked back with such a force that his legs flew into the air and his groin slammed into the rope. The sudden burst of pain caused a reflex in his throat that squealed around the chasm walls like the call of a banshee. As he came to rest and his feet found solid ground, he closed his eyes and waited for the pain to recede. He thought that his ears were ringing from the jolt, but as he began to regain his wits he realised that the noise was coming from elsewhere. He looked up into Tia's face, a face contorted as she collapsed in fits of laughter. She let go of her line and helped loosen his wrists from the pulley.

As soon as his hands were free, the pulley swept back over the ravine. Faversham looked back at Jack who was pulling it back towards him. The agent stopped for a moment to lift his hand in apology.

"Sorry old chap. A little enthusiastic I'm afraid."

Tia burst out laughing again

67

J ack took the pulley from the line after transporting Mitch, the last of the able bodied of the party, to the other side of the ravine and began adding more rope.

"You are a remarkable man, Mr Case. I can see why the Sheikh trusts you with such an important task."

Gordon Nightly had been watching him closely at every opportunity. He was thorough, strong, single minded. He liked that in a man and he thought he had that with his Head of Security, but Mitch had proved to be a disappointment. Perhaps he had been too hasty to ask for his head now that he had lost Mitch and Aya was disabled.

"I'm here to save his son and the countless others that you have given this thing to. I am not remarkable, I have a job to do and trust me Nightly, once this is all over, you will pay for what you have done."

"Oh…you misunderstand, Mr Case. Like everyone else you think my intentions are purely for my own gain and you are wrong. I will be seen as a saviour of the human race. We will prosper, develop and grow with the promise of life eternal, all illness eradicated. A utopia dreamt of by many, but it will be us, you and I who will be the pioneers of a new world."

He stopped what he was doing and stared at the weak, seriously ill man sitting against the wall.

"Don't involve me in your fantasies and fairy tales, Nightly. We need to defeat only two diseases…The plague that is killing people around the world and the parasite that caused it. In that order."

Nightly said nothing as Jack continued to work with the ropes. But he would show him, he would show them all. He had dealt with the uneducated and the naive all of his life. Ever since the Pharaohs ceased to control their people, failed to maintain discipline, started to show weakness, the world has become fractured…Not anymore. He was the true Pharaoh, the next ruler, the man to show the world the way.

In a few hours they will see for themselves and bow to their one true god…the light of all life…RA.

Jack thread three strips of rope into the loops on the pulley and tied them off creating a much larger loop, big enough to fit a body.

Sitting Nightly into the newly crafted loop he separated each rope, fitting one under his bent knees, one at the top of his thighs and the other on his backside, creating a swing. Once in position he used the last piece of rope to wrap around the scientist's chest, securing it tightly to the sides of the swing, and pulled the man's hands up to hold on to the cable to add stability.

"Now keep hold of the rope at all times and sit still."

Jack eased Nightly out over the edge and feeling his weight begin to slide away from him, he grabbed the trailing rope and taking the weight, fed the cable through his hands, being careful to let the cable run smoothly, gripping it occasionally as the swing began to sway, easing off again as it levelled out.

. . .

Aya was next, she remained silent throughout the whole process, allowing Jack to manoeuvre her into a seated position, securing her into the swing and positioning her one good hand to grip the side as he lowered her gently across the ravine.

Mitch and Jenson freed her from the pulley and attempted to rest her against the wall. But she resisted, preferring instead to stand. She may have been drugged sufficiently against the pain, but her mind was still sharp and her independent, strong personality had very much returned to the surface.

With everyone safely transported across, Jack pulled the swing back one last time. He sat in position and held the trailing rope after throwing it over the line behind him to add friction, ready to use as a brake when he reached the shelf opposite.

He left the canyon edge and began to slide over the ravine, pulling on the trailing line, relieved that the swing slowed. Satisfied, he let it slacken and began to speed up. It took only minutes for the slide to reach its destination.

Once on terra firma Jack left the swing behind, cutting the trailing rope and looping it onto his shoulder. A length of rope may come in handy.

Mitch was already at the entrance, shining his torch into the tunnel.

"Shall we get this over with?" He entered without waiting for an answer, disappearing into the darkness.

Nobody in the group noticed the object fall from Nightly's pocket as he was positioned on the swing. It was a tiny blue porcelain disc, an artefact from a bygone era. It was a sun disc.

She saw it fall with her one good eye and remained focused on it until the last of the group entered the tunnel.

Putting it in the pocket of her jeans she pulled her belt loose and throwing it over the cable, tightly wrapped the leather around each hand.

Gabrielle leapt off of the edge and out over the ravine.

68

The descent down the tunnel was slow and in some places treacherous. It was pitch black even with the Maglites flickering around the craggy surface, as if the darkness was battling with the light, fighting to force it away.

It wasn't a steep gradient but saturated with the water seeping from the cracks and crevices that pock marked the ancient walls, it was treacherous. The passage filled with the sound of boots scraping loose gravel along the uneven floor as one after the other slipped.

"Jesus, guys….there's no rush." Mitch pushed back several times as he was shoved in the back by either Faversham or Tia sliding into him.

"Sorry old chap, but I think we are all struggling here… oops…bugger!"

Faversham slid again catching Mitch on the calf, sending the American's right leg forward and with no purchase on his left he couldn't stop his body from crashing to the ground, sending him sliding forward on a bed of loose shale and gravel. Frantically trying to dig his heels into the ground to stop his slide, the stone floor remained impervious to his boots, if anything it made him speed up. He could do nothing more than wait until he stopped, wherever that may be.

He burst from the tunnel onto a smooth polished floor, closing his eyes for an instant as the darkness of the black stone changed into bright torch lit marble.

Mitch slowed to a stop and as his eyes adjusted to the light he stared all around in wonder at the magnificent hall of statues.

Faversham whistled as he left the tunnel and scanned their new surroundings.

"Wow, this is remarkable...Oh...Sorry about that old chap by the way."

He bent to help Mitch off the floor, dusting at the back of his trousers to brush away flecks of grit. Mitch slapped his hand and stepped away, leaving the professor to circle the room and examine the carved inhabitants.

The majority were male, carved in basic tunics. Some holding tools, some carrying an array of things from representations of vegetation and fruit to more industrial stacks of tiles, sticks and branches. The few females within the display carried water vessels on their shoulders, dressed similarly in basic garb.

"It's a depiction of ordinary Egyptian town folk." Faversham went through his normal practise of placing his glasses on his head as he examined each figure, removing them again as he moved in to get a closer look.

"Where is this supposed to be?" Jack was studying the painting of a walled city of circular turrets behind a body of water that covered the whole of the west wall.

"Could be anywhere..." Tia joined him to take a better look.

"...Egypt was made up of several enclaves, many enclosed for cultural or religious reasons. It was widely accepted that with the worship of many gods along with cultural differences within each territory, the Pharaoh's could allow the factions to self govern. Each city continued to abide by the laws of the land and by creating their own constitutions, became easier to manage. The Pharaohs only had to pull the strings of the governing body of each enclave rather than the people within it. "

"Well perhaps this gives us a clue to what we have here." Mitch wandered to the end of the hall, to an ornate door within a decorative architrave full of hieroglyphics.

Pulling himself away from his studies, Faversham looked over the writings. Some were beyond his scope of learning but he was able to make out a single phrase that seemed to make sense, although menacing in its message.

"All I can confidently make out is…*it is made known the unworthy shall never leave*…the rest I'd need a little time…"

The crash of stone on stone made them face the tunnel entrance, now sealed by a slab of rock.

"Well I guess you'd better be quick…" Mitch turned back to the professor.

"…because I think we are about to find out what it all means."

Gordon Nightly was grateful to be lowered on to the medipac to rest. It kept him no more than eight inches off the floor, but it was far more comfortable than cold stone.

His organs were beginning to fail. He could feel the mucus filling his lungs as pneumonia began to creep around his system, his cough spraying bloody sputum into his hands, down his clothes and congealing around his mouth. His travelling companions had no idea that the air was full of the Y pestis that would eventually infect each and every one of them.

The pathogen had mutated to such an extent that it could not be stopped. The watery sputum it forced from the lungs of its carrier was so fine that it could now travel through the air with ease, searching for more vessels to help it develop and grow.

They had little more than two hours to find the field of reeds. He was determined to survive, he had to survive. From there he would regrow, re energise and develop the antibodies to obliterate the disease.

He would then become the most powerful man on earth, the messiah, the saviour of mankind.

He coughed another bluster of fluid and blood, this time he struggled to take in a breath. A tiny amount of air expanded his lungs before they decided to reverse and expel what little they collected. He felt himself begin to choke.

Through teary eyes he searched for Stacy to help him stand. But she was crouched on her haunches, holding her hand to her breast, struggling to breathe herself. Aya was sitting against the wall by the old tunnel entrance, her breathing shallow, head bowed as she also gasped for breath. Jenson was bent over her, his hands on his knees as his chest pumped furiously, struggling to draw in air.

Light from the torches dimmed as the flames began to shrink.

"Everyone take a deep breath…hold your nose as you breathe in if it helps you to pull in air! Breathe in as deep as you can…"

Jack had been through this before, his ears began to pop as pressure began to surround his body. He shouted instructions as quickly as he could, his voice carrying clearly within the confines.

"…Oxygen is being sucked out from somewhere…keep your lungs expanded as much as you can or they will collapse…then breathe in and out in short bursts keeping your lungs as full as possible…"

Mitch had also noticed the change in the air and like Jack, had filled his lungs and encouraged the professor to do the same.

" We..need..to.. get this…door..open." Faversham raised his eyebrows at the American to confirm that there was nothing like stating the obvious.

He stood and looked over to Tia who was holding her nose as she continued studying the drawing of the walled city with Jack. He left her to it as he knew she would shout if she found a connection.

He should check the statues again, see if there was something that linked them. There must be a reason for them being here.

He walked from one to the other, stopping occasionally to exhale and inhale in short bursts, trying as best he could to keep his lungs full, but it was becoming increasingly difficult the more he moved.

As the lack of oxygen began to lighten his head, he studied the figures through increasingly blurred vision. Looking at the way they were posed, the items they carried, a scythe, an ancient tiller, swords, knives, hammers. It seemed to be a depiction of the people and their roles at the time, nothing out of the ordinary.

The light was failing making it increasingly difficult to see any finer details.

A dull thud from the direction of the tunnel caused Faversham to look up just in time to see Jenson come to rest on the floor, collapsing as his lungs failed him. Aya was behind, slumped against the wall, her head flopped onto her shoulder. Nightly sat on a medipac his chin resting on his chest, his head too heavy to support without the help of oxygen. Stacy was prostrate in front of the unconscious scientist, her head buried in her arms that were splayed in front of her as she tried to break her fall. Everyone was dying…

Slumping to the floor as vertigo took hold, Faversham crawled along the cool marble floor. He was hoping that it wasn't a trick of the eye, it was three figures along, something he hadn't noticed before, perhaps a clue.

It was the figure of a man wielding a machete, a machete that had been carved strapped to his hand, cord carefully crafted around his closed fist, criss-crossing up his wrist and tied off at his forearm. The reason for the strapping was clearly evident as there was no left hand, the carving stopped at the end of the wrist with a bandaged pad crafted on the end.

He noticed several fingers missing on the figure next to him, a man holding a spear, both hands on its shaft, stubbed fingers scrunched at their tips to show a basic repair of botched stitching.

. . .

"Rhinocolura! Of course…"

With a strength that was borne from the adrenalin of his discovery, he pulled himself up on the fingerless spearman and looked into its stone face, at the bearded blank stare of a criminal from a bygone era.

Taking his maglite he smashed the shaft into the stone face, sending the nose to the floor. Even before it landed on the marble, Faversham pulled his own nose towards the hole in the face of the spearman and breathed in beautiful, sweet, clean air.

"It's the noses….Smash the noses off the male statues!" He shouted across the hall as he methodically walked the line sending broken stone noses clattering across marble, relieved to hear the hiss of air as it burst from shattered faces. Light filled the room as the torches reignited.

He stopped short for a second as heads from the figures opposite exploded into showers of splintered stone. He saw the Glock appear as Jack Case slowly rose to his feet, blasting several heads into dust until he emptied the clip. Tia was using her maglite on the rest, feeling all of her strength return as the hall filled with oxygen.

The door slid away from the ornate architrave revealing the exit to the next chamber.

"Well, I gotta say, prof…That was well done… but how did you know?" Mitch chipped away the last of the noses on his way to join the rest who were helping revive Nightly and the others.

"As is always the case. Once you crack it you feel a fool as we should have seen it from the start. "

"Three thousand years ago, thieves were punished based on the severity of their crimes, some would have fingers removed as a lesson, others would have a hand removed as a harsh punishment and forced onto the streets to beg for forgiveness for the rest of their days. But it soon became clear that Egypt was rife with poverty away from the hall of kings and they began to realise that the punishments were creating more disabled than able bodied men to assist in the construction of their cities and temples. So, it was decided to create a prison in the form of a walled city near the city of Gaza which they named Tharu, later renamed by the Greeks as Rhinocolura. "

"The punishment for anyone caught stealing from then on was to have their noses removed from their faces and condemned to live in the city for the rest of their lives. It enabled the Pharaohs to guarantee able bodied men when needed and at the same time ensure thieves were removed from the streets, because if they escaped they would be immediately recognised for what they were and returned to Rhonocolura…"

The party began to recover as the air flowed freely through the hall. Nightly was getting worse, his breathing laboured in between coughing spasms, but they all knew he would need to complete the journey if there was to be an end to this.

Aya accepted a shot of morphine from Jenson and waited for it to take effect, giving Faversham time to complete his tale.

"…The inscription on the door *'it is made known the unworthy shall never leave'* meant that to exit the chamber we would need to leave the unworthy or in this case, the thieves, behind. So we needed to create the inhabitants of Rhinocolura with the clues being the image of the city on the wall and the previously punished criminals within this group of statues. Quite simple really."

Jack added a fresh clip to his Glock and racked a bullet into the chamber.

"Well, we should move on everyone. We have ninety minutes left to find this field.

Keeping an intentionally slow pace to allow everyone to stay together, he led them past the noseless and headless criminals and through the ornate architrave to discover their next challenge, daring to hope it was their last, only to inevitably face the disappointment of yet another task.

69

T he first thing that struck them as they entered the new chamber was the smell, a mix of earth, vegetation and a putrid undercurrent of decay.

"Jesus…smells like shit in here." Mitch had only just got used to breathing clean air again. He had smelt farms better than this, even after the manure had been spread.

Through the dim light Jack could see the dark shapes of torches suspended on the walls close to them. In all of the other rooms the torches had lit on entrance, these sat suspended like dark sentinels watching and waiting.

The floor seemed to disappear six feet ahead of them, as eyes adjusted to the darkness the top steps of a stairwell came into view.

"Looks like we've found more water." Faversham looked over the edge and watched the gentle sway of the floor undulating in small waves.

He reached for his maglite to get a better look when the harsh sound of rock grating against rock resonated across the room. Light emanated through the opening on the far wall revealing a doorway as the stone slab disappeared into the floor.

Torches erupted along the walls as rich oxygen diluted some of the stench, illuminating the chamber in an instant. The room suddenly filled with a rhythmic ticking, as if the light had started a thousand clocks. It increased in momentum until it became more of a buzz as all sound melded into one.

Faversham backed away from the edge…

"Holy Christ almighty!"

Tia and Jack moved out of his way as he retreated past them, stumbling back until he hit the chamber wall.

"What is it, Iggy?" Tia felt the hairs prickle on her neck, she knew Iggy well and very few things phased him, but he looked genuinely terrified. His expression, his whole demeanour was enough to put the fear of god in her.

"Oh fuck!" Mitch backed away from the edge and faced the group.

" Anyone got some bug spray?"

"What is it?" Tia looked from the American back to Iggy.

"Deathstalkers. Hundreds and thousands of deathstalkers."

"Oh this place just gets better and better." Jack hated scorpions.

Looking over the edge, his stomach lurched as he stared into the undulating lake of yellow. A lake made up of thousands of death stalker scorpions fighting for space, climbing over each other, the ticking buzz growing louder as tiny jagged feet scrambled over each other's bony carapaces.

Apart from four shrubs of vegetation covering the arthropod's access in and out of the chamber, there was nothing else visible until stone steps rose towards the exit fifty feet away.

Jack had enough rope to stretch, but not enough to carry the wounded in a makeshift sling. It would make no difference anyway as the torches were poked into slots formed within the smooth walls.

"There's only one thing for it…we will have to walk across."

"We'd better get a move on then." Tia pulled a flaming torch from its housing and headed to the stairs. She could tell that not one of the tough guys really fancied being first.

She was used to them after fighting her way through several tombs, caverns and arid landscapes during her adventures. Even though the deathstalker was one of the most dangerous of the species, they were no different to every other arachnid. They feared a flame.

From the bottom step she lowered the flame towards the floor. A path of sand and grit appeared as scorpions climbed over each other desperate to escape the heat, leaving a two foot circular space for her to step into. Keeping her eyes on the floor she swept the torch in a wide arc around her as she moved forward at a snail's pace being careful to put the flame behind her occasionally as arthropods began to reform and head towards her.

"This is the best way to do it guys, they will stay away long enough for you to move forward. Just remember to sweep behind or they will be on you quickly. One bite would be fatal."

Although that wasn't strictly true, one sting wouldn't kill a full grown adult although it would be extremely painful and the venom, a powerful mix of neurotoxins would cause the body to collapse. On this floor it would be curtains.

Tia felt her foot give way as she took her next step, the floor was crumbling in front of her. Instinctively leaping forward, she landed on solid ground squashing a number of scorpions as she slid to a stop on her knees. She waved the torch frantically around her, panic taking hold as she watched the arthropods close in.

Scrambling to her feet she regained some composure and swept a wide arc of flame around her, pushing the scorpions away. Hundreds of them hurtled into the two foot hole that opened in the floor, looking like a pool of yellow sludge disappearing into a drain.

They appeared to increase in speed as anger flowed through them, a hiss filling the air as they roared a call to arms, their severity growing as tails flipped upright, stingers aimed forward waiting for the perfect moment to strike.

She could see the steps no more than fifteen feet away, the path blocked by a growing horde of scorpions scrambling over each other to get to the invader of their lair.

The torch sparked as the bravest of the arthropods exploded, caught in the sweeping arc of the flame.

First instincts were to run for the exit, her whole body tense, every sense wanting to flee, every hair rising on her body, prickling with fear.

But letting her experience rule her head, she edged forward torch extended, sweeping slower, seeing the horde thin out as the heat began to reach towards them.

Her foot gave way again five feet from the stairs, the floor disappearing in front of her.

Pushing forward to leap to safety her body sank and followed the sand, stone and rubble into the void. She threw the torch away as her body fell, with no foothold she kicked her legs furiously trying to gain some purchase, only to kick dust as it rose from the widening hole.

Thrusting her arms forward, Tia instinctively stretched her fingers and grasped for anything that would stop her. Both palms smacked against the bottom step of the stone stairwell, momentum pushed her legs forward and her boots kicked into the pit wall threatening to pull her hands away from safety.

She dug her fingers into the stone as she felt her hands slip backwards, gritting her teeth she pulled hard, taking all of her weight on her forearms in an attempt to halt the slide. Her fingertips held fast.

Before her muscles gave out, she pulled with her right arm and hooked her left forearm over the step and using it to take her weight, brought her right arm up. Using the tips of her boots to scrabble up the pit wall, she managed to pull herself onto a second step and with one final effort pulled her legs to safety.

She took the steps two at a time grateful to be away from the horrors below.

Turning, she sat on the top step, pulled her knees up and hugged them.

Tia closed her eyes, taking deep breaths to bring her heart rate down as it pumped painfully in her chest.

She looked over to the group and even from fifty feet away could see the concern on their faces.

She waved, assuring them she was fine, but she wasn't sure who she was trying to convince.

"So this is how we'll do it. I'll take Nightly...Mitch you take Stacy...professor, you and Jenson help Aya across. Follow the route Tia took, no deviation. Let's get out of here."

Jack cut a short length from the rope and tied Nightly's hands together. The scientist was in no fit state to cross the floor on his own and, like it or not, he was tasked to ensure that they reached their goal.

Taking one of the remaining four torches, Jack lowered himself on his haunches and waited for Stacy to assist Nightly to place his tied hands over the LARA agent's head and around his neck. The scientist was too weak to resist and once Jack stood with Nightly hanging on his back he couldn't believe how light the man was.

Like a five foot four limp rucksack, Nightly offered no resistance as Jack took his first step onto the chamber floor. Legs bent and leaning forward to keep his passengers feet clear of the scorpions, Jack dragged the torch across the floor in front of him taking many arthropods with it. Occasionally a scorpion burst into flames and ran back into the hoard setting fire to several more, a strategy that kept them at bay long enough for Jack to make good progress across the floor. It was more than useful as it allowed him to stand to his full height and stride over the first hole in the floor with ease.

Tia was waiting for them on the bottom step as Jack cleared the final path to the edge of the hole. It had grown by a foot since first uncovered by Tia, widened by the hundreds of eight legged arthropods that were continually scuttling in and out, their hooked claws scraping new soil into the void at each pass.

Pulling Nightly's arms from around his neck, Jack turned the scientist to face him. He laid the torch behind them, relieved to see the arachnids push back from the flames. He needed the extra seconds to complete the crossing.

"I need you to lock your fingers and hold on tight."

Nightly did as he was told and interlaced his fingers, the rope connected to his wrists hanging loose between his forearms.

"Now lift your arms above your head and keep them there, stand as straight as you can at all times...Oh, and trust me."

As Jack began to lean Nightly backwards over the pit the scientist kicked out and screamed at the top of his voice...

"NO! DON"T....You need me....PLEASE...NO!"

Jack pulled Nightly back towards him, pulling him so close they could touch noses and focused ice blue eyes into the madman's.

"Don't be an idiot! If I wanted you dead and believe me that is how you should be, I'd have shot you when we first met. Now stay still and do as you are told."

Nightly stiffened at the rebuke and although raising his arms as he was told, he focused on Jack as he was lowered, imagining the blood soaked head that he would fix to a pole once he was immortal. There was a world to lead into a new future and Jack Case was not going to be part of it.

Jack nodded to Tia as Nightly was eased over the edge towards her. Tia, already in the program, took hold of the rope tethered to his wrists and held on as Jack bent to lift the scientist by the ankles. With him now horizontal, Tia ascended the stairs backwards pulling the scientist with her. Once Jack had stretched as far as he could, he let go of the mans ankles allowing Tia to pull the scientist clear of the pit and safely onto the steps.

Jack stepped across and together they helped Nightly towards the exit, resting him against a wall as they waited for the others.

∼

Stacy remembered way back in the meeting room before all this began that Mitch had addressed her as 'Stace'. She hated the man ever since.

"Are you ready?" Mitch bent down with his back to her and offered his arms to wrap around her legs.

Having watched the previous crossings by the girl and Gordon Nightly with the agent, she was terrified and panicked more than she expected. The thought of the scorpions climbing all over her gave her the creeps. She had never been good with creepy crawlies and even the smallest of spiders had her running for the hills. She would not be able to put her feet anywhere near the chamber floor without wanting to run. She would fall, she knew it, and they would be on her in seconds.

The more she thought about it the more she freaked. So it was no surprise that she climbed onto Mitch's back and let him piggy back her down the stairs and onto the writhing floor.

She buried her face into his neck, clamping her eyes shut as he swept a swathe of fire in front of them.

"Come on you bastards! Suck on this."

Whether through bravado or genuine fearless confidence, Mitch made her feel safe. Even when he stooped forward to attack more arthropods, jabbing the torch forward like a sword, bringing her closer to the floor, she knew he would not let her fall.

Jack watched from the bottom of the stairs as the American dodged and weaved across the chamber shouting expletives as scorpions burst into flame. The young scientist bobbed and jostled around his shoulders as if in a rodeo, clinging on for dear life, hoping that it would be over soon.

He had grown to like the man even though they had an issue that needed resolving. He was a man after his own heart, resolute, determined and focused, even if his Americanism did sometimes exacerbate the situation, he stood by his convictions.

As Mitch reached the edge of the pit he bent low as scorpions leapt from the darkness, jabbing with the torch, clearing a path to get closer.

Jack held his hand out to help with the three foot void between the chamber floor and the steps.

Throwing the torch into the pit, Mitch locked forearms with him and taking a wide stride hopped onto the base of the stairs. Scorched air rose from the pit as hundreds of arthropods ignited upon contact with the discarded flame, the acrid smoke stung their eyes and entered their nostrils causing them all to gag.

"Jesus. Smelly fuckers!" Mitch coughed as he moved his free hand to his shoulder to help Stacy dismount, releasing his other arm from her leg to allow her feet to reach the steps.

A scorpion crawled over his fingers and headed for Stacy's face as it searched for an escape from the carnage below.

Screaming, she let go of Mitch's neck and fell backwards pulling him with her. Mitch managed to grab her leg as momentum caused her to kick it into his armpit and held on as they both tumbled into the hole.

Jack caught Mitch's foot and held on with both hands, his legs planted firmly on the stone steps. He leant back to compensate for the impact as Mitch and Stacy crashed against the pit wall.

Tia raced down to help and caught the other flailing boot of the American and together they eased backwards ascending one slow step at a time.

Stacy's screams echoed around the cavernous hole as her head stopped a foot from the bottom, hot glowing embers of dead arthropods singed her hair and falling scorpions flicked over her face as they fell to their deaths, unable to scale the walls to retreat the carnage.

She shook her head vigorously as she felt herself being lifted.

She was unable to close her eyes and watched hundreds of scorpions scaling the walls, some jumping towards her, landing on her chin as they tried to hitch a lift out of the pit. Being upside down she tried to keep her hands close to her chest, brushing relentlessly as she felt the touch of tiny hooked feet scuttling over her body.

Strong hands grabbed her wrists and yanked her up and onto stone steps.

"There you go. You're safe now."

She looked into Jack's eyes, his calming voice immediately confirming she was clear of danger.

Mitch was resting on the stairs next to them, his head back staring at the ceiling, breathing heavily as he calmed his heart.

Standing over him she looked down at his ruddy complexion, his stubble now a deep black stain around his jaw. He smiled at her and for reasons she would never understand, she fell on him and began to sob.

Mitch closed his arms around her and kissed her forehead.

"Don't worry Stace…I've got you.'

Watching each member of the party tackle the chamber before them convinced Faversham that they were about to meet with a catastrophe.

The sting from a deathwatch is a pain that he hoped he'd never have to experience again. He was stung on a dig in Libya and even though an antidote was given within the hour, he was hospitalised for three days. The neurotoxin had paralysed his left side, culminating in the loss of use of his left leg. Five months of debilitating therapy and a re-education of certain aspects of his gait later, he was back to full health apart from one lasting condition. Occasionally, his left leg would seize when crouching, causing it to collapse and need a minute or two of rest before it became fully functional again. It hadn't gone for a few years now, but with his half empty pessimism it was at the forefront of his mind that it would happen again halfway across this chamber.

.   .   .

With a torch each, Jenson took the lead with Aya's good arm wrapped around his own while Faversham swept a wide arc of flame behind them. The damage to her shoulder meant that there was no way to transport Aya across the floor other than walk her across. Jenson insisted on the escort as he wasn't convinced that she was as strong as she said she was and they could not afford to lose her now they had come this far.

Faversham was drenched from the exertion, his flowing hair stuck to his face and occasionally he wiped the sting of salty sweat from his eyes.

As well as the torch flame he began to kick and stamp at the scorpions as they continued the relentless assault on them. It appeared that the more they cleared a path, the scorpions multiplied by the time they returned to continue their attack.

Clearing the first smaller pit with relative ease Jenson stopped a yard from the tiny chasm that continued to grow in front of the stairwell.

"There is no way we can make it from here."

The hole grew wider and was overflowing with arthropods as more and more poured in over the ones pouring out, their illuminated bodies created a yellow hue that seemed to bubble across the surface like molten lava, rising and falling across the surface.

Jack and Tia were stamping and kicking them away from the steps on the other side as they began to rise towards them, soon they would take the stairs.

"We'll need to navigate around the pit and get to the stairwell from the side."

Faversham continued to sweep the flame across the floor as he followed Aya and Jenson's feet, sweeping across his path and to the rear as the scorpion activity seemed to accelerate, they had sensed that they were changing course.

As they arced around the pit to approach the open stairwell from the side, the arthropods followed. But the humans had the advantage as there were no entrances into the chamber from the south wall which meant the onslaught was initially only from the north. It allowed Faversham to concentrate on one direction while Jenson manoeuvred Aya around towards where Jack was waiting on the third step three feet from the floor.

Jenson crouched to Aya's right, lacing his fingers to provide a foothold for her as Jack leant forward offering his hands to grab her good arm to pull her onto the steps.

"Get a move on guys, these bastards are spreading out."

Faversham was spreading his torch as wide as he could but many of the creatures, being wise to his reach, began to lead several legions around the range of heat and flame.

Aya pushed her foot onto Jenson's hands and with Jack holding her wrist she was lifted into the air.

The pain that shot through the medic's body hit him like a bolt of electricity. Jumping away from his crouch sent Aya flying towards Jack who was already braced to support her. Letting go of her arm he managed to move his hands to her waist, catching her safely and sat her next to him out of harm's way as he turned back to Jenson. He caught brief sight of the medic before he disappeared into a sinkhole as the ground fell away from under him.

The medipac flew out of the hole passing hundreds of Scorpions as they scuttled in after the medic. The container of morphine slid across the floor squashing a number of the arthropods before coming to rest by the side of the steps.

He saw the scorpion fall from his calf as he jumped backwards. It had escaped the swathe of flames and climbed onto his fatigues, injecting him with venom as Jenson crouched to lift Aya.

As the floor gave way he went straight down, shattering his ankle as it turned on loose rock, unable to straighten as the rest of his body plummeted ten feet to the bottom.

Being less than two feet wide, Jenson was wedged in place unable to move. Pain racked through him as the neurotoxins began to effect other parts of his body, his head exploded with pain making him cry out.

He could feel the hooked feet of scorpions as they clambered over him, it was as if he was caught in a downpour, feeling all eight legs of each and every arthropod as it landed on him and scuttled to find a clear space of its own. The first of the stings caught him by surprise as he was pierced in several parts of his body. He took four in the thighs which made him scream in agony, but nothing compared to the ones in his neck, his skin exposed, stings piercing relentlessly in a frenzy.

In agony, convulsing with spasms and with confusion filling his senses, he managed to muster enough strength in both mind and body to throw the medipac free of the pit. On its way out the case struck the sidewalls and several more scorpions fell onto him, their anger piercing the skin all over his body.

He looked at the opening above and saw the face of Jack Case looking down at him, he tried to scream for help but as he opened his mouth two scorpion ran deep into his throat, stings reigned on his tongue, his cheeks and as he swallowed he felt his larynx erupt.

Gagging, he stared at Jack unable to move as he watched him lift his hand towards him. His vision became blurred with an obstruction which he tried desperately to clear, opening and closing his eye to try and focus. As his pupils began to work for the final time the obstruction became clear, it was the five segmented tail of a scorpion the barbed sharp point of its aculeus aimed directly at the centre of his eye.

He watched fascinated as it quivered to attention, its point moving closer as he continued to stare. He watched it crack through his cornea and sink into the pupil, but it was the flash that came with it that surprised him the most. It took away the pain, helped him relax…made him forget.

Jack put the Glock back in his jacket. Jenson was now out of pain, it was all he could do to help him. The man was wedged and by the time he got to him, scorpions had filled the sinkhole up to the guy's chest.

"You…you shot him!!"

Jack grabbed Faversham underneath one arm and lifting him fully to his feet, pulled him along towards the stairs.

As they passed the sinkhole, Jack pushed the professor's head over the edge.

"I had no choice, he was gone. He would have done the same for me."

Faversham let Jack drag him to the stairs and push him onto the steps as his mind tried to extinguish the image from the pit.

The image of an eyeless head, mouth wide open overrun with scorpions as several ran in and out of the fleshy cavern, pulling segments of throat with them.

Nobody spoke as they ascended the stairs and made their way through the exit. Jack came up the rear with Aya as they followed the others down a winding slope of sandstone. Tia and Faversham walked together several feet ahead of them with Mitch and Stacey supporting Nightly from the front, disappearing occasionally as the curve in the slope became more acute.

"Thank you…" Aya spoke without taking her eyes from the sandstone ahead.

"He was a good man and I would have done the same to save his suffering."

It was the first time that she had spoken since her injury and it took him a little by surprise. He was impressed by her strength and resolve since coming round from a drug induced sleep. Her arm remained strapped to her side but she seemed to take it in her stride, which considering the mess of her shoulder meant she either had the pain threshold of a superhero or the drugs were working.

"I had no choice, he was gone anyway…" He didn't feel the need to justify his actions and really had no intention of dwelling on it.

"…How are you? I've no idea what your boss has planned for you, but are you feeling up to it?"

She continued to look straight ahead, a steely determination etched over her face.

"My heart is in far more pain than a bullet could ever cause…"

She was referring to the revelation that Nightly was her father. Something that was not only a surprise but had appeared to blow her world apart.

"…I will do what is necessary and will see where the consequences lead us."

Nothing more was said as they rounded the bend and caught up with the rest of the group who were congregated at a dead end.

Inscriptions filled every inch of the walls, both image and hieroglyph in browns and reds, enriching the deep yellow of the sandstone.

Two intricately carved cobras grew from the wall directly in front of them, their hooded heads staring down at a grooved track containing four symbols; the sun, the moon, a star and a scarab beetle.

Nightly stood on his own, looking up at the engravings, running his finger along some of the grooves within the crafted images, mumbling to himself.

Faversham met them as the floor levelled out.

"I think we should take a little rest. Perhaps recharge our batteries."

Jack narrowed his eyes.

"…And what makes you think we have the time for a rest?" According to his timing they only had forty minutes before midday.

"We've found it. The hall of Maat, the final task to enter Aaru… The Field of Reeds."

70

"Fascinating…" Faversham continued the routine of lifting his glasses, returning them to his nose, removing them and putting them on again as he studied the many inscriptions on the walls surrounding the main cobra wall.

"…This is a collection of maps of the underworld, different routes, different challenges but all leading here…see?"

The walls were covered with tiny images of the people of the times. Some Pharaohs, some gods and some of servants and guides. Hieroglyphics and symbols followed tracks through various areas on the map inscribed with scorpions, snakes, lions, elephants and a variety of earth symbols, fire, water and air.

"…These show the tasks…Look this seems to be our route or part of it at least. Clever…It appears that the underworld is procedurally generated as you pass through each chamber. So there was never a right or wrong way of completing it, the underworld decides it for you."

Tia stood beside Nightly, studying the symbols below the giant cobra carvings. They moved along a grooved track with four branches leading up the wall towards the head of the snakes.

She was surprised how smoothly they moved along the track, only a slight scrape as she positioned the sun symbols into the top branch…

"NO STOP!" Faversham moved past Jack and grabbed both Tia and Nightly, pulling them back by their shoulders. Nightly, weakening all the time, collapsed backwards, only the quick reactions of Stacy catching hold of him before his head crashed against the stone floor, saved him from any serious damage.

Fire exploded from the mouths of each cobra hitting the floor where the two had been standing. The force of the flames sent glowing embers of sand into the air stinging their skin as it sprayed over them.

It stopped as fast as it started. Only the heat remained, filling the hall with a malevolent silent warmth and a sense that there was more to come.

"Jesus! What was all that about?" Mitch dusted himself off as he got back to his feet.

"This is the final gate, the gate of Desert-Baiu. Guarded by the goddess Isis and her sister the goddess Nephthys…"

Tia moved back towards the cobras and pointed to the hieroglyphs that bordered the wall ascending from both sides of the snakes…'*The great god comes forth to this gate, this great god enters through it, and the gods who are there praise the great god*'

"The goddesses are the guards of the halls of Maat. It is here that they test the purity of the subject before they are judged. Isis is also known as Nebet Neseret, the fiery one, the Lady of Flame, the fire spitting uraeus cobra and protector of the Kingdom of Osiris and the afterlife."

Faversham joined her and continued the story…

"We have to prove our worthiness to pass through the gates…."

He moved to the loose symbols and began to place them up the track towards the four meandering branches. Moving the Scarab into the top branch and lifting the sun symbol, Tia took a step back keeping her eyes on the mouth of one of the cobra carvings, just in case.

Faversham placed the sun symbol on the second branch and started to move the star.

"I hope you know what you're doing, Iggy." This was beyond Tia's understanding.

"So do I…" Faversham finished positioning the star on the third branch and went to the last symbol, the moon.

"…When the gates of the afterlife is finished, the sun rises on the world in the form of the sacred scarab, Khepri, the deification of the morning sun. That is of course, if I have translated it correctly"

As soon as the moon symbol was set onto the fourth branch, the air filled with the grating of stone on stone as the two cobra carvings slowly moved inward. As they sank into the sandstone the wall slid aside.

"I guess I got it right. Behold ladies and gentlemen…The Hall of Maat."

∾

71

The hall was pure white, almost clinically clean with no impurities on the floor, walls or ceiling. It glowed so brightly that it pained the eyes if stared at for too long.

A gigantic solitary statue stood before them. The body of a muscular man dressed in only a short shendyt of pure gold wrapped around his waist, covering only his modesty to expose vast muscular legs, standing at least thirty foot tall, holding a staff with a Cobra at its tip. He had the head of a growling jackal, angular snout and sharp pointed ears adding to the malevolence of the creature, pure black save for tiny golden globes for eyes.

Aya backed away in awe as she stared at the growling wolf like head of the god that had became a legend from her past, an object of many of her childhood nightmares. This was becoming too real.

"Anubis…" Gordon Nightly moved forward, his head raised as he stared in awe at the eyes of the deity.

"The overseer for the judgment of the dead. Son of Osiris and Nephthys…" Faversham gave the explanation to anyone who listened.

"…His role is to weigh the heart against the feather of Maat."

. . .

A golden bath sized bowl sat either side of the statue, backed with the intricate design of mechanical scales etched into the wall. Shade and reflections had been expertly crafted to create a near perfect 3D rendering.

Nightly, seemingly in a trance, began to climb into one of the bowls.

"NO!..." Jack, already on edge as he prepared for the next challenge, reached Nightly before Faversham's warning shout stopped echoing around the walls, pulling the scientist out before he had time to place both feet.

"No! ...wait... I must. It's my destiny. I need to prove the purity of my soul."

Even though he was weakened, Jack still had to keep hold of the man as he continued to struggle.

"I'd think twice before proving your purity if I were you, there's near on eight billion people who would beg to differ."

He handed Nightly over to Stacy, pushing him towards her by the shoulders until she had him in her arms.

"Keep an eye on him until we know what we are up against."

Stacy hated being ordered about. She was a colleague of the scientist, not his carer. But seeing Jack's face, his expression leaving no room for negotiation, she moved Nightly away from him.

Faversham nodded thanks to Jack for his quick action.

"The book of the dead gives accounts of the weighing of the heart. It states that should the heart prove heavier than the feather, then it is full of evil and thrown to Ammit, the devourer of the dead, who would eat it and doom the sinner to eternal hell. Ammit was part lion, part crocodile and part hippo."

"Of course he was..." Jack had given up being surprised at anything thrown at him in here.

"...So how do we work this thing?

. . .

"You don't....You watch me pass through before you die..." The group turned to face the entrance, straight into the terrified face of Tia as she stood next to the bandaged woman who had her by the throat with a gun pointing at her temple.

Gabrielle Millson was smiling. Unfortunately, the nerves completely destroyed on one side of her face made it more like a grimace, teeth fully exposed along with part of her jaw bone as the skin had rotted around it.

Pressing the pistol firmly into the archeologist's temple, she used her other hand to caress the pert backside of the pretty young thing and found what she was looking for. She drew the scroll from the back pocket of the khaki shorts.

72

"Gabrielle. Don't be stupid, we've got this far, we can fix all this. Even you, look at you, you need help. Let's do this together."

Mitch took tentative steps towards her.

She had no reason to trust him, she had every right to hate him and looking at the mess that was now her face, again his fault, he wouldn't be surprised if she blew him away right now. But he had to do something or all this shit will be for nothing.

He could feel the pressure begin to build in his head, he could hear the explosions from a war that had transformed his life, had caused him to murder his mother in law, had ruined the life of the woman in front of him.

The beautiful blonde with the red flash in her hair, the confident fun loving minx with dreams of a perfect life with the man she loved…

"Fuck you, Dawson. Come any closer and this pretty little head explodes. You deserve nothing, you all deserve nothing. This is my time and I am going to enjoy every single second."

"You can't…" Gordon Nightly moved Stacy aside and stood as straight as his weakening body would allow.

"…It is destined that the one true descendent of Amenhotep IV shall lead the world towards the sun. That the great almighty Ra, God of Light, will allow all men to live when he shines."

"Ooh, ladi dadi ladi dar…..Who made you in charge, dickhead. I think you need more than just a birth certificate to complete this little puzzle, Mr Nightly…Something like this." With her hand still holding the scroll, Gabrielle reached into the top pocket of her shirt and withdrew the tiny sun disc lifted from a museum in England some weeks ago.

Nightly backed away, his eyes wide with terror. It was if he had been shot as he staggered backwards and crumpled to the floor.

"Well, that was easy." Gabrielle allowed herself a little smirk as she pulled Tia towards the statue of Ammit while the group ran to help the old man.

Jack pulled his Glock as the woman dragged Tia towards one of the bowls. She was good as he had no clear shot, positioning herself directly behind Tia, keeping stride with her as she was pushed sideways. He would need to bide his time.

"You have to stop her…she has no idea." Nightly had been helped to a seated position. He pointed at the two women as they closed in on the statue.

Stacy was amazed at how old he looked as the disease took hold of him in earnest. His breathing was laboured, his voice weak and fragmented and his skin had developed a deathly pallor. If they didn't find what they were looking for soon he wouldn't be around to see it.

"Oh I wouldn't worry yourself too much, Nightly. You'll all be helping…You see, I can't do this without you. Now Mitch, bring Nightly and climb in that thing with him." Gabrielle pointed to the bowl on the opposite side.

Mitch could see that he had no choice but to comply for the

moment as Gabrielle held all the cards. Tia was trapped and looked terrified, she held herself stiffly as if any movement could prove her last.

"Do something somebody, for God's sake. You can't just stand in the scales, that is not how it works. Tia tell her."

Faversham was helpless and seeing the gun at Tia's head made him wish he carried a weapon more often. He made a mental note for future reference, but for now he had to think of something else.

"Oh don't worry, pretty boy, I won't harm your girlfriend as long as you all do as you are told. And you are wrong by the way, it is exactly what the scales are meant for."

"Careful Gabi, don't give too much away. I'm waiting for you on the other side, nobody else. This is our time my baby girl...come to me."

Gabrielle smiled at the apparition standing within the bowl next to her. Barbara wore her favourite spring dress, the one with the flowers, the one she wore on the day she made her favourite chilli salad, that balmy spring afternoon at the house. The same balmy spring afternoon that her son in law stabbed her with the knife she had used to slice the tomatoes, the spring onions, the zucchini. The day Mitch Dawson ruined her life forever.

"Get your goddamn hands off of me!" Nightly fought with Mitch as he led him towards the statue. His Head of Security had a strength that overpowered him when healthy, in his current state it was a pointless protest.

"Shut up old man. She has no idea what she is doing, just play along until we get Tia away from her."

Nightly stopped struggling as Mitch lifted him into the bath sized bowl, sitting him on the edge as he climbed in himself. The floor of the bowl was engraved with the intricate design of a feather, its vane swirling around the base giving the surface a delicate soft appearance.

"The feather of Maat." Nightly stared at the design, an exultant rush of adrenalin coursed through his body as he realised that he was so close to the fulfilment of a lifetime.

Gabrielle manoeuvred her leg over the side of the bowl engraved with a human heart on its base while using Tia's shoulder for support, ensuring the barrel of her gun continued to press against the girl's temple. She positioned her outside the bowl as a human shield.

Faversham took a few furtive steps towards the women, focusing on Gabrielle as he moved.

"You do realise that this won't work Gabrielle, don't you? I can understand why you are using Mr Nightly and Mitch as the feather, which would prove heavier than you as the heart. But the ritual is based on the purity of the seeker of Aaru, not just the heart being lighter. It will not let you pass."

Smiling back, it appeared that she hadn't noticed he was closing in on her.

"That is one theory, pretty boy. But there are just as many theories as there are gods. My former boss for instance, was from a different boys club, part of the cult of Amun, and his theory is that the key to our goal is within this parchment. It has to be there at the end, like a passport. You don't really think that you have to rip your heart out to gain entrance surely?"

"Probably not, but we have our theories and we don't have that long to work through them. Please let us work with you Gabrielle, we can do this together. The whole world is depending on us."

Faversham held his hands forward, both beseeching and empathetic, attempting to gain enough trust to give him the chance to get Tia away from her.

"Don't let them do it to you again, Gabi. This man is like all the others, he is trying to make a fool out of you. Look at the pathetic

fool, grinning at you like a moron. He thinks he can use his looks to get the better of you...look at him Gabi...LOOK AT HIM!"

Gabrielle raised her hand. She could tell that mother was getting angry, she didn't want that, not now.

"Move one more step and I'll blow your girlfriend's brains out. You can either hold her whole or gather her up in pieces, your choice. Now back the fuck up and shut your mouth."

Faversham backed away again until he was alongside Jack, as the woman climbed into the bowl and let the scroll fall to her feet.

"Get ready to grab Tia." Jack whispered in the professor's ear as he prepared for what might happen next.

Nightly was with Mitch and he could cover Stacy and the professor, Aya was well away from them all, unmoving against the far wall, her eyes fixed on the statue. But Tia needed help and he had to trust that the academic was ready to move.

He wasn't surprised when the professor changed his stance and leant forward on his leading foot as if waiting for a starting pistol. The one thing he'd learnt about Faversham throughout this whole adventure was that subtlety wasn't one of his traits.

Everyone held their breath and waited. The deathly silence became more uncomfortable as seconds passed, moving into minutes.

Gabrielle could feel mother next to her as her eyes moved to the opposite scale, the bowl containing Mitch and Nightly.

She studied the man she had given her life to. His strong features, the way he carried himself, the way he looked at her now, the concern on his face, the same concern he showed in Helmand when surrounded by insurgents with no chance of escape. The way he carried the responsibility for getting them trapped in the tiny farmhouse and the tenderness he showed when they had made love, thinking it was their last night on earth. It had been explosive, exhilarating, leaving a determination to survive, a reason to live.

. . .

"What now?" Mitch's sardonic tone cut through her like a knife. She hated him, hated him so much.

Dropping the small sun disc, she held out her hand to feel for her mother as the tiny ceramic rattled in the bowl around her feet.

She stared up at the enormous legs of the statue, following the rippling muscles over the short skirt and up through his toned torso, following the snout of the snarling wolf, stopping at the fearsome, angry eyes that stared down from the ceiling at those who stood before him. Looking for a sign, a hint of what she was meant to do.

The bowl began to vibrate, light at first, tingling through her feet. It pulsed and churned, growing in intensity, vibrating through her calves. She began to feel unsteady on her feet as the floor began to shake, causing her to place her hands on the side to steady herself.

Jack, seizing his chance, ran at Tia leaving Faversham still in the ready position. Tia, having the same idea, ran towards him. As they converged Jack pulled Tia to the floor, the bullet smashed into the marble, a foot away from them.

Gabrielle steadied herself as best she could and took aim at the fallen targets…the floor disappeared from beneath her feet.

Falling forward she plummeted into a pit, with her good eye she could see the tips of the steel spikes hurtle towards her. She turned her head just in time to avoid the point thrusting through her retina, instead it pierced her temple, another through her cheek and yet another through her neck, pinning her head to the side. Numerous steel pins pierced her arms, torso, legs.

There was no pain as she felt the weight of her body slide down the shafts of the spikes, only a sickly squelch as blood and steel began to play a tune, a single tone, squealing to a stop inches from the stone base. Then the pain began, Gabrielle could feel every puncture, through her skin, through her innards, through every nerve and sinew the steel had penetrated.

It was impossible to move, but she could scream, which she did, as loudly as she could, full of terror, fear, pain and utter despair. But the spike through her larynx meant her screams filled her head, leaving her mouth as nothing more than a bubbling whisper of blood.

Mitch was the first to reach the bowl, looking down at the carnage below. He didn't move or utter a word. He just stared at the red mess that flooded the floor below the torn body of his ex wife, suspended on the thin needle sharp spikes.

"We need to retrieve the scroll and the little statue." Jack approached Mitch, staying a couple of yards away in respect. He could see that he found the image disturbing by the look on his face, one of horror, but also of devastation.

"I'll do it." Mitch kept his eyes on Gabrielle, at what he had caused.

Guilt hit him like a train, the time in Helmand when they first connected, how his pursuit became all consuming, he was using her as a reason to live, a reason to fight. He had to marry her because he needed her, but did he really want her? She was the safety he needed, the Afghan experience had made her stronger, she was his rock. She was there at every episode, his attacks, his breakdowns, the shoulder to cry on.

She showed him a better life, a normal life and he threw it back in her face. Barbara's death changed them both, but he should have taken his punishment. He should have taken the mental rehabilitation, accepted the treatment available to him. Not to accept the easy way out, become an experiment for a megalomaniac and throw all the care, support and love straight back into his wife's face.

"I don't think that's a good idea." Jack couldn't afford any more delays and definitely no more mistakes.

"Then it's a good job it's my fucking idea and not yours. I'll take the responsibility. She's my wife!"

As Mitch confronted the LARA agent he stopped short of attacking him even though the hairs prickled on the back of his neck. He was on the verge of losing it, ready to attack the enemy

before him. He tensed every sinew he could as he fought back,
trying to keep himself at bay. It was starting again.

Jack braced, ready to defend himself, hoping he didn't have to.

"That's why it's not a good idea, Mitch. She was your wife, we need
to retrieve the items and the likelihood is that they are close to her
body. I wouldn't wish that on my worst enemy. Let me do it for
you."

Mitch studied the man in front of him. He was everything his
profile indicated. Highly trained, focused, strong and ruthless. But it
wasn't until now that he was able to see the man for who he really
was. He could see that however much he protested, whatever he
came up with to try to stop the man, Jack Case was not going to
allow him to enter the pit.

"How do we do this?" Winning his own personal battle, pushing the
aggression as far away as his mind allowed, he conceded for two
reasons. They were running out of time and any delay could be
catastrophic and he still had to own up and tell Jack the truth, but
now wasn't the time.

~

With the rope secured around the substantial ankle of Ammit, Mitch
and Faversham lowered Jack into the pit.

It was no more than twenty feet to the base, but after fourteen
feet the tips of the spikes blocked any straightforward descent.

The scroll was easy to find as Gabrielle had fallen past it as she
plummeted to her death. The parchment swayed gently in the breeze
as it followed, coming to rest against four of the steel tips.

Placing it in his pocket, Jack pointed the Maglite around the
blood soaked floor in search of the tiny statue, trying as best he
could to look past the body suspended four foot below him. It
proved impossible as Gabrielle dominated the view, her death fall
captured forever, suspended a foot from the floor. She was pierced
throughout, resembling a macabre pin cushion with at least thirty

steel rods through her torso and her arms pierced from shoulder to palms as she'd extended them to break her fall.

The floor was thick with her blood, by the look of the carnage it seemed she had retained very little of her ten pints. What was left still tried to join the rest, dripping occasionally from the body.

He saw the small turquoise statue and watched, trance-like, as one of the thick drips rippled through the surface, the red rings fanning out until they were disrupted by the object blocking its path.

"Any joy?" Faversham's voice echoed down at him.

"I have the scroll, just take my weight and I should be able to grab the statue."

Jack squeezed between the steel rods horizontally, using his hands to ease himself down the tubes towards his goal. They gave slightly as he squeezed himself through, becoming tighter the nearer he slid towards the floor.

He stopped an arms length from the sun disc and weaved his arm through the spikes to retrieve it. He was level with the decimated face of Gabrielle Millson and however much he tried, he couldn't take his eyes from the sight before him.

Her head had been pierced three times, the one closest to her mouth had displaced her exposed jaw and pushed it over her cheek.

His fingers felt through the sticky fluid, feeling for the object as he continued to stare at her face… Her already damaged eye escaped from its socket and was laying out of the skull hanging by tendrils of optic nerve, arteries and veins…He felt the small circular disc with his fingers and wrapping his hand around it, pulled it from the sticky blood….Gabrielle opened her good eye, the pupil looking all around in a weird dance as it frantically searched its surroundings. It locked onto Jack who froze as his heart jolted in surprise. The half of the jaw still connected to her head moved slowly up and down trying to communicate…It was joined with the faint sound that pushed through the exhalation of bubbling blood, over and over again.

·   ·   ·

Transfixed, Jack watched and listened, trying to understand what she was saying. She was repeating the same thing, labouring to form a word, eventually slowing until Gabrielle's time ran out, but not before she made one last effort. With her dying breath Jack was able to make out what she was trying to say…'Mother'.

"Jack, move your arse. This thing is closing."

The creaking of gears echoed through the walls. Jack could see the circular gap he had climbed through begin to take the shape of an oval, it was sliding shut.

Thrusting the disc into his back pocket he began to scale the rope, pumping his arms and legs as fast as he could. He slipped down three feet as the rope slackened…

"Jesus Christ…hold the damn rope!"

"It was me Jack, don't worry the professor has you. But this thing is closing fast…get a move on and I'll hold it as long as I can."

He saw Mitch's legs come into view, pushing against the edge of the base as it continued to close. Bare legs then joined as Tia sat next to him and added her boots to the pressure as Jack ascended. The rope swayed erratically with the effort and several times he missed his footing, slowing him down as he climbed. The thought of being trapped in the darkness with the cadaver caused him to panic a little, putting him off his stride several times.

Elation filled his body as his head came into view of the temple, its bland white surface a welcome sight.

Heaving himself up between them both he managed to grab hold of the sides and lift his legs free, just as Tia and Mitch pulled their legs clear as the base slammed shut.

73

"This is incredible…Look."

Faversham passed the scroll to Tia, as they sat together on the plinth supporting the statue of Ammit.

"Some of the hieroglyphs have gone…How can that happen?" Tia instinctively turned the parchment over even though she knew they wouldn't be there.

"It looks like they've just dissolved. There isn't even an outline of where they were…completely gone." She looked over to the bowl that had swallowed Gabrielle.

"You don't think…"

"…That the letters dissolved and caused the bowl to open." Faversham finished her thoughts for her. He had been thinking the same thing.

"Could it be some form of chemical reaction? I mean you explained the phosphorus when the torches lit by themselves." Jack was theorising again even though it was beyond his scope. But he needed to focus on something other than Gabrielle's face.

"That might be the case…" Faversham agreed.

"…Except for one thing. The message has changed, these Hiero-glyphics are totally different to the ones that led us here."

Tia looked closer, her finger running over each vertical list, checking and rechecking.

"Well I'll be…!" Tia looked up from the script and shook her head.

"It's the Judgement of Osiris…" She returned to the hieroglyphs.

'Homage to thee, O great God, Lord of Maãti, I have come to thee, O my lord, that I may behold thy beneficence. I know thee, and I know thy name, and the names of the Forty-Two who live with thee in the hall of Maãti, who keep ward over sinners, and feed upon their blood on the day estimating characters before Un-Nefer. Behold, I have come to thee, and I have brought Maãt….'

"It then recites the passages of purity before finishing with *'I am pure. I am pure. I am pure'*…Over and over again."

"Hang on a second…" Jack was finding it hard to keep up.

"…Are you sure I picked up the original scroll. Could there have been another one down there and I grabbed the first one I saw?" It certainly made sense to him anyway.

Tia turned the parchment over and showed the markings she had used to find the location of Duat from the Temple of the Oracle only last night.

"This is definitely the same document. It's just altered itself."

"It's the key. I need to take it from here. Stacy, give me a hand my dear."

Nightly, with the help of his assistant, walked unsteadily to the feathered bowl and with some awkward manoeuvres managed to climb over the edge. Stacy kept hold of his hand until she was satisfied that he could stand unaided.

"Now if you could place the scroll into the other bowl please." The scientist spoke softly, almost hesitantly, as if he was unsure himself.

"Are you sure about this, Mr Nightly?" Faversham wasn't, he

felt it required more investigation. He wanted to study the document a little more.

"Do as he says." Aya approached and stood at the edge of Nightly's bowl, her head raised high as she continued to stare at the bestial head of Ammit.

"We are fifteen minutes away from midday. So I suggest we give it a try or all of this is for nothing."

Mitch had a point. If it didn't work they would have little time to try anything else. Tia took the scroll and leaning into the heart inscribed bowl, laid it carefully in its centre, deciding to lay the Hieroglyphics face down to touch the surface.

It was unfortunate that the plague had begun to shut down his organs as he should be elated at this moment.

Gordon Nightly watched the other bowl, the heart bowl.

The key to Aaru, The Field of Reeds and eternal life were about to be revealed to him. In his head he was running around the temple screaming with excitement and bouncing off the walls. He could feel tears well in his eyes as he thought of the adulation that was about to be imposed on him.

He would be seen as the saviour of the human race, like a second coming. Healing the world of pain and suffering.

He coughed another racking throat full of bloody phlegm, which he held back as best he could. He wasn't going to present himself as a weak subject, not as he was about to be presented as a disciple of RA.

He felt the vibration through his feet, rising in momentum until his calves began to quiver. He rode it as it grew in strength, ignoring the urge to grab hold of the sides. He had seen the woman plunge to her death in similar circumstances and he began to fear that he was about to meet the same fate.

He searched for Stacy to help should he need to be pulled free before the floor gave way. She was with the others and she was backing away from him...they were all backing away...their eyes focused on the statue of Ammit, staring up at the beast's head.

The statue was moving.

The plinth moved across the floor, the vibration from stone scraping against stone rocked the very foundations of the hall as it transported the thirty foot behemoth away from the wall.

White light emanated from the floor as the statue uncovered an underground entrance, growing wider as the plinth continued its journey. Soon a set of stone steps appeared leading down to what Nightly knew was Aaru...Entrance to the Kingdom of Osiris.

74

Tia was the last to descend the stairs after collecting the scroll from the heart bowl.

While the rest of them were rushing to catch up with Nightly, who had disappeared down the hidden entrance before anyone had a chance to stop him, she couldn't resist a chance to study the scroll. She wasn't disappointed, the hieroglyphs had altered again. The new script was more of a prayer than a chant and directed at RA.

She felt her own sense of excitement as she imagined what was yet to come and all but skipped down the stairs as she rushed to share her discovery with Iggy.

She wasn't prepared for what she saw…The others had moved no further than a foot away from the stairs by the time she reached them. Like her, they had stopped to stare in wonder.

It was paradise within a colossal domed cavern. Green luscious grass spread around them infused with colour of the flora of the world; cherry blossom, roses, poppies, lotus, marigold, a plethora of scents filling the air. Bees busied themselves pollenating as they flitted from flowerbed to flowerbed and tiny white butterflies bobbed from petal to petal.

A stream fed from a waterfall, cascading from a ledge several feet above, flowed around a small hillock within the centre of a field of reeds swaying in a gentle breeze that carried through the air.

Air that brought with it a warmth from the sunlight that burst through a cavity in the cavern roof. It sparkled off of the rough calcite riddled granite, lighting sections of the ground creating a weird spring feel to the whole landscape.

Jack's ear fizzled into life

"Jack, there you are. How are things down there?" Sara had been trying every few minutes to get a reading on him and saw nothing for hours.

"I'm afraid we're not in Kansas anymore, Toto..." Jack, struck by the scene in front of him was still trying to come to terms with it.

"Sorry?... did you say Kansas?" Sara couldn't see what he was looking at.

"Never mind...We've come to the end, I think...Or we will be in ten minutes once the wizard has done his stuff. Can you get a fix on us Sara, I think we might need a lift out of here. We are in some sort of dormant volcano or some natural chasm, there is a break in the ceiling, I'm guessing close to one hundred feet above us. Send a chopper down to collect us, I'll signal you when we're ready."

"I'll do what I can Jack, but here's the thing. I have you on screen but there is no sign of any rock formation and I have you pinpointed forty miles from where we lost contact. According to the image you are on a flat desert terrain."

"Forty miles? That's impossible, if I was to hazard a guess we would have travelled no more than a mile, two at most." LARA used the latest satellite tracking systems that could pinpoint the movement of an insect if it needed to. This was getting weirder.

"Nope forty miles, Jack, trust me. It's all here on surveillance."

Forty miles was impossible, that would take at least ten hours to walk at a steady pace without any stops. They had spent more time in each location than they had walking in between.

. . .

"Ok, we'll see when you get here. How are things out there. Much happened while we've been away?"

" *Yes, It's bad Jack...Over two million have died so far. Hospitals are at breaking point and borders are closed in every country. It's a bacterium Jack, it has no preference to age, race or health. But it seems to be hitting the young the hardest, the twenty to forties are the registering the highest rate of deaths.* "

"And the sheikh's son?" He needed some good news but he wasn't sure if their employer could provide it.

"*He's holding on. They have him in an induced coma, surrounded by physicians. It's only a matter of time before decisions need to be made however, as his respiratory organs are beginning to struggle. He's in a better position than most, but it may not be enough.* "

Not great news but there was still hope. They can only wait and see if the madman comes through.

"*One last thing, Jack. There has been quite a firefight back at the entrance, many casualties, but not one of them female. Have you caught sight of the Millson woman? I think she may be on your tail.* "

"I'll tell you all about it when we're done here. Needless to say, she won't be bothering us from now on."

Nightly began to walk towards the stream, followed by the others.

"Let me know when you are nearby. It looks like it's showtime here... Out."

Jack followed without knowing what to expect. But as he felt the soft grass beneath his feet, smelt the sweet aroma of the flora and listened to the soft trickle of the small stream in a location that wasn't on any map, he was ready to open his mind to anything.

The stream was no more than a yard across and a few inches deep. Crystal clear, moving slowly around the knoll like a tiny moat.

Nightly undressed, throwing his clothes off with a boyish enthusiasm. Stacy helped Aya, avoiding her damaged arm, easing her top away from the bandages that criss crossed her torso.

"Do we have time for a swim? " Mitch could do with a clean up himself after the grime of the previous few hours.

"We are cleansing ourselves in the stream of Duat, before presenting ourselves to RA with a purity that has allowed us audience. This is also as far as you are permitted to go. Do not cross the stream." Nightly kept his focus on removing his clothes, choosing not to look at his former Head of Security. One of the first to pay for his treachery once he became one with RA.

Naked, they knelt in the stream and while Nightly bathed, Stacy assisted Aya to ensure that every inch of her uncovered skin had felt the water.

In the centre of the hillock stood a pedestal with a gold crescent moon glistening from its top. It was 11.55AM and the sunlight was gradually climbing toward it, lighting half of the marble base.

Soaked and shivering, Nightly and Aya approached the pedestal leaving the others to watch as the ill, slightly emaciated man and his severely wounded daughter trudged towards their destiny.

"Jesus, God help us all if this pair are all we've got to turn this crap around." Jack was a pragmatic man and normally if anything is too good to be true, it generally is. He had, however, seen enough through the past few days to not come to any conclusions…just yet.

"I have a feeling we haven't seen it all. There is more to come that may just change everyone's perception of what is real."

Tia, seeing the changes in the scroll, believing that there was more out there than man has yet to discover and having stranger than fiction experiences of her own in the past, was open to the fact that something momentous was about to happen.

Taking the sun disc amulet from Aya's good hand Nightly placed it into a rectangular slot on top of the pedestal. The disc was a perfect fit as it clicked into place in front of the crescent moon, its face in front of the concave curve, the tiny hole aimed into the body of the crescent as it sloped towards it.

"Come my dear, we need to become one with the earth."

Nightly pointed to two bare patches of earth, devoid of any foliage, next to the pedestal and beckoned for her to follow as he stood in one of the patches, grinding his feet into the earth to ensure that he was fully in touch with the ground.

Aya, avoiding his touch as he tried to help her, stood within the second patch and followed suit, she knew what she had to do.

Holding the scroll in front of him, feeling his heart begin to flutter, Nightly began to speak, his voice loud enough to travel across the chasm and echo off the granite.

" Behold, I am in thy presence, O Lord of Amentt. There is sin in my body. I have not uttered a lie knowingly. I have no duplicity. Grant that I may be like the favoured ones who are in thy train…"

The sun moved towards the centre of the dome, its rays beginning to light the crescent, licking the tip, ready to move into the concave slope and the sun disc.

Nightly continued, knowing that he would finish as soon as the sun positioned itself to release its midday glow.

"…I am purified from evil things, I am free from the wickedness of those who lived in my days; I am not one of them. I will not decay, nor rot, nor putrefy, nor become worms, nor see corruption. I shall have my being, I shall live, I shall flourish, I shall rise up in peace"

. . .

An explosion of light hit the pedestal as the sun's rays flooded the highly polished concave body of the crescent moon. The light rebounded off the surface hitting the sun disc, a thin laser like beam shot out from the hole in its centre and bombarded part of the granite wall to the east.

Jack watched on, unable to assist. But he made the decision to move the group to the west, aligning themselves behind the light show. As the heat began to grow in the air he wasn't sure if moving would make any difference. Something was changing in the atmosphere and they could very well be wrapped up in it all.

"We need to move back, I have a feeling this could get a bit hairy."

"It won't touch us. It is intended for the two on the hill and will concentrate around the sun disc. We will be perfectly safe." Stacy knew enough to know that she had to be on standby should she be needed and she was almost sure that they were safe.

As she watched the molten lava slowly creep down the wall underneath the sun powered beam, she hoped she was right.

The thin hot UV light emitting from the hole in the sun disc hit a seam in the rock wall. It contained a waxy residue, a mix of calcite, manganese, alumina and fine clay that fell apart as soon as heat began to burrow through its surface. It opened a fissure that began to bleed, an orange seeping ooze of lava.

The heat became oppressive as it carried on the breeze, bees and butterflies disappeared as the flowers wilted and the air singed delicate petals and leaves curled in protest.

A thick mist followed, drifting clear of the fissure, a white maelstrom swirling towards the sun disc, carrying with it fine black ash of carbon, tiny bursts of electrons exploding like minuscule fireflies, along with slivers of silver white veins of calcium, forced to the surface from a pocket deep in the depths of the earth's core.

Rolling across the grassy knoll like the fog of a damp early morning, it remained within the border of the stream.

As if held back by an invisible wall, the mist climbed within the confines of the knoll. Once it reached a height that came into contact with the natural air from the hole in the ceiling it rolled back in on itself creating a barrier of mist, enclosing the pedestal, the sun disc, Gordon Nightly and Aya within.

Jack looked on aghast at the scene in front of him, thankful that the temperature had returned to normal once the mist formed into a giant globe of haze, but powerless to intervene.

"Anybody have any ideas of what's going on here?"

He could see clearly the shapes of Nightly and Aya, unmoving as the mist swirled around them, but what was happening was well beyond his experience and without a strategy or an exit plan, he was as good as useless. He needed an idea of what was happening.

"It's the prophecy…" Stacy offered her explanation as far as she could fathom from the research and discussions with Nightly and his knowledge of the underworld.

"…It is said that once the subject completes the journey and the heart is weighed and they are sent to the field of reeds, they are provided with the gift of eternal life. Well, here it is, brought from the earth itself."

"You are kidding me. They're getting eternal life from a fog… Whoa!…now what?" Mitch stopped in mid sentence as he watched the action developing in front of him.

Electrons began to bombard Nightly and Aya, exploding on impact. Neither moved as they flashed into them, disappearing as if absorbed. Dark specks of carbon surrounded them both, a ghostly black cloak draping its aura around them.

. . .

"It's happening…"

Stacy tried a little to explain something that, although she had been coached by Nightly, was herself taken aback as she actually experienced it in front of her own eyes.

"Tell me Mitch. Are you a religious man?" It was a loaded question but one that was easy to answer.

"No, not really, why?"

"Well I guess you know some of the stories of the bible, know people who are deeply religious and surely you have been to a church at least once in your life. You were married for God's sake…" Stacy stopped short, wishing she hadn't said the last part, not with what had just happened to Gabrielle.

'Sure, I know people who are religious, sure. And yes, I have been to a church, what's your point?"

Thankfully he hadn't taken offence.

"Well there are people who believe in a god, whose son was murdered by Rome and resurfaced three days later, resurrected. A son who turned water into wine, can feed five thousand people with five loaves and two fish and gets out of a boat and walks on water. Only a few examples of what the religious call miracles, and yet not one person alive today could have ever witnessed this, yet some still believe that it happened.

You have to keep an open mind Mitch, as I believe you are about to see one of those very miracles that in a thousand years time, others like you will not believe this ever happened, because they weren't here."

Mitch wasn't going to argue and he had to admit something was happening, but it didn't make things any more logical.

Gordon Nightly looked at Aya. He felt alive, invigorated, healthy… he could feel the disease being destroyed inside his body, feel the regeneration of damaged cells, feel his heart growing, pumping new life into his veins.

Aya looked more beautiful than any other woman he had ever seen, naked in front of him with an aura that consumed him, his daughter, his legacy, his world.

He pulled away the bindings from her damaged shoulder, taking away the bandages, removing the thick gauze that covered the wound. Taking away the dressing from a perfectly healthy, perfectly formed, undamaged shoulder.

Aya instinctively raised her hand and felt around the smooth unbroken skin. She raised her arm away from her with no pain at all.

She looked into Nightly's eyes and for the first time in a long time, she smiled.

"You have done it." Her voice breaking half way through as she choked on the words she spoke to her father. A father she never knew she had. She too felt alive, more than she had ever felt in her entire life. A health in mind, body and soul. It was hard to explain, but for the first time in her life she felt complete.

Black flecks landed on her skin and as she brushed them away, they disappeared inside her. Tiny sparks hit her body and again disappeared inside her and each time she felt the exhilaration as they became part of her.

"We have great work to do, Aya. The world is ours, we need to take it, cleanse it, rule it. We are immortal, we need to lead the world away from misrule, govern how they want to be governed, need to be governed…"

She looked at him and narrowed her eyes. He sounded different and to an extent looked different. She was sure that it was a trick of the mist swirling all around them, but he looked hazy in her eyes, a little blurred. She tried rubbing her eyes and refocused, but it was still the same, as if he was surrounded with some sort of aura, a glow.

"What has this done to us?" She wasn't sure if she looked the same but what she saw in front of her scared her a little.

"It has given us everything we have ever wanted, Aya. A chance to start over, rebuild a better future, help people like them." He pointed at the hazy figures of his former companions as they stood on the periphery looking in.

"Come, let us meet our subjects." He turned and walked away leaving Aya to watch as the confident stride of her father seemed to flicker. It was as if she was watching a film where part of the reel had been damaged.

75

"Behold, I have come before you all as the saviour and ruler from now and forever more."

Jack found it hard to keep a straight face as the naked man stood in front of them all, surrounded by mist at the edge of a stream, his arms wide and his head held high as he barked his greeting.

"You're looking better Nightly, and you've returned with an ego bigger than the one you started with…" He just wanted the guy behind bars now.

"…So what's next? How do we get the cure for this thing you started?"

"We need the antibodies…" Stacy went through the next stage.

"…If we are right, Mr Nightly should now hold the antibodies that can regenerate and contain the ability to tackle any foreign body within the human organism."

"Any foreign body? What, any illness?" Mitch wasn't sure he was hearing right.

"In theory, yes. If we can extract the antibodies from the plasma it could be possible to adapt the Y proteins to tackle any disease."

"So, where do we go from here?" Faversham was still reeling

from what he had seen and he was loathe to leave as it certainly required more investigation.

There were more questions than answers, an archeologist's dream. They couldn't just leave it here.

"We need to get back to the lab and work with Mr Nightly and Aya to extract some of their antibodies. But I should take a sample of blood from both of them before we leave, to take samples at differing stages of it growing in their bodies."

Stacy opened the medipac and withdrew two syringes and vials to preserve the blood for the trip back to Frisco.

"Look! Her arm…" Aya stood beside Nightly and Tia noticed the perfect complete shoulder that she had seen blown apart back in the buggy as they drove away from Gabrielle.

"Fascinating…" Faversham put on his glasses, removed them again, trying to see through the misty images, moving forward to get a better look.

"Wait!…" Nightly screamed at them. His face flush with anger, veins straightened, protruding from his neck as the venom built inside.

"…We are not here as your guinea pigs. We are your saviours. We decide what is to be done and the first thing we need to do is to notify the world of my existence."

" Notify the world of your existence? The whole fucking world will know of your existence I can guarantee that. You have already killed millions and many more will die unless we get the samples needed to provide the cure. Now get your arse off of your little island and let's get out of here."

Jack had now had enough. He fulfilled his part and ensured the madman got to the source of a cure, now it was time to revert back to basics. Complete the mission, stop people from dying and get this prick locked up.

"You are in no position to dictate anything to me, Mr. Case. You realise that I hold the fate of the world in here…" Nightly punched his chest to emphasise.

"…And before I go anywhere, discussions are required. The

world leaders need to know that I will govern them from now on as they need to be aware that I will outthink them all, outmanoeuvre them all and when all is said and done, outlive them all. The sooner this is understood, the sooner the world can recover."

Mitch could feel the hairs rise on the back of his neck. The bastard had this planned from the beginning and he'd helped him do it. He knew Nightly was power mad and he'd monitored the growth of the ego over the past few months, but he'd missed this, like he'd missed the Aya thing. He needed to step up his game.

"Get out of there, Nightly, this is madness. Come on we have a world to save"

He grabbed Nightly's shirt and walked into the stream, with any luck he still had a little influence to calm this before it got any worse.

The bolt of electricity that coursed through his body cramped every muscle instantly, his jaw locked as he spasmed and the jolt crashed through his brain making it feel that his head was on fire. He was unaware that he was flying through the air until he lost all the oxygen in his lungs as he crashed to the floor four yards from the water. He gasped for breath, struggling to get air into his lungs, his mouth still open wide in shock.

Stacy was the first by his side, she worked quickly, rubbing his chest vigorously as she assisted in helping him breathe.

She was relieved to see him sit up, coughing violently as his rasping gasps began to draw in the oxygen he needed.

"What the hell happened?" He spluttered in between gasps for breath.

"Static…" Stacy helped him get to his feet.

"…with the amount of friction created by the rolling mist of matter, it must have reacted with the surrounding water."

"Ha, Ha. What did I tell you fools? You are dealing with not just a living god but the very land you exist on. Now you can see my power you know that I am speaking the truth." Energy surrounded

Nightly and seemed to accelerate its penetration. More and more materialised, sparking all around him as it entered his body.

Jack was sure he saw something as the sparks flew around the scientist, or more like saw something through him. It was as if, as the lights flashed around him, Nightly became translucent.

"I cannot do this..." Aya moved away from Nightly and walked to the edge of the knoll to cross the stream.

Her mind was in turmoil, she had been given this gift from her father, a man she never knew. Through the haze of pain and morphine she seemed to drift from location to location as if in a dream.

Now, wide awake, in fact more awake than she had ever been in her life, the reality of everything that was happening around her was beginning to hit her hard. All of her life she had felt that there was something missing and had never known what it was. It had caused issues with her growing up, fitting in.

She rebelled at every opportunity as a young teenager until she joined the military as part of the Caracal battalion, an Israeli force to assist in securing the Egyptian border against drug smuggling and terrorism. This was where she found her independence, her skills in combat but never the answer.

With Nightly, she felt she was getting close to the knowledge she needed. Not quite knowing why or how, but she found herself trusting him, never questioning his orders or requests.

But now, having been reborn, with the knowledge of who he was, of what she had done to enable him to get to this and the monster he was becoming, it was too much.

She found what had been missing and now wished it had remained hidden for all time.

She was now invigorated, refocused and complete. She was on this earth to help people...She alone was the saviour.

Nightly grabbed Aya before she could enter the stream and pulled her back with such force that she fell on her back. She struggled, kicking him away as he tried to hold her down and crawled towards the edge of the knoll, moving as fast as she could on all fours, hoping to rise to her feet as she entered the stream.

. . .

"No…Aya, No!.." Nightly grabbed her ankle, pulling her back. Pain racked her leg as the scientist's new found strength squeezed her foot, the metatarsals crunching together as his grip turned vice-like.

"Nightly, leave her alone…" Jack had the scientist in his sights, his Glock aimed at the arm pulling Aya's foot.

"Jack! NO!… You'll destroy everything…" Stacy ran to him, her arms waving wildly to get him to stop.

"…Any damage to him could be devastating to the development of the antibodies. We cannot let that happen."

Jack pulled his gun away and glared down at Stacey.

"This needs to stop NOW! We are here to do a job and either Aya or Nightly need to be out of there and I don't care which one it is."

"Well shooting one of them isn't going to help. We need as many chances of developing a vaccine as we can get. You need to think of another way."

"Sara, how close are you?…" He needed a contingency and the one he was planning would need a quick escape.

"… *According to the screen five minutes, Jack. Josh has you on fix, do you need me to brief him on anything before he gets to you?*"

"Not sure yet. But I guess we will need a quick getaway…Oh and a decent medic…possibly."

"*Possibly? how do you mean possibly…You either do or you don't. What are the injuries?*"

Typical of Sara, always the finer details.

"Can't tell you Sara, I haven't done anything yet. I'll let you know when I have…Out."

"*Jack…Jack!…what are you up to…Jack?…*"

Raising his Glock again he aimed at Nightly's head and although the temptation made his trigger finger twitch as the madman continued to pull Aya towards him, he moved it a few degrees higher, slightly further to the left and fired.

The velocity of the bullet seemed to accelerate as soon as it entered the swirling mist, a trail of blue light followed the shell as it cut its way through to its target.

The crescent moon shattered on impact extinguishing the beam instantly, the bullet continuing its trajectory until exploding into the granite wall.

The mist appeared to stop in its tracks, falling from the ceiling like rain, thinning as it fell. It then began to flow back inside the fissure as if being sucked in by an invisible vacuum.

Gordon Nightly, eyes wide with fear, squealed as tiny sparks began to pop around him, some lighting inside his body before exiting and swirling away to ride on the mist as it retreated from the knoll.

Aya screamed. She looked up at her father as he started to glow. Every part of his skin was pulsing, a golden glow that illuminated fat and tissue, leaving veins dark as night, a network of thin lines criss crossing his golden silhouette.

Scrambling on all fours she scampered towards the stream, clearing the knoll as the entire area erupted in a thunderous roar.

The mist spiralled into a tornado sweeping up calcium, carbon deposits and electrons. It surrounded Gordon Nightly, splitting him into minute pieces of matter, he exploded into nothing more than a dust cloud of black particles, sweeping his remains into the tumultuous cloud before disappearing into the wall.

"Oh my god…NO!" Stacy watched open mouthed as Nightly disappeared before her eyes. She then caught sight of Aya laying face down on the bank of the stream, unmoving, her face pushed into the damp grass. Her scientific responsibility overtaking the shock of what she had just seen, her instincts taking precedence.

She ran to her with the discarded clothes she had collected, pulling off her own jacket as she slid alongside Aya's still body, covering her as best she could.

"Bring the medipac quickly." She shouted at no one in particular.

Tia ran with the bag, placing it alongside her.

"What the hell happened over there." The archeologist was still trying to register what she had just seen. The man literally disappeared in front of them.

. . .

"All I can think of is that the transformation was incomplete. When the beam was broken it stopped the process of building the cells it required to make a mortal into an immortal. I can only think that as it reversed the process it had already changed too much of Gordon to leave anything behind."

Stacy took the two syringes she was intending to use on both Nightly and Aya, drawing blood from the neck and main artery of the left arm, capped them and stored them in the chilled section of the medipac. Now they needed to get her out of here as fast as they could.

"Well I guess he got his wish of eternal life, but I doubt he thought it would be as a cloud."

Stacy looked up at Jack with such derision that he felt the acid bite of her tongue even before she uttered a word.

"Hilarious, Mr Case...And thanks to you we may just have managed to sentence the world to death."

"Hang on a minute. You saw that he wasn't going to play ball, he was going to hold the world to ransom. That wasn't what we signed up for and he knew it, he never intended to save the world as he put it, he only ever intended to gain the power to control it. Even Aya saw that in the end, so at least we have saved the one who wants to do this for the right reasons."

He wasn't going to take the hit for this, although Nightly dissolving wasn't in the plan.

"Oh and you know that Aya is all we need to create a vaccine, huh? Well mister, I know better than you...let's hope you are right and Aya has the antibodies we need, or at least part of her anyway..."

Stacy moved the shift away from Aya's waist to expose her lower half.

"Oh my God!" Tia gasped in horror. Jack just stared, words were superfluous even if any could come out.

Aya had escaped the mists of Osiris as she cleared the stream, but not until it had claimed as much as it could.

Half of her was missing, from half way down her buttocks there was nothing but an inch of glowing embers as cells, skin and bone fought to fuse back together something that was no longer there. It rolled within itself like a band of orange molten, resetting and re rolling, trying to form the missing parts.

"We need to get her to a hospital as soon as possible. If we can't save her, we need to save the plasma."

Jack walked away as Faversham and Mitch arrived, he had no desire to listen to Stacy's declaration of their chance of failure. He needed to get this thing done.

"Sara, we need Josh now and you need to have a hospital on standby as close to us as possible…"

"What have you done, Jack?"

Typical, she always assumed that it was something he'd done.

"No time for that now… Get Josh down here as soon as you can. Where is he?"

"Searching, Jack. We have you on radar, but we can't see you. We're just seeing desert."

"That's impossible, Sara. We're inside a bloody great mountain, volcano or chasm of some kind. There's a hole the size of four football pitches one hundred foot above us. Just look for a gigantic hole and you'll find us.

"That's what I keep trying to tell you, Jack. There is nothing five miles in either direction of your location except lots of sand."

Jack had no idea what was happening. How can they not see the hole, he can definitely see blue sky.

"Sara, I have no idea what is happening but I need you to send these instructions to Josh. Get him to land directly on my location, but tell him not to reduce velocity. I know it might sound odd, but you need to get him to trust me. He'll know what to do, he's a good pilot."

"He's a good pilot because he doesn't deliberately set out to crash his helicopter. What are you asking me to do, Jack?"

"Sara, when have I ever let you down…No, don't answer that… Just trust me will you? We need to get Aya to a hospital as a matter of urgency. Tell Josh to land on top of me and keep it steady. If I'm right, he won't crash."

"If you're right?…"

"For fucks sake, Sara…TELL HIM!"

76

C aptain Josh Adams could see Jack's icon flashing directly below him but on his monitor he could see only sand.

The Sikorsky hovered at one thousand feet, scanning the area for any signs of the him. To no avail.

"I can see you Josh, bring her down…"

Adams squinted into the monitor and saw only sand.

"Jack…I don't know where you are. You're a dot on my screen, but the monitors see no sign of you. Wave your hands or something….I can't see you."

Jack stood in the centre of the knoll beside the shattered crescent moon and stared up at the Black Hawk in the centre of the blue sky directly above him. He could tell by the size of the craft that he was still far above his location and was holding position. He waved frantically, although from that height he would be hard pressed to see any movement.

"Jack, I'm telling you. I can't see you, just sand."

"Well I guess you'll just have to trust me and land. Just do yourself a favour and keep your eyes peeled as you come in, you are in for a surprise."

~

Adams brought the chopper down, checking the instruments and the external monitor as the ground rose towards him.

Ten feet from the surface and still no sign of Jack or any of the group.

He hovered at eight feet as he noticed something that made him lean in to the screen. What he saw made no sense.

He could see the surface clearly, soft golden waves of clear desert sand, untouched, still and calm.

There were no signs of any footprints which, apart from confirming that Jack could not be here, was not as disturbing as the knowledge that the sand was untouched, still, unmoving. There was no rotor wash.

At eight feet from the ground the rotors should be forcing sixty to eighty miles an hour of wash through the ground, sending sand in all directions at a radius of at least one hundred feet. As he rose to look out of the cockpit it became even stranger, sand was kicking up in the air in small undulating wisps just over a hundred feet away, the tail end of the extent of the wash in normal circumstances.

Looking at his instruments, he realised what was happening and why he couldn't see Jack.

The altimeter flickered frantically between 6ft and 130ft which could mean only one thing...Light refraction.

As he brought the Sikorsky down to three feet the ground disappeared to be replaced by the entrance to an enormous chasm, his instruments settled to 128ft as he continued to spiral down towards the green carpet below.

Due to the angle of the desert floor meeting with the sun's rays, the refracted light showed nothing but sand, a mirage. Thankfully his instruments never lied and although his eyes were looking at an image of sand from elsewhere, his altimeter couldn't be fooled the closer it came to the refraction.

.   .   .

"Jack I have you now, but I think you will need to get everyone together and fast."

The granite walls began to tremble and drip as the helicopter moved deeper into the chasm. From the cockpit Adams could see the grey dust of crumbling stone create small drifts along the crevices, sending sediment cascading into the valley.

Jack saw it too, the roar of the helicopter filled the chasm with a deafening rattle as each rotation of its blades boomed across the void, bouncing off every section of cavern wall sending shards of granite into the ground. More troubling was the rumble that began to vibrate through his feet.

He ran to the others who were doing their best to make Aya comfortable, shouting as he approached over the cacophony of engine noise.

"We need to get ready to leave immediately, the place is falling apart and the helicopter won't be able to land."

Heat began to grow around them as parts of the ground broke apart, throwing steam into the air. Boulders crashed against the walls as the granite fell in on itself and the orange glow of lava started to fill the seams as cracks appeared spreading throughout the surface.

From the monitor Adams could see streaks of orange spread through the green surface, a large seam began to grow, the lava slowly crawling towards the small group huddled together watching him descend.

"Jack, I'm not landing, you'll have to use the ladders. We'll send two out to you, but get in as quickly as you can, the heat will affect the rotors if we stay too long."

"Negative Josh, we have a casualty and trust me…they won't be using a ladder. Once we have everyone else on board you'll need to get your ship down as close as you can for thirty seconds tops."

.   .   .

The crew threw two ladders from the sides of the Black Hawk when they were twenty five feet from the ground. Adams fought with the controls as the heat began to affect the lift, sending the chopper into a rocking motion.

Tia and Faversham were first to climb aboard, scaling the ropes with ease as the chopper was steadied to a gentle sway.

Stacy finished administering morphine and headed to the helicopter.

"We've made a hammock of sorts for her. Make sure you don't go anywhere near the wound, it would be catastrophic if you touch it."

Tia and Stacy put Nightly's shirt, jacket and Aya's robes together to construct a makeshift blanket which doubled as a hammock style stretcher.

Aya's body had been crudely covered with a mix of bandage and Faversham's leather jacket. The pulsing wound that was Aya's entire waist had been loosely covered with gauze and bandages which had already stained black.

As Adams brought the Black Hawk as far down as he dare, the two crew men leapt onto the top rungs of each ladder and wrapped their shins in between the aluminium rungs and the fabric frame.

Their legs locked in place, they reached down to take the hammock from Jack and Mitch, carefully easing her into the chopper where Tia, Stacy and Faversham helped lift her to the back of the craft.

Lava began to pop out of the ground sending sprays of molten liquid into the air, a fist sized drip smacked into the tail of the Black Hawk forcing it forward as a hole appeared in the tail fin.

As the ship flew forward Adams had no choice but to climb while he wrestled with the controls to bring it steady.

Jack and Mitch watched the helicopter climb away from them.

"Jack, I can't get down, the heat and damaged tail fin is stopping us from moving any further. I can hold position, if you can get to higher ground."

A spurt of lava launched several feet into the air and spread across the cavern splattering into a steaming line of molten along the floor, joining with other seams and spitting into the air once again as heat sources reacted.

Jack could see the stream of water bubbling within the channel of heated earth and followed it to the waterfall. It was still forcing cool water into the cavern, its spray mixing with rising steam creating a fog that began to roll towards them.

"Come on, let's do this."

Mitch followed as Jack leapt over molten seams, rode some of the loose earth as it bobbed within molten puddles and leapt into the waterfall. Luckily footholds were plentiful as the water had eaten into granite over time.

Water cascaded over them as they climbed, but with a slow deliberate pace the narrow channel proved an easy thirty foot ascent and they were soon standing on a shelf with water wrapping around their ankles as it made its way to the edge.

The helicopter had risen further as the heat thermals battled with the downdraft and it was still steadily rising.

"Nothing I can do Jack...The ladders won't reach you, we'll need to throw you a line. Get ready as you'll only get one shot.

"What a way to go." Mitch shouted over the noise of the propellors.

There were scattered pockets of grass left on the knoll as it clung on to its last breath of fertility before it too succumbed to the orange and black molten lake climbing steadily towards them.

Two cables dangled several yards in front of them, the ends clearly visible a few feet below. It became clear that Adams was struggling to keep the helicopter from rising as the ends of the lines were now level with their feet.

.   .   .

Both men stared at each other for a moment. Jack, his chiseled features as determined as always, had to admit he liked Mitch. There was still something nagging at him about the man, but he felt he could trust him.

Mitch liked Jack from the get go, he was his type of guy. Which is why he should own up to him if they get through this. He didn't feel guilty as it was necessary, but he wished he'd let him know from the beginning.

They nodded to each other, a good luck and a silent show of respect.

"Well...It's now or never...After three...Three!" Jack leapt forward with Mitch only seconds behind him.

They both grabbed hold, wrapping their wrists around the cables to lock themselves on as they swung across the chasm like pendulums riding the thermals.

Adams lifted the Sikorsky clear of the mouth of the chasm and out across the desert towards Cairo.

Within minutes both men pulled themselves into the cockpit, the ladders proving a lot easier to climb than cables.

77

"S he's gone." Stacy removed her mask and slipped out of her gown, throwing it onto one of the seats in the waiting room as she approached the others.

It had taken just over an hour to arrive at the hospital in 6th October City and a further thirty minutes to arrange all of the necessary equipment to stabilise Aya as best they could.

Jack put his fourth coffee under his seat, having wished he hadn't drunk it like the previous three, but it helped pass the time. He stared up at the ceiling and exhaled loudly.

"Shit…what about the cure." He blamed himself in part for the destruction back at the Field of Reeds, but he had to act or they would have been held to ransom by Nightly without any guarantees.

"We have the plasma and we've managed to identify some B-cell receptors that look promising. But it will take a while before we can be confident that we have enough for a cure."

"You say a while…How long are we talking?"

Stacy was used to timescales and she was well aware that they were racing against time. But this was well beyond the knowledge of the people she was standing in front of and was loathe to commit totally.

. . .

"All I can say is that I will stay behind and extract all we can from the body. I have a flight scheduled back to the lab at six and should have answers within the next twenty four hours. I have a good team waiting who will work as fast as they can. We know what is needed."

She could see from the faces, particularly Jack and Mitch, that it wasn't enough. She didn't care, but she needed to work fast and had to get rid of them.

"Look…I've already spoken with our president and he will handle any further dialogue with those that need to know. Now please excuse me, I have work to do." She turned and made her way back to theatre.

She had to work fast and away from prying eyes.

"Well, I guess we will just have to wait and see, won't we." Faversham watched her go, surprised after all they had been through that she didn't want to at least say goodbye, let alone offer some thanks.

" I think she knows what she is doing. We just have to trust her."

Tia gently rubbed Faversham's arm as she spoke. Jack noticed how their relationship had blossomed during the adventure. He guessed that this was only the beginning.

"I'm sure we'll know soon enough. What do you two have planned? Back to England?"

Faversham could tell that Jack suspected that they had rekindled an old relationship and tried to be as matter of fact as he could be.

"Quarantine I'm afraid. There are no conventional flights to the UK due to restrictions…"

"…And I have accommodation at the Grand Hyatt, I'm sure they will have a room for Iggy." Tia cut in before the professor did his usual with his size tens.

"I'm sure they will..." Jack gave a knowing smile. He looked around the waiting room.

"...Where's Mitch?" He hadn't noticed the man leave.

"He took a call a few minutes ago. There he is..." Faversham pointed to the window.

Mitch was pacing outside, his mobile to his ear, in deep conversation. He noticed Jack looking at him and held up a finger indicating he was on his way, moving out of sight as he walked back to the waiting room.

"Well I must say, Jack, its been an adventure, something I will not forget in a long time. Thank you for giving me the opportunity." He grabbed the LARA agent's hand with both of his and shook it furiously.

Tia slapped his hand away and holding Jack by his shoulders, kissed him on the cheek.

"Thank you for everything, Jack. It could have been so different without you."

She meant that she could have lost Iggy and Jack took it as such.

But he was still troubled by the way it ended. Should he have waited to see what happened with Nightly, waited until the process had run its course and transformed the man into an immortal? Or had he doomed the earth to an incurable disease?

∽

Mitch said his goodbyes to the archeologists as they crossed paths by the waiting room entrance. Faversham, having his hands slapped away again by Tia, who thanked Mitch with the same peck on the cheek.

Jack's eyes narrowed as the military man approached. He had a look of consternation on his face, as if he needed to get something off his chest. He handed the mobile phone over.

.   .   .

"Somebody wants to talk to you." Mitch sat on one of the waiting room chairs and stared at the wall opposite.

"Who is this?" Jack thought it best to get straight to the point, he hated surprises.

"Hello Jack. I hear congratulations are in order."

He recognised the voice immediately. Smooth, professional with a Middle Eastern lilt.

"Hello Abu…"

Sheikh Rashad Bin Al Sharraf knew there was no need for any introductions as Jack would recognise his voice. He was slightly disappointed however, that the surprise seemed lost on the LARA agent.

" How's Sami?" As soon as he said it he wished he hadn't. If it was bad news, all this was for nothing.

"He is still holding on, Jack. He is in an induced coma and I have been assured that his vitals are responding well. And now I am much more optimistic after speaking to Mitch. I understand you have uncovered what is needed for a cure."

Jack was trying to process the information in front of him. Mitch was one of Abu's men. Why wasn't he told? Who else knew? Ryker?…Sara?

" I can tell by your hesitation that I need to explain a little more…"

"A little more…I need it all, Abu…who knew of this?" He looked over to Mitch who avoided his glare, preferring to count the floors on the hospital map.

"Nobody else knew, Jack. If you recall when we first discussed this with Ed, I explained that I had an inside man within the 24. I couldn't risk anybody knowing that it was Mitch. For a start, it would jeopardise his own life. He was Nightly's Head of Security and right hand man, his information was key to discovering what the madman intended.

Once it was found that Nightly was deliberately infecting people Mitch was more than happy to help. Don't get me wrong, Mitch is a loyal man, a man to be trusted. But he is also an honest man who has done his service to his country in saving many lives. He would have no part of a plot to infect the world with a manufactured disease. I too wanted to ensure that LARA were given as much help as possible without jeopardising the mission, so it was decided to keep it quiet. When Nightly ordered Mitch and the Aya girl to kill you, Mitch was there to ensure that it didn't happen. He was guarding you, Jack."

Jack recalled the time Aya was stopped from shooting him in the Cairo prison by Mitch standing in front of the gun. How many more times he couldn't be sure, but it was clear that without Mitch, he could be dead by now.

He didn't know how to react. He certainly wasn't happy that he'd been kept in the dark, even though he understood the reasons, it just wasn't the way he worked.

"Jack, it's ok. I needed you to succeed and, had you known, it may have affected your judgement. I needed the Jack Case who saved my daughter's life. The one that I knew would also save my son."

He was good. Jack had to admire the Sheikh for his diplomacy, no wonder he was used for negotiating with the superpowers on behalf of the Middle East.

"I just hope we have done enough to save Sami, Abu. Only time will tell."

"I have faith in you, Jack. I always have."

The phone went dead.

"Sorry, Jack. I couldn't say anything." Mitch stood a few feet away from him. Not knowing him well enough, he felt better at a distance.

"No harm done." Jack lied. He didn't blame him, he just couldn't cope with being kept in the dark. He preferred to be the master of his own destiny. Once he relied on others he was a dead man.

"So where do you go from here? " He realised that Mitch had finished his assignment. He had no Nightly to report to and the Sheikh now had no need for him. The pay off, knowing the Sheikh, would be a handsome one. So employment probably wasn't of primary concern.

" Back to Frisco…I have a bungalow to fix up."

Jack had Josh waiting to get him back to the UK. It was only a short hop to Libya, he could arrange for a flight to the States from there.

He held out his hand which Mitch accepted. The shake was firm, affirmation that everything was good..

"Come on. I'll give you a lift."

78

Sunshine, coffee and Cornwall, an ideal start to some much needed R&R.

Jack, showered and rested, took his coffee into the conservatory overlooking Mount's Bay.

Every opportunity he had to hide out in the safe house in Marazion as the unassuming IT consultant Matt Collins, Jack made sure he savoured every second. Although LARA were only one call away from a world of espionage, murder and mayhem, his home town was as far removed from that world as Mars was from Earth.

A pie and a pint at The Fire Engine, savouring the new selection of real ales while bathing in the glorious rays of the sun glistening off of the bay, would allow even the most stressed to re-evaluate their lives and realise it was too short to waste in worry.

He switched on the radio, relaxed in the armchair and flicked through a selection of magazines on his tablet.

'Here is the national news, with Brian Andrews…Good morning… Latest figures from the World Health Organisation show that the global vaccination is on track to ensure every man, woman and child will have been inoculated by the end of the year. The BCR drug program has also provided one hundred percent success at eradicating the bacterium and is particularly successful

throughout the third world. It has also been reported that there has been no further deaths attributed to the plague in the last two months.

Chief scientist and CEO of BioTane Pharmaceuticals, Stacy Mickelson has confirmed that the rollout of both vaccine and drug program has reached the stage that a cure is now available for every person in the world today, with a supply in reserve should there be the unlikely event of any recurrences.

In a statement given to WHO and The United Nations during yesterday's conference, Ms Mickelson also claimed that they have found, after intensive tests and research, several cancer reducing drugs that BioTane are ready to launch into the mainstream. In a claim that is bold if not, as some quarters call, foolish, she has guaranteed that half of all cancers will be eradicated within the next ten years...More from this story as it comes in...In finance...'

Jack switched off the radio to answer the buzz from his PDA.

"Have you heard the news?" Sara hadn't spoken to Jack for a few weeks now and thought it was a good chance to catch up.

"Just heard it. Seems our Stacy has made a name for herself over the past few months. Sounds promising."

"Well I wouldn't say promising just yet. It appears that the plague is over and we are sure that it shouldn't return. But our science bods have explained that during the sequencing, they think that all she has done is turn off the switch that enabled the bacterium to spread and mutate. They don't have all the facts, but worryingly, BioTane are keeping everything close to their chests. WHO have tried to send in delegates on several occasions to review the plants, but have been tied in red tape every step they take. Needless to say we are keeping our eyes on her, with any luck she'll prove us wrong, but we can't afford another Nightly."

Jack had to agree that the scientist he left in the hospital wing in Cairo four months ago didn't seem to have it in her to take BioTane to where it is today. It did strike him that she seemed a little distanced as she broke the news of the death of Aya. She definitely had more on her mind.

"Oh...and another thing. Officials excavated the area Josh picked you up from to look for the series of chambers you guys went through. Professor Faversham and Tia spent a month with them to assist in the search. They found nothing other than a disturbance in the earths mantel within the shelf to the west of Qara. A geographical phenomena that happens every million years or so when the earth shifts on its axis. Just a vast area of hardened lava creating a new rock formation. There was nothing Jack...apart from a tiny blue disc stolen from the Egyptian Exhibition in Manchester, according to Faversham the sun disc that was in Nightly's possession. The stones that you entered from were also missing within the reed oasis. Tia said it was as if they were never there. Weird huh?"

The whole thing had been weird, so it didn't really surprise him. Perhaps Nightly had been right after all. The more he thought about it, the less he wanted to know.

A wry smile did cross his face however as he thought of Faversham and Tia, their excitement mounting as they dug deeper, to come up with nothing. It wouldn't stop Faversham from dining out on the story for years.

It would be good to catch up one day, he'd like to hear of the archeologist's heroism.

"Well, best laid buried as far as I am concerned. At least we found the cure. How's the Sheikh's son, Sami by the way?"

He hadn't altogether forgiven the man for duping him with Mitch, but he couldn't help like the man and after all, his kids were innocent.

"Fully recovered. He is clear to return to MIT when the lockdown ceases next month...I have to ask you though, Jack. Why aren't you answering the Sheikh's calls? He's hounding Ed weekly, do we have a problem?"

"No problem, Sara. I just have no reason to speak to him at the moment and I'm certainly not speaking to him during R&R. Tell Ed I will get in contact with him by the time I get back there in a couple of weeks."

"Ah, yes. Your return to HQ. I think you'll enjoy it. Buzz has been working overtime on your new toys." She allowed herself a smile as she could already see his reaction before he said anything.

Buzz was the techno whizzkid of LARA, he made all the gadgets, tweaked existing and effectively screwed every agent once he had been given carte blanche.

"Great...I can't wait. Tell him to make some manuals this time, so that I can read them as and when." Jack was not looking forward to this. He couldn't think of anything worse than sitting all day in a classroom listening to technobabble. He just needed to know what it did and how to switch it on, after that, trial and error. Hadn't let him down so far...well not seriously anyway.

"You'll have to sit the test Jack and you know full well Ed will keep you back this time. You flunk every time...and he is determined to set an example. The budget has quadrupled and the investors want results. Even if it just shows the agents are on the ball...one time Jack, that's all he asks. Ed wants to get them off his back like you want him off yours...quid pro quo, Jack...quid pro quo."

He had to smile, Sara was great. She was his confidante, his conscience, his mate, his mother...his lover at one stage and his eyes and ears. She was the one person he could never let down.

"For you, Sara, anything. Now leave me alone. The sun's out, the tide is out, the beach looks inviting and I have a beer waiting to cool me down after I've done fifteen miles or so."

"Absolutely, of course, don't worry about me checking the world for trouble, cooped up with Buzz while I put the program together. You enjoy yourself. See you in a couple of weeks."

"Looking forward to it."

. . .

After locking up, Jack put the headphones in his ears, selected Metallica 'And Justice for all' on his PDA and began to jog towards Mount's bay just as the haunting introduction of Blackened filled his ears. He started sprinting as the first chord of the thrash metal rift crashed through his head.

Today was going to be a beautiful day.

79

EPILOGUE

As the elevator came to a stop in the basement she turned to the aluminium hand rail to the rear and felt behind for the recess. Placing her key card into the slot she waited for the panel to slide away to her left.

After walking into the hidden elevator she waited for the panel to close and pressed SUB3 on the keypad.

After dressing in the bio suit, passing through the antibac shower and navigating the airlock, the lab burst into life as soon as she began to cross the mesh bridge over the tanks.

After exiting the second airlock she walked over to the screens.

"How are things, Gerard?"

The scientist finished writing up his report and using the touch screen, threw an image onto the wall sized monitor.

"As you can see from the figures, we've managed to stabilise the melanocytes and we've eradicated most of the melanoma's. I think we've done it, Stacy…I think we have found its Achilles heel…We can stop skin cancer developing."

Stacy Mickelson checked the figures, double checked the notes and nodded slowly as she began to see all of the figures adding together.

"Good...this is very good. Shall we take a look?"

"Sure..." Pleased with himself, Gerard moved to the operator screen and accessed pool 234.

Two ultra bright LED panels lit above one of the circular pools within the network of tanks, lighting the water as it began to bubble and fizz.

A figure burst through the surface, bobbing lazily in the wash, tubes and cables surrounded it in a network of vital data, nutrients and life giving organisms. The figure resembled a tiny fly caught in the middle of a vast spider's web, each strand piercing the skin, suspending it, feeding it, analysing it.

The top half of a woman, her arms outstretched, lay perfectly still, eyes searching the ceiling, neither seeing or reasoning.

The screen zoomed in to the breast they had infected. There were no signs of the dark brown fist sized melanoma that had began to grow virulently only a few weeks ago. The skin was ruined, a grey mass of scar tissue, but clear of disease.

"Well done, Aya." Stacy shouted through the comms, her voice echoing through the lab.

"You are saving many lives and your work has only just begun. Your father would be so proud."

Stacy nodded at Gerard to extinguish the light, sending the body back into the depths of the biochemical solution, allowing it to regenerate ready for the next test.

"Great, let's wrap up for tonight. I assume the culture is formed for the pancreas?"

Gerard nodded, smiling to himself. He had nailed it.

.　.　.

"Yes indeed. All ready to go. We'll implant on Monday and hopefully within a week she will show signs."

"Excellent." Stacy helped switch all monitors off, checked the instruments and signed them off, leaving Gerard to go through the procedurals until he joined her on the mesh bridge.

"Come on, Gerard. I'll buy you a beer."

The lights extinguished as they left the lab and entered the elevator. Another day another dollar.

∽

It was there again...Bright, flashing in her eyes. What it was she didn't know. Things hurt, pain...lots of pain...but never knowing what or why.

Floating, covered in something...but what...never knowing. Things sounded in her ears, noises, a noise she once knew...never knowing what.

She makes a noise...that never sounds...but bubbles flow...lots of bubbles...she pushes them out...never knowing the noise.

Sometimes, she sees the bright things close, no water above, her nose brings in a strange thing, no fluid...makes her chest move up and down. ...never knowing why.

She makes the noise..it is loud...shrill...hurts her ears...never knowing why....

It is now dark...the noise are bubbles once again...she makes the noise...it helps the pain...makes the pain...causes the pain....

The noise still comes...but only bubbles...

If the noise had no bubbles...was shrill...hurt her ears... someone might hear.

THE END

DECLARATION

This is a work of Fiction. Names, characters, places and incidents either are the product of the author's imagination or are used fictitiously and any resemblance to actual persons, living or dead, business establishments, events or locales is entirely coincidental.

KISS OF THE PHARAOH ©
Book Two of the Case Files

Coming Soon

TOMB OF THE EMPORER ©
Book Three of the Case Files

Printed in Great Britain
by Amazon